CROSSING THE LINE
April 1942

Papillon Books
Saint Paul, Minnesota, USA

Library of Congress Control Number: 2023921293

ISBN: 979-8-9889592-0-5 (paperback)
ISBN: 979-8-9889592-1-2 (hardcover)
ISBN: 979-8-9889592-2-9 (ebook)

MMXXV I
Printed in the United States of America

The events of this novel are either a product of the author's imagination or used
fictitiously. Any similarities to actual historical events or organizations are entirely
coincidental and not intended by the author. Apart from known historical figures,
the characters and names are also fictional.

PAPILLON BOOKS

For Drake, Alexa, and Bonnie

CROSSING THE LINE
April 1942

J.D. Maxwell

Novel Map Area
North Central France

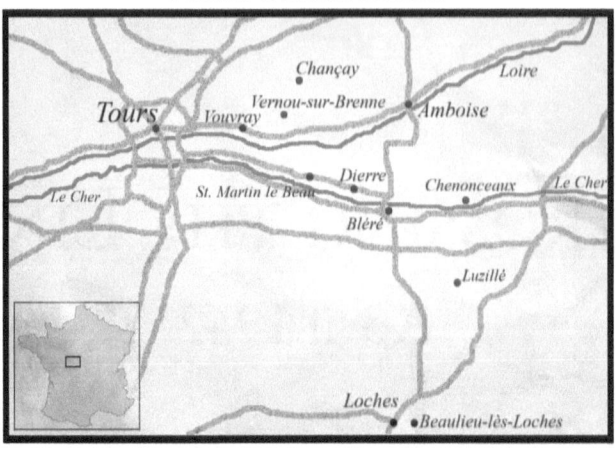

<u>Name Pronunciation Guide (Approximate)</u>
Marcel Bouchet > Mar.sehl Boo.shay
Colette Dubois > Koh.leht Doo.bwah
François Dubois > Frahn.swah Doo.bwah
Giselle Dubois > Zhee.zehl Doo.bwah
Louis Dubois> Loo.ee Doo.bwah
Henri Flamand > Ahn.ree Flah.mahn
Auguste Gagnon > O.goost Gah.nyon
Jean-Paul > Zhahn.Pohl
Violette Lebon> Vyaw.leht Leh.bohn
Simone Menier> See.mawn Meh.nyay
Georges Perrin > Zhorzh Pay.rahn
Philippe Renaud > Fee.leep Reh.noh
Charles Touchard > Shahrl Too.shar
Regina Viard > Reh.zhee.na Vee.ahr

CHAPTER ONE
Northwest of Amboise, France
April 16, Morning

COLETTE LOOKED OUT the weathered panes, returned her plate to the dirty dishwater, and smiled at her little brother scampering across the south field. She loved how he greeted each day with unbounded spirit.

The morning fog sparkled in the sunlight, and small dew-drenched branches glistened as though slathered in honey. The bitter winter had slogged its way into a miserable spring, but today, Mother Nature was softening her stance to the benefit of all—especially Louis. Colette, meanwhile, had yet to change out of her nightgown, and tangled waves of long, black hair still awaited a careful brushing. Watching him, she supposed the world seldom disappointed a ten-year-old boy. Despite being seven years older, she, too, had few objections to their pastoral life in central France, and the arrival of the Germans had done little to corrupt her outlook.

She lay in bed many nights, imagining what surprises awaited her. Before crawling under the covers, she liked to sit at her bedroom window and ask her favorite stars for advice. She had straightforward questions: *What should I wear tomorrow?* And more difficult ones: *When should I ask Papa if I can go to the dance social?* Of course, it was silly, but she'd await their replies and consider them. Simple questions got simple answers; difficult ones had mixed results. No matter. If one response didn't suit her, the next star inevitably told her what she wanted to hear.

She and Louis were often reminded how their father knew

everything about everything. Her mother would shoot them a wink, and they'd smirk as she craftily steered her husband toward revised, more accurate versions of his knowledge. He, in turn, would nod in agreement, claiming that's what he'd been saying all along.

In an unusual twist, Colette overheard her parents agreeing and sounding equally concerned about the weather. But three days had passed, and last night's drizzle hardly counted. *Spring's finally here*, she thought, *thanks to La Mère de la Terre*. As a child, she liked the way it rhymed and still addressed Mother Nature that way. Outside, Louis was a testament to their misjudgment, and today's sun would surely gobble up the fog in no time.

Heavy footsteps at the kitchen side door made her whirl. "Hi Papa, when did you get home?"

"Good morning, Bunny," he said, tossing his hat on a hook. "Let's just say it was later than I like."

"You look tired. Maybe you should get more sleep. Mama and I can take care of things." She looked back out the window and smiled.

"Just what are you so pleased about this early in the day?" he said in his deep, soothing voice.

"Oh, nothing. It's just that Louis always makes me—" Her smile faded. "Hey Papa, I think something's wrong."

"Huh? What do you mean?" he grumbled, lumbering around the large kitchen table.

She squinted. "I think Louis looks scared, but I don't see any reason for it. Are the wasps out already?"

Her father turned and squeezed her shoulders. "Do you know where your mother is?"

"Yes, Papa, I...I saw her from my window heading past the old shed. Maybe she went to gather wood."

"Listen close, Bun. Do you remember everything I showed you

and Louis about the hiding place?"

It was a foreboding question. "I think so, Papa," she stammered.

"That's great. I need you to go down there and clear things away. Open it up and wait for me. I'll be right back to—"

"But Papa!"

"It's probably nothing, but I need you to do it. Quick now." He was out the door before she could resume her protest.

~ ~ ~

François heard his son holler but couldn't understand him. They soon met on a path bordering the south field.

"They're coming, Papa." Louis panted.

"What? When?"

Louis took a deep breath. "I think they're coming, Papa!"

François patted his son's shoulder. "Where are they now?" he asked, scanning the horizon.

"At Paul's! I went the back way, and three cars drove up in front just when I got there. I sneaked up and listened at a window, and a mean-sounding man was yelling. I heard him say your name, and I ran home as fast as I could. They might be coming here, Papa!"

François hoisted his son like a small sack of goose down and lowered him. "You did great, Louis. Now listen to me close." His son stared wide-eyed and nodded his head. "Your sister saw Mama heading to the woods past the shed. I need you to run and tell her what you told me. Okay?"

"Yes, Papa."

"Then, Louis, this is most important. I want you and Mama to run and run and run until you get to Monsieur Touchard's. Don't run too fast, and don't run slow. Run like I taught you so that you can run far.

Stay off the roads, and don't stop until you're sure nobody's foll—" François caught himself. "No, assume somebody's following even if you don't see or hear them. Just keep going. But if you see anybody, hide. Not being seen is even more important than getting to Monsieur Touchard's." Louis kept staring. "That was a lot to remember. Can you do that for me?"

"Yes, Papa. But what will you and Colette do?"

François heard some concern in the boy's voice, but also a confidence that reassured him. "I'll take care of that. Now go." Louis spun and ran for the north woods. François hastened for the house, then turned. "Remember, Louis," he shouted. "Stay out of sight!"

"I will, Papa! You can count on me!" came the already distant reply.

~ ~ ~

Colette grabbed a beat-up lantern off a shelf next to the cellar door and lit the wick. Looking down at the dirt floor below, she cringed. She peeked back, hoping to see her father returning with a smile and word of false alarm. The cellar was unpleasant enough, but the grave was a place of dread. Her father tried to reassure the family that it would probably never be needed. "Probably" was a poor word choice.

Germany's sudden invasion almost two years ago caused widespread commotion, concern, and fear among the adults. But their arrival didn't seem that terrible to her. Both sides confiscated animals and machinery, and there was a shortage of many things that were always available before. Still, her mother and father adapted to it without excessive grumbling and explained that it was temporary.

Most of the war chatter was hazier than the morning fog, and it was easy to shrug off much of it. The tales she'd heard of atrocities were surely exaggerations or imaginary. The few Germans she'd encountered seemed pleasant, at times even charming. Studying her French-German translations or reading German books she borrowed from her teacher long ago was now a pastime. She figured it might come in handy if they couldn't understand her or were puzzled by certain words and phrases.

Reaching the bottom stair, she went to the far corner and found a flat surface to set the lantern. Just last week, her father again made the family watch as he covered the hole with two wide boards. He then placed items on top: a stained, half-rolled woven rug, a bedside table on its side, a handful of rusty tools, a broken floor lamp, rolls of wire mesh, and other random things. It looked like a dumping ground for household junk.

But rarely had her father's voice sounded so urgent. Moving the musty rug aside, she considered the remaining boards and hesitated. Kneeling, she slid them away and held the lantern over the pit. Her whole body quivered. *What's Papa thinking? I can't go in there. It's like being buried alive!*

Seven months earlier, with the help of his neighbor and best friend, Roland Viard, François dug out the hiding place from the dirt floor. Colette and Louis helped haul away the excavated earth. Good dirt was dumped in the vegetable and flower gardens and spread around with rakes. Clay clumps got carted to the fallow fields, and rocks were spread randomly throughout the woods. Everyone was tired and desperate for a wash at the end of the day. It always took her father substantial effort to get the grime out of his dense black beard. Louis wouldn't have noticed his own condition if it weren't for his mother's attempts to improve it.

The hole in the cellar floor was big enough for anyone to fit through and sufficiently deep to ensure the earth above wouldn't collapse. It could accommodate two adult men or three petite people, and François intended it as a place to hide his family or fugitives in an emergency. Wood braces supported the dirt ceiling at the corners. Double-thick quilts lined the floor and walls and were tacked to the corner beams to keep the occupants somewhat dry and warm. Regardless, the hole was more than unpleasant; it was terrifying.

"Colette!" a voice boomed from the kitchen.

"Down here, Papa!"

Her father hunched to avoid banging his head and made his way across the room to her. "They're on their way," he sighed, "and I don't think it's a social visit."

"What do you mean, Papa? Why here?"

He was distracted while considering the junk around him. "I need you to hide."

"But—"

"We don't have time. They could be here any minute. I don't know their intentions, but we can't take the chance."

"Papa! Please, no! I can't go in there. I...I'm sure it's fine. Maybe they want to meet us," she begged.

"You must, honey." He hugged her and grimaced. "Be brave. I'll send them away and come right back for you."

"I can't do it," she said, choking up.

He let out a sigh. "I'm sorry."

"But what about Louis and Mama?"

"I sent Louis to find her. They're going to run and hide."

Colette sensed his seriousness and knew she had no choice. She also trusted him. He helped her into the hole. Standing in the clammy pit in her nightgown and slippers, she looked up.

"Think of it as the greatest hide-and-seek place ever," he tried. Her eyes beckoned back at him. "Sorry. Okay," he started over, "I know you're scared. But we've talked about it and practiced. You'll be fine. Remember most, no noise. You can't cough or hiccup. Easy breaths.

Not fast, not slow. There's plenty of air, so take a deep breath if you feel the need. Remember how we close our eyes and listen. Concentrate on what you hear and try to remember it. If they ask me to leave with them—"

"What?" she interrupted, her mouth quivering.

He put a finger to his lips. "Shh. Just in case they need my help with something. If you hear nothing for a long time, count in your head the animals on the farm and the names you have for them. When you're done, push the trap door up slowly. It won't be too heavy. Believe in yourself. You can do this." Colette stared back, speechless. "It won't take long. I'll come to get you as soon as they're gone. Lie down now and close your eyes. Try to relax and listen. I love you."

"I love you too, Papa," she whimpered. She shuddered, then crouched down and stretched out on the quilt. Boards clunked overhead, and all went black.

She could hear him covering her up with clutter, and the clattering had just stopped when three faint knocks came from upstairs. Heavy footsteps followed.

"François Dubois!" a man with a thick accent hollered.

She gasped.

"Who is it?" her father roared back.

~ ~ ~

Louis could hardly contain his emotions. He was excited, nervous, and scared. But most of all, he felt important and was eager to make Papa proud. His mind raced while he ran, trying to remember: *Find Mama. No yelling. Don't run too fast or slow.* Passing the old shed, he snuck a peek over his shoulder and saw two cars approaching the house. He stumbled, caught himself, and didn't look again.

He found his mother stacking kindling in the woods. Catching his breath, he relayed everything he'd seen and what Papa had said.

"What about Colette, Louis? Did you see Colette?"

"Papa said not to worry about her!" They both looked toward the farmhouse. A distant vehicle was coming their way. "Let's hurry!" He took off running, slowing twice to let her catch up.

"Go that way, Louis!" his mother called to him, pointing.

He turned left and soon entered a dense wood.

"Good thinking, Mama. He can't follow us in here." The driver veered left. Louis had him figured out. "He's trying to catch us coming out the other side." They snuck back to where they entered as the car disappeared around the tree line. "Let's go, Mama!" he whispered, sounding more enthusiastic than scared.

They doubled back across the field, turned north, and ran up a small knoll. Louis heard the rumble first and slowed to look back. The car was a long way off but heading for them.

The far side of the knoll sloped down to a marshy hollow. Years ago, his father built a simple wooden footbridge in the only place that made sense. The old thing had deteriorated and was mainly forgotten —except by Louis and his friend Paul. The two loved the marsh. They grabbed their little nets each spring and ran off to catch tadpoles. In the summer, they spent entire days searching for frogs, butterflies, dragonflies, or anything fun to chase. They often sat on the bridge, dangling their feet in the stagnant water, eating cheese sandwiches, and crunching on carrots. When they finished snacking, one would yell, "Time!" Pulling their feet out, they would count the attached leeches and award bonus points for any stuck between the toes. A winner was declared and got full bragging rights. The loser had to remove all the bloodsuckers—unless a tie forced another round.

"This way, Mama," Louis waved, running down the slope. After crossing the footbridge, he waited for her. "He'll never get over that," he beamed.

"Head for the tracks, Louis!"

~ ~ ~

François grabbed the lantern, threw a roll of wire on his shoulder, and headed for the stairs.

"Halt!" he heard from above.

He stopped and peered around the mesh. A short, stocky soldier stood silhouetted in the doorway above. The Nazi directed him with two flicks of his pistol. Without a word, François dropped the roll.

He stepped into the kitchen and extinguished the flame. The gun-toting private and a beefy sergeant standing in the corner were unfamiliar, but the sight of the man with his back to him gazing out the window made his skin crawl.

"How may I help you?" François asked, breaking the brief silence.

The officer pulled his gloves off and turned. "Monsieur Dubois?"

"Oui."

"My name is Lieutenant Schmid. May I have a word with you?" The voice was both gentle and unsettling.

"Of course." The man's reputation preceded him, and his cursory gesture toward the table suggested a lack of choice. François accepted the offer and took a seat.

The lieutenant reached into a jacket pocket and strolled over to the cellar stairs. *Scritch*. François turned his head imperceptibly at the distinct sound of a struck match.

"Private Ott?"

"Sir?" the private responded, stepping over to his superior. Seconds later, the lieutenant returned to gaze out the window.

"Your French is quite good, Lieutenant," François said, trying to feign indifference to the near-deafening sound of boots clomping down the cellar stairs.

"My German's even better," Schmid jibed, "but I suspect it will do little good here. I have a busy schedule today," he said, still looking out. "But that's nothing new." He paused and nodded as though agreeing with himself. "I've come out of my way to see you, Dubois." He returned to the table. "Anyhow, my visit is necessary, so I'll get to the point." He pointed at a chair. "Do you mind?"

"Please," said François.

The lieutenant sat and drummed his fingers on the table as though deciding how to begin. "To be fair, Monsieur Dubois, I may need you to come in for further questioning if things don't work out as I'd like."

François stayed composed as the lurking sergeant stepped next to Schmid. "How may I help you, Lieutenant?"

"Oh," as though it had slipped his mind, "I meant to ask if anyone else is in the house this morning." He pulled out three photographs, took a cursory glance without revealing them, and slid them back into his breast pocket.

"No," François said. His experience taught him to offer up no more than was asked.

"Hmm, I thought not. One of my men saw someone running off on our way in. Your son, Louis? Or Colette, perhaps? Likely saw us and got frightened. Any child might do the same. Anyway, I sent him to find out."

François seethed inside. He never imagined a Nazi would concern himself with children. At a minimum, it meant Schmid or someone had researched the area residents. More disturbing was the specific knowledge he had of the family. The desire to squash the little man was building, and he understood how others might lose their cool in his presence—to their detriment.

Lieutenant Schmid had a slight build and lacked remarkable physical traits. His dirty blond hair looked like it had been drenched in cooking oil, but the two-inch scar on his right cheek was so well-suited for his face that one hardly noticed it. François studied him while listening to each word that spewed from his mouth and knew it wasn't his physique that supported such brash arrogance, but his weapons, stooges, and position as a Nazi officer.

"Your son, I suspect," Schmid continued. "Perhaps he can help me, too. But not to worry. I mean him no harm, of course. You say you haven't seen him?"

"Oh, I've seen him, Lieutenant...the way one sees fireflies. The boy's ten. If I could get him to stop playing or running around with friends, I'd get more done around here. He's supposed to help me repair the coop and corral the hens this morning. If only I could corral him first."

Schmid appeared to understand. "Fair enough." His face turned serious. "Monsieur, have you been here at your home all week?"

"No, I returned just last night."

"Returned? Where from?"

"Amboise."

"I see. What were you doing in Amboise?"

"I go there on occasion. It's the nearest town of consequence."

"I'm aware. You had business there?"

"I did."

"What kind, if you don't mind me asking?"

He minded. "I go to buy supplies. This time, I was also hoping to solve a problem."

"And?" the lieutenant asked with feigned anticipation. "Was your mission a success?"

"I'm hopeful."

"So, what's this problem of yours?"

"More like an inconvenience, I suppose. The French army requisitioned most trucks and horses, including mine. If they hadn't, the German army would have done the same. Don't get me wrong; I understand. I'm reminded every day how valuable they are. Even if I could share a truck with others, there's no petrol. My only choice for travel comes down to my cart and my feet." François glanced down at his worn boots.

Schmid rolled his hand. "Please, feel free to get to the point."

A crash came from the cellar. François ignored it and continued. "It takes at least three times longer to get to Amboise pulling a cart by foot than by horse. I met with some merchants, hoping to convince them to meet me between here and the town. My body would greatly prefer it."

Schmid remained attentive, unblinking. François expected the non-verbal aspect of the interrogation and had heard how the lieutenant relished it. Tales of the man's memory for detail were remarkable, and stories of citizens being mistreated, imprisoned, or even vanishing after stating simple lies weren't uncommon. Yet, as intimidating as the man was, François had the benefit of recounting undeniable events. Truthfully, he had gone to Amboise and had the conversations he described. If questioned, others could corroborate his story. He ordinarily traveled for legitimate, explainable, and verifiable reasons—even if his trips had more purpose than he let on.

"So, no other reason for going into town?" Schmid went on.

Answering with a lie might haunt him. "I prefer to accomplish as much as possible when I go, so I purchased some materials to make repairs around the farm." His brain raced, wondering if he should mention going elsewhere. He held off.

"Understandable," said Schmid. "And your wife? Is she around, or did you leave her in Amboise?"

François let himself smirk. "My wife would never let me live that down. No, she stayed home. As far as her whereabouts this morning, I've been wondering that myself. I was up and out at dawn, but she was up earlier. I haven't seen her since I got out of bed."

"If you've been out," he pointed to the stairs, "or down in the cellar, how do you know she's not in the house?"

Another loud clang came from below. François was troubled by the questioning and hoped the conversation didn't switch to his daughter's whereabouts. "Lieutenant, my wife and I have lived together a long time. I can assure you she's not in the house. For better or worse, it's her nature to make me aware of that."

Schmid grinned. "Do you mind if I look around? I'm always interested in how you French live."

"Please." François motioned with an open hand.

The lieutenant stood and walked to the cellar door. "Private?" he yelled down. "Give me some light." He started down the stairs.

"Watch your head," said the private. Schmid arrived at the bottom. "All clear down here, Sir."

"Must be the maid's day off," the officer grumbled, stumbling on some wire.

François followed him down. "Sorry. I admit it needs some work. I was bringing things up to repair the coop."

"If I had a wife, I suspect she wouldn't tolerate this," Schmid scoffed. He began kicking things around. "Then again, she wouldn't be living here, would she?"

He felt sick thinking of Colette lying below. *Stop moving things!*

After seconds that felt like an eternity, Schmid asked, "May I take a look around upstairs?"

"Upstairs? Certainly. Anywhere you like." François did his best to sound confident and relaxed—as much for his daughter as his visitors.

Schmid took a final look around and left. François followed. It was all he could do to avoid showing his relief when reentering the kitchen. But it was short-lived. The unmistakable *pop-pop* of two distant gunshots consumed him. He raced for the door.

"Verdammt," Schmid cursed.

CHAPTER TWO
East of Tours, France
The Prior Night, 2:00 am

HENRI FLAMAND GRUDGINGLY tolerated the relentless drizzle. He could only blame himself. He wore the requisite dark clothing, but his short jacket had glaring shortcomings compared to the full-length raincoat and hood effectively sheltering his cell leader, Marcel Bouchet. Regardless, they each preferred the dreary weather, and April in northern France was often accommodating whenever one hoped for rain. Moonless nights helped, but the rain had additional benefits. Bored German sentries and local police were apt to stay sheltered, and citizen collaborators were inclined to take time away from their snooping ways.

At two o'clock in the morning, with dawn well off, he and Marcel waited beneath the dripping leaves on the northern bank of the River Cher. The wooded area was small but remote, and the low branches hid them well.

The packages they brought were unaccustomed to discomfort. Henri glanced at the two sitting on a wet log a few meters away. The husband and wife looked cold, exhausted, miserable—and scared. He pitied them but knew their hardship kept them huddled and quiet. Meanwhile, he and Marcel strained their eyes and focused upstream, hoping to spot changes in the black water wending their way.

"The guy's a crook as far as I'm concerned," he grumbled to Marcel without averting his eyes.

"Well, the couple behind us might say he's worth every penny," Marcel whispered.

"How about he does it for France...or his own damn conscience?"

"So you wouldn't charge a fee or favor to risk your life for people you don't know?"

Henri gave his leader a bewildered look. "Aren't *we* risking our lives for people we don't know?"

Marcel raised his eyebrows and acknowledged the point. "Now that you mention it."

Henri remained sour. "It doesn't suit him," he said, wiping water from his face.

"How so?"

"He's old, he's fat...and he's fidgety. Nervous as a mouse at a cat convention and not an agreeable bone in his body. Acts like he doesn't even want to help. And I don't know how he does it. He'll have a heart attack one of these times and really screw us."

Marcel considered it. "He's stressed. Has a lot to lose, including his wife and his life. He wants to do his part, I suppose. Might as well get something for it. Anyhow, he's got a boat, knows the area inside out, and hasn't failed yet. Do you know of another way? Anyway, I hope the high water isn't giving him trouble."

"I hope it's his only trouble," said Henri. "Whenever there's a delay, the packages grow more anxious, restless, and miserable. Not to mention me." He peeked back at the two huddled together. "I sure don't envy them. The trip upriver could be grim."

"They'll be fine. The rain's starting to let up."

"I'm not talking about the weather. I couldn't spend ten seconds in a boat with that asshole."

They fell silent as a dark shape slid around the bend fifty meters upstream. Henri pulled a flashlight from his jacket, sent two short bursts, and waited. The reply came seconds later. He and Marcel walked over to the couple.

"Stay positive," Henri urged.

"We can't thank you both enough," the husband said.

Marcel shook the man's hand. "Thanks for your patience. Before long, this will all be behind you."

"Are you sure you can't say where he's taking us?" the wife pleaded.

Henri shook his head. "Nobody knows. For the same reason, you don't know where we are now. The less any of us know, the safer. If questioned, we can't divulge your destination, right?"

"We understand," said the man. "It's just hard not knowing."

"Be sure to thank that kind, big man for us," the wife added.

Henri knew what she meant. Their week-long stay at the safe house was uneventful, but packages were always uneasy. François Dubois hadn't spent much time with them, but he did well navigating their transfer into his and Marcel's hands.

"We will," said Henri. He gave a reassuring look and asked them to sit tight.

~ ~ ~

Alone on his weathered rowboat, Auguste Gagnon frequently craned his neck toward the shoreline, looking for the signal. His hair had become a matted mop. It stuck to his forehead like leeches at a blood bank as he continued pulling on the oars. Two short blasts of light cut through the gloom. He stopped rowing, fumbled for the flashlight hanging around his neck, and gave a single return flash. He dropped it back under his cloak and pulled on the oars.

Cell members often referred to him as River Man. He couldn't care less what they called him as long as he got paid. Fruitful opportunities were abundant in wartime, and he planned on making the most of them. He despised the work, but it was too lucrative to resist. His price was steep, and if people didn't like it, good luck finding another option.

Auguste spent his entire life farming nearby and knew the river and surrounding landscape better than anyone. This was the best spot for a clandestine transfer: far from city lights, well-hidden, lazy waters, and no garrisoned dams to skirt. He hated the late hours, but it was the only way. And tonight, he was eager to get his hands on his reward. He callously referred to certain packages as "jewels." Tonight's shipment was a perfect example: Jewish, childless, wealthy, and willing to pay anything to flee Nazi persecution.

Nearing the landing, he saw another muted flash to guide him. Despite his cape, he felt drenched as his waterlogged boat brushed against some low branches. He remained seated while Henri grabbed the bow and pulled it onto the muddy flat.

Marcel approached. "Everything okay? You're a bit late."

"I know," he snapped. "Would you rather do this? The weather's been lousy ever since I left the house. How are the...jewels?" he asked, knowing how Marcel and Henri hated the term.

Marcel glanced over at them. "The *packages* are wet, tired, and stressed but otherwise fine."

"Who isn't?" Auguste's eyes darted to the two waiting passengers. He measured them up. "Do they have the toll?"

Henri got close to his ear. "I've got it here, you greedy bastard."

He stepped back and tossed a cloth pouch. Auguste bobbled and dropped it. Bending over, he lost his footing in the mud and flopped onto his stomach. He grabbed the bag and stood up. Henri shook his head and gave Marcel a look that said: *See what I mean?*

"How are things on the other side?" Marcel asked, changing the subject while deliberately avoiding specifics.

"It's turning into a cesspool. Full of overzealous police and greedy collaborators trying to score points and make ends meet. You can't trust anyone."

Marcel looked thoughtful. "I heard even the Nazis are amazed at how efficient our police can be...rounding up Jewish folk and turning them over faster than they can ship them out."

"Free France, my ass," Henri grumbled.

Auguste tried wiping the mud off his cape, but only smeared it around. "It's true. I may have to change things to avoid sending them through Loches. But it's not great anywhere. I fear the day may come when none of this will have been worth it. Is there a next shipment?"

"The twenty-fifth. One person," Marcel whispered.

"One? We've never done just one," Auguste griped. "Is it even worth my while?"

"It's a big fish, and it can't get caught," Henri said through clenched teeth. "A pilot. It'll be worth it, all right."

"Okay, okay. The twenty-fifth. Same time."

"How was the last run?" Marcel asked. Auguste expected the question. He got it every trip.

"The usual. I wash my hands of them and let others deal with it." His answer was intentionally unhelpful. Marcel didn't pry. "Anyway, the trip back upstream is the real pain in my butt, and time's wasting. I don't get paid by the hour, but people sure gripe if I'm not on time."

Marcel waved over the husband and wife. The pair gave their two guides wet hugs and stepped into the boat. They huddled together in the only space available—a narrow bench seat near the bow with a view of their oarsman's back. Henri shoved the stern, and Auguste pulled on the oars. As always, the boat rocked slightly as the couple gave a last wave to two men they would never see again. The dank gloom soon enveloped them.

~ ~ ~

It surprised François when he was approached in the fall. He was only somewhat acquainted with Marcel Bouchet but had heard how the cell leader's integrity, character, and unwavering patriotism were unquestioned. It wasn't until later that he learned Marcel had sought him out for the same reasons.

François stood out in a crowd. He was tall. He was big. With his full beard, he could make a child believe in giants. But Marcel explained how his gentle demeanor was a bonus and insisted he'd be an asset to the resistance. After two days of self-debate and reasoning with his wife, François couldn't say no.

Tonight's assignment wouldn't require his size or appearance. He and his friend Roland Viard would be tracking River Man after he left Henri and Marcel with the packages. Unbeknownst to the boat occupants, the two sat upstream on the Cher's northern bank, hidden within a small cluster of trees. They had patiently looked on as Auguste came downstream by himself. Now, they awaited his return.

Over several months, a network of brave patriots had helped others embark on a similar journey. Unfortunately, nobody ever learned the result of their efforts. For them, the story ended each time River Man departed upstream with the packages. François wasn't alone in feeling hopelessly ignorant about the fates of those he helped. Like everyone else, he could only move on to other matters.

River Man's explanations were always vague. All that was known was that after heading back and landing on the southern bank, he would stash the old boat, make his way south, and have the passengers briefly lay low before moving them on. That was it. Auguste claimed to have no knowledge or interest in what happened next. He, too, asserted it was best not to know what others were doing or where they were going.

François understood that keeping track of the bigger picture was Marcel's job, but news of outside activities was sporadic and inconsistent. Out of extreme caution, Marcel preferred to limit contact with other cells. Everyone agreed it was safest that way. Tonight, François was asked to take a small step, and if watching River Man meant improving their understanding, it felt justified. The cell leader wanted a team of two. François agreed to the request and suggested Roland Viard as the second. The two worked well together, and Roland's reliability was undeniable. Marcel approved it.

He planned on staying an extra day away from the farm and told his wife. As usual, Giselle shared her fears and pleaded for him to stay home. He gave no specifics about the assignment but reassured her as best he could. The reality was that there were risks with almost anything. For starters, it wasn't unusual for the Germans to lay mines in various fields, including the vicinity where he and Roland were asked to work tonight. Fortunately, the explosives were seldom a surprise. Affected farmers would complain to local officials that portions of their land were no longer usable and their property was now overtaxed. It was a reasonable and compelling argument. Field-verifying the complaints wasn't in their job description, so to adjust for the inconvenience, an official would note the mine locations based on verbal descriptions. Not only was the taxable acreage adjusted, but copies were passed along by a civic official sympathetic to the cause. The cell cartographer would mark up maps accordingly. These were then reviewed and memorized by anyone given a field assignment.

Tonight, François and Roland confidently sloshed across the wet fields. To avoid detection, they kept well ahead and inland, returning to the shoreline upriver of Auguste's boat to wait, watch, and listen before moving on again.

"Damn, he's not the quietest rower," grumbled Roland. "All that clunking could wake Hitler himself. You'd think he'd be better at it or at least more careful."

François nodded. "River's done this enough times. Maybe he's gotten comfortable with what to expect. Perhaps too comfortable."

"Then again, maybe we're a bit on edge," Roland reasoned.

"I prefer it that way," François whispered, his eyes locked downstream, waiting for the boat to come into view.

"Any idea how long we'll be tracking him?"

"Nobody knows, but Marcel suspects he doesn't go far. He's not in the best shape for a long trip, especially rowing upstream with passengers. His farm's on the south side, and I suspect he'll make it as easy as possible. Maybe he stashes bicycles."

"I sure can't picture him on a bicycle," Roland muttered.

"Anyway," François continued, "it must be somewhere before Dierre. The dam nearby would end his trip, and I doubt he'd risk getting close to it. They're patrolled. Can't blame them, I suppose."

François and his friend moved farther upstream and waited at a bend on the northern bank where a narrow road neared the Cher. They again heard the boatman before they saw him. A shape soon loomed faintly against a dark backdrop of trees. River Man was hugging the far shoreline. The boat slowed and came to a stop. Wanting to avoid the muddy slopes, François and Roland stayed crouched among a copse of trees. François squinted through the drizzle as the passengers stepped out. The two packages sat on what appeared to be a large stump. The man sat hunched with his arm around his wife. François tapped his friend on the shoulder and pointed as Auguste returned to the boat and began resetting the oars.

"What the hell's he doing?" François whispered as much to himself as to Roland.

The boat departed upstream just as another figure appeared

seemingly out of nowhere. The female passenger rose and hugged the shorter newcomer.

"Is that a woman? I think that's a woman," said Roland.

"Hmm," grunted François. "I think you're right. Stay here and watch what happens. I'll follow River, and maybe this will make sense somehow. I'll be back as soon as I can. Then we'd better head out."

The sun wouldn't be up for a while, but their long trip home would require caution. Moving slightly inland, François kept an eye on the rear-facing oarsman.

~ ~ ~

Roland sat against a tree trunk and focused. Shortly after François left him, the three on the opposite shore disappeared into the trees. He strained to see through the dark and drizzle. It was no use. Fifteen minutes passed, and he saw nothing more.

"What are you doing here?" came a high-pitched voice.

Roland's heart leaped into his throat as he wheeled around. He tried gathering his wits.

"Damn, you startled me," he said to the stranger. "I didn't hear you." He realized his fixation on the far shoreline was careless. Recovering, he pretended to show interest in something downriver. "I thought I heard noises out there."

The stranger paused. "I don't hear anything. And that doesn't answer my question," he barked.

The policeman looked too young for the part—maybe eighteen years old. A raincoat covered him well, but his outdated, flat-topped Kepi cap was unmistakable. He held his pistol in a way that indicated he didn't feel threatened but thought it best to have on display.

Roland was out after curfew and too far from home to be visiting a friend on foot. It wasn't wise to reveal a friend's name anyway. Such a lie could be discovered and put any named person in the precarious position of not knowing what to say when questioned. From training and experience, he knew not to trust the policeman's allegiances. Although there were many trustworthy local officials, some even essential to the resistance movement, he'd also heard the stories of police welcoming Nazi bribes of food, coffee, perfumes, money—and family security. In exchange, they assisted the Germans with anything. Being interrogated wasn't an option.

"You aren't supposed to be here," the young man scolded. "Papers!"

He was French, but his Nazi manner was transparent. Roland moved toward the road and glanced back across the water. He hoped to look more like a curious passerby than a threat. He approached the policeman in a disarming way.

"I was just on my way home from seeing a sick friend when I thought I heard—"

He lunged, hoping to catch him off guard. His right fist landed squarely on the youngster's jaw, knocking him down. The pistol tumbled off the road. The officer recovered, and the two wrestled in the gravel and mud. Roland sprang to his feet, sent two hard kicks into the man's ribs, and turned to run. A leg swung around, caught him above the ankle, and sent him tumbling. His hat flew off, and he scrambled to his feet. He grabbed the knife from the leather sheath around his calf without thinking. The policeman was on his feet and rushing at him. Roland thrust the blade deep into the man's stomach, pulled it out, and stabbed it into his chest.

"Wha..., why did you do that?" the young man stuttered, slumping to the road.

He was dead within seconds.

Stunned, Roland stared down at the lifeless body. Without

thinking, he took off running in the direction of home. But home was a long way off.

~ ~ ~

François plodded along undetected as Auguste Gagnon continued upstream. The boat rounded a bend and beached next to a wooded area on the far bank. François worked his way behind a large willow, then over to a mass of tangled brush directly across from the landing. He was well hidden, watching through a gap in the branches. As expected, River Man was stashing the boat. Dragging it up the muddy slope, he slipped and landed face-first. Recovered, he pulled the boat out of sight.

That's pretty good, François thought. *Best not to keep the boat in the same place you drop your people.* He wondered how Auguste would get back to his passengers. *Could be a shortcut through the woods. Maybe uses a bicycle?*

River Man walked eastward near the shoreline. François followed on his side. After a minute or two, Auguste waved his hand several times above his head as though batting at flies. Flickers of light danced in the tree branches. Two dim beams pierced the murky darkness across the river to François' left. *That would be the road from Bléré.* He considered warning Auguste, but caught himself. *Maybe that's who he's signaling.* He stayed crouched and motionless. The lights grew brighter, and the low rumble of two motorcycles breached the calm. François recalled a trick Louis told him about. He wasn't sure it worked for humans, but took no chances and squinted his eyes to keep them from reflecting light.

Is this the transfer? No. Too loud. Was the signal meant for somebody else? Is he caught? The engines stopped, but the headlights stayed on. He sat unblinking as Auguste began conversing with them. Simple. No animation. No sign of danger. The glow from the headlights was sufficient to reveal Auguste handing something over. *The woman's purse? For safekeeping?* The driver turned his back and appeared to be examining the contents. *Is he throwing it back at him?* Auguste dropped the tossed bag and bent to pick it up.

One of them pointed a gun at River's head and, just as quickly, holstered it. *What the—?* The other walked up and put his arm around River's shoulder. *What in the hell's going on?* That was the end of it. One motorcycle headed back east; the other went south. In seconds, all was dark again. François made out River Man trudging south. *Why did they leave him there? Is anyone going to get the packages?* François made a mental note of the landing location. Carefully looking around, he began his trek back. *What the hell was that about? Maybe Roland has some answers.*

Several minutes later, he saw a dark mass on the road ahead. He crouched. A sickening thought struck him. Hearing nothing, he whisper-shouted toward the body. "Roland?" No response. "Roland!" Ignoring the risk, he ran to it. "Merde." He tried again. "Roland!" Silence was all he got in return.

Looking down at the dead body, he saw a knife handle sticking out of the policeman's chest. "Jesus, Roland." It made a horrid sound pulling it out, and he ran to the river, throwing it wildly. A glance across to the passenger drop revealed nothing. He slipped and nearly fell. Something didn't feel right. Blood covered the soles of both boots. *Damn!* Stepping into the river, he used both hands to try scrubbing them. *Enough! Get out of here. Go home. No, don't go home.* He tried slowing his brain. *Where did he go?* Dawn was coming. *Stick to the plan. Get home. Tell everything at the meeting tomorrow.*

CHAPTER THREE
South of the River Cher
April 16, Dawn

AT FIRST AGITATED, the longer Auguste waited, the more he worried. It was nearly morning when his wife, a stout woman in her late forties, walked through the front door. River Man groaned and stood up from the high-back armchair he'd been sitting in for two hours.

"Well?"

She removed her hat and hung it on a hook. Wavy, salt-and-pepper hair fell around her shoulders as she pulled a cape over her head and draped it on the hallway chair. After removing her shoes, she entered the living room and slumped onto the sofa.

"That took longer than usual," he said with growing impatience. "How did it go?"

"It's done," she said, "and thank heaven the rain finally stopped."

"So, no trouble?"

"No, but those two souls have no idea what lies ahead."

Auguste sank back into his chair. "They never do. But neither do we, right? Honestly, we don't know. Maybe they'll be fine?" he suggested, as though it were a question.

Flora glared at him but let it go. "Am I being paranoid? I feel like everyone's watching. Iris poked her nose out again. Always asking questions, that one. Why is she even awake at this hour? Her snooping may be the death of me...or her."

"She's harmless."

"I don't know," Flora sighed. "I'm not sure about anyone anymore."

She looked to the kitchen. "I can't sleep yet. I'll put on some coffee."

Auguste was pleased with the idea. "Your coffee would be the envy of France."

"But nobody will ever know about it," she replied. "We'll be keeping that a secret, won't we?"

Auguste followed her and sat at a small, round breakfast table. Flora brought a bowl of sugar cubes and returned to the stovetop. When ready, she poured an espresso into two porcelain cups, added a dollop of steamed milk to each, and set one in front of him. He plucked a cube from the bowl, dipped it in his café crème, and popped it in his mouth. They sat in their thoughts.

"How was the river?" she finally asked.

"Miserable. Wet, cold, tiring, stressful. The usual."

"How's your back?"

"Killing me," he grumbled.

"Auguste?" She set her cup down and waited for him to look up.

"Mmm."

"I know I keep saying it, but we've got to figure a way out of this. It's too much."

He closed his eyes and wiped a hand down his face. His wife had the same distressed look every time they had the conversation.

"Jesus, if it were that easy, we wouldn't still be here, would we? You need to stop bringing it up."

Flora heaved. "It's just that it's gotten to the point where we have more than we could ever—"

Auguste was exasperated. "I know!" he interrupted. "I know. I know. But we can't do anything with it. Not yet."

She stared blankly at the tabletop. "I'm afraid our luck will run out. I don't know how it'll happen, but I have a bad feeling we'll never get to spend any of it."

He tipped his head back and looked toward the ceiling. "I don't see another way...short of sneaking out of town in the dark of night with nothing but sacks of money and jewels on our backs. And you know how it is. Nobody can sneak anywhere anymore. Some people around here are worse than the damn Nazis."

"I just don't know," she groaned. "Maybe that's exactly what we need to do."

"No. We need to hang on. The war will be over before you know it, and we'll live out the rest of our days like royalty."

"Hah, not here, we won't."

"No, not here," he agreed, knowing what she meant. "It's not our fault we're smarter than them."

"Well, they sure know how to resent it. I feel like I'm walking on eggshells every time I go out. It's misdirected. The Germans are their enemy, not us."

He thought about it. "Citizens make for easier targets." They sipped their coffees in silence. Auguste finally perked up. "Hey, Flora! It was a long night, but we did well. The best we've ever done!"

"I'm exhausted," she sighed, taking one last sip. "I'll remake the room. There's little to do. Never enough time for them to—"

"Do you need help moving the bookcase?"

"No. I'm fine."

"Should we stock it with more books? Make it heavier? Is there a chance somebody could discover it by accident?"

She considered it. "Seems a waste of time now. What if we—" She stopped to think. "What if instead of hiding people in there, we use it to store...you know...other things?"

His head kept bobbing as he stewed it over. "Yeah. That makes sense. The packages are rarely here long enough to matter. Even if they stayed in the guest room, they'd never discover the passage. Safer to store things there than under our bed."

Auguste pulled down the shades in the bedroom and changed into his pajamas. After resetting the hiding space behind the guest room, Flora crawled into bed and soon snored at his side. He replayed the night in his head before joining her in the noise-making.

CHAPTER FOUR
The Dubois Farm
April 16, Mid-morning

THE GUNSHOT ECHOES still hung in the air as François raced outside. He ran around the corner of the house but saw nothing. The sergeant and private came up behind. The lieutenant walked up moments later.

"Where in the hell's that driver?" Schmid snapped.

"Not sure, Sir," said the hulking sergeant.

Seconds later, a Kübelwagen appeared over a low ridge to the north, the driver waving at the group with his pistol.

Private Ernst Wegner was excited and breathless as he pulled up. "Warning shots, Sir!" The young man's military papers verified he was eighteen, though he could've passed for fifteen. "Someone was running off. Then I saw another. I went after them, but a marsh got in the way. I fired shots in the air, hoping they'd stop."

François felt a surge of relief course through his body.

"Idiot," the lieutenant sneered. "Did you get a good look at them?"

"No, Sir, but it looked like a woman and a child."

"Boy or girl?"

"Um...boy, I'm pretty sure."

"Which direction?"

"North, toward a rail line."

"Nobody else?"

"No, Sir. Just the two."

Lieutenant Schmid turned to François and raised his eyebrows. François shrugged, so relieved at the boy's story that little else mattered. He stood idly by as Schmid addressed the driver.

"What's your damn name, Private?" the lieutenant barked.

"Wegner, Sir. Ernst Wegner."

"How did you end up with me today?"

"I don't know, Sir. It was last-minute. I think somebody was sick."

"Uh huh. Lucky me. So, are you trying to make me look bad?"

"Sir?" said the confused private.

"A new major is arriving today." Without waiting for a response, Schmid drew nearer. "Rumor is he thinks things are getting too soft around here. I've never met the man, but without exception, I hear he's a real son of a bitch!"

The lieutenant paused, and François wasn't sure if the driver was supposed to respond.

Private Wegner seemed just as unsure. "Umm...yes, Sir, I...I heard one time he—"

"Shut up and listen, you shit. I'm attending his welcome dinner this evening. And, believe me, if he finds out about it, he'll wonder how I let a woman and CHILD slip away!" Schmid backed off a couple of steps and calmed himself. "I can gladly offer your name, but that won't matter. He'll hold us both responsible for your incompetence. Damn it, I'll deal with you later." He motioned for François to follow and walked into the house. Private Wegner followed at a distance before standing rigid inside the kitchen door.

"It seems my idiot has discovered the whereabouts of your wife and son," Schmid muttered, sitting at the kitchen table.

François nodded. "He may have frightened them off."

The lieutenant turned his head and glared at the young driver. "Hopefully not for long. I may have some questions for them. By the way, Monsieur Dubois, have you seen your daughter recently?"

The question made him uneasy, but François acted indifferently and continued to stick with factual statements. "I saw her earlier, but not since."

The lieutenant motioned at his men to search the house, then sat in thought. François knew that assisting them was beneath the officer. He remained silent, waiting for the two subordinates to return.

"Well?" Schmid asked the returning private.

"Nobody here, Sir."

"Your daughter's not home either, Dubois?" François shrugged again. "Do your children ever help you around here?"

"Tracking them down to help with chores is a chore in itself. Just ask my wife."

"Perhaps I will if someone could track *her* down." He glared again at his driver, then paused as though considering his options. The others waited patiently. "I have some questions your family might help me with. Unfortunately, they've all gone missing. But no matter, I'm sure we can find them soon enough. I do, however, have a few more questions for you."

"I'm not sure what I—"

The lieutenant held up a finger to cut him off. "Sergeant Protz?" He snapped his fingers twice and held his palm out.

The sergeant walked over, pulled an item from his coat pocket, and handed it over. Schmid tossed a dirty leather cap onto the table.

"This was found on a road late last night. Do you recognize it?"

He did. "It's not mine."

"No, I'm sure it isn't." The lieutenant turned it over and pointed to some writing inside. "The name's a bit worn, but 'R Viard' is what it looks like to me."

It wasn't a question, but François sensed Schmid expected him to speak, and playing stupid wasn't sensible. "I've got a neighbor, Roland Viard. He says his wife loves labeling things, so I suspect—" He studied the hat again. "Yes, I'm sure it's his."

"Pretty careless of him, don't you think?"

"I suppose," François answered. "But I'll admit, I've been known to lose things occasionally."

"I don't doubt it, but that's not quite what I mean. I'm saying it was careless to have his name in it."

François furrowed his brow. "Seems more precautionary than careless. I'd probably benefit from labeling some things, too."

"Yeah, maybe someone could do the same for me. But I just came from the Viard place. I'll tell you the same thing I told him. The problem I'm having is that it was found far from anywhere he claims to have been."

François raised one eyebrow. "I suppose that is odd."

"Viard attempted to explain it," Schmid continued, "but I wasn't convinced." He drummed his fingers on the table, staring at François. "On a different note, I wondered if there's any reason why someone would say they saw you with him yesterday?"

François understood the question was designed to unnerve him. *It's what he does. That's why he's here. But if Roland folded to questioning, this conversation would've ended long ago.* More likely, it meant Schmid knew little and was fishing for more. He remained calm. "Lieutenant, *why* people do or say things often escapes me. On the other hand, if you're asking me why someone *did* tell you that, I wouldn't know. But, if you're asking me if somebody *might* tell you, I can help. I came across him on my way to Amboise. I'm not the best with details." He paused as though considering. "Yes, I believe he was wearing a hat." He thought again. "I suspect he could have worn and lost it...or had it stolen. Where did you say it was found?"

Schmid leaned back in his chair and shook his head. "I didn't, but that's where it gets interesting. It was found near a dead policeman in the middle of nowhere...far from here, and far from Amboise. Another Frenchman killed at the hands of his countrymen." He smiled with his mouth, not his eyes. His tone soured. "You're cleverer than most, Dubois, but I'm wasting my time. We'll continue this in Tours." He stood and walked out without another word.

Stunned, François called after him. "Tours? How can I be of help to you in Tours?"

Private Ott looked pleased to have the opportunity to show off his gun again. He waved it at François to go outside. Desperate to have them off his property, François complied.

Hoping to warn his daughter that he was leaving, he turned and yelled to the private. "If we're going to Tours, could you grab my coat off the chair?"

The German obliged.

CHAPTER FIVE
Giselle & Louis
April 16, Mid-morning

GISELLE AND LOUIS ran eastward along the rail line, staying in the shadows when possible. Exhausted, she waved her arm to get his attention and ducked into a hedgerow opening. She sat down in the shade, satisfied nobody was following.

"I just need to catch my breath," she panted.

Louis remained standing. He poked his head out, looking left and right. "Mama, I don't think they're coming. Papa said to keep going."

She nodded. "We should be getting close. Maybe half a kilometer. One at most."

Louis busied himself, keeping a watchful eye for a minute or two. He peeked back at her. "It's still clear," he whispered.

She took a deep breath. "I'm ready. Stay quiet and keep to the sides. If you see or hear anything, hide. I'll follow."

"Okay, Mama."

"Let's go."

It wasn't long before she waved for Louis to stop. A worn cart path crossed the rail line, running south across a barren field and up a long slope.

"I think this is it." Crossing the open area worried her. If enough seed was available, the field would be lush by late June and could provide some cover. But not now. They had no other option. She exhaled. "Here we go."

Louis was well ahead of her when a distant gunshot rang out. He went down.

"Ahh!" Giselle screamed, running to him.

He peered up at her. "Shh, Mama. Get down."

She landed at his side. "You scared me to death. Don't do that!"

"Oh, I thought it was the best thing to do."

"Well...it was. I just—" Another shot stopped her.

"It's far off," he whispered. "I don't think anybody saw us, but we can't stay here."

"No," she agreed, scanning the horizon. "Now!"

Over the crest, the Touchard place stood out in the distance.

"Run for the barn, Louis. Behind it!"

They reached it, and he squatted beside her as she peeked out from the corner. The farmhouse was thirty meters away. She studied it, unsure what she was looking for. "Louis, you stay here. No, bad idea. Come on." He sprang up. She grabbed his wrist and pulled him back. "Stay with me. No running now."

Her small knuckles took the brunt of the exchange when she knocked on the solid oak door. There was no response.

"I'll try, Mama." Louis pounded on the door—still nothing.

Giselle reached for the handle.

"May I help you?" She and Louis both jumped at the calm voice behind them. Charles Touchard gave them a welcoming smile and slipped a shotgun sling from his shoulder. "Ah, Madame Dubois, I thought it was you."

"Oh, Monsieur Touchard, you startled me," she said, putting fingertips to her throat. "I'm so glad you're home."

She had never visited without her husband, but the man showed no surprise or concern. "Please come in," Charles offered, opening the door. He set the gun inside the entry. "I wouldn't dare carry it in public, but it helps with the squirrels. The red ones are a real nuisance. So, tell me, where did you two come from? Is François with you?" She shook her head. Sensing her distress, he peeked back outside before closing the door.

In the dining room, Charles listened intently as Giselle explained all she could remember about the morning. Louis chimed in often, excitedly embellishing or contributing points of clarification.

"What's going on?" she sobbed when finished. "I have no idea what's happened to François and Colette. He got home so late last night. What's he gotten himself into?"

"Everything will be fine," Charles tried reassuring her. "He might even be sitting at home, anxious for me to bring you two back. The worst that could happen...and it's not even that bad...is they may take him in to question him about something."

"Why? What would he—"

"It's not unusual, but I'll get to the bottom of it."

Louis jumped up. "What about their guns, Monsieur Touchard? Why were they shooting at us?"

"No, no. I'm sure they were just warning shots in hopes you would stop. They didn't want you and your mother running away. You did well. Your father will be proud. By the way, young man, how did you know the soldiers were coming to your house?"

"I just got to my friend Paul's, and I saw the cars and heard yelling inside. I ran home to tell Papa. I ran all the way without stopping."

Charles turned his eyes to Giselle. "Paul being the son of Roland and Regina?"

"Yes. Does that mean anything to you?"

"I'm not sure. I need to get to your place and find out what I can. Most important now is making sure your husband and daughter are fine and letting them know you two are safe."

"I'm going with you."

"Giselle, please come to the kitchen. Louis, I need you to wait here

38

a minute. Is that okay?"

"Yes, Sir."

In the kitchen, Charles explained himself. "Let me make sure the coast is clear back at your place. Whatever is going on, they may also want to question you and Louis."

"But what could a little boy possibly—" Her voice drifted off.

"I don't know. But we need to keep you out of harm's way. You can help that happen by remaining here for now. Get some rest in the spare room upstairs. Keep quiet and stay away from windows." He pointed to the pantry. "Have a bite to eat. You two must be hungry."

"What will you do?"

"I'm going to get a friend. We'll make the rounds and find out what we can."

"Charles!" she cried, as though seeing a ghost. "The cellar!"

"I know. If I don't see anyone, it's the first place I'll look." He put his arm around her and walked her to the door. "Be sure to bolt the lock behind me. Eat and drink whatever you like, and please get some rest. I should be back late this evening."

He hugged her, shot Louis a heartening look, and was gone.

CHAPTER SIX
The Viard & Dubois Farms
April 16, Early Afternoon

CHARLES TOUCHARD'S CLOSEST friend was Georges Perrin. Both were in their early fifties and eager to help undermine the foreign presence in and around Tours. They admired their younger cell leader, Marcel Bouchet. He was passionate but levelheaded and calculating. Their pride wasn't hurt when he withheld them from more rigorous tasks, assuring them their experience and knowledge could benefit the team in other ways. Georges knew the entire region and was adept at assimilating and coordinating information. Marcel made him head of intelligence and data gathering.

Charles told his friend everything he'd learned from Giselle and then listened to Georges explain last night's field assignment on the north bank of the River Cher.

"I don't like coincidences," said Charles.

"No. And, it's safe to say that the two getting questioned the morning after an assignment isn't a coincidence."

"Roland's place is on the way to the Dubois farm. We should stop there first."

"You're right," said Georges. "Let's go."

They crept up behind the Viard house like mice wary of conspicuous cheese. Snooping in the windows, they saw nothing.

"The way Roland says it, Regina is cooking in the kitchen almost every afternoon," Charles whispered. "It's not a good sign." He thought for a second. "Don't they have a dog?"

Georges understood. "We should have seen or heard something.

Should we try getting in?"

"We'd better keep moving. I don't feel good about this."

They walked and jogged, nearly retracing the back way Louis had taken that morning. Entering a dense wood southeast of the house, they separated to get different vantage points. Five minutes later, Charles returned to his friend.

"It's like the Viard place."

"Deserted," Georges agreed.

Charles shook his head. "On the off chance we find Colette, she could be a mess. François desperately feared his kids ever having to experience that pit."

Approaching, Charles tested the kitchen door handle. Unlocked. He made a rapping motion at Georges to get his thoughts about knocking. Georges shook his head. They stepped inside.

Charles ducked his head going down the cellar stairs, and pointed up as a warning.

"I heard all about it but haven't seen it," said Georges, following close behind. He looked about. "It looks like my cellar. Hell, it looks like anybody's cellar."

Charles began clearing junk away. "That's the idea. And he didn't build it for himself. It was to hide his family or those in need. Here, set these over there."

At last, moving a worn rug to one side, Charles knelt beside the remaining boards and listened, but heard nothing.

"Anyone here?" he called softly. Getting no response, he tried again. "It's Monsieur Touchard. Is anyone here?" He moved the boards aside, grabbed the lantern, and held it above the opening. He gave Georges a thumbs-up. "Don't be afraid. It's Monsieur Touchard." She didn't speak or move—as though paralyzed. Her eyes opened and clenched back shut. He understood and set the lantern to the side.

"Your mother sent me, Colette. Let me help you out of there."

Her breaths were short and rapid as he eased her out. He let her cling to him, quivering and weeping silently. She felt clammy. He slipped off his coat and wrapped it around her. Georges motioned to him, touched his eyes, and pointed up. His movement toward the stairs startled her.

"Who's—"

"It's alright. That's Monsieur Perrin. He's here to help, too."

"I...I didn't see him." She rubbed her eyes. "It was so dark in there. Blacker than—"

"Let's get you out of here," Charles whispered.

Colette eased her grip on him and sniffled. "Did you say my mother's okay?"

"Yes, yes. Safe and sound at my place. But how are you doing?"

"I'm cold. I must have—" She shook her head. "I must have fallen asleep. The Germans were coming. Papa told me to wait and count the —. Monsieur Touchard, where's my father?"

"I'm not certain yet, but I hope to see him later this afternoon. In the meantime, it's my privilege to escort you from this cellar. I think you've spent enough time down here for one lifetime, non?" She sniffled again, and they went up to the kitchen.

"Nice and quiet outside," Georges noted as the two entered. "It's good to see you, Colette. I'm very sorry about your eventful morning."

"We both are," Charles added with a forced smile. "But today's our lucky day. We get to spend the rest of it with you until you're reunited with your parents." He pulled a kitchen chair toward her and patted the seat.

"What about Louis?" she said, sitting down.

"He's fine and with your mother."

Georges continued to peek out the windows. He motioned with

his finger for Charles to join him. "We should leave here now to get to the meeting. And those Nazis could come back any time."

"Right. We'll bring Colette. She isn't cleared, but given the circumstances—" Charles looked toward the cellar. "First, we need to put that back together."

Colette was still in her nightgown and slippers and asked to go change. He and Georges went down to conceal the pit and put everything back into disarray.

"She should have some useful insights," said Georges as they finished. "Let's get moving. It's more than an hour's walk the way we'll need to go."

Returning to the kitchen, Colette asked, "Where are we going, Monsieur Touchard?"

Charles continued his upbeat approach. "Well, we're heading toward Chançay to see if we can't find out more about this crazy morning you've had. We'll go the back way so we don't bother those annoying soldiers."

They walked northwest across a field, through some woods, and up an embankment to the rail bed. After several minutes, Colette stopped and stared blankly at the ground.

"Monsieur Touchard, have you ever been buried alive?"

"Uh, no. I can't say that I have."

"Have you Monsieur Perrin?"

She didn't look up, but Georges just shook his head.

"I have. And I don't plan on it ever again. It wasn't cold at first, but it seeped into me. It kept seeping. And I've never seen black like that. I don't even think you can call it seeing. I put my hand right in front of me and saw nothing. It seemed lighter when I closed my eyes. Is that even possible?"

"I—" Charles began.

"I don't think the cold and blackness were the worst part. It was the sounds."

"Like voices?" he tried.

"No." She shook her head and slowly looked up at him. "Not voices. More like centipedes fighting. Or...maybe maggots swarming over a dead mouse. I kept thinking things were on my face, but my hand never felt anything."

Charles didn't know what to say. Georges broke the silence.

"Hey, Charles. I haven't seen any good wildlife around this spring. How about you?"

He picked up on the attempt. "Maybe Germany gave them a daytime curfew."

"The animals!" Colette suddenly cried. "Messieurs, we must go back! I need to tend to them!"

Charles looked to Georges for help.

"Colette, they'll be okay," Georges tried reassuring her. "I'm sure your mother and father cared for them this morning. Skipping lunch might even do them some good."

"But Monsieur Perrin, what if Jessible starts biting Clarice again?"

Time was pressing, and Charles stepped in. "Jessible and Clarice?"

"My geese. They're best friends but can fight like jealous sisters. One time they—"

"Colette, they'll have to work things out," he interjected soberly and in a tone he hoped she'd understand. "Today, we need your help more than the animals do."

They continued walking, remaining wary at road crossings. Halfway there, Georges stopped, closed his eyes, then opened them. "Train," he said, pointing eastward. "Two minutes at most."

Charles took a quick inventory of the surroundings. "Over here."

He guided Colette across the tracks and down a shallow,

overgrown ravine. They crouched low and waited. A short four-car train sped past.

Georges glanced at his pocket watch. "Not scheduled. Important though. I'd say the new major has arrived."

The three gathered themselves and continued walking.

CHAPTER SEVEN
Tours, France
April 16, Afternoon

THE MAIN ENTRANCE to the Gare de Tours was a magnificent blend of architecture and art admired by locals and visitors alike. Four massive stone columns were adorned with sculptures giving tribute to the rail-connected cities of Limoges, Bordeaux, Toulouse, and Nantes. Above the two pairs of entry doors, enormous semicircles were inlaid with rectangular glass panes. Over the years, an impressive radial clock centered high above and set into the stone facade reminded outbound passengers to pick up the pace.

Today, the stunning exterior received little notice. Sightings of local citizens were negligible, but the interior was teeming with Germans and had been all morning. It was the model of organized chaos. There were burgeoning reports of resistance activity coming out of Paris, and tighter security was becoming commonplace throughout France. Local security officials had arrived hours ago and were performing their third sweep. The handpicked welcoming committee was at the station far earlier than necessary. Others continued reviewing the details of transporting Major Holtzer from the station to his headquarters. Primary and alternate routes had been well-planned and secured, and a local detail would assist the bodyguards arriving with him. The logistics team continued sifting through the minutiae to ensure no glitches. The major's residential accommodations were in order days ago, and the baggage handlers had received an obnoxious repetition of instructions. Two handlers chosen by his assistant would bring his personal belongings. A larger team would rush volumes of office supplies, papers, and various furnishings to anxious office staff awaiting at headquarters.

At 2:04 in the afternoon, one minute ahead of schedule, the train carrying Major Viktor Holtzer pulled into the station and screeched to a halt. The conductor rolled his eyes at his chief engineer and heaved a sigh. The engineer, dripping sweat, shook his head and wiped his forehead with the back of his arm. Everyone on the platform remained glued to their spots. The forthcoming bustle of activity was to wait until security escorted him from the area.

Two imposing figures boarded the train. Three minutes later, they returned. A thin woman wearing spectacles and clutching a briefcase appeared next. Holtzer stepped off the train behind her.

His uniform wasn't misleading. He was neither a general nor a colonel; he was a major. But his stature and deportment exuded charisma, leadership, and authority. He looked lean yet solid and stood taller than the two brutes who preceded him off the train. He paused on the platform, looking left, then right. He might have been reviewing or studying his surroundings, but it seemed more like he was allowing his surroundings the chance to observe him. Beneath his rigid, perfectly placed cap, his blond hair looked like he'd received a professional cut only moments earlier. His face and sculpted jaw were clean-shaven. His jacket, pressed and crisp, was decorated with some medals, but in an understated way. It lacked the excessive embellishment and ostentation of the average German officer's uniform. His polished black boots gave the conflicting impression he'd never worn them, yet was born wearing them. To understate it, he was impressive—captivating was more like it. There was an air of inaccessibility, but his controlled demeanor and impressive appearance had a calming effect while revealing little about the man. Was he intense, cold-blooded, merciless, or none of that? Should he be admired and respected—feared? Did it matter who you were? Perhaps time would tell. But if there was any doubt before, there was none now. Major Viktor Holtzer was in charge. In charge of what was the question on many minds.

If the crowd of well-wishers annoyed him, he didn't let on. The transportation detail soon whisked him to the waiting motorcade, and within minutes, the Gare de Tours returned to its more customary, sleepy status.

CHAPTER EIGHT
Chançay, France
April 16, Afternoon

COLETTE, CHARLES, AND Georges reached a quiet, dusty road on the eastern outskirts of Chançay. The old house ahead was well off the main route through town.

"Where are we?" she asked.

"The owner left last year and asked if someone could look after it for him," said Georges.

Charles shrugged. "I don't know if he'll be back, but it's the least we can do."

Colette looked forward to seeing her father as they walked a rutty brick path to a side door that seemed desperate for a new coat of paint. Georges knocked in a purposeful pattern. A single knock came back. Five seconds went by, and the door opened. The watchman swept his eyes across the landscape, motioned for them to enter, and closed the door. Staying next to Charles, she scanned the faces in the living room. A couple seemed familiar, but none was her father.

"Sorry we're running late, Marcel," Georges apologized.

A man who appeared to be in charge approached. "Ah, not to worry. We're still waiting on a couple more. And welcome, young lady." The inquiring look he shot Charles didn't escape her. "What a pleasant surprise. Is your father close behind?"

Georges motioned to the cell leader with a finger, and Marcel excused himself. Colette remained with Charles.

~ ~ ~

"We need to talk," said Georges plainly.

Marcel led the way to a den down the hall. "What's going on?" he asked before the door closed.

"We're not sure. Roland isn't here?"

"No. I thought he and François might come with you. We're anxious to know what they learned at the river. Jean-Paul let me know when he saw you walking up. Why Colette?"

Georges rubbed his chin. "Can someone preoccupy her while Charles and I tell you what we know?"

"Hold on." Marcel stepped out and soon returned with Charles. "Okay, she's in good hands. What's going on?"

The two filled him in: The arrival of Giselle and Louis at Charles' house and their story; the visits to the Viard and Dubois farms; the discovery of Colette in the cellar; and the train sighting on their way to Chançay. Charles added that Giselle and Louis were resting alone at his place and that he and Georges were staying upbeat with Colette regarding her father.

When finished, Georges asked, "They were with you last night. Can you make anything of it?"

Marcel shook his head. "Just surveillance on River's return trip. They were reporting their findings here today after getting some rest. When I saw you with Colette, I thought they'd be close behind."

"Well, the Nazis visited them both first thing this morning, so something went wrong," said Georges. "We just have no idea why or what kind of trouble they're in."

They gave Marcel a moment as he thought about it. "Well, we need to find out. I'll send everyone out to make inquiries and get word to Henri. But this house is no longer safe. It could be compromised, and I need to—"

"What?" Charles interrupted. "Those two, of all people, would never give us away."

Georges understood Marcel's point. "No, he's right. Never is a tricky word."

Marcel clarified. "We don't know what's happened. Are their families now in danger? No, we need to leave. And I need to speak with Colette."

"What could go wrong with a little surveillance after hours?" Charles wondered aloud. "At worst, they'd be detained for being out past curfew. But we know they made it home."

"I thought it was routine," said Marcel. "I hope I didn't put them in harm's way. Charles, I need you to take Colette to her mother and brother. The rest of us need to get out there and find out what happened to Roland and François."

CHAPTER NINE
Colette & Charles
April 16, Late Afternoon

CHARLES KNEW MARCEL was right; he had to reunite Colette with her mother and brother. She was sitting beside Philippe Renaud on the living room sofa and laughing. It was good to see her mind occupied. He approached them from behind.

"Prove it," he heard Colette say.

"What do you mean?" Philippe asked.

"You say you're witty. Prove it."

"What? It doesn't work that way."

"I thought that was exactly how it worked."

Philippe scrunched his nose. "Hmm, you may have a point. Well, I'm a good storyteller, anyway."

"You are, huh? You'll have to convince me."

"I don't think I can."

"Why not?"

Philippe shrugged. "I only tell *unconvincing* stories."

Charles cleared his throat to interrupt. They both stood and turned. He saw the anticipated question in Colette's eyes and smiled half-heartedly. "I'm sorry. No word on your father yet, but we're sending people out to get to the bottom of it." He cocked his head, and Philippe took the cue to join the others receiving their assignments. Charles remained with Colette as Marcel gave a version of his usual wrap-up.

"Remember, plenty of people will support us, but enough others make it difficult to know who to trust. Be careful out there. One more thing...we won't be meeting here anymore. Report back to me in Vouvray. The usual place."

Jean-Paul gave the all-clear. Everyone departed alone or in pairs, took varied paths, and went out to learn what they could about their patriotic friends François Dubois and Roland Viard.

Marcel walked over and managed a cheerful look. "I'm sorry about your missing father, Colette. But we'll find him."

He sat and listened as Colette rehashed the details of her day. When she finished, Charles patted Marcel on the back. "We'll get going to my place. I appreciate your help with François."

"Not at all. Helping people is what we do."

"After you, Mademoiselle," Charles said, standing and motioning toward the door. "Our friends here can look out for your father. You and I can go say hello to your mother and brother." His reassuring tone had the desired effect.

"Merci, Monsieur."

Charles and Colette set off in the direction they'd come from. They reached the rail line and followed it eastward. It would skirt the north end of her home and continue the way her mother and Louis had taken that morning. They stuck close to hedgerows, shrubs, trees, and trenches. When approaching road crossings, Charles motioned for her to stay low while he took a peek. He preferred to keep out of sight, regardless of who anyone was or their supposed allegiances. Only once were they forced to take cover as a boy led two scrawny, reluctant goats across the track fifty meters ahead. As they neared the Dubois farm, a pair of ducks swooped down to land on a pond.

"Monsieur Touchard!" Her sudden outburst surprised him. "I must tend to the animals! They've gone all day, haven't they?"

He'd forgotten about her earlier concern and kicked himself for not avoiding the area altogether. "It's too risky, Colette. And don't you want to see your mother and Louis?"

"I do, and I'm excited to, but it won't take long."

"The longer we're out here, the better chance of being seen," Charles countered. "Not to mention the Germans could come back."

"Yes, but maybe they've already brought my father back."

Charles thought it was unlikely, but her good-natured spirit prevailed. "Okay," he said, "but on one condition. You stay out of sight while I check things out."

"I promise."

After several minutes, he was sufficiently satisfied and waved her forward. There was no sign of her father.

~ ~ ~

To Colette's relief, she saw no strewn feathers or pervasive evidence of savage conflict. Jessible and Clarice were lounging comfortably on a bed of matted grass near the front door. She rewarded each goose with a scoop of corn.

Her thoughts raced while she tended to the animals as fast as possible. She understood Monsieur Touchard's concerns but wondered why today was so much different than every day before. The more she thought about it, the more she considered that maybe it wasn't. *Have I been blind?* She felt foolish.

When she finished with the animals, she went to her room to pack a change of clothes. After throwing a few items in a small sack, the two left out the back. They passed the old shed, crossed an open field, and descended the slope toward the footbridge. Back on the rail bed, she felt relieved at their uneventful detour. They'd taken only a few steps when she stopped and looked back. The feeling of relief had vanished, and her expression and manner soured.

"What's wrong?" Charles asked. He waited but got no answer. "Are you okay?"

She turned to him. "My life changed overnight, didn't it?" Not waiting for a response, she added, "Yesterday, I hardly had a care in the world. Now my father's missing, and I'm sneaking around my own house. Why?" Charles opened his mouth, but she continued. "These soldiers have no right being here." Her short-lived, menacing look had already faded, but there was a coldness in her voice. "No right doing this to us...or anyone."

"No," Charles sighed. "They don't. But this is exactly what they do and will continue doing as long as they're here." He put his hand on her shoulder. "As long as we let them."

"I've had my head in the sand," she said, looking back at the property. "Naive. Going about as though all was right with the world. My world, anyway. I've been a fool, Monsieur Touchard."

"Come now; it's not as simple as—"

"My father's fighting back, isn't he?"

Charles gave it some thought. "What your father and others are doing is highly guarded. If anyone messes up or makes a slip of the tongue, lives can be endangered—even lost. Do you understand?"

"I'm proud of him."

"You should be."

"And I trust him."

"You're not the only one, young lady. Now, come on, let's be on our way. I know some people who will want to see you."

Walking along the corridor, Charles grinned at her. "This is the same route your mother and Louis took this morning while you were relaxing in the cellar."

She stopped and playfully slapped his arm. "Don't ever bring that up again!"

~ ~ ~

The Touchard place felt eerily quiet. Despite it being his house, Charles knew that barging in unannounced would be unwise. He gently knocked on the door and stepped back to make himself visible from the windows on both floors. Colette followed his lead. There was no answer.

"They may be napping," he said. "Let's announce ourselves."

He inserted his key, but the door was already unlocked. They stepped inside.

"Giselle!" he called. "It's Charles. And I brought you something." He looked at Colette and put a finger to his lips. Again, no response.

"Mama! Louis! It's me!" she shouted. "Where are you?"

They made a quick pass through the house. The bed upstairs looked ruffled, and the kitchen had seen some use, but there was no sign of trouble.

Charles was confused. "I instructed them to stay inside and keep out of sight."

"Monsieur Touchard, if I know Louis, I'd guess he's playing in the barn. Mama would be out there with him. What do you think?"

"I'm not sure what there is to play with, but—." He gave her a reassuring look and led the way outside. The main barn doors were closed, but they found a smaller door open around the back.

"Well," said Charles, "somebody's here...or has been. I haven't used that door in months."

He motioned for her to follow. The inside was an enormous expanse with stalls along two walls. There were no animals, but the smell of long-gone hay filled the cavernous space.

"Mama?" Colette called out.

"Is anybody here?" Charles' voice bounced about the rafters. "Giselle, it's Charles. And I've brought Colette!"

Colette tried again. "Mama, where are you?" She waited. "Louis?"

"Let's make a loop around the old place," he suggested. "I'm pretty sure they've been here."

After checking each stall and returning to their starting point, Colette pointed at a colorful cloth folded on a wall girt near the door.

"That's mother's kerchief!"

Charles walked over and grabbed it off the two-by-four. A piece of paper with a scribbled message fell to the dirt floor. He read it, hesitated, then handed it to her.

Nazis here. Sent Louis running. Find him!

Colette crumpled the paper in her fist. He stepped over to console her, but she held up a palm, stopping him. Her serrated voice sliced the stale air. "Oh, I'll find him, alright." The note fell to the dirt floor.

Charles picked up the scrap, and they walked back to the house. He saw the fire fade from her eyes.

"It's my fault," she lamented.

"What? What's your fault?"

"I made us stop for the animals. If we'd gotten here sooner—"

"Colette, the Germans could have come at any time. But if they were just here, there's nothing we could have done. We'd all be in the same boat."

She looked up at him. "How did they know to come here?"

Charles shook his head. "I don't think they did. My guess is they looked for her and Louis all over and eventually arrived here."

"My brother's out there somewhere. We need to find him."

Charles agreed, but the day had been physically and emotionally draining. Within minutes, adrenaline boosts were fading. Her eyes were drooping, and he wasn't doing much better.

"The sun's setting," he said, looking out the window.

"Searching about in the dark makes no sense, does it?" she asked, her voice full of disappointment.

"We need to eat and get a good night's rest. Tomorrow's a busy day," he said, trying to sound upbeat.

"I could eat a horse if I wasn't so tired."

Charles went to the kitchen, put together two plates of meat, cheese, and bread, and poured two glasses of watery milk. When they finished the meal, he showed her to the same bedroom her mother and Louis used. He adjourned to his room, slipped under the covers, and was asleep within seconds.

CHAPTER TEN
Tours
April 16, Evening

THE GUEST OF honor had yet to arrive, and the welcome dinner wouldn't begin for another thirty minutes. People were biding time with idle chatter or wandering the reception hall admiring the artwork. Nobody paid attention to the string quartet's lackluster attempts at Schumann, Straus, and Mendelssohn—least of all Lieutenant Schmid, who was further bored by the dull conversation surrounding him. He recognized some officers at the back wall and walked their way.

"But why Holtzer?" he heard one say. "I'm confused. He used to be Abwehr, right? Is he still?"

"Regardless, isn't he wasting his time out here?" said another. "Why even agree to it? I would think the major tells people where he's going, not the other way around."

Schmid caught on quickly and chimed in. "There's growing concern at the top about increased resistance activity in this sector. Perhaps he came here to help root them out."

"Increased activity?" came an agitated voice. "It's nothing compared to other places. It's overkill. Anyway, things are about to change for everyone. We'll all be on pins and needles, and I, for one—"

"Disturbances are escalating fast in Paris," another cut in. "There are always little things, and there will always be rebels, but intelligence warns that subversive activity will soon be knocking a lot louder here." He turned to Schmid. "Lieutenant, didn't I hear about you dealing with something just today?" The others turned their eyes to him.

"A policeman was killed late last night in the middle of nowhere." Schmid waved his hand randomly. "Somewhere east of here. We already have a good lead, and we're questioning suspects."

"What's the motive? And why was the policeman out there in the middle of the night?" asked an unfamiliar face.

"Why he was there is beside the point. I've got two men working on the motive as we speak." The group all smirked, but Schmid maintained his hardened expression.

"It's like wringing water from a baguette with these Frenchmen," someone said.

"You can rest assured my men will do what it takes. I've been asked to brief Major Holtzer tomorrow," Schmid added, not bothering to suppress his vanity.

A tinkling bell signaled that the major would soon arrive, and the group went to their assigned tables. The room was called to order, and a general clamor ensued when chairs screeched back in unison as everyone stood. Schmid knew how these things went and was prepared to remain standing. The grand ramble praising the man's accomplishments, accolades, and righteous qualities would inevitably be followed by a blustery speech from the guest of honor. Early into the introduction, he saw Holtzer lean down and whisper something that caused the speaker to stop.

"Well," the man announced. He cleared his throat. "Major Holtzer has something else in mind. He'd like you all to please sit and get started enjoying your meals."

Schmid was relieved at the news and shared bemused looks with his dinner companions. Still, nobody sat until Holtzer looked over the room and motioned with his hand to sit. Within minutes, a Captain Eicher began escorting the guest of honor around, introducing him to the various officers and VIPs dining throughout the ballroom. Some introductions led to brief conversations, some held the major's attention longer, and others brought moments of levity. Before long, Schmid found himself standing and shaking the man's hand.

"Lieutenant Schmid, Sir," the lieutenant said proudly, making Captain Eicher's introduction unnecessary.

"How are you, Lieutenant?"

He opened his mouth but withheld his reply. Major Holtzer had already diverted his eyes and moved on. Stunned, Schmid fumbled for his chair, hopeful others hadn't noticed the exchange. Of course, everybody in the room was scrutinizing the new VIP's every movement.

Someone at the table behind him snickered, but he did his best to feign indifference and took a bite of lukewarm mashed potato.

~ ~ ~

Spending time with the major after dinner would have been his preference, but there was little chance he'd get a word in over the competition. More importantly, he needed to prepare for his morning meeting. The better prepared, the more he could impress. Schmid slipped out during a gap between the main course and dessert and found Private Wegner standing alert next to the car. Still walking on eggshells after letting the Dubois mother and boy escape, Wegner jumped when his superior ordered him to drive.

Schmid's earlier discussions with François Dubois yielded little. In his gut, he felt Dubois knew more than he was letting on. Then again, the man might be nothing more than a commoner trying to eke out a meager living. Playing the family blackmail game wouldn't work; he had no idea where they were. He'd let him continue fretting in the local jail. In the meantime, his two henchmen should be getting to the bottom of some nagging questions.

An unlit deserted road on the edge of town led between a row of abandoned warehouse buildings. The darkness swallowed whatever glow the approaching headlights offered. Schmid saw a parked vehicle where he expected and had his driver pull up behind it.

"Stay here," he growled, stepping out, "and try not to get lost!"

He walked up the crumbling cement stairs and disappeared inside.

"How's it going?" he asked, removing his overcoat. The two grimy, half-uniformed thugs look nervously at each other. "What? You've got nothing yet?"

"It didn't go as we hoped," said Sergeant Protz.

"He was a stubborn one for sure," Private Ott added.

Schmid took a long look at the two. "What do you mean *was*?"

They led him to a stark room equipped with the usual single chair. The neglected warehouse hadn't seen electric light in years. A pair of wax-dripping candles made the room flicker. Bound to the chair with heavy rope was a slumped figure. His jaw hung open at an unnatural angle, and blood had pooled on the floor. Schmid approached and pushed on the man's shoulder.

"He's dead, Sir," said Sergeant Protz, stating the obvious. "I'm not sure how. One minute, he was alive and defiant. Then Ott here took another good crack at him, and, I don't know...he died."

"Morons! Did you find anything out?" The two subordinates exchanged glances. "I'm giving a report tomorrow. Please tell me you learned something, anything!"

"He said he wanted to go home," Private Ott offered.

Schmid's agitation grew. "Oh, he's gone home, alright. Jesus! What about my...what about the dead policeman? Did Viard give you answers? Was he out there alone? Were there others? For Christ's sake, what did you learn?"

Sergeant Protz shrugged. "As Ott said, he was a stubborn one. Usually, they come to their senses quicker."

Schmid stared at the body, trying to decide the next step. "I needed information from this one," he said at last. "Then I planned on making an example of him. This shit can escalate." He looked again at the body. "Take care of this," he snarled. "Then get out there and find the Dubois wife or son—SOMEBODY!" he shouted in a near rage.

"Where do you think we should look, Sir?" the sergeant asked.

"I don't fucking care. Figure it out!" He left to find his driver, ignoring the two subordinates saluting the back of his head.

CHAPTER ELEVEN
Saint Martin le Beau, France
April 17, Early Morning

NESTLED NEAR THE ligne de démarcation but on the wrong side, the small town of Saint Martin le Beau awoke to the news of a slain policeman west of town near the Cher. Before sunrise, townsfolk took short detours down a small backstreet near the city center to witness the gruesome consequence. They came quietly, stared briefly, lowered their eyes out of respect, shame, or aversion, and departed without speaking. As the morning progressed and the village came to life, more felt compelled to witness the beaten, mangled remains of the dead man in a tree, his half-clothed body secured by ropes tied around his wrists, arms, and ankles. A bloodied note with bold letters was held in place by a knife stuck in his chest.

Ne sois pas stupide comme moi.
Don't be stupid like me.

Shortly after 8:30, a café door opened, and a lanky man entered. At a prominent table near the front, two middle-aged men sat immersed in a game. A younger man, straddling a chair backward, watched intently. The newcomer hung his trench coat on a hook and paused to consider the board. He removed his gray fedora and scratched his forehead.

"Mmm, mate in four," he said, unmindful of spectator etiquette. The three glanced up and returned their focus to the board. The man playing black kept a finger on his knight, returned it to its starting position, and mulled longer. "Touch-move?" the newcomer asked. The three nodded. "Ah, never mind then," he said, losing interest. He scanned the room, sat at an adjacent table, and skimmed over the small breakfast menu.

Another man walked in, looking agitated. He approached the game table and sat in the only remaining chair. "Rumor is somebody betrayed him," he grumbled.

"Rumor?" the man playing white asked, looking up.

"Probably that Jew innkeeper," the young observer suggested, eyes still glued to the board.

"Come on. He's been here longer than you've been alive," said the man playing black. "He's only half-Jewish anyway. The mechanic's son, though. Hell, I don't know if he's a communist or what, but I don't trust him."

The tall customer accepted a coffee from the young waitress. He attempted to order from the menu, but it was too late. She had already turned to join the discussion.

"Talk about not trusting," she chimed in. "What about that coquette all the boys fawn over? I mean, does anyone truly know her? Mysterious that one."

The white player pushed a rook to the far rank. "What did the note say again?"

"Don't be stupid like me," his playing partner mumbled.

"Mmm. Advice worth heeding."

Two chattering and distressed-looking women entered. "He probably had it coming," one of them snapped. "And how dare he bring attention to our little corner."

"God-fearing, I am," said the other, "but these Germans are a close second when we don't mind our business. So far, they've been tolerable, but—"

"Mother, has anyone learned who he is?" the young spectator asked wide-eyed.

"No. And thank God for that," the first woman huffed. "If he were from here, there'd be hell to pay." She turned and scowled at the stranger sitting alone. "Who are you? You homeless?"

He looked up at her. "No, madame. Just passing through."

"Mmm-hmm," she scoffed before leading the other woman to a table in the back.

"I feel bad for the poor soul," said the man playing white, "but it's best to keep our heads down. Things will get ugly fast if we don't." He put his elbows on the table, rested his cheekbones on his fists, and concentrated on his next move.

The stranger rose, adjusted his hat, set a coin beside his mug, and looked down at the board. "Ah, mate in three." He grabbed his coat from the hook and walked out.

The young spectator turned his attention back to the board and studied it. "Which color?"

The man playing black considered it, then reached out and knocked his king over.

His opponent smiled. "Another game?"

CHAPTER TWELVE
To Vouvray, France
April 17, Dawn

CHARLES AGREED WHEN Colette insisted they eat breakfast on the go.

"I have no doubt when you say your brother's slippery," he said, placing some crackers, cheese, and two canteens into a sack. "But I still think he'd want to get home."

"I tossed and turned last night," she said. "He'll be sneaky about it, but that's where I'd want to be, too."

Walking west along the rail bed, he shared thoughts, and Colette showed little emotion. "Your mother will be fine. She's done nothing that would put her in danger."

"Maybe," Colette countered, "but they came to our home for a reason. My father was gone that night. Something happened, but I guess he wasn't enough. Why do they want both of them?"

"It's probably just a routine—"

"They think he did something," she interrupted. "Or maybe saw something. He'd tell his wife. They'd assume so, anyway. I still don't know how they found her."

"They may have seen her and Louis run for the tracks. They likely made a sweep of the area."

Colette stopped and looked up at him. "I hear they also have ways of making people talk."

Charles had no intention of going down that path. "Well, that's mostly hearsay or reserved for real criminals. I'm certain they're just trying to get to the bottom of something." Colette nodded in an unconvincing way and continued walking.

After crossing the footbridge and nearing the house, he followed suit when she knelt where the north woods opened onto a field.

"Somebody's been here," she whispered.

"What? How do you know?"

"Claude's eating apples."

The answer did little to improve his understanding. "Who's Claude?" he whispered, "and why would that—"

"Over there. See how he eats? Weird, isn't it?" A roan-colored donkey stood behind a wire fence twenty meters away, munching on something. She turned to him and smiled. "He loves apples and won't stop eating until they're gone. Mama buys them whenever she finds a bargain and stores them in the cellar."

It was roundabout, but the explanation satisfied him: Claude wouldn't be eating apples unless they were recently given to him.

"Papa, Louis, or maybe even Mama is here—or has been," she said.

Before yesterday, he only knew her as the daughter of François Dubois. But he was learning more with each passing hour, impressed at how she noticed, considered, and interpreted everything.

They approached the house, announced themselves, and searched every room. Returning to the kitchen, she pointed at the cellar door and made a face. "You don't think he'd—"

Charles lit a lantern and headed down. Colette followed.

"Something's changed here," he mumbled. "We left in a hurry yesterday, but I know Georges put that mesh on top, not over there."

Colette called out for her brother but got no response. Charles did the same and soon cleared the clutter that concealed the hiding place. He slid the boards aside and looked down the hole.

"Well, he's been here, alright." He waved her over; she reluctantly peered into the pit. There was a pillow, two apple cores, several cracker crumbs, and an empty glass. "Now, how in the world could he have covered himself?"

"I told you he's slippery," she said offhandedly. "And the Germans wouldn't have covered it back up. He did." Charles began concealing the pit. "Where are you, Louis?" she muttered. "Monsieur Touchard, Louis spent the night in there. But he wouldn't stay down there in the daytime. I think he'd be watching for somebody to come home. Not only that, Claude's been fed recently, right?"

"Agreed," he said, replacing the last of the junk.

Colette lit up. "I have an idea!"

"I'm all ears."

"Outside," she chirped.

Stepping into the kitchen, Charles said, "Well, outdoors is a big place, and we need to keep an eye open for more than just Louis. What's on your mind?"

"Here's what I'm thinking. We came here from your place, right?"

"Right."

"And we were quiet...at least until inside the house, right?"

"We were." He hoped she'd come to the point but enjoyed her participatory manner.

"Well, there's a tree fort in the south woods. Louis likes it because it's hidden, and he can see who's coming and going on the road. But he couldn't have seen us. We didn't come on the road, did we?"

Charles was intrigued. "No. No, we didn't." At the window, he considered the woods she spoke of. Somewhere beyond was the main road. A dirt driveway bisected a field between the woods and the house. They would be visible in the open. "We need to be quick."

They jogged across the field and arrived at the edge of the woods.

"Follow me," she said without looking back. She soon slowed and looked up. "Louis!" she called out.

Charles followed her eyes. In the tree ahead was a crudely constructed platform with assorted wooden planks on three sides. A rotting canvas tarp covered part of it. Colette was about to call out again when a head popped over the side. Before either could shout out to him, Louis put a finger to his lips and motioned for them to get down. They did as instructed and seconds later heard it. The boy had a better view from his perch, and Charles kept his eyes on him.

Louis peeked back over the fort wall, held up two fingers, and indicated that the vehicles turned into the drive. In seconds, he scrambled down imperceptible footholds nailed into the tree. Colette gave him a big hug.

"I think they have Mama," he said.

Colette nodded. "She'll be fine...won't she, Monsieur Touchard?"

"Of course, but we'd better get moving. What's the safest way out of here? No roads."

"Where do you want to go?" Colette asked.

"Vouvray. It's on the way to Tours."

"Then follow me," Louis whispered.

Colette's expression suggested her brother knew what he was talking about. Charles felt surprisingly reassured while letting Louis lead them through the woods and away from the house. Reaching the roadside, they stopped and listened for more signs of trouble. The trees on the other side were dense. The three scrambled across the road and disappeared into the thick cover.

They followed Louis along an overgrown, stick-strewn footpath. After several minutes, Charles stopped in a small clearing to survey the surroundings. Feeling safe, he had everyone sit down on the trunk of a fallen tree.

"Great job, Louis."

"How far to Vouvray?" Colette asked.

He thought about it. "Two hours at least. Maybe more if we run into trouble."

"Really?" Louis piped up. "What kind of trouble?"

"Hopefully, none, but we'll need to take some roads to get there, and we could see Germans. Keep your heads if we do."

"Okay," said Colette, "but no law says we can't be out enjoying a walk, is there?"

"No," Charles agreed, "at least not in the middle of the day. But we don't want to stumble across anyone who recognizes either of you."

"Do you suppose those were Germans?" she asked.

"They sure were!" Louis blurted. "They're the only ones driving big trucks anymore. It was a truck and a car."

"First Papa, now Mama. What do they want with us?" Colette wondered aloud.

"They have Papa?" Louis asked, surprised.

"Yes. They took him!"

"Now, now. Let's keep calm," Charles jumped in. "We'll see your parents in no time."

"They never bothered us before," Colette grumbled. "And I'm not so sure about that."

"About what?"

"I appreciate you being so positive, Monsieur Touchard, but I'm worried to death. Being taken away by Nazis can't be a good thing."

Charles was unsure how to respond. He fixated on a tick crawling over Louis' hand. It traversed each finger before Louis carefully set it on a dead leaf. "These Germans seem to be crawling everywhere," Charles said. "Let's get going."

"What's in Vouvray, Monsieur Touchard?" asked Louis.

"Some friends that can help us. But it's a long walk." Charles patted the boy on the shoulder. "Maybe we can find something to snack on along the way."

"I don't know about food," said Louis. "But there's a creek not far from here if we get thirsty."

"I'm not sure how you know that young man, but it's good to hear. Lead the way."

While walking, Louis filled them in on what happened at Monsieur Touchard's place.

"Mama and I heard a truck while exploring the barn. She told me to run. I stopped a lot to listen, but finally got home. I hid in the cellar most of the night, fed the animals when it got light, and climbed into the fort."

Charles suspected Colette wouldn't want to hear about it, but he had to ask. "Just how did you cover yourself in the pit?"

"Oh," Louis perked up. "It wasn't perfect, but I set the boards on the rug and covered them with junk. Then I stood in the grave and pulled the rug over and down onto me. I adjusted the boards from underneath." Charles looked at Colette. She was shaking her head, eyes closed. "I used the rug as a carpet *and* a blanket to stay warm."

Twenty minutes later, the three came to a shallow stream. Charles had them all stop and encouraged his companions to drink what they could. Five minutes later, they emerged from the woods.

Colette recognized an old barn in the distance. "I've been here! See that weathered barn way out there? Papa and I once brought the wagon this way. There's a road on the other side of the field."

Charles surveyed the surroundings and also recognized where they were. "The fields are dry enough, but we'll look out of place stomping around out here. Let's get to the road and see how it goes."

They were out in the open now but had little choice. Charles gave his young travelers simple instructions if they encountered Germans: Act normal. Nervous is fine, but don't be fearful or look suspicious.

We're just out for a walk. Be sure only to give your first name if asked. It'll be fine.

Louis scampered ahead tirelessly, always well out front. He'd glance back when reaching a junction, and Charles would indicate the way. Their journey through the countryside was pleasant. With the passing of time and distance, the vehicles that had approached their home were forgotten, and La Mère de la Terre was smiling upon them. There wasn't a cloud in the sky, and it wasn't too warm or cool. Colette seemed upbeat since finding her brother and remained hopeful of seeing her parents soon. Charles was still concerned about the limited natural protection, but felt good about their progress and the lack of traffic.

"I've never seen the sky so blue," Colette said, looking up. "Not since Honfleur, anyway."

"Honfleur?" Charles said, looking skeptical. "I've been there twice and never saw the sun once."

"Oh, then you must go back. It was my favorite vacation ever. There was a little chocolate shop...candy shop, really. I hope it's still there. Well, I do remember it rained a lot. But one day, the clouds just vanished. We took a day trip to Trouville, and the sky and sea were so blue I couldn't tell where one stopped and the other began. I'm guessing it's just like that today."

Whether the Normandy coast, the French Alps, or the Côte d'Azur, Charles knew it was unlikely any had the same weather as Indre-et-Loire. He chose not to burst her bubble. "I suspect Paris is lovely today, too," he said.

Louis dashed off the road, disappearing once again.

"I hope it's rabbits," Colette sighed, "but it's more likely snakes."

Reaching the spot, they called out but got no answer. Moments later, Louis inexplicably appeared on the road fifty meters ahead.

Charles and Colette traded looks, shook their heads, and continued their walk.

"I guess he's in his element," Charles said, chuckling.

"He loves it outside and never gets tired of exploring."

"Now, where's he off to? I motioned to go straight. He went left."

"Oh, he'll be back. He saw you just fine."

Nearing the crossroad, Colette stopped and put a finger to her lips. "Shh, listen."

The rumble was faint but getting louder. Charles' instinct was to hide, and the best spot was where he last saw Louis heading. They went that way, but the boy was nowhere in sight.

He thought better of it. "If it's Germans, let me do the talking. Hopefully, they won't bother stopping."

"Oh, it's them," Colette said with palpable disdain. "And I'm sure they see us."

"Well, we can't hide now. Keep calm."

The two stepped to the roadside and waited.

~ ~ ~

Louis braced his hand against a large stone and leaned forward to peek inside the culvert at the bottom of an embankment. The entire passage was big enough to get through if one crawled or crouched and waddled like a duck. He found a solid stick and poked it into the ground: wet, soft, but not terrible. He stepped in front of the opening, and his right foot sank in the mud past his ankle.

"Stupid," he scolded himself.

When he pulled his foot from the muck, his shoe failed to come with it. He grabbed the sopping, brown mass and sat on a flat rock to remove his sock. A small pool of water gurgled beside him, and he started rinsing things.

The sound of a distant motor was unmistakable. Hiding had worked best so far. He decided to stay out of sight rather than come up to find the others. He removed the shoe and sock from his other foot and ducked into the culvert. Cold mud oozed between his toes.

~ ~ ~

The Kübelwagen stopped, and a burly soldier in the passenger seat stepped out. The stumpy driver remained seated and ogled Colette from top to bottom.

"What are you two doing here in the middle of nowhere?" the sergeant asked, as though out of habit.

"Just out for a walk," Charles answered, faking a smile.

"It's a beautiful day," Colette added.

"Mmm, I hadn't noticed," the sergeant replied with little interest.

The private slipped off the driver's seat and continued assessing her from a better vantage point.

"Papers," the sergeant said, holding his palm out.

"Certainly," Charles said. "Wouldn't be without them."

He read the name aloud. "Charles Touchard."

Colette realized the address could be a problem. Being on a casual stroll so distant from the Touchard place was unrealistic. Then again, she expected the meddler wouldn't recognize the geographical nuance. He handed the papers back without raising a concern.

"Who's this one here?" the private piped up, still looking over Colette. He ran his hand under her dark curls and down her neck.

"My niece," Charles lied, grabbing her hand.

Still addressing Charles, the sergeant said, "She fits the description of someone we're looking for. What's her name?"

"Colette," she sneered. "What's yours?"

The infatuated private was too consumed to catch on. "Mine's Ott," he whispered so near that his breath made her wince. His twisted smile revealed the source of the stench.

The sergeant was more astute than his plump sidekick. "We're looking for a girl with that very name. You wouldn't happen to have a last name, would you?"

"Just what is this—" Charles began.

"Dubois!" Colette trumpeted. She knew Charles would think it foolish, but these Nazis were her best chance of finding her parents.

"Dubois?" the private shouted.

The sergeant ignored him. "We've been worried about you. Our lieutenant will be happy to know you're safe. He's been looking forward to meeting you."

Charles came to her defense. "What could anybody want with her? She's done nothing and couldn't possibly be any help to you."

The sergeant let him finish, then pulled out a pistol and pointed it at his face. "Shut up." He turned back to Colette. "We're also looking for your brother. Any idea where he might be?"

"I was hoping you could tell me," came her indignant reply. She trusted Louis was aware of the unexpected encounter and had hidden.

Just then, the private called out. "Hey, Sarge!" His eyes were focused on something down the embankment.

"What the hell is it?"

The private pointed down the slope. The sergeant strolled over.

Colette grabbed Charles' arm and followed. "Hey, if you want to question either of us about anything, we've got nothing to hide," she said, hoping to redirect their attention.

The sergeant ignored the distraction and focused on the ditch.

"Odd place to leave a shoe, wouldn't you say?" said the private.

Without answering the obvious, the sergeant motioned for him to check it out. Ott made three attempts to get a grip on his pistol.

"Think you can handle it?" the sergeant said dryly.

Nervous while awaiting the inevitable discovery, Colette was surprised by a sudden idea. The sergeant had a casual grip on his gun. She could try grabbing for it, but wouldn't know what to do next. Even worse, it could put Louis in more danger with the private. She grazed Charles with her elbow and used her eyes to indicate the possibility. Charles caught on and gave the slightest nod.

~ ~ ~

Louis heard the crunching of dry grass and froze.

"Looks like kid shoes!" someone yelled.

Inside the culvert entrance, he gripped his stick like a security blanket. Scurrying on all fours and out the far side crossed his mind more than once, but he figured it wouldn't help. Instead, he sat tense, listening to the approaching footsteps. They stopped.

With a startling splash, a German landed in front of him and peered in with a toothy grin. Louis lunged, thrusting the end of his stick and catching the Nazi in the left cheek. The man cried out and dropped his pistol. With his boots immersed deep in the sludge, the blow caused him to fall backward—his entire backside sinking into the muck. Louis leaped out, grabbed the mud-caked gun, and threw it. He turned and scampered through the tunnel on all fours.

~ ~ ~

Hearing the cry of pain from below, Colette reacted. She clenched her fist and hammered it down on the sergeant's wrist. His Luger fell to the road. He stooped fast to retrieve it just as Charles slammed into him from behind. The force knocked the man down the embankment. Colette grabbed the gun and thrust it into Charles' hand. The sergeant scrambled to his feet and readied to charge uphill, but stopped.

"Ah-ah, use your head," Charles stammered, pointing the gun.

The sergeant stayed put, his face turning crimson with rage. "Oh, you're not going to shoot me," he growled at Charles, "but you're a dead man."

"LOUIS!" Colette screamed.

"Over here!" her brother shouted. She spun and saw a mud-encased figure pop up across the road.

"Get in, NOW!" yelled Charles.

He didn't need to repeat it. Colette jumped into the passenger seat, and Louis scrambled into the back.

"DEAD MAN! DEAD MAN, YOU HEAR ME!" the sergeant roared from below.

Charles threw the vehicle into gear, and the tires kicked up rock and dirt. A dust cloud followed them down the road.

CHAPTER THIRTEEN
Tours
April 17, Afternoon

LIEUTENANT SCHMID HAD been inside German headquarters many times, but this was different. He felt uneasy, even agitated. His usual arrogance and air of superiority were off-level. The plan to waltz into Holtzer's ring of trusted confidants was unrolling slower than expected, and the clammy reaction at last night's reception wasn't how he'd envisioned their first encounter. Capturing a murderous rebel and efficiently extracting valuable information was something to tout. Now, he wasn't even sure what to say. On top of that, the major's receptionist informed him that his captain couldn't join them. Schmid sat alone in the receiving room, listening to the ticking of the wall clock. After thirty minutes, he approached.

"If Major Holtzer is busy, I'm sure our business can wait. I can return at his convenience."

Angela Fassbender slipped her glasses off her thin nose, let them dangle by the neck chain, looked up, and smiled. "I'm sure he'll be with you shortly." She fussed with some bobby pins in the loose bun piled on top of her head, settled the glasses back on the bridge of her nose, and resumed typing. Schmid returned to his seat. Ten minutes later, hearing the clicking of her heels, a feeling of apprehension swept over him.

"Follow me, please, Sir."

He'd never been in the room but gave it little notice, directing his attention to the man seated behind an imposing mahogany desk. The major was reading a letter when Schmid snapped to attention and saluted with a ramrod straight arm. Holtzer returned a nonchalant salute and remained in his well-worn burgundy leather chair. Schmid expected an offer to sit down or stand at ease, but got neither.

The major sighed. "Lieutenant, do you know why I'm here?"

"Not entirely, Sir."

Holtzer reached for a cigar box, plucked one out, held it to his nose, and rolled it between his thumb and index finger. "There's subversive activity going on in these parts. It needs to be dealt with. I'm here to see that it stops."

Schmid was uncertain if a response was expected. "Sir," was all he could muster.

"My skill set may be useful," Holtzer added, propping the unlit cigar on an ashtray.

"Yes, Sir...and welcomed."

The major ignored the feigned attempt at flattery. "You're here today because I understand you're involved and have recently apprehended some individuals concerning the death of a policeman somewhere east of here."

Schmid perked up. Trying to avoid sounding boastful, he answered, "I have, Sir, yes."

Holtzer showed no sign of gratitude or appreciation. "Good. I suspect these individuals may be helpful to our intelligence efforts. What have you learned?"

Schmid again felt uneasy. Trying to buy time, he continued. "Sir, we picked up two men for questioning. We hoped for more to report on short notice, but we'll get you a full accounting soon." There was a brief silence as he felt the major's eyes burrowing into him.

"I'm not sure who you mean by 'we,' Lieutenant, but I want you to report directly to me. There's no need to go through your captain on this. I've got other important matters for him. Understood?"

"Sir!" said Schmid, pleased at the invitation to correspond directly.

"That's all," Holtzer said without standing.

Schmid saluted and returned to the receiving room to retrieve his overcoat—relieved at having gotten out unscathed.

"Lieutenant Schmid!" Miss Fassbender called out as he headed for the door. He turned. "Sir, Major Holtzer needs you a moment."

She escorted him back in. Holtzer stood behind his desk, looking pensive, his left arm across his chest, his right hand cupping his chin.

"Lieutenant, I like to delegate. I believe it can embolden and motivate people, and I can get stretched pretty thin."

Schmid liked what he was hearing and anticipated the major's next move. Unfortunately, he was off the mark.

"On the other hand," Holtzer continued, "I also like to insert myself in new situations and settings. It helps me come up to speed quicker. It may be more hands-on than most. Some like that, some don't. How do you feel about it?"

Schmid didn't like where it was going, but it wasn't a trick question and had only one safe answer. "I completely understand your thinking, Sir, and I admire it." He tried steering the conversation back to where he wanted it. "However, if you're looking for someone to reduce your workload, you can count on me."

The major maintained an unrevealing expression. "Maybe I'll get to that someday. I've got a full schedule, but I'd like to squeeze in a visit with the suspects you've detained. Bring them to me this evening at eighteen hundred."

Schmid was stunned. He'd gotten nothing from Dubois so far, and Viard was dead. He tried altering the course. "Sir, believe me, I can save you time. Let me handle it and get you a detailed report rather than waste your time."

"I don't consider it a waste of my time, Lieutenant. And to be crystal clear, it wasn't a request."

Schmid sensed a growing sternness in Holtzer's tone. It was too late to tell him one of the suspects was dead. He could have already made that clear. *Verdammt, I even said they were being interrogated, and I'd handle it.* He needed time to think of a way out.

"Yes, Sir. Eighteen hundred." He snapped to attention and gave his best Nazi salute.

The rest of Schmid's day was unproductive from a military standpoint as he spent his time brooding over a handful of unappealing options. An idea formed by late afternoon. He summoned his driver.

~ ~ ~

Private Wegner shrank at the news. Sergeant Protz and Private Ott had wasted little time picking up on Schmid's attitude toward him and felt licensed to match the same contempt their lieutenant showed. Today, he had relished their absence and didn't care where they were as long as it wasn't near him.

The boyish driver learned they were gone all day on assignment, but he had no idea where or whether they had returned. One tip led to another, and he stopped in front of a stale tavern not far from quarters. A bartender was refilling their empty mugs.

"The lieutenant wants to see you both," he reported.

Sergeant Protz turned his head, rolled his eyes, and returned to his beer. As usual, Private Ott had something to say.

"Look here, you little shit. We've had a day. I just got cleaned up, my face hurts, my feet are killing me, and we have full beers." His anger swelled. "We're not wasting them! Crawl back to the lieutenant and tell him he can—" Ott caught himself from completing the thought and reached for his beer.

"It sounded urgent," Wegner said, ignoring the large bandage covering Ott's cheek.

"Fuck," Protz grumbled into his beer. He rose from his barstool as though the time of reckoning had come and poked Ott in the chest. "Not a word about the daughter."

Wegner had no idea what he was talking about and didn't care. He was ordered to pay the tab and followed them to the car. He drove the fifteen minutes back, thankful for the unusually subdued demeanor of his two passengers.

Stepping out, Ott snarled, "Go do something useful...not like that's even possible."

Protz spun around. "Hey, what's the idea?"

"What?"

"It's my job to treat him like shit." They walked away snickering.

Ernst Wegner closed his eyes and thought of his grandmother's coffee cake muffins.

~ ~ ~

Lieutenant Schmid was pacing when Sergeant Protz and Private Ott walked in at four-thirty.

"Where the hell have you two been?" he started. "Any luck finding the Dubois kids, or am I wasting my breath even asking?"

"Sir, we looked everywhere," said Protz.

Schmid spared himself from listening to the forthcoming excuses. "Never mind. Both of you sit down. I have a plan." He noticed the bandage covering most of Private Ott's cheek. "Should I even ask?"

Ott began his rehearsed reply. "Sir, you see, I was—"

"Shut up," snapped Schmid, "I don't care about your damn face. Now listen. I'm meeting with Holtzer this evening, and I want you both there." The two looked uncomfortable. "As you know, I'm supposed to tell him what we've learned. But there's been a change. He's asked me to bring in the suspects. You fools have made that impossible. But I've got an idea." Protz and Ott perked up. "We'll bring Dubois along. I'll let him tell his story straight to Holtzer and see what kind of shit the major hits him with. The bigger problem is Viard, thanks to you idiots. Not only is he dead, but you learned nothing from him." He shook his head in disbelief. "So here's our story. And if you ever deny it, I'll personally see to your miserable futures." He paced a circle around the two before stopping to look at Ott. "You're the moron who killed him, so you're the one that *accidentally* let him make a run for it. While being chased, he jumped off a bridge and splattered on the pier below. Then you saw the dead body flop into the river and disappear. It all happened earlier while I was away on other business."

Ott squinted, his bushy black eyebrows becoming one. "So, we need to get his body and throw it off the bridge?"

"No, you dimwit, that's the story I'm telling Holtzer. It doesn't *actually* happen. Leave the body wherever you buffoons put it, and nobody will know the damn difference. Jesus!"

Private Ott returned a blank stare before turning to Sergeant Protz, looking for help.

The confused expression didn't escape Schmid. "What's the matter?" he snapped.

"Uh, nothing, Sir," Protz jumped in. "I understand. I'll run it past him until it sticks."

Schmid put his right thumb and index finger to his eyes as though his brain was percolating. "I could play it that Viard ratted out Dubois. But if Dubois wasn't involved, that might bite me in the ass later. The wrath of Holtzer is best to avoid." He cocked his head as he constructed his next thought. "I think Dubois is involved somehow. I'd bet on it. But I've decided to let the major bust his balls. For some fucking reason, he's eager to be hands-on." He thought some more. "The Viard wife and kid are useless to me. I kept them as leverage, but they don't know shit. And I can't threaten Viard with their safety anymore because...he's dead!"

After a short silence, Sergeant Protz spoke up. "What time do you need us there, Sir?"

"Pretty damn soon. Eighteen hundred, but be early. I need you two to pick up Dubois. You'll need the guards to release him. Use Wegner for transport."

"You can count on us, Sir!" Private Ott shouted, thrusting his right arm forward. Sergeant Protz followed a bit less enthusiastically.

Schmid rolled his eyes. "Dismissed."

CHAPTER FOURTEEN
Vouvray
April 17, Late Afternoon

AN OLD STONE church on the outskirts of sleepy Vouvray was ideal for secret meetings. The road to it was sparsely traveled; the thick outer walls were as good as soundproof; there were discreet vantage points to see outside, and people seen coming to and from a place of worship wouldn't cause suspicion. It didn't hurt that the priest was sympathetic to their cause and, more than just looking the other way, equipped the basement to make it more accommodating.

Marcel had directed Charles Touchard to reunite Colette with her mother and brother and tend to their needs. By mid-afternoon, others had returned to report any news on the whereabouts of Roland and François. Most had learned nothing, but one late-returning group had information from an operative in Tours. Although everyone in the basement agreed it wasn't grave, it wasn't promising either: François was in jail awaiting an interrogation. The good news came from overhearing two Nazis grumbling about learning nothing from him regarding the dead policeman and nothing linking him to other activity in the area. The bad news was their babbling about a new major who would soon end Dubois' silence. Marcel thanked the men for their efforts and told them to get some rest. While waiting for the last group to return, he and Georges discussed what, if anything, they could do to help François.

Henri Flamand and Philippe Renauld had traveled together to Amboise to learn anything they could. Marcel suggested Philippe could benefit from traveling with his second in command. In the late evening, the two finally returned to the church basement. Their somber expressions were foreboding, and their report couldn't have been worse. Marcel and Georges were staggered. After bowing their heads in silence, Marcel asked the men if they would recount their heart-wrenching story.

"We made inquiries in Amboise but learned nothing useful," Henri began. "We were about to leave for Tours when we learned of an occurrence in Saint Martin le Beau."

Philippe was staring at the floor. "It was a long walk, but I tried to stay optimistic."

Henri put his hand on the young man's shoulder. "I wanted to, but the report of a dead body on display didn't sit well. When we arrived in the village, it was no longer there. Finding no contacts in town, all we could do was ask around."

"It was strange," said Philippe. "Many just ignored us. Then, a hunched woman in a shawl shuffled past and told us that—" He turned away, unable to finish.

Henri shook his head slowly. "Word has it a citizen unstrapped a leather sheath from the man's leg. 'R Viard' was inscribed on the back of it. It tore through us. We soon learned about the policeman and Roland's supposed admission."

"Some townsfolk were furious with the Nazis," Philippe added, "and just as many feared repercussions."

"Most didn't say a word," said Henri.

~ ~ ~

Marcel departed for Tours to help the team learn anything about François. Georges looked across the room at the two remaining figures in the church basement. Henri sat on a sofa, staring glumly at the footstool before him while Philippe paced, his eyes red and swollen. Though usually upbeat and playful, he had taken a hard jolt, and Georges saw him struggling to digest a reality to which he was unaccustomed. He called them over to the table, figuring a slight distraction couldn't hurt.

"Philippe, do you know how this new major got his nickname?" he began.

The young man looked up from the table with glazed eyes. "Der Jager? I think it means 'The Hunter.' Is it from hunting Jews?"

Georges shook his head. "No. It has nothing to do with the Nazis or even the war. He's been called that since before anyone can remember." Henri gave him a confused look, and Georges continued. "Do either of you remember the picture I circulated?"

"Sure. I can see why the German command likes him," Henri grunted. "He's everything they brag about with their relentless Aryan race bullshit."

"Yeah, I suppose he is. But did you notice his left hand?"

"Not at first, but I did when you said he was missing some of it."

"That's right. He's missing some parts. But w*hy* they're missing is the interesting thing."

"I don't know how you know the things you know," Philippe said, the conversation helping to distract him.

Georges held up a finger. "It's my job to know what I know. Anyhow, Viktor Holtzer's twelve years old and out in the woods one morning with his mom and sister. A farm deep in the Black Forest somewhere southwest of Stuttgart. They accidentally surprise a massive Russian boar. The males can be violent bastards. Well...it charges." He had Henri and Philippe's full attention. "The boy gets knocked aside, but his little sister isn't so lucky. Word is a tusk ripped through an artery." Georges paused to let the image sink in. "Then the thing turns on him and his mom. He's back on his feet with his hunting knife in hand...a treasured gift from his father. Maybe the only thing he has to remember him. The kid's twelve but already tough as a cornered badger. He tears into its neck with his knife. Blood spewing everywhere. Kills the massive thing. Think about that. The kid kills a charging wild boar with his bare hands and a knife. Got a rib or two broken, and parts of a finger and thumb on his left hand were dangling by some skin. Rumor is he just grabbed hold with his other hand and tore them off."

"Holy cheese," Philippe mumbled.

"Seems like he's been hunting ever since," Georges continued. "Doesn't matter what: wild boar, us, mosquitoes, maybe Jews. I doubt he takes pride in it because I don't think he cares. Just does it and moves on."

Henri looked stumped. "Again, how do you know all this?" he asked, repeating Philippe's question.

"News, stories, digging. You can learn a lot about someone when it's your job."

"His sister?" Philippe asked with hope-filled eyes.

"Dead within seconds, more than likely."

"But he saved his mother?" Henri asked.

"Yeah, I guess he did. Not much good, though. Seems she lost her marbles at some point and was sent off to a state ward. Maybe the trauma of losing her daughter. Little more is known about her, but I doubt she's alive. These Nazis aren't exactly sympathetic to their own if they aren't perfect specimens."

"Compassion isn't their strong suit," Henri scoffed.

"What about his père?" asked Philippe.

"His father died in the first war," Georges answered. "That couldn't have helped his mother either. He was gone at the front for two years before getting it. What's more, Holtzer was born after his father left for the war. He never met the man. I hear he still carries that knife with him to this day."

"He's a mysterious one, isn't he?" said Henri. "A lot of hate brewing, I suppose."

"I'm not sure," Georges went on. "I don't think it's hate. He hunts as though he couldn't care less. Smart bastard too. Thinks everything through. Cool-headed."

"It's weird...creepy even," Philippe whispered. "I heard he's calm and stays professional when anyone else might be boiling mad."

"I believe that's so," said Georges. "But that's what I'm saying. People who hate kill with emotion. Not him. No need to get all riled up or even proud about killing if you don't give a shit. Anyway, he's got one hell of a reputation. And make no mistake...it's deserved."

Philippe again stared at the floor in thought. Georges nudged him on the shoulder, and he looked up. "So, what's he doing in Tours?"

Georges frowned. "I'm responsible for knowing the million-dollar answer to that, and I don't. I know some about the man, but I don't know that. Not yet."

"Shhh!" Henri turned his ear and held up a hand.

They heard a faint, coded knocking. Philippe bounded up the stone steps to tap the reply while Georges and Henri watched from below in anticipation. Hearing the expected response, Philippe opened the door. A weary-looking Charles Touchard stood with a disheveled Colette Dubois at his side—her arm draped around the shoulder of her mud-caked brother.

Louis looked up. "They got Mama."

~ ~ ~

Henri offered Charles, Colette, and Louis water and a bite to eat before having them recount their day. Charles started with the uneventful trip to his place yesterday, and how things took a bad turn when they arrived and found Giselle and Louis missing. Colette jumped in whenever she thought he passed over something significant; Louis chimed in whenever he got excited. She talked about spotting her brother in the tree after they searched the house and found evidence of him in the cellar. Philippe sat mesmerized, hanging on every word as they described their harrowing escape on the country road. When they finished the account, Charles praised Colette and Louis for their extraordinary bravery, and the three received hearty congratulations and hugs from the avid listeners.

"Finding your mother and father is our top priority," said Henri. "We already have a team in Tours to do just that." His words had the positive effect he hoped for. There were still plenty of questions and concerns, but he withheld them until he and Georges could speak privately with Charles. "Philippe, show our young guests to the wash basin. I think they'll appreciate it." Colette smiled, seeing her brother nodding his head.

Walking off, Philippe rustled Louis' hair and laughed when dried mud chunks fell to the floor. "I've never seen anybody so dirty!"

Henri motioned for Georges and Charles to join him.

"Well," he started in a hushed voice, "the first thing we need to do is find out what's happened to Giselle and Regina."

"Based on the note Giselle left, it's a certainty the Nazis took her," said Charles. "And with Louis' story, coupled with our findings at the Viard place, it's safe to assume the same is true of Regina."

Henri dropped his voice to a faint whisper. "Something happened at the river the other night, and the Nazis won't hesitate using those two women as pawns."

The three sat mulling over likely scenarios. At least they had a starting point with François. With little or nothing to go by, finding Giselle and Regina would be difficult at best.

There was a secondary issue troubling Henri. "Charles, they may not consider you a threat, but you're a marked man." Charles bowed his head in understanding. "You know where I'm going with this. Not only can you be recognized, but you've pissed them off. Don't get me wrong, you did the right thing, but they don't like being made fools of...and they don't easily forget."

Georges put his hand on Charles' shoulder. "It's also possible they'll remember your name and address."

"He only glanced at my papers. I doubt—"

"No, Georges is right," said Henri. "It's too risky. It may not have been those two, but somebody came by your place, and you can be sure the Germans now associate you with Giselle. You can't return home or be seen in public. Not for a while, anyway." Henri could see Charles absorbing the reality and knew it stung. "We'll come up with something, but we must put the group first. Our efforts can be jeopardized by the smallest of things."

"What happened with the Kübelwagen?" Georges asked. "What did you do with it?"

"I ditched it. I didn't like that Louis was barefoot, but I couldn't risk getting closer to Vouvray. A Frenchman seen driving two kids around in a German army vehicle wouldn't have gone over too well."

Henri chuckled. "No, no, it wouldn't."

"We stuck to farm roads, taking a detour to avoid the château."

"Jallanges?" Henri asked.

"Right. Nazis are always crawling around that place. Instead, I took a road south of there. Sorry, I don't know the name, but it runs mostly east-west, just north of Vernou-Sur-Brenne. There's a rundown shack several meters off the road on the north side."

"Hah," Georges laughed. "Believe it or not, I think I know the place. That's where you stashed it?"

"Yeah. There was too much clutter to hide it inside, but the overhang in the back with the junk around it was perfect. Nobody's going to stumble across it any time soon."

Henri commended Charles for making good decisions and getting the children to safety. He apologized for having to reassign him to more discreet roles.

"It's alright," Charles said. "Marcel will feel the same."

"There's still plenty you can help with behind the scenes," Henri reassured him. "Marcel and I have been noodling something important, and you may have just solved it for us." Turning to Georges, he said, "Let's get two men to the Kübelwagen tonight. Strip it: wires, engine parts, wheels, everything. One never knows what we could use. Have them siphon any fuel...and check for spare tanks."

"Got it," said Georges. They turned at the sound of laughter across the room. "They're sure taking their day in stride, huh?"

"I'm telling you," said Charles, "I've never seen kids like this. And I swear Colette is a different person than when Georges and I found her in the cellar yesterday morning."

"How so?" asked Henri.

"Oh, she looks the same. Just as pleasant, maybe just as naive. But there's an edge to her I didn't expect."

"What do you mean?" Georges asked.

"There's a fire in there. She doesn't curl up and whimper at bad news. I'd say it's the opposite...at least regarding family. She gets angry. Not so much outwardly; more like smoldering. But it doesn't consume her. Five minutes later, she's back to her usual self. I don't know if she's stuffing it down inside, or she's so damn positive she assumes it'll turn out fine."

"A good quality," said Georges.

"Another thing," Charles continued. "Maybe more surprising...to me anyway. She has an acute awareness of what she sees. And she sees a lot. Not just what she's looking for. She takes it all in."

"Like what?" Henri asked.

"I don't know. She's quick to recognize and understand what her eyes tell her. The meanings and possibilities pop into her head fast."

"Did something happen?" Henri asked, pushing for more.

"Yes, I mean, no. I—" He paused a second. "It's not like she saw something once and formed a thought. It was every time we came across something different or unusual."

~ ~ ~

After extended effort, Colette got most of the mud off her brother's hair, face, hands, feet, and knees. She would work on finding him some clean clothes later. When Louis was mostly recognizable, Philippe led them to a worn, comfortable couch. He was fascinated by their story, almost envious.

"You two sure have a knack for dramatic adventure," he laughed, shaking his head.

Colette looked at her brother. "You have a lot of practice, don't you?" A big grin broke across his face.

"And you," said Philippe, looking admiringly at Colette. "Disarming a Nazi? Seriously? Are you kidding? I'm a kidder, but tell me you're kidding."

"Just another beautiful day in paradise," she joked.

It took only minutes for Louis to go from being an active participant to fast asleep in the corner of the couch.

"I thought I had a day, but my little brother has me beat," Colette said. "He eluded capture at the Touchard barn, spent the night in a black pit of horror, was up a tree at sunrise for scouting duties, led us on a long walk through the countryside, and fought off a Nazi in a muddy ravine."

Philippe looked over at him. "How old is he?"

"Ten."

"I'd say his nap is well-earned."

Colette was also weary but still invigorated by the day. It had been like no other, and the two gabbed nonstop. Any pauses could be attributed to Philippe as she watched him frenetically search his brain for another question.

He paused longer than usual, then lit up. "Colette, you should be a part of our team!"

"What?"

"Well, for starters, you seem smart. We can always use smarts. Hell, almost everything we do requires using our brains."

"So, what do you need me for? I suspect you're all pretty smart."

"Um, thanks. Yeah, I agree. It's just that you—" He started over. "Well, you have certain advantages over the rest of us."

She squinted. "What kind of advantages? I don't know a thing about what you do."

"No. Right. But you're a...I mean...you're a woman."

She snickered. "Okay. I'm vaguely aware. Is there more?" She watched Philippe adjust himself on the couch. "May I get you a pillow?" she asked wryly, aware that there wasn't one to offer.

"No. Thanks. I...I hope this doesn't offend you. I prefer not to offend people if—"

"Try me."

He looked down. "It's just that you're...well, you're...pretty."

She tapped him on the leg to regain his attention and suppressed a smirk. "That wasn't as offensive as it could have been."

He continued to bumble along. "I mean, you're prettier than the rest of us. Hell, you're prettier than all of us combined."

Colette held up her palm to stop him. "Philippe, thank you for not offending me, but what are you getting at?"

Her tone seemed to put him at ease, and he spilled it. He explained how he thought women had advantages over men when communicating with the enemy and believed that the prettier they were, the more they could get away with.

"What do you mean? Get away with what?"

"Well, for instance, you could approach a patrol, and they might spend all their time flirting with you. But with me? Forget it. They'd interrogate me, demand my purpose, and shake me upside down until my pockets were empty...pretty much anything they could think of to make my life difficult."

"But why would they treat a girl differently?"

Philippe threw his hands up. "Because they're men! And, I don't know your age, but you're sure no girl."

She smiled at his initial emphasis and the awkward attempt at another compliment before looking down at herself. Her arms, legs, feet, and hands were still filthy. Her clothes were dusty, and she could only imagine how her face and hair looked.

"Oh, I can do better than this."

"Yeah...I don't doubt that for a second."

Are we flirting? she wondered.

Philippe explained that she might get past barriers others wouldn't and how she could take advantage of her qualities to accomplish essential tasks. She caught on quickly.

"So, you think I'd make a good...spy?"

He looked sheepish. "Um, yeah, I guess that's the gist."

"Hmm," she feigned consideration, "I can't tell if you're giving me another compliment or if there's some reason you want me dead."

"Oh no, I didn't mean to...I mean, I would never—"

"Philippe, I'm teasing you. But," she continued, "I was wondering...Do you do a lot of dangerous stuff?"

"Good question. It's hard to know what's dangerous anymore. But we're still growing. So far, it's mostly information gathering, moving people, that kind of thing. We're not out there blowing up bridges or assassinating world leaders."

"Yet."

"Yet," he said, holding up a finger.

Her tone changed. "Is my father in danger?"

"Colette, your father's going to be just fine. He'll be back with us in no time."

"Mmm, yeah. Okay. So, how big is the team, anyway?" she asked, switching subjects.

"I'm not allowed to say, but small. And others help us. I can't say who, but we count on them to keep an eye open or lend a hand. We want to grow. Marcel's open to suggestions but always cautious about bringing someone on...even your father."

"Well, he might be especially cautious about a seventeen-year-old girl. And, I must tell you, Philippe, your idea could have problems."

Seventeen, huh? "Problems? Like what?"

"Well, for starters, would it be dangerous? I don't know how well I'd do if it was. I've never done anything like it before. Zero experience, you know?"

"Yeah, I know, but none of us do...did...do. We learn as we go, and you'd be taught."

"Hmm, you're saying I'd be taught by someone who hasn't done it? Sounds promising."

"Ugh, I know. I'm blowing it. Let me run the idea past the others." He stood. "Stay here with Louis. I'll be right back."

"I'll be right here," she humored him. "By the way, it all sounds quite exciting, but there's one other thing you should know that might be important."

"What's that?"

"My father wouldn't let me do this in a million years."

~ ~ ~

Philippe was determined not to let it take the wind from his sails. Despite knowing the man reasonably well, he hadn't considered the obvious hurdle. Wagging a finger at Colette as if he'd just solved the problem, he left to pitch his idea to Henri, Georges, and Charles. When welcomed into the conversation, the three happened to be on the subject of François.

"You're doing a great job, son," Henri said, "though it seems you've bored Louis to sleep."

Philippe looked back and grinned. "He's had a whale of a day. His sister, too."

"That they have," Charles agreed.

He saw an opening and jumped on it. "Speaking of Colette, I have an idea I want to run by you."

Nobody had ever considered having a woman on the team. But, after much discussion and salesmanship by their newest team member, they had to acknowledge the possible benefits. Five minutes later, Philippe was sure he'd sold them on it.

"Except for the obvious problem, right?" said Henri.

"I know, I know. She already brought it up. There's no way her father would ever let her. But there must be something she could help us with, right?"

Georges nodded. "From observation and messenger standpoints alone, I can think of several."

"Gentlemen," Henri cut in, "it's one thing to tinker with the idea, but it'll be meaningless once François hears of it." None dared suggest that François might not be available to oppose the idea.

"Hmm, what if—" Georges began, staring at the ceiling and formulating an idea. "What if we let it be for now? We don't tell François. Instead, we pitch the idea to Marcel, and then we all convince François that it's for the good of France. Nobody's more patriotic than François, right?"

Philippe liked what he was hearing. "Vive la France."

"But enough of that," Henri broke in. "We've got far more pressing concerns right now, and Georges needs to get men out to that Kübelwagen."

~ ~ ~

The longer the men discussed her, the more Colette thought about Philippe's suggestion. Her initial dismissive reaction was softening. Possible dangers were a concern, but it sounded intriguing—and thrilling. She was convincing herself she should try it when she saw Philippe heading her way. His expression revealed little.

"So? How did it go?" she asked as he settled onto the couch next to the sleeping Louis.

"Well, they're not exactly opposed. Of course, your father was mentioned...more than once."

"Not opposed, huh? Is that something like being in favor?"

"Let's just say they're open-minded about it."

"Open-minded is a good start," she said, patting him on the knee. "Maybe you'd make a good salesman."

"I think I made a good case. Anyway, it was worth a try."

She took his hand. "Keep trying."

CHAPTER FIFTEEN
Tours
April 17, Late Afternoon

MARCEL REACHED THE government building in Tours just before closing. Trivial visits were frowned upon, but this was urgent, and his contact there was the best chance to confirm what he'd heard.

"I'm here to file a complaint," he declared to the woman at the receiving desk.

The clerk finished filing some papers and stepped over. "Let me guess, livestock and landmines?"

"Only the latter," he answered, pretending to be agitated over his contrived inconvenience.

She asked him to complete the necessary form and take a seat. He finished and waited to hear his name called. It didn't take long.

One level up, he knocked on the usual door and was met by a frail man in his late thirties with a beaked nose so prominent it announced his forthcoming arrival. Any remaining wisps of hair were matted and pressed to his skull—whether intentional or out of neglect was anyone's guess.

Marcel stepped inside the cluttered office. The man looked up and down the hallway, scurried in after him, and closed the door. "I thought I might be seeing you," he squeaked.

There was no place to sit, but Marcel didn't plan on staying long. "I've been asked to try and ascertain the location and condition of some ordinance that may or may not have been removed from a property owned by a fellow named Dubois," Marcel said quietly.

"Right, good. Uh, I do recall the matter. It came to my attention just this morning." The spindly man rifled through a pile of papers on his desk. "Ah, yes, here it is." He picked up a blank sheet of paper. "It appears the ordinance is in good condition but is being delivered to German headquarters at six this evening for further analysis."

"Thank you for your assistance," Marcel said.

It confirmed what he'd heard. He knew where to go and left the office without another word spoken.

~ ~ ~

François spent the time in jail agonizing over his family and friend. The way he'd left Colette mortified him. Over time, he convinced himself she'd be fine. Though innocent and inexperienced, she was sensible. Surely she'd go to the Viard place or continue to nearby neighbors. She might even reunite with her mother at Charles' home if she went further. He also had unwavering faith that Louis would come through. He admired his son for his grit, keenness, and natural competence—traits he didn't find especially common in young boys.

It was prudent and expected to distrust Nazis, but aside from having to sit in a stuffy jail cell, he was surprised at his humane treatment. Lieutenant Schmid had ordered the guards to isolate him, which suited François fine. He wasn't the type to pursue or welcome small talk with cellmates and knew that idle chatter could lead to unintentional slips.

As evening approached, his thoughts were interrupted when the cell door clanged open. The two soldiers who visited his house the day before slapped undersized handcuffs on him and shoved him down the hall. They didn't say where they were taking him, and he didn't ask. The car stopped in front of German headquarters, and the sergeant yanked him out.

Private Ott slammed the door shut. "Try not to get lost!" he admonished the driver.

François felt uncharacteristically nervous. He'd heard tales of Nazi methods and was sure the subject of Roland would come up. He had no way of knowing what his friend might have said under interrogation and would need to improvise and summon whatever cleverness he could.

The sergeant muscled him through the main door and down the entry hall. François had never been inside the building and glanced around, hoping to learn anything useful about the place and its occupants. The foyer and main hall were grand and well-kept but lacked customary adornments. Dusty outlines remained where large paintings had hung on the now stark walls. Statues and busts were conspicuously missing—all undoubtedly removed by the Germans in the name of safekeeping.

He was led to a receiving room and saw Lieutenant Schmid pacing. A woman seated at a solitary desk looked up. He was sure she smiled at him before averting her eyes. The sergeant jerked on his arm and pushed him onto a chair.

~ ~ ~

Schmid was certain Dubois knew something about Viard and the policeman. Worse, he may have seen other things he shouldn't. They locked eyes briefly. Looking scornful, the lieutenant turned away and said nothing. The prisoner was out of his hands now. The major could do with him as he wished.

After a brief wait, the woman at the desk walked their way. All four stood in anticipation.

"Hello, gentlemen. My name is Angela Fassbender. Major Holtzer wishes to see Lieutenant Schmid first."

He turned and glared at his two thugs as a final reminder to stick to the plan. The three sat back down.

Schmid was surprised to find himself alone. With his hat tucked firmly in the crook of his left arm, he stood erect and considered the room for the first time. The dark wood throughout, combined with the burgundy carpeting, book-filled shelves, and warm glow from a few antique sconce lamps, gave the room an academic library feel. Schmid shook his head. It was an impractical place for interrogations: Far too comforting, and the dim lighting was hardly sufficient for revealing wary glances, tics, and other enlightening expressions.

A thundering gunshot disrupted his critique-filled thoughts. He jerked his head toward the back corner of the room. Moments later, a door opened, and Major Holtzer entered. Schmid snapped to attention and saluted. The major walked to his desk and set down a nickel-finish Smith and Wesson .357 magnum revolver.

"Hello, Lieutenant," he said without expression. "I apologize for the delay. I was preparing the inner courtyard. Have a seat." He motioned toward two chairs facing his desk.

"Thank you, Sir," Schmid said, removing his focus from the gun. "I wasn't aware of a courtyard." He sat down and hoped some small talk might ease his nerves.

"There are two doors to it, including the one behind me," Holtzer said. "It's not a secret, but it doesn't get a lot of press, so I suppose most wouldn't know. It may come in useful today, though I hope not."

Schmid wasn't sure what he meant. He waited as the major pulled two thin files from a right-hand drawer and set them on his desk. One was labeled 'Dubois' in bold black, the other 'Viard.' Schmid still needed to figure out when and how to reveal Viard's unintended demise, but he hoped for an opening to address it before it became increasingly awkward.

"Anyway," Holtzer continued, "I've been looking forward to this. I've already had more administrative meetings than I can stomach."

Schmid felt uneasy as the major settled into his chair and seemed to be considering him.

"You may think it beneath me, Lieutenant, but I like to get to the meat of things. The best way to do that is to get involved."

As he did yesterday, Schmid cringed inside, thinking about how this newcomer could interfere. He adjusted himself in his chair and replied in his most sincere tone. "I'm pleased you're here, Sir." He was deft at adapting to his audience despite seldom having the need. He opened his mouth to speak of the dead suspect just as Holtzer picked up one of the files.

"Viard," said the major. He pulled out a photograph. "Roland Viard. So this is the guy, huh?" he asked aloud, not indicating he expected an answer.

"Sir—" Schmid started.

"Well, let's do this," Holtzer said, pressing the intercom button. "Miss Fassbender, please show Monsieur Viard in."

The dreaded time had come. Schmid had no choice. "Sir, about Viard. He isn't here. A problem arose that I wasn't aware of until just recently." Holtzer stared at him without saying anything. "But we have the other prisoner here for you to interrogate," Schmid added, hoping to soothe his predicament.

"Fill me in, Lieutenant. What's this problem that arose?"

Schmid hoped to limit the details while boosting the major's ego. "He's dead, Sir. I'm sure he feared that you—"

"Sir," came a woman's voice over the intercom. "There is no Monsieur Viard here."

Holtzer pressed the button. "No, no, I suppose there isn't. Thank you." Holtzer glared at Schmid. "You were saying?"

"Uh, yes, Sir. Viard committed suicide. I understand it was right after learning of his upcoming meeting with you. I'm sure he couldn't bear the thought of facing you."

Holtzer stood, stepped behind his chair, and faced away. After a long delay, he asked, "Why are you just telling me this now, Lieutenant?" He turned to face his subordinate.

"Sir, I apolo—"

"And just how did you let him kill himself?"

Schmid launched into his fabricated story. He recounted the escape, the jump from the bridge, and the vanishing under the water as told to him by Sergeant Protz and Private Ott. He blamed Ott for the prisoner's mismanagement and clarified that it never would've happened if he hadn't been away on another matter.

Holtzer scowled as though doubting the last comment. "I assume you have no other witnesses to corroborate this tale?"

"Not that I'm aware of, Sir."

"So, your understanding is that the body was washed away and never recovered?"

"Yes, Sir."

"I see. Well, I guess that's that." Holtzer sat down and took a slow look around the room. "So, what did you learn from Viard before he... went and killed himself?"

Schmid didn't love the line of questioning, but it was inevitable and going reasonably well. Unable to trust Protz and Ott to give consistent answers under pressure, he needed to proceed cautiously. "Viard was apprehended when making his way home after curfew and was detained for questioning. The policeman was found shortly after, less than two kilometers away."

"I'm curious. Why was he patrolling out there at that time? Was he expecting something?"

"It's still unknown, Sir. I was woken and brought in to question the suspect. Viard initially denied everything but soon admitted to stabbing the policeman in a panic."

"Did you find out what he was doing out there after curfew?"

"No, Sir. We were working on that when...well."

The major eyed the second file and picked it up. "Was he operating alone...or with this Dubois?" He flung the file back on his desk. "Or maybe I'm getting ahead of myself. Is Dubois even alive?"

The ridicule was palpable. Schmid took offense but hid it.

"It's uncertain if Dubois is involved, Sir. But he is here. He hasn't admitted to anything, but I wanted to give you a chance to interrogate him. You expressed an eagerness to get involved."

"It's not an *eagerness*, Lieutenant," Holtzer articulated. "It is so that I can learn more. Come up to speed as it were; perhaps determine the level of competence or incompetence I've inherited here...rewarding the prior, *weeding out the latter*."

Schmid said nothing as a sour taste developed in his mouth. The plan to maneuver into the major's good graces and subtly sway, mold, and guide him was in jeopardy. Holtzer's questions continued.

"If you learned nothing from Viard, why are you holding Dubois?"

"His property is near the Viard place, Sir."

"And?"

"They knew each other, Sir."

Holtzer looked miffed. "Being neighbors, wouldn't you say that's a bit predictable? Did the policeman scuffle with multiple attackers? Was another man seen in the area following the attack?"

"Not that I'm aware, Sir. But Dubois was away from his home the same night, and I have a feeling that—"

"Feelings can be wonderful," the major interrupted, "and intuition is often helpful. But for now, I'm trying to ascertain the facts."

The comment stung. Schmid prided himself on his ability to infer, deduce, reason, and solve—and believed nobody did it better. He had used the wrong damn turn of phrase. The implication that feelings dictated his actions was an insult. Having to swallow his pride was infuriating, but he did.

"So, Lieutenant, before I bother speaking with your men, I'd like to see this...Dubois. You can wait out there with the others."

Schmid was relieved to be dismissed. As he departed, Holtzer called after him.

"Lieutenant, is he cuffed?"

"Of course, Sir."

"Remove them."

~ ~ ~

François heard Miss Fassbender acknowledge a request over the intercom. She approached and asked him to follow her. Though unaccustomed to feeling so unsettled, he turned and thanked her before she closed the door behind him.

"Come in, Monsieur Dubois," he heard. He turned toward the voice, taking in as much of the surroundings as his racing brain permitted. "Please have a seat," the German officer said in perfect French, motioning to the empty chair across from him.

François sat down, and they held each other's gaze briefly. He didn't get the sense it was a power play. It was more like the man was gathering first impressions of the suspect before him. Major Holtzer's face remained expressionless and revealed little of how he would conduct himself. His steel-blue eyes narrowed, and one corner of his mouth crept upward. François was disturbed to see the man smirking.

"Dubois, you've inspired me." François didn't know what to make of the surprising comment. But, as it wasn't in question form, he remained silent. Holtzer continued. "Since I've arrived here—" He looked at the ceiling and slowly returned his focus to François. "Hell, since the start of this whole damn thing, you are the first person to thank my assistant when shown into an office of mine. And I don't mean people in your position who may feel anxious. No, you're the first *anyone*." He reflected on that a second, then added, "From now on, I'm having others follow your example. Common courtesy isn't too much to expect during a war, is it? I've never said it before, but the woman is a blessing. I ask her to follow me from one place to the next. Always amenable. I ask her to do one thing after another. Never complains. I ask that she make no mistakes. Reliable as can be."

François weighed his preference to remain silent against the major's demeanor and decided to speak. "Perhaps she thinks you're telling instead of asking," he said in a deep, humble voice.

Holtzer leaned back in his chair. A smile slowly formed. "Yes, Dubois, you have inspired me."

François cocked his head slightly and turned his palms up. He wasn't sure what would come next and remained leery. The man and his reputation couldn't be separated, and his pending arrival had unsettled everyone. Discussions about him always touched on his aura, imposing stature, or eerily composed wrath. Now, François was getting a first-hand taste of it and hoped Holtzer's present demeanor wasn't masking any ill will.

"But, moving on," said Holtzer, leaning forward in his chair, "let's talk about you."

~ ~ ~

Marcel Bouchet sat on a park bench facing the building's main entry. He feigned interest in a newspaper while racking his brain to figure out why a major in the German army was involved. *The man must have more pressing concerns than a dead policeman.* Without more to go by, his thoughts got him nowhere.

A few minutes before six, a driver and three passengers pulled up to the main entrance. He peered over his paper as François was brought up the steps. It heartened him to see his colleague in good physical condition, but he was worried that could soon change. The driver stayed with the vehicle, and Marcel suspected François would be sent back to jail—or worse. After what felt too long, he walked past the front entrance. Several people were out and about, and there was no need to remain in the shadows. Pacing or loitering wouldn't be wise, but he could blend in with other citizens going about their lives. Strolling past the driver, it struck him how young the lad looked.

People were entering and leaving the building, but nobody caught his eye. He moved to a bench near the far street corner to get a different vantage point. Pretending to read more of his paper, he waited again. Several minutes later, his curiosity soared. A large man was walking away from the rear of the building. From the back, it looked like François. He wasn't keen on taking his eyes off the main entry, but he had no choice. If it wasn't François, he needed to return to his post. Then again, it could be a trap. It would be foolish to engage a man the Nazis had just interrogated. After following for a few blocks, he determined the man on the other side of the street was indeed his compatriot. It was all he could do not to call out.

Preoccupied with tracking him and anticipating their reunion, Marcel wasn't mindful of his surroundings. The middle-aged, lanky figure following a half-block behind wore a long, charcoal-gray trench coat and matching leather fedora despite the pleasant weather. Marcel may have noticed him under normal circumstances. Then again, although the man's ensemble set him apart, plenty of unique people were roaming the world. To Marcel's thinking, those who stuck out warranted less attention than those lurking in the shadows.

It didn't take long to realize that François intended to walk home. Marcel used the cover of pedestrians and street vendors to get beyond him. Where the city streets neared their outer limits, he stopped and leaned casually against a building corner. François looked lost in thought as he approached.

"Hello, stranger." Marcel's voice startled the big man.

"Oh, hello. Wha—?" François rushed over and wrapped his arms around him. "What are you doing here?"

Marcel smiled while scanning the area. "What do you mean? This is my favorite street corner. I never know who I might run into." They continued northward.

The tall stranger a block behind, turned and walked back the way he came.

~ ~ ~

Marcel first comforted his friend by telling him that Giselle and Louis had made their way to the Touchard place. He then explained how Charles and Georges found Colette and that she was doing fine. François nearly slumped with relief.

"I knew I could count on that boy, but I was worried sick about her. I tried to tell myself she'd be okay, but leaving her in that pit made me ill. What kind of father does that?"

"You were trying to protect her," Marcel reassured him. "What kind of father *doesn't* do that? I also asked Charles to reunite Colette with Giselle and Louis just before I came looking for you. I've been away and haven't heard more, but I suspect they're resting comfortably at his place and anxiously awaiting your return."

"I can't tell you what a relief it is to hear they're safe. It was the weight of the world on me. Thank you."

"You're welcome, my friend. You'd have done the same for any of us." Marcel wasn't sure how to proceed with the bad news and held off. "So, the new major. When I caught wind of your meeting, I feared the worst. But here you are. What the hell's going on?"

"Good question. Lieutenant Schmid visited me at my place after going to Roland's and had me spend time in a jail cell. The next thing I know, I'm standing before Major Holtzer."

"And?"

"And I never thought I'd see the light of day again. But he was cordial. Speaks damn good French, too. Said that his grandparents on his mother's side only spoke French."

"Okay, but what did you two talk about?"

François gave a long exhale, shook his head, and reflected. "Not much. He asked about the wife and kids. I presume Schmid told him about them. He wondered about the war's impact on the farmers and asked if he could get me a ride home. I told him no, but thanked him. It was weird but strangely pleasant."

"Did he mention Roland?"

"I thought for sure he'd have questioned him and would look for holes in our stories. He never said a word about it."

Marcel began to fidget and failed to hide his heartache.

"What don't I know?" asked François. "What is it?"

"I'm sorry. I've put it off long enough, and there's no good way to tell you. Roland is dead."

The news devastated François, and it was distressing when telling him what the Nazis did with his body. Marcel consoled him before adding that Roland's wife and son were missing.

"I'll take care of those Nazi bastards if it's the last thing I do," François said coldly.

Marcel understood his friend's need to vent. He also knew that vendettas, though understandable and commonplace, could endanger resistance efforts when pursued recklessly. He'd discuss more rational options another time. They walked on.

"What happened out there?"

"I don't understand it," François said, slowly shaking his head. "I've been wondering the same ever since."

They put in a few more strides when Marcel offered a suggestion. "Let me walk you through what Henri and I did that night; then you can describe the things you did. We'll try to piece together whatever we can."

François listened. Marcel even mentioned that the Jewish couple asked him to thank the 'kind, big man' who helped them.

François bobbed his head. "They're good people."

"You did well by them and made them feel safe. After pushing them off, Henri and I separated as agreed, made our way home, and reconnected at the afternoon meeting. There wasn't much more to it. Walk me through your side."

François took his time to reflect and talk through each step. Finally, Marcel asked him to stop. "Let me get my head around this. So, you said that one person met the Jewish couple at the drop, right? And it was a woman?"

François hesitated. "Yes. Yes, I'm sure it was a woman. And Roland thought so. I didn't see anyone else before I continued following River Man upstream."

"Okay." Marcel looked down and contemplated the scene in his head. "There are some odd things. First, the bag. You say River handed over a bag, and then they returned it?"

"That's how it looked."

"Did they empty it, then hand it back to him?"

"I can't say for sure. It happened quickly."

"Could they have exchanged bags?"

François mulled it over. "I don't know. I guess."

"Now, the motorcycles," said Marcel as they continued walking. "Some things are troubling me."

"I'll do my best."

"You're doing just fine. It's mostly my brain trying to catch up. Why were there two motorcycles? You say neither gave a ride to anyone, right?"

"Right. One appeared to head south, maybe in the direction of Loches. I don't know the roads down there. The other went back east toward Bléré, possibly on to Amboise. There's no way to be sure, but that was the direction they came from."

"So neither picked up the two passengers he dropped off earlier?"

"No. It's unlikely, anyway. While sitting in that jail, I had plenty of time to think. I can't figure it out."

"Here's another thing nagging at me," Marcel continued. "That's no way to be discreet. Who sneaks about the countryside at night on a motorcycle, let alone two of them?"

"Nobody," François agreed.

"So, who's comfortable taking motorcycles out in the middle of the night?"

François frowned. "Only Germans would be riding around at that time. I've thought about it, but it doesn't add up. I know he's a stick in the mud, and nobody cares much for him, but he's helped us repeatedly and always comes through. What's more, he's making out like a thief with what these people pay. He's got everything to lose if he messes up."

"But, based on your description, it wasn't like he was caught. You said his encounter with the motorcyclists was uneventful, right?"

"Yes." François bit his lip. "Hold it. There's one more thing. Before leaving, one pointed a gun at River's head for a second or two. Then, the other guy put his arm around his shoulder before the two drove off. Strange, non?"

Marcel had heard enough. "He met Nazis, not relay men."

"Why would he—"

"He can't be trusted, whether of his own doing or forced into it. There are a few possibilities, but try this one out. What if he's handing over their valuables, or some anyway, to the Nazis?"

"Why would he do that? And why would they let him go?"

"Maybe they have something on him. Or they caught him at some point, and he and his wife are being forced. And I say Nazis loosely. What if it's just a few rogue ones on the take?"

François let out a deep breath. "Shit, they're all bad in my book, but I know what you mean."

"Or," a parallel thought occurred to Marcel, "what if it was, in fact, an exchange?" He was vocalizing thoughts as they came to him. "The Nazis reward him with something in return for delivering the packages to them. A win-win, right?"

"So, you're suggesting River gets paid by the packages and then also gets paid by the Nazis?"

"Maybe," thought Marcel. "The Nazis wouldn't know he's already getting paid...especially if they caught him at it early on. They would expect a patriotic Frenchman to be doing it for the cause. You know, rowing the passengers to freedom out of the goodness of his heart."

"But hasn't everything been smooth sailing until now?"

"We've always assumed so, but maybe it's been too smooth. I asked you to follow them because we never know what happens after they leave. We've taken it for granted that they're handed off for the next stage. Whether or not they reach their final destination is out of our hands. Maybe I've been blind."

"Holy shit, Marcel. Then what's happening to the packages?"

Marcel shook his head and stared at the ground. "If you were those Nazis, could you afford loose ends hanging around?"

François looked sick. "I can't imagine. Do you believe that?"

"I don't know. But with what you've told me, it's possible."

François stopped walking. "Marcel, I'm so sorry. I have no idea what happened. Maybe we were tailed. I like to think I'd have noticed. Seems like a strange time and place for local police to make a random pass. Was it a coincidence?"

"It's possible," Marcel said. "But coincidences worry me... especially when friends get killed. Maybe he was watching River. Maybe he's been watching all along."

"Merde," François muttered.

"I hope I'm wrong, but we need to know much more before making another transfer."

"What about the woman Roland and I saw?"

Marcel thought for a second. "It's usually the simplest answer. I think it's River's wife. They're likely in on it together. Maybe they're being threatened. Or, maybe they're just getting rich by it."

"She got a big hug from the Jewish woman," said François.

"It's unlikely they were acquainted. She was probably just happy to see anyone claiming to help. And I'm guessing his wife acted her part well. But back to this policeman. It can't be a coincidence. I think he's been watching the drop site, and this is the first time he's stumbled across anybody."

"I keep thinking if I hadn't left him alone, he'd be—"

"You did the right thing, François. Roland is gone, but your decision was right. There's no way you could have foreseen it."

It was dark, and curfew was in effect when they came to a split in the road. François was anxious to see his family, but Marcel needed him to meet with the others. François understood. They walked the road to Vouvray.

CHAPTER SIXTEEN
Tours
April 17, Evening

FRANÇOIS DUBOIS HAD disappeared into Major Holtzer's office nearly an hour ago. Lieutenant Schmid, Sergeant Protz, and Private Ott took turns fidgeting in their seats inside the receiving room. Miss Fassbender continued her busy ways and provided the sole respite to the silence by answering calls, opening and closing drawers, and tapping away at her typewriter. While they waited, she declined nine phone requests to speak with the major. Holtzer appreciated her innate ability to know which interruptions to categorize as urgent.

The intercom crackled, and they heard the directive to escort them in. She motioned to meet her at the office door and closed it behind them. The three approached and stood rigid before the grand desk with their right arms extended. Holtzer remained seated and flicked his arm so they could lower theirs. Schmid looked about the room, wondering what had happened to his prisoner.

"How did it go with Dubois, Sir?"

"Sergeant," the major said, ignoring the question, "go ask Miss Fassbender to return."

"Yes, Sir," said Protz, not considering the intercom would've been more efficient. He led her into the room and retook his place beside the lieutenant. Holtzer stood and motioned for her to approach. She did gladly, eager to assist in whatever way she could.

"Miss Fassbender?"

"Yes, Sir."

"From now on, when you usher someone into this office, I expect you to show appreciation when they thank you. And I want to be reminded afterward if they don't."

She gave a curt nod. "Thank you, Sir. I won't let you down."

"You never do."

She turned and saw herself out. Schmid remained silent, digesting the unmistakable undertone. Holtzer said nothing more about it and sat down.

"Now, what was it you were asking, Lieutenant?"

"Sir, I was just wondering about—"

"Oh, right. I had Monsieur Dubois escorted out the back way," Holtzer said offhandedly.

Schmid wasn't sure what to make of the answer. He had just learned of the back way, and all he knew about it was the gunshot he'd heard earlier. Did Holtzer dispense of Dubois in the courtyard? Was he taken elsewhere? Set free? He started with the least likely option, hoping to get clarification.

"Did you release him, Sir?"

"That's correct," said Holtzer.

"I see," said the confused lieutenant. "Did you get the answers you were looking for?"

"No, he told me nothing useful."

Schmid was beginning to think the major was inexperienced with interrogation. "Sir, my staff and I are happy to get your answers."

Holtzer glared at him. "Thank you, Lieutenant. We may have something to learn from Dubois, but it will be much easier if he's alive." The deadpan delivery was a searing jab. The major turned his gaze to Sergeant Protz. "So, I understand a man is missing here today because you let him escape and kill himself."

The sergeant was rigid. "Sir, I regret to say it happened on my watch. It was a desperate and unexpected move, Sir."

"You saw him jump from the bridge, hit the piling, and disappear under the water?"

Under pressure and flustered, Protz began to improvise. "Not exactly, Sir. Private Ott was nearest in pursuit and reported it to me."

Turning for the first time to the private, Holtzer continued. "So, Private, is that what you saw?"

The squat soldier stood next to Protz. His head came no higher than the sergeant's shoulders, and his bulbous nose, bushy eyebrows, and round figure hardly lived up to the master race hype.

"Yes, Sir. That's how it happened!" he blubbered, failing to mask his rehearsed tone.

Lieutenant Schmid was mentally crossing his fingers, skeptical that his two idiots could get through the questioning unscathed.

"Any other witnesses?"

"No, Sir."

"I see. That's what your lieutenant reported as well."

Private Ott attempted a show of loyalty. "Sir, Lieutenant Schmid wasn't present at the time."

The major kept his eyes fixed on the private and said nothing for what felt like an eternity. Finally, he turned back to Protz. "Sergeant, do you carry a knife?"

"Yes, Sir. We all do. I wouldn't be without it."

"Set it on my desk." Protz unsheathed his knife and did as instructed. Holtzer picked it up and inspected it. "I see initials scratched into the hilt. This is your knife?"

"Yes, Sir. Well...no, Sir," Protz backpedaled. "That is, it was issued to me. Most everyone etches their initials to avoid confusion."

Schmid wasn't sure where this was heading, but he waited it out. His mind drifted, trying to anticipate upcoming questions.

Holtzer grabbed a large, unsealed envelope off the left side of his desk and looked up at the sergeant and private. "Do either of you know French?"

"We both know some, Sir," the sergeant answered.

"I thought maybe." The major contemplated the envelope and tipped it. Three items dropped onto the desk: a knife, a chunk of cardboard, and a slip of paper smaller than his palm. Sergeant Protz looked like a man with nowhere to hide. Private Ott turned white. Lieutenant Schmid's unease mounted.

Major Holtzer read the note to himself, then held up the blood-stained cardboard by a corner and looked it over. Setting that down, he picked up the knife and examined it.

He addressed Lieutenant Schmid. "These items were recently brought to my attention. Do you know what they are?"

"Not at all, Sir. I've not seen them before," he answered less confidently than usual.

"I hope not. Because ignorance is probably best for you at this point...though being taken for a fool is hardly a banner achievement."

Schmid wished to speak in his defense but had no idea what Holtzer was getting at. "Sir, I have no idea what you're talking about," was all he could come up with.

"Unfortunately, I'm beginning to believe that." Holtzer pointed the knife at the cardboard piece on his desk. "This bloody thing here... well, Sergeant, do you mind reading it aloud?"

Sergeant Protz stepped forward and cleared his throat. "Don't be stupid like me."

Holtzer nodded and turned his attention to Schmid. "I suspect the author was oblivious to the irony of his words. Anyhow, it's a warning...a threat, one might say. It was directed at the townsfolk of Saint Martin le Beau. The tactic has become de rigueur in Paris and is now spreading like the Loire floodwaters." He turned his attention to the knife in his hand. "And this here? Well, it seems this was used to assist in its display. I understand it was thrust into a Frenchman's chest as one might use a pin on corkboard...though I suspect the effect was more dramatic."

Schmid listened on with a disquieting dread. *Why does Holtzer care about some poor nobody who likely got what he deserved?*

"Then there's this." Major Holtzer put the knife tip on the communique. "This little note clarifies who the mutilated body in a tree was...and when it was discovered."

Lieutenant Schmid looked at Protz and Ott. Their singular, unsettled expressions were sufficient for him to piece together the unthinkable. They didn't dispose of Viard's body at all. They put it on display for everyone to see. The fools hadn't informed him, even when they went along with his story about the suicidal escape attempt. He failed to hide his disbelief.

"It appears your brain is catching up, Lieutenant," said Holtzer. "Welcome to the meeting." His tone had become even more scathing, and Schmid sensed the man's blood boiling beneath the surface. The major turned to address Ott. "Private, your sergeant informs me everyone keeps their knife with them. May I take a look at yours?"

The meeting was unraveling fast, and Schmid watched in agony as Ott fumbled over what to say. "Sir, I lost it, and I...I haven't had a chance to replace it."

"Yes, I expected as much," came the icy reply. "Is it possible that this knife here—" He paused to examine the hilt. "This one with your initials engraved into it...just might be your *lost* knife?"

"Yes, Sir," Ott spouted, then spewed anything in an attempt to rescue himself. "It was an accident. Killing him, I mean. We were trying to get information from him." The private was flustered and couldn't think, but continued, trying to save face. "Lieutenant Schmid said he wanted to make an example of Viard. Sergeant Protz and I took it upon ourselves to make that happen. The lieutenant had no idea. It was an accident, Sir!" Holtzer held up his palm. The private froze.

"What about the escape?"

"The escape?" Ott stuttered. His brain had reached its capacity. "What escape, Sir?"

"Don't you remember?" Holtzer began, his voice full of contempt for the floundering man. "You saw Viard jump from the bridge and disappear beneath the water."

The private turned his eyes to Sergeant Protz, then his lieutenant. Receiving no support, he stammered, "Um, uh, Sir, you wanted to interrogate him, but we knew he was dead, so we...I mean, I—"

The major held up his hand again. Ott stopped talking. Holtzer leaned back, slowly regarded the three men before him, and stood.

"The German people are proud of their country, and they're proud of their fighting men. Many believe you are returning to them what is rightfully theirs. You've been chosen to do your job dutifully, without hesitation...and to do it well. There is no other option. Those who fail to do so are a liability to the homeland."

An uncomfortable silence followed as Holtzer straightened the folders on his desk, holstered his polished .357 magnum, and finalized his thoughts. He directed Sergeant Protz and Private Ott to follow him and led them out the back door into the hidden courtyard.

Lieutenant Schmid was left behind to contemplate the ramifications of what just happened.

~ ~ ~

The three men emerged from a corner door into the windowless courtyard. A brick walkway to the center encircled a large oak and continued to a door at the opposite corner. Three stone benches rested around the trunk of the tree. The remaining area lacked ground cover, and intermittent shrubbery was overgrown and neglected. Wartime clock adjustments to synchronize with German time prolonged the daylight, though the four encompassing walls shaded the enclosure. Shooting targets were secured to the brick mortar in the two courtyard corners without doors.

Major Holtzer stopped a few steps in, scanned the area, and turned to the two subordinates. "Do either of you have a sidearm?" Each did. Taking the standard-issue Lugers in each hand, he examined them together, returned Protz's to him, and slipped Ott's gun into his jacket pocket. Pointing to the target on the far wall, he asked, "How is your aim, Sergeant?"

Protz had lucked out. After losing his gun to Colette and Charles, he had gotten his hands on another. Regardless, his nervousness was justified despite his excellent marksmanship. Without saying a word, he raised the Luger and fired—a near bullseye. Holtzer said nothing and extended his palm face up. Beyond relieved, Protz handed the gun back.

"Private, go stand under the target."

"Sir?" Ott replied wide-eyed.

"You heard me." Holtzer used the weapon to motion him across the courtyard, then handed it back to Protz.

Ott gaped at his sergeant and shuffled off to the far wall.

"Sir, what if I hit him?" Protz pleaded. He looked across the way. Private Ott looked paralyzed, his head just beneath the target.

"You mean to tell me you're only accurate when it doesn't matter?" The major didn't wait for an answer. "And you'll switch places with him if you miss the target." Holtzer thought on it. "Though we may need to raise it some."

Protz took a deep breath, raised the pistol—delayed—delayed longer—and fired. Again, a near bullseye.

Private Ott vomited as small chunks of brick sprinkled down on him. Seeing the result, but also feeling sick, Protz handed it back.

Holtzer wasted no time. "Have you ever fired one of these, Sergeant?" he asked, offering his revolver.

Protz's eyes widened. "Sir, I've never even seen one. I wouldn't trust myself."

"Let me demonstrate."

Holtzer raised the gun, aimed, and fired. The walls amplified the explosion; the roar was deafening—a perfect bullseye. Private Ott wet himself as brick chunks again rained down.

Holtzer handed it over and motioned for him to shoot.

"Sir, I can't do it."

"Are you telling me you won't?" The major moved in front of him and was inches from his face. "Because it wasn't a request." Holtzer stepped back and calmly added, "On the other hand, you may switch places with him if you prefer."

Given the impossible predicament, Protz reconsidered and stared at the weapon. He raised it to eye level, held his breath, and took aim. The gun was substantially heavier than what he was used to, and he worried about the recoil.

He vaguely heard Holtzer say, "Remember to hit the target."

The tranquil evening air erupted. Instantly, blood and brains splattered the target and brick. Sergeant Protz stood horror-stricken as Private Ott crumpled to a heap at the base of the wall. Major Holtzer guided the revolver from the unresponsive gunman's hand and reported the result.

"You missed."

~ ~ ~

Four shots? What in the hell's going on? Schmid had entertained thoughts of being part of Holtzer's inner circle, but his hatred for the man grew every minute. He struggled to envision a way forward.

He was pacing when the back door opened. Holtzer led the dazed-looking sergeant into the room. Protz's swollen, vacant eyes took Schmid by surprise. He had bit his lip long enough.

"What the hell happened out there?" he snapped at the major. Holtzer placed his revolver on the desk corner and set two pistols beside it. Schmid turned to his subordinate. "Sergeant?" A blank look was all he got in return.

Holtzer reached for the intercom. "Miss Fassbender, I need you to arrange a follow-up in area three fifty-seven."

"I've already sent a team, Sir," a pleasant voice replied.

Holtzer looked toward the office door. "She's a godsend."

"Sir, where is Private Ott?" Schmid asked with mounting agitation.

Holtzer sat down and glared at him. "It turns out the sergeant agrees with me. Private Ott was a liability. No longer an asset to his homeland...if he ever was. And I'm arranging to send the sergeant east to get trained in the use of firearms. He'll be reassigned from there."

Schmid was numb. In mere seconds, he'd lost his two loyal stooges. Despite their shortcomings, they'd be hard to replace. He'd have to start from scratch.

The main office door opened. Miss Fassbender poked her head inside and announced, "Sir, they're ready for Sergeant Protz." Hearing his name, the sergeant regained some awareness. He looked to his lieutenant but got nothing in return as Miss Fassbender motioned for him to follow.

Major Holtzer looked stern but otherwise unaffected by the

preceding events. Schmid was stunned and remained rigid, choosing not to press his luck. He thought his horrible day might finally end. He was wrong.

Holtzer spotted an unlit cigar and set it back in its box. "It has come to my attention that others in the Dubois family eluded your vice-like grip the morning you visited them. Is that a fair assessment?"

Schmid somberly regarded the tone and realized the day would continue its downward spiral. He did his best to state the facts while deflecting blame. "Sir, his daughter was out that morning, and my replacement driver let the wife and son escape while I was inside questioning Dubois."

"Thank you for the explanation, Lieutenant. I'm not sure what they were escaping from, but you've clarified your grip wasn't the problem; it was the slippery grip of someone you were in charge of." Schmid remained silent. Holtzer continued. "And does this driver of yours still exist?"

"Wegner? Yes, Sir. He's a nuisance and a hindrance. I've relegated him to menial tasks."

"Where is he now?"

"Outside, Sir. With the car."

Holtzer pressed the intercom. "Miss Fassbender, please have someone retrieve the lieutenant's driver. He's parked out front."

For the next couple of minutes, Schmid sat in uncomfortable silence as they awaited the arrival of Private Wegner. Soon, the door opened and the private entered. He couldn't have looked more uneasy as he approached, failing to salute or greet either officer. Schmid kept quiet while the major regarded the driver.

"Wegner, is it?" Holtzer asked the young man.

"Um, yes, Sir," came the timid reply, looking at Schmid as though hoping he answered correctly.

"I'm curious. How old are you, son?"

"Eight...eighteen," he sputtered before adding, "Sir."

"How long have you been stationed here, Private?"

"Uh, two months, Sir." The private seemed to realize his mistake and corrected himself. "I'm sorry, Sir...I mean two months next week."

"How is the war going so far for you?"

"I'd...I'd say fine, Sir," he answered, again looking unsure if it was correct.

"Do you like driving for the lieutenant?" Holtzer asked as though Schmid wasn't in the room.

"I...um, yes, Sir."

Schmid offered nothing when the private shot him a rattled look.

"Have you a sidearm?" asked Holtzer.

"Yes, Sir."

"May I see it?"

The private moved his hand to his waist but brought it back empty. Barely audible, he mumbled, "I left it in the car, Sir."

Schmid scoffed and looked away in disgust.

Holtzer pressed the intercom button again. "Miss Fassbender, has three-fifty-seven been taken care of?"

"It has, Sir," came the tinny reply.

The major stood and grabbed a Luger from the desktop. "Private, come with me. Lieutenant, have a seat. I'll be with you shortly."

Schmid sat down and exhaled as the major led the anguished private to the courtyard.

~ ~ ~

Dusk was settling in, and the yard took on a gray hue. Private Ernst Wegner followed the imposing man, ignorant of what was happening and why he was alone with a major. Whatever the reason, it couldn't be good. Over his panicky thoughts, he heard a gentle voice.

"Private, I will ask you again, and I expect an honest answer. How do you like working with Lieutenant Schmid?"

Unnerved, he was unsure what to say. "I try to do my best, Sir."

"I'm sure you do, but that's not what I asked."

"Um, I believe I could be put to better use, Sir," he said, staring at the ground. "I'm only driving and running errands. I don't think I'll be allowed to do more." He looked up. "May I be honest, Sir?"

"I'd recommend it."

"I don't think they like me."

The major looked upon the young man. "Private, are you certain you're eighteen?"

The question confused him. "Yes...yes, Sir. I wouldn't lie to you."

Switching subjects, Holtzer showed him the pistol. "Do you know how to shoot?"

Wegner squirmed. "I received some training, Sir."

Holtzer handed him the Luger and pointed across the courtyard. "Show me."

No longer was there blood-splattered brick or a crumpled, lifeless body on the far wall—just a clean target awaiting a result. The private slipped the pistol from the major's platter-sized hand and scrambled to remember what he could. He unsuccessfully tried to steady his nerves—and fired. Holtzer studied the far wall for several seconds, then held out his palm for the gun.

"Is it true you fired at a woman and child the other day?"

Ernst Wegner turned his baby face up, mouth and eyes agape. "Yes, Sir...I mean no, Sir. They were warning shots into the air. I wasn't trying to shoot them."

"That was my understanding." Holtzer looked again at the target and back at the private trembling in his oversized uniform. "But based on what I just witnessed, are you sure you didn't hit them?"

~ ~ ~

Lieutenant Schmid heard the gunshot, leaned forward in his chair, and put his head in his hands. He half expected it this time, but could barely believe all that had happened since arriving. His treatment of Protz and Ott could be called authoritative, even heavy-handed, but they each had a purpose, and he had them molded as he wanted. Relishing their newfound power, they served him loyally in return. On the other hand, he believed his contempt for Wegner was warranted, and having the runt around was convenient when he needed something to kick.

Schmid sprang to his feet when Holtzer returned from the courtyard. As he expected, Wegner wasn't with him.

The major set the Luger on the desktop, sat in his chair, and looked up. "Lieutenant, you no longer have Private Wegner's services."

Schmid couldn't think what to say.

"We're done here," Holtzer announced. "Go find some new men and get back to doing whatever you do."

"Sir!" The lieutenant saluted and headed for the door.

"Lieutenant," the major called after him.

"Yes, Sir?"

"You do know how to drive, right?"

Schmid gave no reply, turned his back, and stormed out.

~ ~ ~

Major Holtzer leaned forward and put a finger to the intercom. "So, how much have I missed?"

"You don't even want to know, Sir."

"Well, let's have it."

Miss Fassbender brought in some envelopes and a handful of well-organized notes, prioritized top to bottom as she saw fit.

"Thank you," he sighed as she set them on his desk.

She glanced around the room. "Is that all, Sir? I feel as though my headcount is—"

"No. There's one more thing." He motioned with his hand to the back door. "In the courtyard, you'll find a young man seated by the tree. He's part of our team now. We'll get him started tomorrow."

"Certainly, Sir. Any particular role in mind?"

"No. Maybe you can help me with that."

"Of course." She headed for the courtyard door.

"Oh, just a second."

She turned. "Sir?"

"Not my security detail."

Angela Fassbender smiled. "I'll figure something out."

CHAPTER SEVENTEEN
Vouvray
April 17, Late Evening

COLETTE WOKE WITH a start and needed a moment to get her bearings. Henri and Charles were coming down the basement stairs. Louis was still asleep on the couch. She saw Philippe walking over.

"How long was I out?"

"Not long enough."

She rubbed her eyes. "I stink."

"Yeah," he chuckled, "we need to do something about that."

Louis lifted his head and leaned on his elbow. "I'm hungry."

Philippe raised a finger. "Messieurs Flamand and Touchard are back and have an idea."

Charles waved them over. "Well, that little nap must have felt good," he said. "I've arranged for you both to get some food in your stomachs and cleaned up better."

She and Louis followed Philippe upstairs and into the church nave. They made their way to a back door that opened to a cemetery. The sun had set, and the dark canopy of several trees made it ghostly.

"The church is so old. How can the gravestones look so much older?" Colette whispered, unconsciously respecting the departed.

"Many of them are," Philippe said. "Plus, they take the brunt, always sleeping outside." She hit him on the shoulder. "This church may be old," he continued, "but others have been on the site for centuries. I heard most burned to the ground."

"By accident or on purpose?"

"Probably both."

"Whoa," Louis breathed, straying toward an imposing monument.

"Ah-ah! Wrong way, Louis," Philippe scolded. "Stick close."

They slipped past a rusted gate in the old cemetery wall. He led them through some woods and soon arrived at a clearing. Across an unkempt wildflower garden, a lantern hung outside a quaint stone house. The glow was hardly sufficient to light the back entrance, but was strangely inviting. Colette shot Philippe an inquiring look.

"It's alright," he smiled. "The Cabanons are Vouvray's finest, and they're expecting us."

Just steps from the door, it creaked open.

"Welcome, welcome. Entrez, s'il vous plaît," said a wrinkled, hunched man with a high-pitched voice.

Colette's stomach rumbled at the smell of warm bread and porridge. Inside, a plump gray-haired woman in a snug apron stepped around the corner.

"Oh my!" she exclaimed. "Come, you two. Follow me, and we'll get you taken care of." She patted Colette's arm. "Upstairs, you'll find a hot tub already prepared for you—second door to the right. I laid out some clothes on a hall table. Plenty there, so choose as you like."

"I can help my brother if you have—"

Madame Cabanon took Louis by the hand. "Don't worry yourself. He needs work, but I'll have him good as new before you know it."

~ ~ ~

Colette entered the kitchen and saw Philippe and the others sitting around the table. Her hair was cleaned, brushed, and draped over her shoulders. She wore a light blue dress with short sleeves, a broad lapel, and a pleated skirt that fell just below her knees. The bodice had three buttons, and the fit highlighted her slender waist. Everything enhanced her black hair, light skin, and chestnut eyes. Madame Cabanon, overseeing the porridge pot, turned.

"I can't thank you enough," said Colette. "Where did you get such fine clothes?"

"You look lovely, dear. They come in handy, non?" The woman gave another stir to the pot.

"When can I return them?"

"There's no need. It's not every day a young woman comes by that we can help. Consider it a gift."

She, Louis, and Philippe ate rapidly and without a word. When they finished the meal, everyone went to the living room. Monsieur Cabanon hobbled in last and was the first to speak.

"I hear it's been quite a day for you two. And I suspect you'll have another full one tomorrow." He looked like he was conjuring more to say, so everyone waited. Colette was about to break the silence when he spoke again. "The only way to follow one big day with another is to rest properly." He looked at her. "You and your brother will spend the night here. A room with two beds has been readied upstairs."

The offer took her by surprise. "Oh my, we couldn't possibly. And there's so much to do."

"You each need a good night's sleep," Philippe interjected. "Henri, myself, and others will be sleeping on surprisingly uncomfortable mattresses in the church basement. I'll come for you in the morning. We have a lot to discuss." Exhausted and thinking of Louis, she agreed without more prodding.

Madame Cabanon entered the room and handed Philippe a basket of provisions. Colette walked him to the back door, kissed him on each cheek, and thanked him for all he'd done. She watched him cross the garden, retracing the path to the church.

~ ~ ~

Philippe gave the coded knock and waited. Henri soon greeted him and led him down the basement stairs. At the bottom, a pleasant surprise awaited.

Seated at the table were Marcel, Henri, Charles—and François. Philippe ran to him. François stood in anticipation and received the boyish hug and accompanying pecks on each cheek. Philippe fired off questions without waiting for answers.

"Where have you been? When did you get here? I just left Colette and Louis. Aren't they great?"

Henri cut him off. "Slow down. They arrived just after you left. Charles and I have already filled them in on all that's happened."

"I'm sorry about your wife," said Philippe.

"I can't say I'm not worried sick about her. But Philippe, I also can't thank you enough for all you've done for Colette and Louis."

"Oh," he blushed, "it was my pleasure. They're great."

François squinted and considered him like a father might a young man taking his daughter on a first date. His voice matched his expression. "Henri and Charles just filled me in about your little idea. Little to some, anyway. Enormous to my daughter and me."

Philippe withered. "I'm sorry, Sir, it was just an idea. It's just that she's really...she has a fantastic ability to...I mean, I never meant to—"

"Philippe?" François waited for the lad to look up at him. "It's okay. I appreciate your kind words. And it will surprise you, but I'm afraid you may get your way on this...for now."

"Huh? What do you mean, Sir?"

"You can cut out the 'Sir' stuff. I've got busy times ahead of me. My wife's missing, and my departed friend's wife and son have disappeared. I can't burden the group with Louis, so he's coming with me. The others are open to your suggestion, and Marcel assures me that anything she does will be low risk. It will help me if you and the others can watch over her for as long as it takes."

Philippe lit up. "You can count on me, Si—, François. I think she's excited to help."

"Hmm, we'll see. But thank you for believing in her. In truth, your idea is a good one. But it's my daughter we're talking about."

Philippe understood but wasn't sure how to respond. Marcel came to his rescue.

"She's in good hands, François. You focus on finding Giselle."

"Thanks, Marcel. You're right. Time's wasting. I'll get Louis."

"Whoa there," Charles broke in. "Time is certainly important. But an hour outside these doors, your son will fade fast...not to mention you. It's been a day. Hard to believe we started it at my place this morning. Hell, Louis started it at your place. It seems forever ago."

"I'm guessing it's safe to say that Louis never had such a day," Philippe chimed in.

"I couldn't agree more," said Marcel. "You'll both do far better in the daylight and after a good night's rest."

François was staring blankly at the table. "I *am* tired."

"You look it," said Marcel, "and it's expected after all you've been through. Sleep well and get a fresh start tomorrow."

CHAPTER EIGHTEEN
Vouvray
April 18, 7:15 am

THE HEAVY BROWN curtains quashed any morning light. Colette had slept well, but she and her brother sat bolt upright at the sound of tapping at the door. It creaked open. She hoped to see Philippe's cheery face but wasn't disappointed.

"PAPA!" she and her brother screamed in unison. Bed covers were thrown clear, and arms were soon wrapped around him, his thick beard unable to mask his beaming grin. She didn't bother asking where he'd been or how he was doing. Instead, she and Louis stumbled over each other, trying to tell him about Mama.

"Don't worry yourselves," he boomed. "I'll find her." They hugged him again.

She loosened her hold and looked up at him. "Where did they take you anyway?"

"They needed me for a spell, but I'm back safe and sound, right?"

"You sure are, Papa!" Louis chirped.

"They had some questions and hoped that I could help. I'm sure it's the same with your mother. You'd think they could come up with an occasional answer on their own." Colette managed a strained giggle. Louis remained clung to his father's waist. "And you," François said, pealing him off and looking down. "Guess what you're going to do?"

The boy's eyes widened. "What?"

"You're going to help me find Mama."

"I'll find her, Papa!"

François chuckled. "I don't doubt it."

"What about me?" Colette asked.

"I've got plans for you, Bunny. We'll discuss it after you two get some breakfast, huh?"

Downstairs, a welcome sight greeted her and Louis. Madame Cabanon was filling the table with an assortment of meats and cheeses. She added four soft-boiled eggs, a basket of bread accompanied by jam and butter, and a breakfast cake—a banquet by current standards. Not a minute after his first bite, their hostess handed Louis a second napkin for his face. She took control of the matter when his efforts only managed to smear the jam.

When the meal was complete, François asked Louis to change and prepare to leave. He had Colette join him in the sitting room. His message filled her with mixed emotions. She was thrilled to have her father back and eager to help find her mother. Seldom away from her home for even a day, she was already missing her bed. But with each passing hour, her enthusiasm and eagerness had grown. The thought of working with everyone was exhilarating. To her amazement, her father approved of it.

"Remember," he said, "only until I get back. Don't get too cozy here. And whatever you do, don't justify my anxiety."

"Oh, I'll be fine."

"Well, don't miss me too much, either. I'll be back with your mother before you know it."

Before departing, he hugged her and whispered a reminder about being good and staying safe. She knew it was the second part that concerned him most.

Standing at the back door and watching them cross the old garden, she shouted, "Remember to feed the animals!"

Louis turned and waved. She watched her father rub her brother's head as they disappeared into the woods.

~ ~ ~

Colette set the washcloth aside, looked in the mirror, and shrugged. She thought the blue dress from the night before would be impractical today and went to the hall table to see what she could find. Pants weren't commonplace in her dresser at home, but they looked intriguing. She tried them on. Rather baggy but comfortable, she cinched them tight and gave the cuffs a couple of turns. The loose-fitting olive sweatshirt needed similar adjustments to the sleeves but was equally comfortable. Before heading downstairs, she made the beds, brushed her hair, and slipped into her shoes.

"Well, how do I look?"

Philippe nearly jumped at the sudden voice, but he quickly composed himself.

"Am I suitable? Or is it too informal for my first day on the job?"

He stood and slowly circled her. She sighed and waited out the exaggerated inspection.

"You look perfect," he said, arriving back where he started. "But I don't think parachute training starts until tomorrow."

"Shut up," she laughed and butted him aside.

In the kitchen, she found Madame and Monsieur Cabanon and thanked them for the lovely night's rest, change of clothes, and delicious breakfast. She gave Philippe a subtle look, reminding him to do the same.

CHAPTER NINETEEN
Tours
April 18, 7:30 am

THE CELL LEADER insisted that his team avoid wandering about in groups. Dining with a couple of friends was one thing; roving about town like a pack of wild dogs was another. After his two breakfast companions left the café to take care of morning assignments, Marcel took another frugal sip of coffee and glanced around the room. He tended to be suspicious of others and needed to remind himself that not every stranger was nosy or sinister. Still, sitting in the back and facing the entry while pretending to read the paper permitted him to see all that transpired. Thus far, the habit had no benefit other than putting him at ease or ensuring he wouldn't miss a friendly face. Today, he sat at a table suitable for four and declined the waiter's offer to clear the dishes. The café was getting busy, and a messy table might help deter strangers from asking to join him.

April had predictably reverted to its unpredictable temperament. Each time the door opened, the blustery squall outside persuaded one to take notice of the passersby battling their umbrellas. It happened once again as a tall fellow entered the café. His trench coat and gray fedora made him an effective walking metaphor for the weather. The brim of his leather hat seemed to dump liters of water over his shoulders, which his long coat effectively dispersed onto the already-soaked wooden floor. Marcel took notice of his uncommon attire but saw nothing else of consequence. The man found a ledge to stand by at the window, set his hat down, and began reviewing the pared-down menu. Marcel returned to his newspaper. Intermittent inbound customers led to more discreet glances.

The door flew open again. An abrupt change swept through the room as a uniformed man removed his cap and took in the surroundings. Staff and patrons recognized him at once. His greasy blond hair and fitting cheek scar presaged the smug air of self-importance they all expected. He looked toward the man immersed in a newspaper in the back corner. Marcel felt his scrutinizing eyes while pretending not to notice the approaching German officer.

"Bonjour, Monsieur. Marcel Bouchet, n'est-ce pas? Excusez-moi," he continued, "and pardon my accent. My name is Schmid. Lieutenant Schmid. I was told I might find you here."

Marcel tried to appear unaffected. "No need for the introduction, Lieutenant. Your reputation precedes you."

"Is that so? Merci, I'm flattered."

Marcel remained expressionless. "A man in these parts must be a French Rip Van Winkle not to know who you are."

Schmid chuckled. "Well, I trust even he will catch on once he wakens." Marcel gave in to formality and motioned for the lieutenant to join him. "No, but thank you anyway. It turns out I have a request of you. Well, I suppose it's more than a request. I'm to escort—. Rather, you have been invited for an informal visit."

Informal? Marcel didn't like the sound of it. Invited by whom? And why him? It didn't sit well in his gut. For the German military to know about him and where he was dining this morning was beyond concerning. Then again, he saw no upside to refusing the request and didn't expect he had a choice.

"Have I done something I shouldn't have?" he asked bluntly.

"Hah, I suspect you Frenchmen are always up to something. I suppose only you know that...for now. But, as to your question, I'm unaware of any transgressions. My major merely wishes to acquaint himself with the people of this community he now serves."

"I see," said Marcel, not believing the line for a second. "Does this major who wishes to serve our community have a name?"

"Indeed!" Schmid piped up. "Major Viktor Holtzer. He's new to the area, but he has a fine reputation. I'm sure you'll be impressed."

Marcel looked around the room. The clanking of dishware by a single waiter severed the unnatural silence. "I haven't heard of him. New, huh? Well, I have nothing pressing this morning...and if he's as great as you say, why not?"

"Ah, excellent." Schmid pulled some money from his pocket and gestured to the table. "May I?"

"Merci, mais non. I've taken care of it."

Marcel tried to appear calm while battling a range of thoughts and emotions. He was curious, nervous, apprehensive—even fearful. Holtzer's reputation justified his active imagination, and Schmid had a slimy and untrustworthy history at best. But somewhere in the tone of the conversation, he sensed he might see the day's end. Schmid led him to an awaiting car that soon disappeared in the dense shroud of rain. Every patron rewarded themselves with a deep breath.

Ignoring his full cup of coffee, the tall man in the trench coat grabbed his hat, placed some coins on the counter, and walked out.

~ ~ ~

Although he felt it beneath him, Lieutenant Schmid accepted the assignment of bringing in a civilian. The reason for the task was unimportant. At this point, he was willing to do almost anything to help him save face with Holtzer. He had corralled his new driver and performed the menial role, hoping it was good for something. Now, he looked forward to the meeting, unsure what the major had in mind for his French passenger.

Unfortunately, as he sat waiting with Monsieur Bouchet in the receiving room, he was approached by Miss Fassbender, who kindly informed him that the major didn't require him for the meeting. Schmid stood abruptly, shoved his cap onto his head, and stomped out. His new driver would have to bear the brunt.

~ ~ ~

The woman ignored Schmid's display and turned her attention to Marcel. "May I get you a nice cup of coffee, Monsieur?"

"Mais oui, s'il vous plaît," he said, eager for a refreshing change from the watered-down imposters he'd been enduring.

She returned. He put his nose over it, breathed in, and closed his eyes. Taking care not to spill any, he followed her to an office and thanked her again. She smiled and closed the door behind him.

The room was well decorated and almost inviting, but he had no time to familiarize himself. A man of distinction was standing behind a large desk. He was the spitting image of his photos, reputation, and Marcel's expectations.

"Monsieur Bouchet," Major Holtzer boomed, waving him forward. "I appreciate you taking the time to come in. I hope Lieutenant Schmid was tolerable."

Marcel's apprehension made him less than cordial. He gave an abbreviated nod but said nothing as the major motioned to a chair in front of his desk. Before sitting, Marcel took another sip of coffee and turned to take in his surroundings.

"We're quite alone," said Holtzer.

I'm not sure that's a good thing.

CHAPTER TWENTY
Vouvray
April 18, Late Morning

COLETTE RECEIVED A warm welcome from Henri and Georges when Philippe accompanied her into the church basement. The morning got off to a later-than-expected start as they waited for their leader to return from his early outing in Tours. Upon arriving, Marcel wasted no time and motioned the group to a round table where Colette sat squeezed between Philippe and Georges. Marcel and Henri filled the remaining two seats.

"We're excited to have you with us," Marcel began. "Your day will be long, but we won't get to everything. When we wrap up here, Philippe will continue your training."

"Thank you for trusting me with this," said Colette. "I hope I can help somehow."

"Ask questions as they come to you. Whatever Henri, Georges, and I can't answer, I'm sure Philippe will."

Philippe's head was bobbing. "Thanks, Marcel."

"I think he was being facetious," Colette whispered out the side of her mouth.

Marcel winked at her. "Anyway, it may get old, but there are three things we'll always harp on: Safety, trust, and safety."

Philippe tilted his head toward her. "Safety's critical."

"Got it," she whispered back.

Marcel's face turned solemn. "As you know, Colette, we've just lost a good and valuable friend. I let my guard down, and I'll never do it again. I thought it was routine. Worse, I never considered that it might not be routine. None of us can ever think like that again."

"I was there that night," Henri interjected, "and I didn't consider it either. Colette, you should know it could have been your father instead of Roland."

She looked around the table and felt their pain. "Is Monsieur Viard the first to...um—"

"He is," Marcel helped her. "And however safe we try to be, I can't make guarantees. Everything we do involves risk. We always knew that in the back of our heads, but we all fully understand now."

"A large part of safety includes discretion," Georges chimed in. "Philippe will get into some of that with you, but it's wide-ranging: How you look and behave, where and when you gather, where and when you're alone, who you associate with, who you tell things to. The list goes on."

"You must be doing pretty good at it," said Colette. "My father is a part of this, and I never knew it."

"You weren't looking for it," Marcel suggested. "Others are."

"And not just the Nazi's," Henri added. "It's important to understand that many local officials and ordinary citizens are watching and listening too."

"Is it because they dislike somebody or are benefiting somehow?"

"Yes, is the simple answer," said Philippe.

She shook her head. "It just seems hard to believe they'd turn on their own people."

"Even neighbors," said Henri. "It's important you understand that."

"Monsieur Bouchet, you mentioned trust. I assume you're referring to those that are part of this."

"Yes. Thank you for clarifying. I'm referring to our trust in each other. Unfortunately, it cannot extend to those we don't know, but our trust in each other here is imperative. We must trust what we say, what we do, what we teach, and trust that we are all competent in our assigned roles."

"I understand. Any teamwork would be impossible if you were second-guessing one another. But here's what I don't understand... How can you trust me?"

Colette scanned their faces as they all hesitated.

Marcel broke the silence. "It's good to hear you ask the question."

"We can't," Henri broke in. His blunt response was presented gently, but it caught her off guard. "Not yet, anyway."

Georges softened the blow. "There's different kinds of trust. We all trust your integrity, patriotism, and passion. Otherwise, you wouldn't be here. But there are things that we need to help you with. Take discretion. Most people have a general sense of how to be discreet. But we take it to another level, and you'll benefit greatly from what we know...what we've learned."

Philippe nudged her with his elbow. "I'll help you with it."

~ ~ ~

As the clock passed the noon hour, Colette continued to absorb all they covered. In time, she grew comfortable spewing out thoughts and questions and was especially curious about what they'd done in the past and were currently planning.

At last, the one thing she kept forcing to the back of her brain leaped out. "What do you have in mind for me?"

Marcel smiled. "Well, we've got a handful of ideas, but there's much to do before that."

"Oh, yes. I didn't mean to—"

"It's alright," Marcel went on. "Philippe will be training you, and when you're ready, we'll get you started."

She looked at Philippe. He was glowing like a proud father.

"We all think highly of you," Henri chimed in. "You'll be a great asset. Georges here has several needs for observation and information gathering that he thinks will be a perfect fit."

"We all do," said Philippe.

"Information gathering? So...like spying?" she asked.

They all chuckled.

"If you like," said Georges. "We prefer to think of it as legitimate curiosity stuff. Things we need to find out or look into."

"What we do," Marcel said, "and what we've been doing...learning about the enemy and helping people elude their grasp is important. There will come a day when we need to do more, maybe much more. But our work is vital, and we keep a low profile doing it. We never want to draw attention to ourselves. Not yet, anyway."

"Okay," she nodded.

"We have all just been reminded the hard way...the hardest way... that whatever we do can be dangerous. Things can come up. Unexpected things. Never assume something is safe. Never let your guard down."

Colette swallowed and nodded again.

~ ~ ~

They lost track of time in the windowless basement. It was half past three when Marcel adjourned the meeting. He, Henri, and Georges had plenty to plan and discuss amongst themselves, and Philippe got to the task of working with Colette.

She enjoyed his spirit but noticed somber inflections in his delivery and adapted to him. He reemphasized everything the group had spoken about and then got into specific examples. She was pleased to hear how the vehicle they stole was stripped of crucial parts overnight. Suppressing a show of pride was difficult when Philippe explained how the discovery of Private Ott's and Sergeant Protz's papers would be invaluable for forging purposes.

He gave a brief overview of the cell's organization and various responsibilities. He gushed about everyone, how they worked together, and how roles were interrelated.

"Are there others in France doing this?" she asked.

"Yes. Probably many. But we know little. We're mostly on our own, and maybe that's best. Someday, we'll unite when the time is right. For now, keeping a low profile is everyone's priority."

His talk of secretive meeting places, safe houses, and packages filled her head with questions.

"I don't quite understand. If you say you mostly do research, fact-finding, snooping, and that kind of thing...are the safe houses just for the people you're helping to cross the line?"

"Well, they *are* used for that, but also for us. These Nazis frown on large group meetings. And *frown* is putting it lightly. No law says we can't socialize—yet. But it can raise flags when we do."

"So, they're meeting places, too?"

"For large meetings, they can be. We will also meet in small groups of two, three, or four at a café or brasserie, but for anything bigger, you should assume someone is eavesdropping. You can also think of safe houses as safe *havens*. If someone were to get into trouble, these are the places to get to. They're owned or staffed by people who want to help. Secure, in-place communication methods ensure that only the right people can enter. And there is always a rule in place to know if it's safe to approach them or not."

"That explains the odd knocking patterns and strange questions."

"Yes, but even that could be found out through observation. Communication comes in many forms, including subtle ways an observer might not pick up on."

Colette moved forward in her chair. "Give me an example."

"Sure. Now, I'm not saying this *is* one, but it's the type of thing that could be done."

"Go on," she encouraged.

"Well, maybe the pattern was correct, but that safe house also requires visitors to take off their hat and hold it in their left hand while running their right hand over their head."

"Seriously?"

"I'm not saying that we have a house doing that; I'm just saying it's something that could be done for added security."

"What if they don't have a hat?"

"I don't know. I just made it up. They'd need to have another rule in place, I guess. The point is, you'll soon be indoctrinated into a world of new ways to communicate."

Colette was fascinated when he brought up other discreet forms of communication, like using objects to convey messages, subtleties of questioning, and using a nom de guerre versus a real name.

"What's a nom de guerre?"

"Well, you could say it's a fake name...a codename for people, places, or things when we don't want others to know the real name."

"Is there a nom de guerre for me?"

"I doubt it. Not yet, anyway. Marcel comes up with them, but it can take time. I think he waits until he knows somebody a bit better."

She lit up. "Okay then. What's yours?"

Philippe squirmed in his chair. "It's not important right now."

"Come on, shouldn't I start memorizing everybody's codename?"

Philippe scratched his head. "Alright. Le Bouffon," he sighed.

Colette laughed and sat back in her chair. "I love it!" Philippe groaned. "No, I mean it. You're funny, clever, comical, and enthusiastic. The Jester. It's perfect for you!"

Philippe smirked. "Maybe so."

He reminded her never to lose sight of their purpose and emphasized how the continued occupation of France was being accepted as inevitable by too many.

"Most citizens feel helpless. They see no way to fight such a monster, so they succumb to it."

"Isn't there something they can do?" she asked.

The question awoke Philippe's spirit. "That's just it. There is! Many things...no matter how small. Even if it's just keeping hope alive and dreaming about the day they're free again. Believing. Believing in themselves. Believing in their neighbors."

She grabbed hold of his enthusiasm. "Believing in France! We can help them with that...it's another purpose for us!"

They didn't notice the others in the room looking over, smiling.

CHAPTER TWENTY-ONE
On to Amboise, France
April 21, Morning

THREE DAYS AFTER her initiation into the group, there was still no word about Colette's family. Henri asked for her patience and reassured her that everything takes longer during wartime. She trusted him and returned to pestering Philippe for any news of her first assignment. He continued explaining how her roles were essential and would entail a lot of research and fact-finding. Library visits, city office outings, and casual eavesdropping sorties would be the norm. In other words, there were no swashbuckling adventures in her near future. It didn't matter. If Georges needed extra hands and eyes for anything, she was eager to help in any way she could.

At midday, Marcel returned from Tours and informed everyone they had been in Vouvray long enough. Colette and Philippe had nowhere specific to go, so Marcel had them tag along with Henri and Georges. Madame Cabanon told Colette to choose any clothes she wished. Provisions were loaded onto a mule Philippe got from who knows where, and they set off walking for Amboise. Georges and Henri handled the mule and stayed well behind by design.

Philippe continued to teach as they went. Nearing the city, he tested her by motioning at a random person with his head. "Do you think she's trustworthy?"

Colette studied the woman for a few seconds. "Yes, I believe so."

"Strangers can't be trusted," he countered. "You need to know a person first."

"Okay, but don't you sometimes have to go by instinct?"

"Unfortunately, there are those times. But you need to develop and trust your gut. Now, that last woman? My instinct was the same as yours, but never take the chance if you're not feeling right about someone. Then again, if you're in a pinch and your gut says they're trustworthy, you may have to."

She wasn't sure how she'd do and began looking at strangers for practice. "I suppose you should still be wary once you decide to trust."

"You're getting it," he said. "Being pessimistic about people goes against my nature, but it's necessary."

"It does me, too," she said. "I've always been trusting of others."

"It's not bad, as long as you're aware of it and extra careful...extra picky, you could say. Being attracted to welcoming or optimistic people is easy, but times have changed. Put those characteristics aside when forming your judgment. It could very well be a trap. People just can't be trusted nowadays."

She turned and studied him. "Until now, I don't think I've ever heard you say anything negative about anyone."

He scowled. "You'd better get used to it. Most people think I'm a real asshole."

She laughed. "Oh, they do, huh?" Her tone softened. "It's weird, though, Philippe."

"What's that?"

"I feel embarrassed to say it, but I hardly had a care in the world just a few days ago. We're at war, and even though things are different... tougher...I was walking about like it wasn't so bad while others were fighting for their lives...for our lives."

"Well, some parts of the country haven't seen firsthand what's happened. Many don't believe what they hear or choose not to. And things are getting worse."

"That's what I mean. What was I thinking?" she said, sounding disappointed in herself.

Philippe stopped walking and faced her. The tips of her black curls glowed auburn in the sun. The breeze whipped a few strands into her mouth. Her finger effortlessly swept them free. He opened his mouth to speak, but nothing came out.

"What is it?" she asked.

"Um...I was, uh—"

"Yes?"

"Your father. You know he's a big part of this. Well, he would've done all he could to protect you. Probably hid a lot from you. He's a good man, and I bet he stayed pretty upbeat around you and Louis."

"He did. Maybe more than he should have, huh?"

They continued walking and were nearing the heart of Amboise. Both were hungry and thirsty. Spotting a brasserie a block ahead, Philippe grabbed her hand and made a beeline for it.

"Did we lose Henri and Georges?" she asked.

"More like they lost us. Anyhow, it doesn't matter. They're going somewhere else."

"What do you mean?"

"They're meeting later with Marcel. Henri wants us to get settled. You know, clean up, change clothes, and," he pointed at the menu on the chalkboard display outside, "get a bite to eat. We've been walking for three hours."

"What? Are you sure?"

He stayed focused on the menu. "I hear charming company makes time fly."

She had to roll her eyes and shake her head in mock disgust, but she knew he was right.

~ ~ ~

Marcel, Henri, and Georges arrived at the safe house in the evening. Philippe waved them into the living room.

"How are you doing?" Henri asked Colette.

"Great! Any news of my mother and father?"

"Not yet. But no news is good news," he suggested, despite a lack of supporting history. "Any other news, and we would have heard it. Stay positive."

"Thank you, Monsieur Flamand," she said, trying to appear stoic. "If you need me for anything, let me know."

"Well, as a matter of fact—" He looked behind him and waved for Marcel and Georges to join him. "We need to speak with the two of you. Stay seated. Here will work fine."

Marcel appeared, gave hearty hellos to the team's youngest members, and remained standing. His expression turned somber, and Henri and Georges followed his lead.

"I hear things are going well, and you're eager to help."

"I am. I'll do whatever you need."

"That's great." He hesitated a moment. "Well, something has come up." Colette brightened. Marcel did not. "Honestly, it's not what I wanted or what your father would want either. But after discussing it at length, we've decided you're best suited for it." He looked at Philippe. "And I think you'll agree."

"What is it?" Philippe asked with trepidation.

"Well, it's no library assignment." Marcel looked her in the eye. "We need you to do some field observation for us."

"Oh, okay. Great."

"She's perfect for it and ready!" Philippe exclaimed.

"Now, hold on. Hear me out." Marcel glanced at Henri and got a nod in return. "I'm not about to equate eagerness with readiness, but we believe it's our best option. And we're not talking about sitting around a café and eavesdropping." Colette stared at Marcel, begging with her eyes to hear more. "You'd be on your own for most of it, and you'll need to make snap decisions as events unfold. Unfortunately, it's often difficult to anticipate risks."

"What kind of risks do you mean?" She snuck a peek at Philippe to gauge his reaction, but he looked to be withholding expressions until learning more.

"Well, we don't always know. But what we can do is make damn sure we think of as many scenarios as possible."

"And if we miss something?" she asked.

"There's always that chance. If so, then you'll need to think on your feet...which I hear you're good at."

She gave a weak smile and felt her stomach tighten. "I promise I'll try my best."

"I don't doubt that."

She gave Marcel her undivided attention as he described her first assignment, its importance, immediacy, and why they believed she was suited for it. Time passed quickly as they discussed everything imaginable. Over the final hour, she offered as many suggestions and what-ifs as anyone.

"Many of these are out of date," Georges said, spreading photos on the table. "Some aren't too clear, and others aren't in great condition, but it's what I have. It'll have to do."

He gave an account of each person's name, role, and other details. She scrutinized the images, trying to memorize facial and physical characteristics. She spent extra time on those of Auguste Gagnon and took particular interest when Georges pointed to Lieutenant Schmid as the man who took her father from their home. She studied his full-length photo, then moved her eyes to the face shot.

"So that's him. Not very appealing, is he?"

Georges considered the photo. "Oh, I'm sure he'd give a different assessment. He's the definition of smug. People say he can be smooth, even charming. Some make the mistake of buying into it. This one's ruthless, devious, and always scheming."

Colette scowled. Her nose scrunched as she ran a finger over the facial scar.

At last, the dates and times of her assignment were finalized—with the usual acknowledgment that many variables could subject it to change. They all stood.

Marcel put his hands on her shoulders. "I think you know your father would disapprove of this. The last time we spoke, I assured him you'd be watched over."

"I know."

Marcel smiled gently. "But he'd also be the proudest parent this side of the war."

She patted the back of Philippe's hand. "This guy trusted me. It made me want to help."

"You're a good team," the leader said. "Philippe will equip you with everything you need. Tomorrow's a big day, and the day after is even bigger. You need to get upstairs for a good night's rest. We'll rehash details starting first thing in the morning." A low rumbling filled the air. She and Marcel looked at Philippe's stomach. He shrugged. "But first, it sounds like you two might be famished. Get to the kitchen and help yourselves."

CHAPTER TWENTY-TWO
Amboise
April 21, Nightfall

PHILIPPE STARED AT a knot in the pitched wooden ceiling. The dark planks and beams above matched any floorboards not obscured by a small area rug. A narrow bed, nightstand, and dresser were all the room could accommodate. The bedding included a thick quilt, blanket, pillow, and flannel sheets. The quilt wasn't needed tonight—nothing was. The home's natural heat drifted upward, warming the room. He reached to switch off the table lamp. Though exhausted, his brain wouldn't turn off as he stared up at the blackness.

Colette's first assignment played out in his head. Marcel had talked at length about risks, and there was sincere regard and input from everyone, but "routine" fieldwork got Roland Viard murdered. Philippe tried to convince himself that this was an entirely different, necessary, and prudent plan. The more he considered it, the more reassured he became.

In time, his mind gravitated toward more intimate thoughts. He realized he was falling for her. He already had. She was intelligent, witty, playful, and almost his age. That was plenty, but there was more. Over the past days, he had elevated her from innocent and cute to sophisticated and beautiful—even sexy. He closed his eyes and envisioned her. His body responded. His hand drifted down, unclipped his belt, and slid beneath the waistband. He imagined it was her hand. He contorted to slide his pants down and kicked them off the end of the bed. He felt free. Though inexperienced, he fantasized in any way he could.

His preoccupation was cut short by a sudden creak. A sliver of soft light slipped past the door frame. He grabbed a handful of the quilt with his left hand and tried to cover up. He partially succeeded.

"Philippe, are you asleep?" came a whisper.

"Uh, um, no," he stuttered, disregarding that there was only one way to answer the question. His right hand fumbled for the cover, trying to perform the same task his left hand had. "Who is it?" He was too flustered to notice how ridiculous the words were. There was only one female in the entire house.

"Oh good, it's me," he heard Colette whisper. "I was afraid I might wake you."

He panicked that someone downstairs might hear. "Close the door!" he whispered back, not considering it allowed for two options. Rather than leaving, she slid inside and gently latched it behind her.

"I can't see a thing."

"Good. No. I mean, hold on a second." He released the covering and made frantic, unsuccessful attempts to reach for his discarded pants. The left side of the quilt flopped off the bed. He adjusted himself and got the right half to cover him partially. In the dark, it sounded complicated.

"What are you doing?"

"Oh, uh, there's no chair. I'm making room for you to sit. Follow my voice."

She sat down on the bed's edge. "I'm sorry. I can't sleep. My brain won't stop."

He felt her hip against his leg. "Mine neither."

"Is being a girl really going to make a difference?"

"I—"

"What if I let everybody down? And what haven't we considered? Will I know if I'm at the right place at the right time?" She stopped. He waited in case she had more. "Well...don't you have anything to say?"

"I—"

"Be honest, Philippe. Do you think I can do this?"

He exhaled. "I won't lie. I'm nervous too. But it'll be fine. It's normal to be jittery. It's your first assignment, after all."

"I was thinking the same, I guess."

"You'll do great. You might even put some of us out of a job."

"If I do it well, they might put you in charge of all training," she joked back. Her soft hand squeezed his sweaty palm, affecting his entire body.

He said nothing, unsure what to do.

"It sure seems warm in here for April," she said at last. "I wonder if it's always like this."

"I was here a few days in January and thought I was sleeping outside. And I'm only half joking."

Colette swept her hand across the bed. "Aren't you burning up under that heavy thing?" He felt her hand touch his partially exposed leg. "Wait. Are you under it or on top?" Groping for the edge, she flipped it off him. "There. Doesn't that feel better?"

It was pitch black, but he was now wholly exposed, with parts unhindered and beyond his control. Her arm brushed over him. He stifled a gasp. They both froze. His sudden urge to sneeze soon ended the awkward silence.

"À tes souhaits," she said timidly.

"Um, merci. Sorry."

"For what?"

"For snee—. Well, for...I just—"

"Shh, it's okay," she whispered in his ear. "It's a compliment, right?"

He grabbed again at the quilt, doing his best to cover himself. Too embarrassed and nervous to resurrect his fantasies, he stared up, unblinking at the darkness, unsure what to do next. He felt her soft lips kiss his cheek. Her head nestled into his shoulder. He slipped his arm around her, his fingers cautiously petting her silky gown. Within minutes, he felt her warm, steady breath on his chest. His eyes closed, and the rest of the world vanished.

A sudden noise downstairs woke him. "Colette." He jostled her. "Shh...Colette."

"Mmm." She stirred, then sat up in a panic. "What time is it?"

"I don't know. I think it's still dark."

She kissed him, rolled out of bed, and slipped out the door. He flopped back onto the mattress.

CHAPTER TWENTY-THREE
Amboise
April 22

MARCEL, HENRI, AND Georges spent the morning going over details and quizzing Colette at the breakfast table. Philippe interjected on occasion but looked lost in thought. Georges did the talking while reviewing maps for entry specifics and geographical features. Each shared thoughts on possible hurdles, people to look for, handling German questioning, improvising during unplanned situations, and various exit strategies.

Marcel switched subjects. "Colette, speak rudimentary German at the border if you think it will help. You have a sweet, innocent voice, and even hardened hearts might soften when hearing your accent."

Henri expanded on the thought. "If you encounter other Germans, keep your ears open and don't let on that you know their language. You're ideal for eavesdropping without raising suspicion."

"These are odd times," said Georges. "A lot of nosy folks. Strangers might lure you into conversation like they're your friend...asking questions too. Don't trust anyone, especially in Loches."

They'd emphasized it twice before, and she wanted clarification. "How is it that one city is full of untrustworthy people?" she asked.

Georges acknowledged her point. "Of course, you're right. It isn't. The majority are trustworthy and patriotic, but knowing who they are is hard. Loches is teeming with the sweetest, friendliest, most charming, cunning, and ruthless collaborators anywhere in France."

"Hah!" Henri exclaimed. "I doubt a trained psychologist would stand a chance."

Colette shook her head. "How can people help the enemy for personal gain at the expense of their own country? It's infuriating."

Marcel understood. "To you, it wouldn't make sense. But not everyone is like you, your parents, or us. It's not as simple as wanting to help the Germans. What they want is to help themselves and their families. Many will help the Nazis all damn day if they think it will benefit them or their loved ones somehow—even if only to feel safer."

"They are walking a dangerous line," snapped Henri. "When this war is over, and the only Nazis left on French soil are buried in it, the collaborators will get what's coming to them."

"It may seem like everyone is giving up, and self-preservation is all they care about," said Marcel, "but even Loches has patriots. When we put the word out on River Man, they're the ones who fed us the intelligence and are making this assignment possible. Gagnon is in Loches every Friday, and we need to know why. Anyway, I don't foresee difficulties down there. What concerns me more is the crossing. Georges, what are your thoughts?"

"Well, we have three options: Supply her with legitimate papers, forged papers, or no papers."

Colette leaned in. "Which is best?"

"Well, the first isn't practical," Marcel said. "Those near the border have a slim chance. Otherwise, applications rarely succeed, and the red tape is ridiculous. We don't have the time."

"Hold on a second, Marcel." Henri looked across the table. "What is it, Philippe? You couldn't look more distressed if you were wearing porcupine underwear."

Philippe slapped the table. "I'm sorry, but there's no way that we send Colette with forged papers. I won't allow it."

"Well, there you have it," Henri said, turning his palms up. "Option two is officially out."

"Listen," said Philippe, "it doesn't make sense! Being turned away for not having papers presents little to no risk—just a delay in the assignment. Trying to reenter without them might mean a slap on the wrist. But being discovered with forged papers isn't an option. We've all heard the stories."

Unfamiliar with it all, Colette looked around the table to gauge their reactions.

"He's right, of course," said Georges. "I just wanted to lay out the options. And as far as not having papers goes, it's not implausible."

"We know they're more softhearted and forgiving with women," said Henri. "That's just the way it is."

"And that's one of the reasons we agreed Colette has the best chance," said Marcel. "But we need more. We know that crossing guards are more lenient with certain professionals, especially ones they can benefit from."

"Physicians and veterinarians," Georges said, holding up two fingers. "Perhaps some others."

"I sure know more about animals than people," Colette broke in, "but I'm no veterinarian."

"You don't have to be," said Henri. "We just need a legitimate-sounding excuse. They'll never be the wiser."

They ate supper at the same table as breakfast and lunch, and much of the conversation took place with snacks in their mouths. It was drilled into her head to expect the unexpected, and that improvising may be unavoidable. It was late when Marcel ended the meeting. It had been a long but productive day. Everybody agreed that getting a good night's sleep was more important than reviewing it all again.

Back at her bedroom door, Philippe kissed her on the forehead. She squeezed his hand, and they parted. Colette was fast asleep in minutes. He lay awake on top of the covers for another hour.

CHAPTER TWENTY-FOUR
Departing for Bléré, France
April 23, Morning

COLETTE CHOSE A light-cream, three-quarters-length loose-skirt dress for the border crossing. A bicycle was waiting for her in Bléré, and a long dress might get caught in the chain. Anything shorter might give the wrong impression. She intended to distract or inspire, not create a scandal. Cropped sleeves revealed her thin, toned arms, and the imitation pearl necklace drew attention to the cut neckline. She was thrilled somebody had scrounged up a stub of lipstick and some mascara, but it took time to apply. She'd rarely done it, and only then with her mother's guidance. Lastly, she examined the wristwatch Philippe tried to equip with a ladylike band. Unbecoming at best, she placed it in a pouch to pull out as needed. Despite it being April, everything about her looked airy and summery.

All were up early and pacing in eager anticipation. Marcel's eyes widened when she appeared in the living room archway. Georges caught himself and looked away. Philippe stopped what he was doing and stared.

Marcel recovered to break the silence. "You look fine, dear." The understatement was the best he could do. The others just nodded. "I expect it will work as planned at the crossing."

One step into the room, her right foot snagged a lip of the area rug and buckled. Philippe caught her before she could damage herself or the nearby furnishings. She blushed.

After saying her goodbyes to the others and receiving final words of encouragement, Philippe drove her to Bléré on a cart pulled by the same mule he rustled up in Vouvray. It was no faster than walking and far slower than biking, but she was glad not to expend extra energy. Along the way, they were mostly quiet. Twice, she thought of bringing up the night they spent together. Twice, she decided against it. Instead, she studied a list of German words the team had put together. When finished, she moved on to a sheet with translations of French words and phrases the Germans might not understand.

"Colette?"

"Yes," she said, without looking up from her paper.

Philippe slowed the mule to a stop and stared at the reins in his hands. "The other night. I was just wondering. Was I supposed to...I mean, did you want me to—"

"Philippe." She waited for him to look at her. "It was perfect."

"Okay. Yeah. So, if we had, maybe it would've been less perfect?"

She tapped his nose. "Or maybe more?"

"Maybe more," he mumbled. He snapped the reins. "This animal sure is slow."

"You're not kidding. Where did you get it anyway?"

"Hah, don't ask."

They trudged on.

"How did they decide where the line should be?" Colette asked, interrupting the quiet.

"Line?"

"Between occupied and unoccupied France."

"Oh, I'm not sure that 'decide' is the right word. It's all about politics, favors, money, ass kissing...you know, the usual. The damn line fluctuates more than the temperature."

"Could it change while I'm in Loches? Nobody mentioned it."

"No, I don't think it works quite like that, but I get why you'd ask. You'll be fine for an overnight trip."

Nearing the city, she turned suddenly, startling him. "I hoped I'd get a codename before my first assignment."

"Oh...right. Your nom de guerre. Hmm, didn't I mention it? You already have one."

"What!"

"Yes, Marcel came up with it, and we all thought it was fitting."

"You weren't going to tell me? *Nobody* was going to tell me?" she nearly shouted.

"Well, there wasn't a practical way to put it in play on short notice, so...I guess we forgot about it."

"Forgot! How could you forget about it?" Philippe just shrugged. Several seconds went by. "You're kidding me, right?" she wailed.

He burst out laughing. "Okay, okay. If you must know, it's—"

"What if I don't like it?"

"There's nothing wrong with it. I like it. The others like it. It's just a name, anyway."

She paused. "Alright then. What is it?"

"Are you sure you want to know?"

"Yes! I want to know!"

He sat upright and filled his lungs. "Innocent," he said as though it was his idea.

"Innocent?"

"Innocent," he said again.

She thought about it. "Hmm. It's not bad, I guess. I suppose I kind of like it. Do you?"

"I already said as much."

The mule plodded on.

"Innocent," she mumbled to herself.

CHAPTER TWENTY-FIVE
Bléré
April 23, Late Morning

SOME STRETCHES OF the River Cher marked the boundary between occupied and Vichy France. For those near it, the inconvenient line seemed more fluid than the river itself. By a quirk of cartography or wartime whimsy, the city of Bléré was south of Le Cher but still within occupied France. It was as close as one could be to Free France without being free. Nevertheless, the townspeople weren't about to let a complex anomaly affect their pride, and their quaint town reflected that attitude.

The team chose Bléré as her jump-off point. Its location was ideal. Being north of the line, one could access River Man's landing sites to the west on the south bank. A girl on a bicycle could move about freely before curfew, and the city was small enough not to get lost but big enough to keep Nazis occupied with more than people-watching.

Philippe pulled up alongside the blacksmith shop. Marcel suggested it for its patriotic owner and for being inconspicuous—it was also a natural place to stop a mule. The bicycle was leaning against the shop's outer wall.

"Oh! Is that for me?"

Philippe grinned. "You like it? I heard it works well, and they've spruced it up."

"I love it!"

The frame had seen better days, but it had a white wicker basket mounted on the handlebars and floral-patterned saddlebags on either side of the back wheel. The front and back fenders showed some rust but were otherwise polished. A dazzling white bell adorned with boldly painted flowers was mounted near the right-hand grip.

"I convinced everyone that a pretty girl on a bicycle was a distraction worth planning for," he boasted. "Anyway, here we are."

As scripted, he leaned over and gave her a peck on both cheeks to give the impression it was nothing more than a boyfriend dropping his girl off at her bicycle for the day.

"Philippe? You'll be waiting for me, right?" she asked, despite knowing the plan.

His usual playfulness vanished. "You won't see me for a while, but I'll be watching. You be careful."

She grabbed two small pouches, stepped down from the cart, and put one in each saddlebag. The blacksmith, known to the team by the anglicized name "Smith," stepped out from around the corner. He and Philippe exchanged discreet head bobs.

Before pulling away, Philippe gave her an emphatic wave. "Don't forget to eat. See you soon!"

His upbeat attempt didn't fool her. Suddenly alone, she felt a sharp pang of doubt.

~ ~ ~

Yesterday, she'd been presented with a few clothing and makeup options. Like it or not, her beauty would play a part in her assignment. She liked it. The thought of presenting herself at the crossing in a way to gain access or favors was intriguing. After putting on the finishing touches back in Amboise, even she liked what she saw. She had wished upon her stars last night and was pleased that the day turned out beautiful. Not cool, not hot: warm and comfortable. She felt surprisingly prepared and confident. But the crossing attempt would come later. Now was the scheduled time to eat.

On a corner in the city center was the boulangerie described by Marcel. The smell of fresh bread wafted out the door and engulfed the entry. The scents drifted further and snared passersby like flies caught in a web. Whether French or German, those leaving the scene invariably clutched or devoured their recently purchased baguette, croissant, or pain au chocolat. Colette wasn't immune to its spell either. She dismounted, lifted her bike over the street curb, and leaned it against a lamppost. Passing by small tables dotting the sidewalk, it was hard not to notice the staring men and the women pretending not to. Once inside, the pain au chocolat temptation was too much to resist. She hadn't had one in years.

"Is it real chocolate?" she asked the clerk.

"Real enough," came the bland reply.

It didn't matter. She added a café and two baguettes to her purchase and placed the bread in a bag. Outside, she was disappointed to see every table occupied.

"Young lady!" A refined-looking woman, perhaps in her sixties, was waving her over. The woman motioned to an empty chair as Colette neared. "Please join us."

"Oh, merci beaucoup! It's a busy place, isn't it?" Colette glanced around again before sitting. Several eyes looked away. Most continued to gawk.

"You must not be from around here," said the girl seated with the woman. "I've never seen it *not* busy."

She was pretty and dressed in a fine-looking maid or staff uniform. Her blond hair was pinned in a bun, and stray wisps flowed before her ears. Colette guessed the girl was about her age.

"Hello," Colette greeted her. "Thank you for inviting me."

The girl pointed toward the street. "We were admiring your

bicycle. The basket and sidesaddles are darling."

Before she could respond, the woman asked, "How was your first bite, dear?"

Colette gave a satisfied look at her purchase. "I suspect they don't use real chocolate, but it's delicious anyway."

The girl snickered.

"Well, that's the important thing, isn't it?" said the woman, patting the table lightly with two fingers. "Please, let me introduce you. This young lady is Violette Lebon." Violette held out her hand, and Colette shook it.

"Hello again. I'm Colette."

"Enchantée...and this is Madame Menier," Violette said with an anticipatory lilt.

Colette turned and offered her hand to the woman. "Thank you again for your kindness." She paused. "Menier? Hmm...Menier? My father told me about a wonderful woman named Menier. She cared for the wounded at Chenonceau Castle during the Great War. I've never seen it...in person, that is. Do you know if it's far from here?"

"No, it's not far at all," Violette answered. "And it isn't a castle; it's a château."

"Oh, I once saw a beautiful painting of it. It sure looked like a castle. What's the difference?"

"Well, the way I've been told," Violette began, sneaking a look at Madame Menier, "most castles are cold, heartless, stone fortifications. A château is a warm, welcoming home no matter its size."

"Oh. Then I'm glad it's a château. It would be a shame for something so pretty to be cold and heartless." Colette got back to her previous line of thought. "Let me think. Her first name was...hmm, I forget now."

"Simone?" Violette asked in a guiding way.

"Simone? Yes, that's it!" She looked to the woman. "Have you heard of her...or maybe you're even related?"

"I am, in a way," Madame Menier replied with an endearing smile.

"How exciting! She's famous, you know." Colette felt foolish. "I'm sorry. Of course you do if you're related to her."

Violette was enjoying the conversation. She leaned forward. "And did you know that the same Simone Menier who nursed those poor wounded soldiers back to health is also Lady Menier of the château and heiress to the famous Menier chocolate family? You remember real chocolate, I hope."

"Oh my," Colette exclaimed, "I'm sure I knew that. I should know it. And yes, I love, love chocolate! Where is my head today?"

"Don't be silly, dear," said Madame Menier, dabbing her mouth with a napkin. "You surely have more important things on your mind."

Of course, she was right, but Colette was enjoying their company. "Is it true that the castle...I mean, château...spans the River Cher? My father says the water flows directly underneath it."

Violette jumped on it and scooched her chair closer. "Not only does the river flow under, but you can stand in a grand hall and look right down into it."

Colette shook her head in disbelief. "Oh, how I would love to see that someday."

Violette leaned in. "Do you want to know something more amazing?" She glanced at Madame Menier for approval.

"It's certainly not a secret," the woman said, letting her young assistant continue.

"Well, the main entry sits in occupied France. But the other end is in free France."

Colette was astonished. "Are you saying that the château is the dividing line?"

"The river is. Not always, but it is at the château." Violette sat back, seemingly satisfied with her delivery.

They finished eating but continued to sip their coffees and discuss the weather and other superficial topics. Thankfully, the two never asked personal questions about her last name, her parents, where she was from, or even her age. Realizing it was time to get going, Colette stood, shook hands again, and grabbed her baguettes.

"It was so nice meeting you both."

"You are a charming young woman," said Madame Menier. "I look forward to our paths crossing again."

"Merci. Moi aussi."

"Oh, and here, sweetie." Madame Menier dropped three small paper-wrapped items into her baguette bag. "A little something you may like. Do with them as you wish."

Colette returned to her bicycle and placed the bag in the front basket. The bulk of her day was coming, but she felt invigorated. While pedaling away, a pedestrian gestured toward the sidewalk tables.

"Bonjour, Simone!"

Colette turned her head, saw Madame Menier waving back at the woman, and narrowly avoided crashing her bike into a parked car.

~ ~ ~

Madame Menier turned to her young assistant. "So, what do you think of her?"

"I like her," Violette answered, yet to take her eyes off Colette.

"I do too. She's even more lovely than I'd imagined."

"Thank you for bringing me to the city, Madame Menier."

"It is a nice change, isn't it?"

CHAPTER TWENTY-SIX
West of Bléré
April 23, Afternoon

THE CHER MEANDERED through the Indre-et-Loire department in west-central France, running roughly parallel and slightly south of the Loire. West of Tours, its waters spilled into its more famous and prominent cousin and flowed on before draining into the Atlantic Ocean's Bay of Biscay. Many considered the Loire a more natural and logical boundary between Free and Vichy France, but the demarcation line preferred political winds over topographical nuances.

Fifteen minutes west of Bléré, the dam Colette expected was ahead to her right. Not long after, when the road veered away from the river, she stopped and walked her bike to the water's edge. A refreshing breeze from the west competed against the current, causing ripples that gave the impression the river was flowing backward.

Reaching into a saddlebag, she pulled out a folded map. There were no destination markings—a precaution if it fell into the wrong hands. Instead, around the edges were inconspicuous cuts referencing locations within the map. These sites were based on her father's detailed input and made her think of him.

Getting there went as planned, but she wasn't sure what to expect next. A dirt and gravel patch at the road bend looked convenient to park a car or two. A narrow footpath led away from the road and into a wooded area. She followed it westward, wheeling her bike tightly against her. Skirting the river's southern bank, she eventually arrived at a well-trampled space. Just as her father described, there was a sloped clearing ideal for landing a rowboat. Following scrapes and gouges in the dirt, she soon found the craft concealed behind a clump of trees. She peeked around and underneath, taking care not to disturb anything. Several identical boot prints showed in the dried mud, but nothing looked unusual or unexpected—until she turned to leave.

The bark on the backside of a large tree was full of cuts, some fresher than others. She took a pencil and paper from her pouch and copied the newer-looking marks.

Back at the road, sunlight reflected off tiny shards in the gravel. She picked one up, then two more. She pushed them around her palm with a finger. Her eyes widened. It wasn't glass, but three identical diamonds. Placing them in a pouch pocket and reviewing her map again, she set out for her next destination.

After briefly heading south, the road again turned west. Le Cher was no longer visible, but she sensed it beyond the fields. The trees, hedges, and spring grasses picked up the water's scent, infused it with their freshness, and dispersed the earthy potpourri for all to enjoy. Then again, she hadn't seen a soul since hopping on her bike and imagined the locals had grown unaffected by the aroma over time. She closed her eyes and breathed through her nose.

Beside a tilled field, she stopped to recheck the map. The cut marks on the margins suggested a location that wasn't near a road. Figuring there must be a path leading to the passenger drop, she rode on, keeping a watchful eye.

Repeatedly, tall hedges divided one barren field from the next. She slowed to a stop, again straddled her bike, and was disappointed at seeing no signs. *Papa said somebody met the boat and passengers at the river drop. There must be some way to get down there.* Shortly after turning around to retrace her route, a scattering of brush just off the road looked out of place. The sticks seemed randomly strewn, and the landowner may have simply dumped them there, but it was worth a look. Upon closer inspection, she found a narrow dirt path alongside a hedgerow. Suspecting the river was too far to wheel her bike, she hid it under the hedges.

Once in the woods, the path turned east and followed the river. Further upstream, it stopped at a small clearing at the water's edge. The copse of trees she was told to look for was on the opposite shore. *This is it. Well hidden. There's nobody on the road during the day, let alone at night. I can see why River Man drops them here.* She found footprints in the dried mud, but scanning the tree trunks for cut marks revealed nothing this time.

She returned to the road. "They could go anywhere from here," she said to herself. After making light pencil marks on the map borders, she hopped on the seat and rode back the way she'd come.

A vehicle approaching from behind was the first hint of human life since the dam outside of Bléré. Suspecting it was Germans, she reminded herself she was doing nothing wrong. *I'm just a girl out riding her bike.* The gravelly road was narrow, and she pedaled close to the right edge, navigating the loose rock. Without looking, she gave a courtesy wave as it passed. Road dust billowed up. She squinted and turned her head, trying not to inhale it. Forty meters ahead, the car slowed to a stop. A man in uniform stepped out on the passenger side and waited for her.

"My apologies, young lady," he said as she arrived. "I didn't realize how much dust was kicking up."

"I don't think your driver could have done anything about it," she said, brushing some off her skirt.

Looking up again, a sickening feeling coursed through her. She had studied the photos, and here he was: the insignia, the oil-slicked hair, the scar down his right cheek. It was him, all right.

"You're the first person we've seen on this road," the lieutenant said, changing the subject while looking her over. "And I don't know that I need to see another. You are a vision."

"Oh, that's kind of you."

"The women of rural France continue to inspire my senses, but you...you, young lady, have raised the bar to a new level." Colette wasn't sure what to do or say to that. "And your bicycle suits you perfectly. I'd even say the image of it being ridden by you will forever be ingrained in my head."

Contrary to her expectation, she began to feel *more* comfortable, not less. His last comment even amused her. She smiled while pretending not to notice the crass overtone.

"That's so very nice of you to say...um...Lieutenant," she replied, scanning his outfit.

"Ah, you know your German uniforms. I'm impressed."

"Well, it's not like you all arrived yesterday." She pointed at his trousers. "And I see you're not immune to our dirt either." She had transitioned from nervous to confident and wasn't sure why.

~ ~ ~

"Well, look at that," Schmid said, swiping at dust on his pants. "I guess we have something in common."

As always, he enjoyed his position of power and rattling people's nerves, but something was different with this one. He wasn't used to such a laissez-faire attitude. Civilians never acted comfortably around him. More than a right, he felt it his duty to make people cringe, squirm, and grovel, and it was his nature long before he'd achieved any rank of consequence. However, antagonistic behavior could wait for another victim. In mere moments, he'd become captivated. Other beautiful women that he knew were mainly formal, refined, and stuffy.

They were nothing like this.

"Oh, come now," said Colette, "we have more in common than a little dirt. Look, we're at the exact same place in this great big world at the exact same time." Schmid wished to be in a different place with her. Someplace where the word "exact" was far more literal. "And," she continued, "La Mère de la Terre has smiled down on both of us today, wouldn't you say?"

"Who?"

"Mother Nature, of course."

"Oh, of course," he said, moving his eyeballs just enough to take in the surroundings.

"Sir, should we get going?" his driver suggested.

Schmid turned and directed his well-honed look of annoyance at the private, but kept his composure. First impressions were important to him, even if they varied dramatically from one target to the next.

"I'm afraid my driver's right, my dear. I regret having to cut this short. By the way, where are you headed?"

"Bléré, but I'm not in any hurry. I like to stop and smell Mother's nature." She gave him a slow, innocent smile.

Schmid gave her another thorough review and groaned. "Mmm, don't we all."

"Well, I suspect some more than others, don't you?"

"Perhaps," he answered. "And perhaps I'll have the pleasure of seeing you again. I'll be passing through Bléré from time to time."

"Well, I'll be the one riding this," she said, patting the seat.

Schmid looked her over one last time, shook his head, and climbed in. *Lucky bicycle.* His driver pulled away.

"What was her name, Sir?" the private asked.

"Her name?" Schmid squeezed his eyes shut and grimaced.

"I couldn't tell how old she is, could you?"

He glared at his driver. "What the fuck do I care how old she is?"

"I don't know. She looked young and mature at the same time. And she seemed carefree, maybe even naive. You know, innocent."

~ ~ ~

"Pompous ass," Colette mumbled, watching them drive off. "What the hell is he doing out here?"

Pedaling on, she approached an old cottage she had passed on the way out. One more bend around the stone wall, and she'd be back at her first stop. One more quick search for sparkling diamonds, and she'd return to Bléré.

Merde! She slammed on the brakes, skidded to a halt, and inched backward. The lieutenant's car was parked no more than a hundred meters ahead and next to the path leading to the rowboat. Crouched against the old wall, she peeked around and spotted the driver. Schmid was out of sight. At first, she feared he'd seen the path. Then, it dawned on her that he probably knew about it all along. There were only two options: Continue riding—or not. Risking another conversation was the less appealing choice. *Stay out of sight and learn what I can.* She didn't have to wait long.

Schmid emerged from the path, gave two satisfying pats on the car's fender, and hopped into the passenger seat. *He's pleased about something.* When the car was out of sight, she hid her bicycle and re-walked the path, nervously looking over her shoulder. The boat was there. The markings on the tree hadn't changed. Nothing had.

This first assignment was straightforward: Find the two sites on the south bank and look for clues and anything unusual or significant —particularly about Auguste, the passengers, and the motorcycles. Nobody anticipated Schmid. Despite no scheduled rendezvous, she grabbed her bicycle and raced for Bléré.

Skirting the city center, she pedaled to the north side of town. Her bike was easily recognizable, so she stashed it behind the blacksmith shop and knocked on a banged-up metal door shielded by two large scrap bins. Loud noises inside stopped. Nothing happened. She knocked again. A metal slot slid open, then shut. The lock clicked, and the door swung open.

A sweaty man half-covered in ash or soot made a frantic gesture for her to come in. He was lean and wiry yet somehow muscular. Every fiber in his hands, arms, and neck pressed outward against his tanned, leathery skin. She'd heard of people being skin and bones, but never skin and bones—and muscle. The dusky storage room was lined from floor to ceiling with metal shelves overflowing with loose parts, wire coils, boxes, and tools whose purpose defied imagination. He scrambled to clear a pile of papers off a small chair. There was no space on the desk, so he kicked things aside and set the stack on the floor.

"So sorry. Wasn't expecting you. Is everything okay?" Smith asked.

"I'm fine. I was told you could help me."

"Of course. Of course."

Smith was a trusted contact, but she wasn't sure what to divulge.

"I need to send word that a Lieutenant Schmid knows where River Man hides the boat."

"Oh my. That's not good."

"I'm not positive, but tell them I don't think he knows about the passenger drop location. He drove the road leading past it and never stopped." Smith listened without writing anything down. "And there's more." She dug into a bag and handed him her drawing. "These are markings I copied from the trunk of a large tree near the boat...kind of like Roman numbers. They don't make sense to me, but they mean something. I'm sure they're important."

Smith held it beneath the desk lamp.

XXVIV III l
XVIIV III Il

"These looked the newest," she added. "There were other markings beneath these that were older...more weathered."

"This Lieutenant Schmid made these?"

"I'm not so sure. They were already there before I ran into him on the road, and there were no more after I saw him come out of the woods. I think maybe River Man did it."

"Hmm. Okay if I take this?"

"Sure. I've memorized it anyway. And tell them there were more markings...all older."

"I will," he said, staring at the paper. "Sure look like Roman numerals, but they don't quite read right."

"That's what I was thinking."

"Anything else?" he said, folding the paper and putting it in his shirt pocket.

She wasn't sure about mentioning the jewels but decided to share everything—or nearly so. She pulled one of the three from the hidden pouch lining.

"I found it on the road near the path to the boat."

Smith turned it between his thumb and finger and examined it under the lamp. "It's a diamond. You found a diamond there?"

"The sun was shining. It winked at me like it was begging to be found. My father reported a bag being tossed at River Man. Do you think it could have spilled out?"

"Hmm, maybe. Can I pass this little guy on?"

"Please. Do you think someone can make sense of it?"

"Don't know, but I'll find out. Your father will be proud, Colette."

The comment caught her off guard. "You know my father?"

He gave her a toothless smile. "Proud to say I do."

Her expression changed. "He and my brother Louis are searching for my mother."

"Been made aware," Smith said, patting her arm. "Got men in these parts keeping their eyes and ears open. It'll work out."

She'd done all she came to do. They thanked each other and shook hands; his felt like dried driftwood. Smith stepped outside to make sure all was clear. He gave a quick nod, and she slipped out.

CHAPTER TWENTY-SEVEN
Bléré
April 23, Late Afternoon

PHILIPPE WAS ANXIOUS to get to his perch with a view of the crossing. The guards could be old, young, militant, or reasonable. No obvious pattern had revealed itself, so it was anybody's guess. Upbeat when discussing it, he suggested that real assholes were uncommon. He ignored everybody when they looked at him like he was crazy. Regardless, they all agreed to a crossing time that was often busy, hoping the guards would be more inclined to move things along.

The room Marcel arranged for long ago gave a distant but good sight line to the guard station. Philippe entered, made a beeline for the window, and grabbed binoculars off the table. He was pleased with what he saw. Both guards appeared young. As the scheduled time approached, he paced less and kept vigil at the window. Tilting his head down and twisting it left and right, he heard his neck bones crunch. Pressing around his vertebrae to relax the muscles gave little relief. A minute later, he looked out again and froze. There, propped against a lamppost, was the bicycle. Colette was sitting on a nearby bench. The time had come.

~ ~ ~

The baguettes she bought earlier had a purpose. Grabbing the paper bag from the front basket, she peeked inside. She'd forgotten about the items dropped in by Madame Menier. She unraveled one and bit into it. Her heart leaped. *Real chocolate!*

From her bench, Colette confirmed what the team had hoped. The blond guard hardly looked eighteen; the other, slightly older, had dark hair. Even if they were eager to prove their manliness, resolve, and dedication to the Reich, she suspected they might have the usual inclinations of young men.

Three squabbling middle-aged Frenchmen stepped into line. She wheeled her bike up behind them, and a gray-haired couple followed her. As their turn approached, the men spoke softer but continued their bickering. She hoped their demeanor might work to her advantage. At last, they were called forward.

The dark-haired guard began giving the three a thorough inspection. They presented papers, emptied their pockets, and answered questions. While waiting, the younger guard glanced her way a second time, and she lifted her free hand to give a timid wave. He tapped his comrade on the shoulder and motioned to send the men through. His partner looked annoyed until their conversation led him to look her way. The Frenchmen had their papers thrust back at them, and Colette wheeled her bicycle up to the young soldiers.

"Your papers, mademoiselle?" said the older one.

"I'm sorry. I'm so sorry, but I don't have them with me," she answered in her sweetest, broken German. "I work for a veterinarian in Amboise. He's sent me to tend to a sick horse. Nobody down there can help her."

"I'm sorry, but we can't let you pass without pap—"

"It's okay to speak French," the younger soldier butted in. "I can always use the practice." He continued in French as best he could. "I grew up on a farm outside Düsseldorf. What's wrong with the horse?"

The question surprised her. Nobody mentioned that a crossing guard might know about equine ailments. Fortunately, Henri had suggested a possible medical condition as an afterthought.

"What is your name, monsieur?" she asked, hoping to play into his concern for the animal.

"Ralf, mademoiselle."

"Ah, bonjour, Ralf. I'm glad to run into someone who knows horses. From the description, I'm certain she has strangles."

"I'm surprised anyone still owns a horse down there," the other guard said, trying to get involved. "They're in high demand."

"She belongs to my aunt and uncle, but is well past her prime. Knowing what I do, they wrote me in hopes that I could help. And what is your name, sir?"

"Dieter, mademoiselle"

"Strangles. Poor thing," Ralf interjected. "That's a miserable thing to go through...and extremely contagious. You must keep it away from other horses."

Colette smiled at him. "Would you like to come to work with us after the war?"

Ralf beamed. "Hell, how about *during* the war?"

She gave a coy smile and turned her attention back to Dieter. "You know, no animal has done more for the advancement of mankind."

"What about the—" Dieter thought a second. "Hmm, maybe you're right."

"Oh, I know people love dogs. I love dogs as much as anyone. But it's amazing what horses have done for us, isn't it?"

"Warm compresses can speed up the healing," Ralf broke in. "And it should help loosen things up."

"Oh my, your knowledge of horses is impressive," Colette commended him.

"If only more antibiotics were being developed," Ralf continued. "I know animals could benefit as much as humans."

"That's so true. But if my suspicion is correct, I'll diagnose it immediately and instruct my aunt and uncle on what to do. I must return soon. We're up to our eyeballs at the clinic. Everything from cats to cows."

"Oh, I don't doubt it," Dieter chimed in. "When do you plan on returning?"

"Well, it'll be too late to come back tonight, but I must tomorrow. Will you men be here?"

"Oh yes," Dieter said. "We'll be here from afternoon to midnight the next three nights."

Perfect. That's when I'll return. "Wonderful! Maybe I'll see you both again."

The queue behind her was building, but she was pleased with how the encounter was going and gave no regard to their inconvenience. Those waiting seemed unlikely to complain anyway. They kept their heads down, spoke in whispers, and remained patient.

"How far are you going?" asked Ralf.

"Near Loches," she answered, avoiding specifics.

"Oh, you'll be there in less than two hours on that beauty," he said, pointing at her bike.

"You've both been so helpful. I owe you. Oh!" she said, touching a finger to her lips. "Wait a second." She pulled the paper bag from her front basket and handed each of them a baguette.

Dieter's eyes brightened. "Thank you! Nobody's brought us a bite to eat in forever."

"Or ever," Ralf laughed.

"Really? Well, it's nothing." Her eyes lit up. "But I do have a little something!" She handed each of them a small wrapped item.

"Is this—" Dieter began.

She raised her eyebrows and flashed a smile. Their eyes nearly bugged out of their heads. Waving goodbye with a flutter of her fingers and ringing the bell three times, she pedaled off. Those in line had to wait until the guards finished savoring their treat.

Up in the flat, Philippe flopped into a chair, put a hand over his eyes, and exhaled.

CHAPTER TWENTY-EIGHT
Amboise
April 23, Dusk

TEN MINUTES AFTER Colette left the blacksmith, Jean-Paul spotted five horseshoes instead of the usual four hanging outside the shop. The man with limited facial expressions looked like the bodyguard for anyone who wished to outlive their opponent. Today, his brawn wasn't required; he was checking the shop at intervals for the agreed-upon sign. After meeting with Smith, he left for Amboise carrying Colette's concealed messages.

At dusk, Marcel and Georges walked in together. Jean-Paul handed them a tissue-wrapped diamond and Colette's marked-up paper and filled them in on the details. He relayed the news of Colette's chance run-in with Schmid on the rural road and the lieutenant's subsequent snooping at the rowboat landing.

"Did he see Colette go in there earlier?" Marcel asked.

"That's not my understanding. She thinks he knew it was there and was only visiting the site. Word is he looked pleased when returning to his car."

"Her theory about the diamond may be right," said Georges. "It could've fallen out of the bag thrown at Auguste."

"Agreed," Marcel said. "François said it was a strange interaction. And it was dark. It could easily have been overlooked."

Jean-Paul interrupted them to say he'd been away long enough and should return to Bléré. Marcel and Georges thanked him and sat down to study the paper again.

✗✗✔✓ ꠸꠸꠸ ꠸
✗✔✓✔ ꠸꠸꠸ ꠸꠸

"Uh oh," Georges said at last.

"What is it?"

"So, you can see how each line has two gaps. The left group of markings is more complicated. I'll get to that in a second. The second and third groupings on each line may represent numbers or counts—possibly both."

"Aren't numbers and counts the same thing?"

"Often, but maybe not in this case. I think one group represents time, and the other counts."

"Go on."

Georges moved his finger under the two middle groupings and looked at Marcel.

"Time," the leader said solemnly. "Three in the morning. That would be about when he ends his return trips."

Georges pointed at the far right of each line. "And?"

"Counts. Two passengers last time and one upcoming."

"It's possible. Now, look here." Georges pointed at the left-side marks on the lower line. "As a whole, this part doesn't represent a number...at least no number I know. But both groupings end with an I and V, right?"

"Sure. Four?" Marcel turned his eyes to Georges. "Merde. April."

"And the XVI that starts it?"

"Sixteen," said Marcel. "Our last transfer date." His focus moved to the line above. "April 25th. Our next scheduled delivery."

"Date, time, and passenger count all divulged on a tree trunk," Georges said.

Marcel sat back in his chair. The scheduled moving of their next passenger was coming up fast. It was only one person, but the Nazis were hunting for him. Sneaking a British pilot with valuable information back to England was a big deal—to both sides.

"Everything François saw that night is beginning to make sense," said Georges, "and it's a trap."

Henri Flamand walked in and saw their faces. Marcel and Georges filled him in on everything.

"River made the markings," Georges said bluntly. "Nobody else could have known that information."

Marcel nodded. "And the packages were carrying loose jewels."

"Are you saying he's stealing from the passengers after they've already paid for his service?" Henri barked.

"Or maybe the Nazis are paying him?" Georges countered. "Or the other way around? Maybe they have something on him? And we've determined that River's wife is probably involved."

"It's likely," said Marcel. "Speaking of her, we need to assume the worst for the packages."

"We've never heard about anything going wrong down there," said Georges. "Maybe they're letting the packages go through after getting rich on them."

"I hope you're right," Marcel said. "That's the best-case scenario, but I don't feel good about it."

"Where does the lieutenant fit in all this?" Henri asked. "François said there were two motorcycles. I doubt Schmid would go out there in the middle of the night. Was he sending others? And what in the hell happened with Roland?"

"We're just spinning our wheels here," said Marcel. "Everything's speculation. Before delivering any more packages, we need to know what's going on."

"I've always hated that asshole," Henri fumed. "If he had anything to do with Roland—"

"We need to eliminate him somehow," Georges interjected.

Marcel jumped in. "No. We use him to learn more."

"We can't just hand that pilot over to him!" Henri stormed. "It'll be a death sentence!"

Marcel remained calm. "No. No, we can't. We'll need to make an excuse and send River back empty-handed."

"If the Nazis know what we're doing, wouldn't they have come down hard on us?" asked Georges.

"Great question." Marcel chewed on it. "I mentioned this idea to François earlier. What if they don't want to shut it down? Maybe it's not the Nazis. I mean, not the German army, anyway. Maybe it's a couple of bad eggs on the take, and they prefer the status quo. Schmid sure fits the bill. He's shrewd and rotten as they get. Not a good combination. I think those involved have something good going and want to keep it that way."

"That new major," Henri said, looking up. "This all started with the arrival of Holtzer. Maybe we need to eliminate that bastard, too!"

"No. That doesn't add up," said Marcel. "We did find out after his arrival, but Colette reported that these were only the newest markings. There were more. We don't know how many, but they would've all been before Holtzer's arrival here. So far, everything points to Schmid —and Gagnon."

"Damn," said Georges. "One day, and that girl's already earned her weight in gold."

"She knew to go to Smith," said Marcel. "Keep putting your faith in her. Knowing her, she's piecing it together. We could learn plenty in the next two days if everything goes as planned. And crossing into Vichy was the difficult part. The return should go fine."

"Nobody in their right mind or otherwise escapes *into* occupied France," Henri agreed.

"It's tomorrow night that worries me most," said Georges. "Spying on River Man in the dark with Nazis buzzing about won't be easy."

"And if she's caught?" Henri asked.

Marcel shook his head. "Knowing what she knows...they can't risk their secret getting out."

"We need to consider calling this off," Georges thought aloud.

"Maybe," said Marcel, drumming his fingers on the table.

CHAPTER TWENTY-NINE
Château de Chenonceau
April 24, Morning

VIOLETTE LEBON ADMIRED the Lady of Chenonceau's professional and courteous handling of the uninvited guests. Captain Eicher had responded in kind, soothing things over when Madame Menier expressed concerns. Violette also respected how Madame could set protocol aside, taking matters into her own hands to bestow etiquette lessons on select guests.

Before the war, Violette enjoyed being a maid at the château. The environment was uplifting. Its grounds enchanted her daily, and she revered Madame Menier. Violette's loss of both parents at a young age undoubtedly aroused Simone's nurturing ways, and the two were like mother and daughter. One year ago, she was moved to tears when Madame commended her spirit, dedication, and trustworthiness before asking her to be her assistant.

There was much to do, and she was eager to do it. She wouldn't have listened if someone had told her there were better ways to spend a day. Sure, things had changed. Germans moving about the château was one clear difference, but they tended to follow Captain Eicher's cultured example. The number of servants was also reduced per command, causing the grounds to degrade more than anyone wanted, and German staff assigned to the château seemed to give little regard to its condition. The war had a shameful way of dwindling and disregarding much—but not Violette's love of working for Madame Menier.

Waking early as always, Violette tended to her own needs first. She attempted to compose and present herself in a manner befitting her position, employer, and wondrous setting. Once satisfied, she headed straight to the kitchen. As usual, servers were busy attending to the German officers, but an ornate-handled silver tray had been prepared and set out for her as expected. The coffee pot had a wisp of steam drifting from its spout; an adorned, porcelain demitasse sat atop a matching saucer holding two sugar cubes; a delicate creamer was a quarter filled for that rare occasion when Madame was in the mood. A customary cube of chocolate accompanied her scone.

Violette departed for the study with the tray. Removed from the usual bustling areas, she understood why Madame called this part of the château her sanctuary. She tapped on the door.

"Come in, dear," she heard. She picked up the tray from the hall table and leaned her back into the heavy door.

"Good morning," she said with her usual lilt.

"Well, good morning," Madame greeted her. "You look delightful, as always. Did you sleep well?"

The female staff at the château could keep each other up to all hours, giggling and sharing stories. Violette had worried she would miss that regular camaraderie, but quickly grew to appreciate the quiet solitude of her private quarters.

"I did. My new room has advantages."

Madame Menier chuckled. "I don't doubt that. I hope you don't mind that I wanted you near."

"No, this is much better. And I still make time to see them." After spying the usual open area on the desk and setting the tray down, something caught her eye. "Oh, I haven't seen this in months. I think I love it more each time." An embellished, brass letter opener gleamed as she picked it up. "It's unusually long and heavy, isn't it?" she asked, hoping to learn more about it.

"Yes, I suppose it is."

"I've never seen one like it."

"Well, it's quite old, so I suspect you haven't," was all she got as Madame organized some papers.

At this point, Violette typically took a short break. Madame Menier would finalize her calendar, and it might be several minutes before she had the daily plan ready. This time, Violette remained.

"Madame?"

Her mentor stopped what she was doing. "Is there something you wish to discuss?"

"I was just wondering. Do you think Colette is doing okay? She should be in Loches today if all went well. Do you think it did? I sure hope so. Me? I could never do something like that."

"Dear, when speaking of sensitive matters, always be careful," Madame whispered. "You never know who might be snooping."

Violette put a hand to her forehead. "I'm so sorry!"

"Anyway, I understand the checkpoint went well. She's only there to observe, so I see no reason to worry yourself. We have enough to do around here. I'd like you to come back in half an hour."

"Yes, I will. Thank you again for—" She cut herself off, seeing Madame's playful underhanded flick shooing her away.

Thirty minutes later, she returned and pushed the study door ajar. "Are you ready for me, Madame?"

"Ah, please have a seat." Madame Menier gestured to a purple velvet chair across from her. "I'll get straight to the point. I need you to keep doing what you're doing and not feel ashamed that we treat them kindly. Do you remember why we are so accommodating?" she asked as if giving a quiz.

"So they are trusting of us."

"Precisely. Do not confuse etiquette with assistance. Many

throughout France will gladly assist the Germans if it suits them in one way or another. Our compliance and kindness will earn their trust. With their trust comes comfort. With their comfort," she said, walking around the desk to get nearer, "comes opportunity." She spoke just loud enough for Violette to hear.

"But how will I recognize opportunities?"

"You won't always. I just need you to listen. Always listen. You speak and understand German better than the rest of us. Our guests must never know that. So continue being professional, kind, and always listening. Promise me?"

"I promise!"

"They will slip, and I need you to tell me anytime you hear things that sound vaguely important."

"It's exhilarating, isn't it? I could never do what Colette's doing, but I hope I can help somehow."

"I don't doubt you for a second. I never do. You can start by continuing to attend to their needs. Offer them a café. Cigars. The more time spent near them, the more comfortable they'll become, and the more likely you'll overhear something."

"I won't let you down."

"I know you won't. And it's not all on your shoulders. We will all be trying; it's just that we're less proficient in the language. Some soldiers will speak a little French as a courtesy, but in military matters, it's always German."

"I understand."

"One more thing before you go. I would like you to pay attention to the guards watching the river. Specifically, I need you to note their shift changes. Regimented behavior can be expected from them. I'm looking for patterns."

"The times and the personnel?"

"That's right."

"Yes, Madame. I will!"

She felt proud of the trust placed upon her. Outside the study, she leaned her back against the wall—nervous, hopeful, and excited that she might help somehow.

CHAPTER THIRTY
Loches, France
April 24, Morning

AFTER A RESTLESS night, Colette pulled a wad of tightly packed clothes from a pouch and made practical selections for her trip into the city.

The single woman hosting her a few kilometers northeast of Loches welcomed her warmly yesterday evening and didn't ask prying questions. Colette appreciated the discretion, and the trend continued this morning.

"How did you sleep?" the woman asked.

"Oh, très bien, merci," she said, choosing not to concern her host.

"I'm so glad. A good night's sleep makes a world of difference. It's not much, but I've got breakfast ready for you in the kitchen."

The small plate of bread and cheese was a welcome sight. Trying to maintain a semblance of manners, Colette took her time eating. Before leaving, they embraced but said nothing.

~ ~ ~

The fortified city of Loches was the most medieval-looking city Colette had ever seen. The royal town's beauty made her want to discount the forewarnings of distrustful inhabitants. She stepped off her bicycle and gazed in awe at the massive Porte Royale entrance to the old city. Walking underneath the vast stone arch made her feel small. Arriving early and having never been there, she wished to see the sites. She turned left and followed a narrow street. Around a turn, the four octagonal tower peaks of the church of Saint-Ours were like nothing she'd ever seen. Looking up, she wondered where all the stone came from and couldn't fathom how small people could make such enormous things.

"That's a pretty bicycle."

"Oh!" she said with a start. A woman in her forties or early fifties had come up behind her. "Merci. I do get a lot of compliments."

"Where did you get such a thing?"

"A friend of a friend. He fixed up an old one."

The woman examined it closely. "The basket and bell look new."

"Thank you," she said again, hoping the woman would move on.

"I haven't seen you before. Are you from around here?"

Georges' words about collaborators and busybodies in Loches popped into her head. "No, I'm just visiting. I saw this beautiful church from a distance and had to see it up close."

"Where are you from?"

It was too many questions from a stranger. "I'm helping my relatives," she said, trying to control the direction. "They have a horse with a case of strangles."

"Strangles? I've never heard of it."

"She'll be alright. It just takes time." She tried forcing the woman into answering instead of asking. "I was heading up to look at the castle. Is it this way?" she asked, pointing.

"Well, it depends on what you're looking for. The royal lodge is opposite the church. Just follow the road around. I'm going that way myself. It was built by Charles the Seventh, you know. On the other hand, if you're looking for the keep, it's up that way. I just came from there. I come up here every time I'm in town. Are you staying long?"

"Oh, good, I wanted to see the keep," Colette said, ensuring they'd depart in opposite directions. "No, I'm leaving soon. But I hope to return to see more. Is there lodging nearby you'd recommend?"

The woman suggested a hotel in the town center and an inn on the outskirts. Colette didn't bother remembering the names.

"It was nice speaking with you," she lied. "I better get going."

After a short distance, she turned to look. Something in the woman's stare gave her chills.

The fortress city might have felt claustrophobic if she hadn't been so eager to see what was around the next corner. Soon, an imposing medieval structure loomed ahead. Again, she gazed in wonder. *How did people build this?* The sites were beautiful, but the more she walked, the more she was suspicious of those around her. A middle-aged man approached from her left.

"It sure is a lot of rock."

"It sure is," she replied without looking at him.

"I haven't seen you before."

Colette continued admiring the towering wall. "I haven't seen you before either."

"Are you new here?" he asked.

A grassy open space across the way looked devoid of nosy people. She turned and gave him a pleasant smile. "No, not really. I've been here all morning. Au revoir." She strolled away with the bicycle at her side. The man went back to admiring the wall.

Arriving at the top of the ramparts to the old city, she looked out. The scene below looked peaceful. In the distance was the tiny village of Beaulieu-les-Loches that she biked through earlier. *Maybe I'm being paranoid, but the people here do seem nosy. It sure is pretty, though.* She sat down against the trunk of a large tree to think through the rest of her day.

The bicycle was invaluable for getting around and proved a worthwhile companion at the border crossing, but it had a drawback

—it was a conversation starter. Conversations weren't her preference unless she initiated them. She stashed it behind scraggly bushes running along the ramparts near the church. Reaching for a pouch, she pulled out the watch Philippe gave her and slipped it onto her wrist. The time was nearing.

Given the importance of his role, she was surprised how little anyone knew about Auguste Gagnon. Fortunately, Marcel learned that he visited the historic Saint-Ours church every Friday at three in the afternoon—and he never stayed long. Colette's goal was simple: Keep an eye out and learn what she could. If seen, he wouldn't know who she was, but she couldn't be seen again.

The plan was to arrive early and sit in a back pew, but the nave was much narrower than she expected, and anybody seated anywhere was noticeable. *At least it's poorly lit, and it's not like anybody knows what I look like.* Four people were sitting near the front. She chose a spot in back with a good vantage point of the whole place.

The doors behind her opened one minute before three o'clock. Rays of dust-flecked sunlight flitted about the room and quickly vanished. Keeping her head down, she tried to pick things up peripherally, but the dusky room made it difficult. She turned her head a little more and saw a man with an unmistakable face walking alongside the same woman she had chatted with outside the church. The woman glanced her way. Colette forced herself to remain calm, gave a curt nod, and pretended she was there for religious reasons. The woman nudged the man with her elbow. At the front of the nave, they turned left and disappeared.

~ ~ ~

Flora Gagnon elbowed her husband again. "That girl! I spoke with her outside. What is she doing in here?"

"Which girl?" Auguste replied, looking annoyed.

"The pretty girl...woman...whatever. In the back pew. She was outside earlier. What's the chance she'd be in here now?"

"Why shouldn't she be? You're being paranoid."

"Well, I've never seen her before. Doesn't it seem weird she'd be here by herself right when *we're* here?"

"What are you talking about? Did she look suspicious?"

"I wouldn't say that, but I'm suspicious of everyone—and you should be too. And she told me she was leaving soon. So why is she sitting in the church?"

Auguste ignored her and looked at his watch. "Usually, they're here already. But it's the lieutenant this time. We need to be patient."

"I don't know why I had to come," she groaned. "I hate this."

"I don't like you here either," he grumbled, "but Schmid insisted. I suspect he wants to ensure neither of us has second thoughts."

"Second thoughts!" she said, flustered. "Where have you been? I *always* have second thoughts!"

"Jesus, Flora! What do you want me to do? There's no easy way out of this."

~ ~ ~

Despite his best efforts, the replacement for Private Wegner was faring no better than his predecessor. He had yet to learn that doing his best had no bearing on the lieutenant's demeanor. Schmid's order to drive him to Loches came at the last second and literally caught him with his pants down. He was berated for the delay, and slowing for pedestrians at an intersection in town was the final straw. The lieutenant was in an uproar as the car pulled alongside the placid church of Saint-Ours.

Gathering himself, Schmid went to a side door and yelled back, commanding his driver to stay put.

~ ~ ~

Colette thought it through while considering her next step. *I bet that's his wife. Do I wait? Eavesdrop?* Now, she strained to see what the commotion was about. A figure appeared beyond the front pews and crossed from right to left. She stifled a gasp and looked down as though in prayer. Private worshipers and tourists were commonplace in the medieval house of devotion, and the lieutenant made only a cursory note of those seated.

A door slammed. *Schmid's meeting them.* Eavesdropping was beyond risky and could be noticed by those in the pews. If Schmid saw her—well, that couldn't happen. Her less refined appearance and the lack of context might throw him off, but it wasn't a chance she could take. A thought gripped her: River's wife could tell Schmid about the girl outside and now inside the church. It might even be the first thing out of her mouth. She stood and walked out.

It was frustrating to think she was failing her mission, but Schmid's arrival was foreboding. *Nobody else knows he's here.* Hurrying to her bicycle, her heart skipped. A German soldier was crouched by the bushes, examining it. Although unnerved, her only choice was to retrieve it.

Approaching quietly, she said, "Guten tag," in a sweet accent.

The soldier sprang up. "Oh, why hello. You startled me," he fumbled in French.

"Do you like it?" she asked, pointing at her bike.

"Yes. The bell's a real beauty. Is it yours?"

"It is. And perfect for sightseeing, don't you think?" Time was ticking, but she saw an opportunity. "I don't meet many men in uniform. What brings you here?"

"Oh, my lieutenant is here on business of some sort. I'm just waiting for him."

"Well, this is a beautiful place to do that."

"It sure is."

"So, do you come here often, soldier?"

He laughed at her playfulness. "No, it's my first time. I'd never even heard of it, but I understand the lieutenant comes here from time to time, so I may be back."

"Hmm, I wonder what brings a German officer to Loches, of all places?" she asked, as though indifferent.

"Mostly to meet with locals, I guess. I've no idea why. But honestly, I don't plan on asking."

"Don't you like him?"

"Lieutenant Schmid? He tells me where and when to bring him, never why...and I've learned not to ask."

"Well, welcome to Loches. I'm glad you could see it, and I hope you can come again. Are you here long?"

"It's hard to know. He has a couple more stops, but I'll drive him back north later today. Whenever he tells me to."

"Well, I suppose I should be on my way."

The young man scrambled to get her bike dislodged from the brambles and steadied it for her.

"It was lovely meeting you," she said.

"Oh, the pleasure was all mine," said the private.

She glanced back while riding away. The soldier stood transfixed, looking her way as though spellbound.

~ ~ ~

Flora Gagnon jumped when the door burst open. Schmid strode in without acknowledging them. He swiped at the door, slamming it.

"I need a goddamn driver I can count on to be crooked," he ranted. "These goody-two-shoes they keep dumping on me are wasting my time." With nothing helpful to say, Flora and her husband waited. Schmid finally acknowledged them. "My men were idiots, but I had them trained." He looked at her, then Auguste. "I've had to make some changes. Tell me it's still on for tomorrow."

Flora knew the comment wasn't directed at her and tilted her head down, intent on avoiding eye contact.

"Yes. Tomorrow," Auguste replied. "What kind of changes?"

"That damn major took them away from me. I have to find new men I can trust to keep their mouths shut. In the meantime, I'm stuck doing the grunt work. Give me the details."

She and her husband knew the process well and dreaded the idea of Schmid's direct participation. Transport nights were bad enough when dealing with his cronies; the thought of dealing with Schmid was horrific.

Her thoughts drifted. Leaning to her husband, she whispered, "And who has such a nice bicycle *these* days?"

Auguste shot her a look that strongly suggested she let it go.

"Thank you for the interruption," Schmid sneered with oozing sarcasm. "What the hell are you talking about?"

"I'm sorry, Lieutenant. My wife can be a bit paranoid."

"Again, what the fuck are you talking about," Schmid said with mounting irritation.

"It's just...well, she saw a girl outside the church and now again inside—seated in the pews. She's suspicious of people in general. It's the times. Hard to blame her, right?"

Schmid glared at her. His silence was deafening as she awaited his tongue-lashing. It never came.

"Where?" he finally asked.

"Back corner of the pews. The pretty one," she mumbled without looking up.

Schmid walked out and returned a minute later. "Nobody. But thanks, I needed the exercise."

Her husband gave a look that demanded: *Are you satisfied?*

She continued listening as Schmid had Auguste review the upcoming transfer in detail: When, where, how many, and the cargo's value. Auguste assured him the shipment was high-profile. He lacked the details—always did—but believed it was a British pilot.

Flora knew Schmid would savor the ramifications. Such important packages might not be laden with personal wealth, but they would have travel provisions—including some money—and the capture would go a long way toward reinforcing his ego.

"This is just what I've been looking for, Gagnon, so it better go as planned. I can't risk losing our little side business. Neither can you." He moved his eyes. "Or you," he hissed at Flora. "When I have him in hand, I'll come up with something believable for command, but you can bet they'll ask questions."

Her husband was fidgeting, and she saw that Schmid wasn't blind to it.

"Spit it out!" he snapped.

"Sir, as you say, there's a risk. There always is. And this shipment's value...well, it's higher than usual. I was thinking my fee should increase...for this trip, I mean."

The air was sucked from the room. Every muscle in her body tensed as she braced for the storm surge.

"Fee? Fee!" he roared. "Are you seriously suggesting you charge *me* a fee? You sniveling thief! You don't charge me anything. I *reward* you...and only out of the goodness of my heart! Given your lack of options, you should consider yourself *and* your wife lucky that I'm as generous as I am." Schmid scoffed and threw up a hand. "I don't care what you think. The value's what I say it is. The reward is what I decide it is, if anything at all. You're walking a dangerous line, Gagnon. You and your wife can still survive this war, but be damn careful what cards you play."

Her husband backpedaled after playing his card as poorly as she expected. "You're right. I'm sorry. You have treated us well. Please accept my apology."

Flora was relieved that her husband didn't press the subject she'd earlier suggested. It was readily apparent that backing out altogether wasn't an option.

Schmid looked at both of them with disdain and glanced at his watch. "That's all." He walked to the door and, without looking back, growled, "Don't let me down!"

Hearing the door slam, her husband sank into a chair. Flora buried her face in her hands.

~ ~ ~

Lieutenant Schmid found his driver where he had left him. "Next stop," he commanded.

"Yes, Sir," came a perky reply.

Schmid glared at the private. "What's with you?"

"Nothing, Sir. Just a beautiful city. And the people are so nice."

"What do you mean, nice? It's Loches. You don't know shit."

"I suppose. But I just met the loveliest girl. She didn't seem to have a care in the world and was entirely unaffected by my being German.

Had the cutest bicycle, too."

Schmid kept scowling at his driver while his brain churned. Despite the unlikelihood, he had to ask.

"This girl. How old?"

"Oh, um, I'd say seventeen...maybe twenty. It's hard to say."

"Pretty?"

"Oh yes, Sir. Or cute. No, I'd say she was pretty *and* cute."

"Long black hair?"

"Yes. Wavy too. Do you know her, Sir?"

Schmid ignored the question. "What about the bicycle? White basket? A bell?"

"Yes, Sir. And saddlebags. I take it you know her."

Schmid sat staring at the dash. *It can't be. How can the girl west of Bléré be in Loches the next day? Even if she somehow got here, why? But it must be. There can't be two of them.*

"When did she leave?" he barked.

"Maybe ten minutes ago."

"Did she say where?"

"No, Sir. Just said she was sightseeing."

"Which way?"

"Off that way," his driver said, pointing.

"Of course, you idiot! Which way *after* she got off the grass?"

"Um, she went right, Sir. Right. Headed back down the hill. I'm almost sure of it."

The possibility of it being her both puzzled and exhilarated him. He'd thought of her nonstop since their encounter on the country road yesterday.

His driver sped down the hill, and Schmid had him zig-zagging up and down every street. After twenty minutes of fruitless searching for her, he gave up.

"Verdammt! She never said where she was going?" he asked again.

"No, Sir."

He thought out loud. "She could be leaving. Maybe heading north? If her, she mentioned Bléré." Having other matters to tend to rankled him.

Schmid's driver resumed his role of the hapless scapegoat.

CHAPTER THIRTY-ONE
Amboise
April 24, Afternoon

GEORGES HAD HEARD enough and decided to press Marcel and Henri. Anger was building in the cell and needed addressing one way or another. The Nazis killed Roland Viard, and there was still no word about his wife and son. Retaliation, retribution, and revenge were at the forefront of their minds.

"I already told you what I think," Henri fumed. "We need to find who's responsible and cut off their balls! Or we target somebody high-profile. That new major comes to mind."

"Come on!" Marcel snapped. "We do that, and the Gestapo...hell, the entire German army, will be on us like flies on shit. They won't stop until they ferret out every one of us and our families and dump us in a mass grave. But only after the torturing and public display."

"What can we do?" asked Georges. "The anger and frustration's growing, and I'm worried someone will do something stupid."

"But they're right," Henri interjected. "We can't just say, 'Oh, well, poor Roland,' and do nothing!"

"No, you're both right," Marcel agreed. "We need a plan that settles them down before somebody messes up and gets the entire lot of us shut down or killed. But first, we need to get everyone on the same page and stem this by reassuring them we're working on a plan. And they need to know that going rogue or running off their mouths would be disastrous. Let's do two smaller meetings. Georges, I need you to make the arrangements. "

"Of course, but we need a plan. It will be out of our hands if we don't do something soon."

Marcel nodded. "Whatever we do, it needs to look like an accident. At the very least, a random act. Anything that targets specific officers will have us hiding out the rest of the war."

"What about messing with the rail lines?" Henri offered up with a gleam in his eyes. "The derailment near here in January sure caused a mess. And just last month, a line was sabotaged in Pas-de-Calais. It doesn't guarantee an eye for an eye, but it could sure mess things up."

"It's not bad," said Georges, "and the idea's gaining steam across the country. But they're damn quick at repairing rail. Targeting the switching equipment might prove more effective. Anyway, it's probably best for tactical blows like interrupting freight movements. I've heard they're integrating civilian cars into troop trains to discourage rail attacks."

"Bastards will do anything!" Henri was getting more heated as they spoke. "Do they strap babies to the front too?"

"Let me know what works or doesn't work for you both," Georges said. "I'll plan the meetings."

VIOLETTE WAS NERVOUS but exhilarated at the idea of spying on the unwelcome intruders—and she wasn't about to let Madame Menier down. She performed her duties with added purpose, detouring into rooms where Germans gathered, intent on eavesdropping on them. It was easier than expected. All that was needed was to go about her daily routine. Often, she'd have the kitchen staff provide her with tea, coffee, or food trays so she'd have reason to enter their circles. That they found her attractive, liked her pleasant demeanor, and were ignorant of her grasp of their language made it even easier. She felt disappointed if hours passed with nothing significant reaching her eyes and ears. Nevertheless, she enjoyed the practice and began catching on to their accents and jargon.

Shortly after dinner, her ears perked when she brought a replenished box of cigars into a sitting room. Officers were relaxing and casually chatting when she heard it. It wasn't a German word but a name: Giselle Dubois. *That's Colette's last name!* Inventing excuses to stay within earshot, she continued listening. The French woman they spoke of was on her way to Orléans by a lieutenant's orders. The matter seemed trifling to them, and their conversation quickly moved on. But it was enough. At last, there was something to report. Her heart raced, and it was all she could do to exit the room gracefully.

CHAPTER THIRTY-THREE
Return Crossing at Bléré
April 24, Late Afternoon

SHE HAD NO doubt that River's wife told Lieutenant Schmid about the girl with the bicycle. Even if she didn't, Colette worried his car would drive up from behind at any moment during her return from Loches. The veterinary tale wouldn't hold up under scrutiny. She debated whether to get to the crossing as fast as possible or take less-traveled roads. Unfurling her map, it looked like there would be little lost time if she veered northeast toward Luzillé and then northwest back to Bléré. Going that way, the main road could be avoided almost altogether. Schmid's driver mentioned they had more appointments in Loches, so she was hopeful.

The country roads on her chosen route were mainly deserted. Nearing Bléré, she steered her bicycle behind some trees. The guards were so easily won over yesterday that keeping it consistent made sense. She changed into the same cream dress she'd worn, tucked some hair under her sage-colored hat, and slipped into her floral shoes. She biked toward the checkpoint, keeping off the main route as long as possible. Like the day before, everyone was heading south. To her relief, Ralf and Dieter were manning the checkpoint.

At the crossing yesterday, she suspected she looked too friendly with them. Today, she would be cordial but wouldn't dawdle, wary that Schmid might be coming.

The two guards had their backs to her. Each was busy inspecting and processing those trying to cross into free France. Riding up from behind, she announced her arrival with three bell rings. Ralf and Dieter stopped what they were doing, turned, and grinned ear-to-ear. She raised a hand, acknowledging them. They rushed to dote on her.

"Hi, boys," she said after looking over her shoulder.

"We were worried we might not see you!" Ralf blurted.

"I told him not to worry. I knew you'd come," Dieter boasted.

"I'm sorry, men," she said, looking dejected. " I had no time to grab a treat for you."

"Oh, that's okay," they said in unison.

"We're just glad to see you," Ralf continued. "How's the horse?"

"I gave them instructions. She'll be fine."

Colette was already uncomfortable with the delay, anxious to get out of sight. Her concern was warranted.

~ ~ ~

Lieutenant Schmid saw the southbound queue from a distance. "What the hell's the delay up there?" he griped to his driver.

"Sir, both guards are processing someone going north."

"Lay on the horn. Light a fire under their asses."

"It's...It's a woman on a bicycle, Sir."

"What?"

"Different clothes, though. It must be somebody else." The driver squinted. "Although I think I see a white basket and sidesaddles. Now she's pedaling away."

Schmid reached across his driver and leaned on the horn. "Verdammt! Get there!"

He was sure it was her, and she was getting away. She passed the line of people heading south and turned left, disappearing from view. They skidded to a halt at the gate.

"You fools! Didn't you hear us?" Schmid hollered. The two guards stood ramrod straight with their right arms extended. "Who was that?" he demanded.

"Sir?" stammered the dark-haired one.

"The girl on the bicycle, you moron! What's her name?" The guards looked at each other, and Schmid realized neither could answer the simple question. "Don't tell me," he fumed. "It's right there on her papers. What did her papers say, you idiots?" he ended in a roar.

The younger guard seemed paralyzed. His comrade fumbled a reply. "Uh, Sir, she darted past us when we looked away. We didn't have a chance to—"

"What the hell was that girl doing down here?" Schmid ranted.

"A sick horse, Sir," the blond guard finally sputtered. "Tending to a sick horse."

"Raise that damn gate!" Schmid screamed. "I'll be back to deal with you two later!"

CHAPTER THIRTY-FOUR
Amboise
April 24, Early Evening

HENRI FLAMAND WORRIED about the upcoming rendezvous with River Man. Not only might his hatred for the man be unleashed, but he feared the Nazis might know about their package transfer spot on the Cher.

"You do realize I hate the man?" he griped.

Marcel was forced to acknowledge it. "I do, but I need you there. We can't change everything. He'd get suspicious. And when he learns he's making the trip for nothing, he'll be cranky enough."

"Two men that hate each other meeting in the dark of night. Aren't I the lucky one?"

"Henri, you'll be the bigger man down there. Just tell him what we've talked about. Hell, you can even throw in an apology if it—"

"What! There's no way I'm apologizing to that traitor!"

"Hey, he'll get his due when the time's right. We stay the course and learn more for Colette's sake and ours. Tonight must go according to plan. Our plan. I need you to make that happen."

Henri heard an uncommon agitation in Marcel's voice. He settled himself and agreed to be professional. Marcel patted him on the back.

CHAPTER THIRTY-FIVE
Bléré
April 24, Evening

IT WAS PHILIPPE'S role to relay Colette's findings to Smith. He spent most of the day pacing in his flat. As her expected arrival time neared, he rarely blinked while staring out the window. At last, he saw her expedient crossing and pumped his fist. Now, watching events unfold, he wasn't sure what was happening. Her left turn down the first street made little sense. It was the wrong way. And why was she making such a mad dash of it? *Don't draw attention to yourself!*

A gut feeling made him grab for the binoculars. An animated conversation followed by a car speeding into Bléré was clear enough. She was being tailed—maybe chased. The car turned down the same street she had. Philippe ran from the room.

Doing his best to appear casual, he looked down the main roadway, hoping to see her or the car—fearful of seeing both together. Instinct told him she'd work back toward the town center, where there were more hiding places. He soon spotted her crossing an intersection, partially obscured by a handful of people. There was no bicycle now, and she was only a block away. He tried his best to look calm while speed-walking to close the gap.

Turning a corner, he saw her walking away like she was late for a luncheon. She stopped twice near shop entries and glanced his way. He made a small gesture to get her attention, but knew pedestrians wouldn't be her focus. She ducked into a shop. Looking back, he saw the car heading his way—her way. The vehicle continued to troll at the same speed. *They didn't see her. Ditching the bike was smart.* As it neared, a woman with a bag of groceries hesitated at the intersection. A rule-breaking thought flashed through his head. He ignored all traffic and drew attention to himself.

"Here, Madame, let me help you with that."

He grabbed the bag, took her hand, and marched into the street. It slipped from his grip, the contents spilling into the street. The car skid to a stop.

"Get out of the way!"

Schmid reached over and blared the horn as the woman cowered. Philippe feigned surprise and waved frantically as if apologizing, but remained on his hands and knees, acting eager to pick things up. He thrust items into the woman's hands to ensure she fumbled them. She did.

"ARGHH! THIS WAY!" Schmid cried. His driver turned hard left, nearly sideswiping a truck. "You French fuckers are all FUCKING IDIOTS!"

Philippe calmly picked up the remaining groceries and assisted the woman across the street. She gave him a bewildered look. He apologized profusely, pulled some coins from his pocket, and dropped them into her bag.

Down the street, he entered the store he'd last seen Colette slip into. There was no sign of her anywhere. "Damn." He stood puzzled, unsure where to go next.

"Psst. I saw all of that. Poor woman."

He closed his eyes at the sweet sound of her voice. Tingles coursed through his body. Turning, he was baffled to see nobody there.

Another whisper. "You were amazing."

He looked up. "Holy!"

She stood motionless on a mannequin platform: a different dress, blond wig, a brimmed hat pulled low to her eyes, hand on hip with her left knee slightly bent.

"Do you like her?" she asked in a seductive voice. Her eyes didn't blink. Her lips didn't move.

"Um, I think I love her. But I'd better get her out of here!"

She jumped down and rushed to the proprietress. "I'll bring it all back as soon as I can. Merci. Merci, beaucoup!" The woman smiled without looking up.

Philippe motioned for Colette to wait, stepped outside, and looked both ways. Keeping a casual but keen eye on their surroundings, he occasionally slipped into storefronts and peeked back at the streets. Still trolling, Schmid's car crossed the intersection straight ahead and perpendicular to their path. Philippe waited.

"Who the hell is it?" he asked.

"Schmid."

"Schmid! How long's he been after you?"

"Just now. He was coming up behind me at the crossing."

"But why is he—" Seeing an opening, he grabbed Colette's hand and led on. After four nerve-wracking blocks, they slipped into a building and up some stairs.

"Where are we?"

"My flat. We rent it from time to time. The owner's one of us."

They entered a stark room. The only open curtains were at the window he'd become accustomed to staring out. Next to it was a small table with two folding chairs. On an adjacent wall was a kitchenette with a tiny sink but little else. A roughly made bed was squeezed into the space beside it. He told Colette about the shared washroom down the hall.

"It isn't ideal for discretion, but there's a metal washtub if you don't mind rust or having others walk in on you."

"Are there others in the building?"

"We keep this floor clear. Now, what the hell happened out there?"

"I'll tell you. But I'm starving. What have you got?"

"Home cooking, it's not."

He hurried to the window-side table, closed the curtains, set a pair of binoculars aside, and began removing the accumulated clutter. He plopped everything onto the already-congested counter next to the sink full of dirty dishes.

"I've got two clean mugs. I only have water. I downed all the wine earlier," he joked.

"Fill both. I'm parched. You can use a dirty one."

He drummed up what he hoped was enough and set it on the table, unable to pry his eyes off her as she devoured the food. Twice, she looked up, saw him watching her, and continued stuffing her mouth.

"There's some news I need to pass along," he said. "But, first, I'm dying to hear about your journey and what just happened out there. Hell, I spoke with Smith and heard about your encounter on the road with Schmid yesterday. What's going on?"

"I'm not even sure where to begin," she garbled, soggy cracker crumbs spilling from her mouth. "I need to get to the blacksmith. There's so much to relay."

"It's my job to do the relaying, and Schmid's looking for you, not me. It's not safe out there. You have a long night ahead and won't be good to yourself or anyone else without rest."

"Believe me, that sounds wonderful, but people are expecting me!"

"Time is tight. Nobody's expecting you, and I'll relay everything."

She mulled it over. "Maybe you're right. I do need some sleep. Where did you say the washroom is?"

He was still itching to hear about everything, but couldn't deny her request. "Down the hall on the left. The plain door with no numbers."

Fifteen minutes went by. He was getting nervous. Not wanting to intrude but compelled to check on her, he tapped twice on the door. No answer. He knocked louder and cracked it open.

"Who is it?" he heard.

"It's me, silly. Are you alright?"

"Yes. You can come in." He didn't see her at first. "Over here." Around the corner, he found her immersed in a tub of steaming water. "No soap, but I couldn't resist. I was filthy, and it feels like heaven. Any chance you have a towel?"

"Uhh..." He scanned the room. "I don't think so. Will this do?" He removed his shirt, set it next to the tub, and turned his back to her.

"Won't that just get me dirty again?"

"Oh, you're funny."

"Okay, give me a second."

"Uh-huh." He heard swirling and splashing water and imagined it streaming down her naked body.

"I'm ready."

He turned. She was draped in his wet shirt, seemingly unconcerned about fastening the top three buttons.

"Well," she said, pulling a floppy sleeve back to reveal her hand. "Will you help me?"

"Oh, right." He assisted her out, water cascading to the floor. "After you," he murmured, motioning to the door.

Stepping inside the flat, he pulled the door shut. She turned and planted her lips on his. He spun her against the door and yanked the shirt over her head. She grabbed his arm and pulled him to the bed.

~ ~ ~

Philippe planned on waking her soon, but suspected the aromas drifting about would awaken her senses and inspire her to get up. Wrapped in a blanket, she came up behind him and nibbled his neck.

"Smells amazing. What is it?"

"I stepped out to get something more worthy of you. Not sure I succeeded, but I hope you like it."

"You're so good to me."

"It's nothing."

"No," she said, pressing her lips to his ear. "You are *SO* good to me."

He pecked her cheek. "It's almost ready."

While she ate, he explained that her messages to Smith yesterday had been passed along. Marcel and the others were shocked to learn she'd run into Schmid near the river, but gushed at how she handled it. Although it sickened them, her findings confirmed that the lieutenant and River Man were connected. He told her the team had deciphered the tree markings and how they were River Man's way of relaying the dates, times, and number of passengers.

She looked upward, envisioning it. "I see it. The rat!"

"While you were sleeping, I visited Smith. I said you were with me, and I'd get back to him with your findings in Loches."

"There's plenty, and I need you to get the word out fast."

While eating, she filled him in on everything she'd been through. When he wasn't mesmerized listening, he asked questions.

"Schmid and the Gagnons," he said at last. "It makes me sick thinking about it. We were fools."

"Philippe, they can't move anybody else."

"It's already on hold, thanks to you. And what you learned in Loches confirms everything." He pulled a slip of paper with strange markings from his pocket and reviewed it. "I got news from Smith. He got it straight from Marcel."

"It's odd looking. What is it?"

"Just my way of remembering without writing things down. It feels safer that way."

"Any word about my mother?"

"No. I'm sorry. They're still working on it. Smith's an admirer of your father, you know."

"Yes, he told me. Where in the world is she?"

"Your father will find her. If he doesn't, Louis will," he grinned.

"I'm getting more worried every day."

"I know. There *is* something you'll be pleased about, though. I heard Monsieur Touchard is meeting with the team in Amboise right now, but he's been tending to your animals."

"Oh, thank heavens! I'd forgotten. How could I?" she moaned.

"You've been a little busy. Anyway, he's training to be a forger. The need is growing, and Marcel suggested your home as a good spot for him to lay low and work. There's more."

He went over changes for the night. When finished, he asked her to repeat everything. Not only to confirm she understood it all but to be sure he hadn't missed conveying any of his notes.

"So, I get that there won't be a passenger on the boat," she started, "but why wouldn't they want to know who's meeting the passengers at the drop? It was part of the plan. I can find that out."

"Well, it was, but they've reconsidered. The motorcycles, or someone, could be waiting for the boat by the time you get there. And if Schmid is there tonight, we can't risk it. The danger's higher now that he knows you. There's no way you can be seen in the area again. If seen, you're caught. And if you're caught...well, that can't happen."

"But we covered all this. It's why I'm getting there so early. Father said the motorcycles weren't at the passenger drop. River Man signaled them by flashlight upstream at the final landing."

"Maybe. But that's just one time we know about. They've made the decision, and I agree with it. Better safe and helpful than caught. And there's a chain of command. If we start disobeying orders and going off script, lives are at stake."

"I know, I know. But is there another way of finding out?"

"Short of sneaking around and following River blindly in the dark after they split up, I don't see it. The crucial thing is what's happening at the last landing. From what you've told me, it has everything to do with Schmid. How you'll get near enough to see or hear what's going on is what worries me."

"I've got some ideas," she said.

He sighed. "To be honest, we're sick about your safety. Some of us wanted to cancel the rest of the assignment."

"What?" she objected. "I'm the only one who knows firsthand exactly where and what's happening. We need to learn more!"

"I know. We all know. That's why the plan's going forward despite well-founded concerns."

"I'll be leery as a lamb at Easter. I promise." She paused. "Philippe? I don't think I should use the bicycle."

"I agree. I've been thinking the same thing."

"It was a great idea, honestly. It worked perfectly when I first ran into the lieutenant and then again at the crossing."

"Say no more. I get it. Too recognizable. But we need a way to get you out there tonight."

"I'll have to walk. Both ways. I don't see another option. It's probably an hour."

"I don't know. It's too far. Then, an hour back? I don't like it. You'd have to leave sooner and be in the open longer. Curfew's a big enough concern." He stewed on it. "Let me run out and see if I can drum something up."

He had her lock the door behind him. Forty minutes later, he returned with good news.

"I passed along your findings from Loches to Smith. And I detailed your harrowing return at the crossing, Schmid's search for you here in town, and any revised thoughts for tonight. He's passing the word up to Amboise right away."

"Oh, good." She leaned in and whispered, "Did you tell him we had great...you know?"

He chuckled nervously. "Okay, um...no, I somehow forgot. But I did fill him in on the bicycle problem."

"I see. Strictly business, huh?"

Philippe looked her in the eye and shook his head. "Smith wanted to strip it down, but we couldn't find it anywhere. I suspect some kid is making good use of it. He set me up with an old, battered bike instead. At least it works and will cut time off your trip. We're doing a mix...walk in the city, bike in the country. I'll show you."

He marked on her map where he'd left it just outside town. She could dump the old thing if it was no longer needed.

"Ah, almost forgot." He emptied a bag onto the bed. "It's nice outside tonight. No wind, and not cold. But it'll still feel cool after being out there for a while. I grabbed these for you. Not to mention, a change of disguise is needed."

Colette shuffled through a pile of clothes and held up a leather, fur-lined jacket. "This is perfect. And I'd rather not wear the wig I took from the shop. This hat here will hide my hair."

Philippe instinctively turned his back as she dropped the blanket from her shoulders and changed into them. He walked her downstairs to the door, kissed her on both cheeks, and squeezed her.

She pressed her lips to his ear. "When we meet again, I have a favor I'd like to return."

CHAPTER THIRTY-SIX
West of Bléré
April 24, 11:30 pm

COLETTE SET OUT after curfew to find the bicycle Philippe had hidden. Bléré looked like a ghost town; every sound and movement was amplified. Whether warranted or not, it took her five minutes to get the nerve to cross the main street through town. Afterward, she stayed on back ways and narrow streets.

Finding the bicycle in the dark took longer than she had hoped, but there it was. Philippe's 'old' description was an understatement. Alone with only her thoughts, her heart raced, and she tried settling her nerves. Three times she aborted her departure, imagining somebody was approaching. *Come on, silly. It's just dark—dark's good. Okay, here we go.* The rustic thing managed to do its job, but the creaks and rattles added to her stress.

To her right, the Cher glided alongside as she pedaled toward the rowboat landing. She followed the same route west of town as yesterday, though that seemed forever ago. The upcoming dam was a site Henri warned about. Though not a crossing into Vichy, Germans would be patrolling it, wary of nighttime saboteurs.

The bike's general noise-making kept her on edge. One option was to stash it before getting near the dam and walking the remaining distance. It wasn't a bad idea and probably safe, but she'd be without it, and it might come in handy later. Instead, she carried it further downstream until all was pitch black again.

Every flying bug, croaking toad, or looming tree spooked her. *Settle down.* She figured whoever was in charge would likely come from Bléré. The motorcycle that her father said went south would have to turn west or continue over fields. She hid her bicycle beyond where Auguste met the motorcycles, slipped her watch on, and walked to the river to search for hiding places. It was dark everywhere, but headlights and flashlights could quickly end that. Her eyes were adapting to the blackness, but no place looked ideal. An unappealing thought struck her. A narrow, dense strip of vegetation lined the bank between the road and the river. It was a couple of meters wide at most. The problem was that they'd be right on top of her. She'd hear them if they as much as whispered. That was good. But if she broke a sweat, they might smell her.

Finding a tiny gap in the brush, she worked along the water's edge, seeking the best spot. The thick growth was impractical for anyone to get through. Long blades of dead grass from the prior year drooped toward the shoreline and could cover her like a blanket. The river was high, but she found a dry area and settled in. If they discovered her, it wouldn't be from being seen. She raised the watch to her eyes and turned her wrist back and forth, trying to read it. Time passed slowly.

The faint whinnying of a distant horse startled her. *Maybe it's in a field.* She strained to hear more but got nothing. Minutes later, she froze at the sound of footsteps on the gravel road and envisioned River Man arriving to make his downstream trip. The sound of crunching gravel grew louder. She expected to hear snapping sticks or rustling leaves as he veered into the woods to fetch the boat. Instead, the steps grew nearer. He was right above her. Then came a light noise, like the sound of—*Merde, he's pissing.* She didn't get splattered, but her mindset switched. *Disgusting.* It stopped. She heard gravel crunching, then twigs snapping. *He's heading down the path.*

CHAPTER THIRTY-SEVEN
The River Cher
April 25, 2:00 am

HENRI WAS IN a foul mood. He wasn't looking forward to the rendezvous but promised Marcel he'd be on his best behavior. "I'd rather it be raining," he grumbled to himself.

It was the same place on the Cher where he and Marcel waited for Auguste nine nights ago. They exchanged signals shortly after two, and the rowboat soon pulled alongside the muddy flat. Before the oars were secured, Henri could see Auguste's brain spinning.

"Where's Marcel?" he asked, his nervous eyes darting about. "Where's the package?"

"There's a last-minute change. It's only me."

"What the hell do you mean?" River nearly shouted. "Where's the big fish you said was worth my while?"

"Shh. Shut up, and I'll tell you," Henri said, trying to keep his cool. "The fish is alive but not doing well," he lied. "He may not make it." He suspected Auguste would relay that information, which might ease or even eliminate the hunt for the pilot. "The Nazis are thick, so it's probably for the best."

"What? For the best? Are you telling me I risked my ass coming down here in the middle of the night for nothing? How am I going to explain it to— "

"Keep it down," Henri demanded. "What do you mean?"

"Uh, to the transfer team. They'll be waiting. What am I supposed to say happened?"

"Tell them what I told you, damn it. They'll understand. We're all making sacrifices. They're not in it for the money like you." Henri reached into his jacket pocket. "I figured you'd be all bent about it. Marcel told me to give you this for your troubles."

He placed a crumpled tissue in River's hand. Unwrapping it, Auguste held it near his eye and turned the diamond between his thumb and index finger.

"Well," his voice softened, "tell him I said thank you. Where did you get it?"

"I couldn't say. And you need to know that things are picking up. We have our biggest move yet. Don't ask how or why, because I don't know, but a British spy and an American officer are somehow tied together on this. The Nazis don't know shit about it. We can't have them hunting like they are for the pilot, and we've got to move them fast." He continued to improvise. "Oh, and Marcel wanted me to tell you they'll pay double your normal fee." River Man raised his eyebrows. "Don't get greedy," Henri went on. "It's just this once." He had Auguste's full attention.

"Hey, I'm here to help however I can," River said. "When do you need me?"

"Three nights. The twenty-eighth. But we need to start an hour earlier. One o'clock instead of two. Can you make that happen for us?"

"I can, and I will," Auguste said.

The false patriotic rhetoric was almost more than Henri could stomach. "One other problem. We may need to get a third person onto that boat of yours. They could have a guide or translator with them. I'm not sure yet."

The third person he referred to was as fictitious as the other two. He got the idea while waiting and was curious how the markings on the tree might look if the count was uncertain.

"That's a full load, but I can make it work if they aren't weighed down with too much crap."

"They travel light," Henri ad-libbed.

"Okay. The twenty-eighth at one. Two or three passengers. Got it."

Henri helped push the boat off and glared as Auguste Gagnon pulled on the oars and disappeared upstream.

~ ~ ~

Don't let me down! Schmid's words in Loches tormented Auguste the entire return trip. He tried calculating how best to temper the man's wrath. The news about the upcoming transfer of a British spy and an American was his only chance. The more he rowed, the more he hoped it could save him.

Approaching the first landing, he spotted his wife pacing. He knew she dreaded it. They both hated pretending to care for these people—and that was with fleeing civilians. The prospect of interacting with a combatant had made her a nervous wreck the entire day. He felt relieved, knowing her night was about to become uneventful. *We won't get the money, but she'll be pleased.* He was right.

Upon landing and explaining it to her, Flora slumped her head. "Thank God," she heaved. "I've been a mess all night."

"I know. I'm sorry. I'm dreading Schmid, but he'll feel better when I tell him what's coming in three nights."

His wife shook her head. "I don't know, Auguste. The man's reactionary. Don't count on him rejoicing."

Auguste only grunted, knowing she was right. He sat down in the boat, looked up at her, and gave a reluctant pull on the oars.

~ ~ ~

Not far upstream, Colette remained hidden near the river's edge. The Cher flowed noiselessly past as though aware of Mother Nature's preferred rest time. The black stillness was making a good impression, and she made herself a promise to get outside more often after dark. She could see that La Mère de la Terre had much to offer between sundown and sunrise.

Her eyes were shut, hoping it might sensitize her hearing. A wave of panic hit her when a faint rumble filled her ears. She scolded and encouraged herself simultaneously. *Come on, you expected this. Relax and listen. It's a good hiding place.* Headlights lit up the trees. Her father said the motorcycles appeared after Auguste signaled them. This was different. He hadn't returned from the woods yet—and it wasn't motorcycles. A car stopped at the road bend and sat idling. *It's fine. It's good. I'll hear voices over the engine. It'll drown out other sounds.*

The engine stopped, and all went dark again. A door opened and closed. Someone was walking into the woods. *That's not right.* She had to think. *I won't hear what's happening.* Following was too risky; if anyone stayed with the car, they might spot her.

She moved inches at a time to get to her knees and peer through the brush. She couldn't see anybody. Hidden by the grass and brush, she could make her way along the river's edge, hoping to get close enough to overhear them. Unfortunately, she had no idea what obstacles she'd encounter. The choice between caution and obligation consumed her, but not for long. Staying low, she checked her footing and headed for the landing, hugging the shoreline.

The night was again dead silent. It worried her but would also help her hear better. The dense grass and shrub cover soon gave way to only trees, and she paused with each step to listen and feel the ground with her foot. There was no sign of anyone yet, but she was sure she was nearing the landing. Hearing the clunk of oars downstream, she knelt behind a tree—the tar-black Cher lapping at her heels.

River Man pulled the old boat onto the shore and dragged it to the usual spot. She soon heard scratching noises and envisioned him carving new marks in the tree.

"I don't have all night."

Her heart nearly stopped. The voice was clear as day—and the pitch and condescending tone were unmistakable.

"Jesus, you startled me," River blabbered.

"No, not Jesus," came the caustic retort. "Sir will suffice." A shadow stepped from behind a tree. "It's about time I got Holtzer on my good side, and this will do it. I brought a little extra for you. Don't get used to it, but I thought it might keep a slimeball like you eager and dishonest."

"Sir." Auguste hesitated.

"What is it?"

"He's been injured and can't travel. It sounds like he won't survive. They only just told me at the pickup."

"Hold it. What? Who?" Schmid snapped, and then the realization hit him. "You didn't bring him? You didn't fucking bring him?"

"He wasn't there. They didn't bring him to me, and—"

"What are you saying? Tell me you're joking! No, of course not."

"Sir. Sir, I do have good news."

"Good news? There's no good news. I just wasted an entire fucking night coming out here for nothing!"

"Sir, I think you'll like this."

"For your sake, I sure as hell better, Gagnon."

"There's a new date. Soon too. And it's even bigger."

"Bigger? What do you mean?"

"A British spy and an American officer."

Colette could hear the hope in River's voice as he gave the news.

"Together? The same time?"

"Yes, Sir."

"When?"

"Tuesday. One hour earlier. I just marked the tree."

"Who are they? You said an American officer. Army?"

"I don't have the details, but it's big. They say the Germans know nothing of it."

Colette kept still as the night, listening to every word. River Man was a traitor in every possible way, and the people he'd been transporting were likely getting tortured, killed, or both. And for God's sake, he was likely getting rich from it—paid by his passengers *and* the Nazis.

Without warning, mud under her right foot gave way, and her leg splashed into the water. She froze. The interruption in their conversation was a bad sign. A beam of light swept her way. Running wasn't an option. Her only choice was to slink back into the water.

The icy cold shocked her entirety, and the heavy current took over. Attempting to swim or scramble ashore wasn't an option. Struggling would give her away. The river swept her away in seconds. Trying to float on her back to ride with it was a mistake. Her hat was torn off; her soaked clothes began pulling her under. Removing her shoes was impossible, but her fur-lined jacket was the bigger problem. Contorting in every way, she finally dunked herself underwater and wriggled out of it. The current rushed her downstream and further from the shore. She swam for her life and hoped the struggle was out of earshot.

A small branch brushed her head. In the blackness, she never saw it coming. Her face slammed into a large limb jutting far into the river. She was sucked under. Her hand shot up, grasping for anything, but found nothing. Her head popped up, and her lungs gasped for air.

"Uhhn!"

Her torso slammed into a submerged log. The Cher tried equally hard to push her over and under it. Neither worked, so it threw its full might against her. She was in trouble and had to do something. Over and under were the same. Either way, she'd be swept downstream and farther from the shore. The rushing water made it impossible to plant her feet. She fought the current and inched to her left. With each attempt to move, the river seemed determined to prevent it.

A dry offshoot stuck out of the water. It was almost within reach. She lunged, clutched it with her left hand, and pulled with any remaining strength. It snapped. The torrent pulled her under before she could breathe. She again flailed a hand in hopes of finding something. A thin, wet branch sliced her palm. She threw her other hand up and found another, slightly thicker. It held. Coughing up water, she inched toward a sturdy limb. Minutes seemed like hours before she made it to shore and collapsed. Her relief was short-lived. Still coughing, soaking wet, nearly frozen, and unsheltered, she understood the need to do something fast.

"Louis might have done better at that," she muttered through chattering teeth.

~ ~ ~

Back upstream, Auguste followed Schmid's order to investigate the sound. He pulled out his flashlight, shined it all around, and returned.

"It might have been a fish, bird, or some other animal. There's nothing there," he reported.

"Mmm," Schmid grumbled without pursuing it further. "Well, there's nothing more to do. This might work. Meet me again in Loches the day after tomorrow. Same time."

Given Schmid's softened tone, Auguste remained hopeful. "Yes,

Sir! The day after tomorrow." He hesitated. "Uh, do you mean the twenty-sixth or twenty-seventh, Sir? I mean, technically, it's just turned the twenty-fifth."

"For your sake, this better not happen again," Schmid called back.

Auguste didn't press it. To be safe, he resigned himself to going to Loches on the twenty-sixth, too. He followed well back of Schmid and heard the tires kick up rock as the car wheeled around and sped off toward Bléré. He lumbered back to the road, aware his night could have gone far worse.

~ ~ ~

The options whirled through Colette's head. Her clothes were soaked. Returning to get shelter under the overturned boat wouldn't be enough. She wanted to recheck the markings on the tree, but it was too risky, and she was in no condition to try. Dashing back to Bléré on the bicycle was also too dangerous. Curfew was one problem, and maybe the least of them. Unconvincing answers were likely if she got stopped and confronted with questions. She thought of the old cottage she'd passed the day before. It was around the corner from her bike and her best chance to get warm.

Stripping down, she wrung water out of everything as best she could before putting the clammy clothes back on. She felt her way south through the woods, away from the river. The dirt road couldn't be far. Finally finding it, she ran eastward, barely able to make out the road's edge. She guessed the cottage would be vacant, or River Man wouldn't have his landing so near to it.

After running for several cautious minutes, the house ahead loomed dark and looked deserted. An old trick Louis taught her sprang into her head. She gathered three medium-sized stones from the roadside and crept behind a row of shrubs. Holding the rocks in her left hand, she practiced throwing motions with her right. Now, doing her best not to shiver, she threw them in quick succession. It sounded like somebody knocking. A curtain in a corner room glowed faintly. Her heart sank. She stayed crouched and peered through a small gap in the bushes. The front door flew open. An older man pointing a shotgun stepped onto the stoop.

"Who's there!" he hollered.

He looked eager to discharge the weapon as his head swiveled back and forth. The door slammed shut. Hearing two bolts latch, Colette filled her lungs. It dawned on her: The cottage might not need to be vacant if River Man knew the owner.

The shivering wouldn't stop. It wasn't freezing out, and the air was calm, but the wet clothes had taken a toll. She had to keep moving.

CHAPTER THIRTY-EIGHT
Stuttgart, Germany
April 25, 3:30 am

ANITA HOLTZER WOKE her daughter in the middle of the night. At four years old, Sonja had seen hundreds of trains—perhaps a hundred too few. She shot out of bed like Christmas morning and had yet to slow down.

"Mama, when can we see the train?"

"If you don't stop squirming, we may never see it. Now sit still so I can finish putting this bow in your hair. Your father will be pleased to see it on you."

"It's so bright. Pink is my new favorite color. I look pretty in it, don't I?"

Anita Holtzer leaned back, tilted her head, and tweaked the big bow again. "There."

"Don't I, Mama?"

"Oh, I'm sure you'd look pretty in any color, but you look lovely."

Sonja swished her head back and forth to see if it would stay put. Her blond locks swayed from side to side.

"I've never been up this early, have I, Mama? Or is it late?"

"It's both, dear. But let's say it's early since we just woke up."

"Is it far to see Papa?"

"Tours is quite far, but remember, we stop in Paris first."

"I remember. I can hardly wait to see it. Is it far too?"

"Not as far, but we'll have to revisit it. We won't be there long enough to see it properly."

A tall man in his thirties stepped into the room. His gray woolen suit was well-tailored, his black shoes polished, and his fingernails recently manicured.

"Anita, we're ready whenever you are."

"Thank you, Thomas. We're coming." She motioned with her eyes toward her daughter. "Finally."

A uniformed man opened the back door of the waiting car; Anita, Sonja, and Thomas climbed in. The station in Stuttgart was only three kilometers away, but Sonja asked her mother incessant questions about everything they passed. Anita was used to it and instinctively knew if she needed to appease her daughter with an answer or if the child was talking aloud in wonderment.

"Uncle Thomas, will Papa be awake when I get there?"

"Oh, I think you can count on it."

Sonja seemed content and went back to staring out the window.

"You've only just got back, and here we are leaving you," said Anita, brushing lint off his shoulder. "We never even talked about where you went. Sonja missed you so much, and I never know when we'll see you again."

"Ah, we both know I'll be the last thing on her mind long before you reach the border."

Anita smirked. "You're probably right. There's a whole world out there with no idea they should be bracing for her arrival."

Throughout much of southern Germany, train stations were a frenetic hub of activity during the day but, so far, managed to get a reprieve in the late-night hours. The terminal at Stuttgart was no different. Three apprehensive-looking men in uniform approached as the car came to a stop.

Climbing out, Anita felt a twinge of embarrassment.

"Thomas, must we have all this?"

"If you were going shopping in Munich, I'd say no. But you're traveling across France today and—"

"Yes, I know where we're going," she said in an exaggerated tone. "It just seems a little—"

"Viktor wouldn't take it too well hearing that his wife and daughter were fending for themselves on a trip across France...if you know what I mean."

She heaved. "Okay, my husband may be over the top about many things, but he's usually well-intentioned. Honestly, he's not as fearsome as everyone seems to think."

"I'm inclined to agree with you, but warranted or not, his reputation does put people on edge."

It began to drizzle. Thomas opened an umbrella and held it over her. She moved closer to share it.

"Oh, I do so wish you could come along. You make it more comfortable for us, and Sonja loves it when you do."

"I'm sorry I can't this time, but—"

"I know, I know. I'm being selfish. And you must love the peace."

He snickered. "On the contrary. I'll be counting the hours until I see you both again."

"Well, please don't bother counting. I'm uncertain when we'll return, but I'll send word as soon as I know."

He nodded. "Fair enough."

"And someday," she said, adjusting his collar, "I'm picking out a new coat and hat for you."

"Why, what's wrong with these?" He pinched the wide brim of his fedora. "You never know when it might rain."

Sonja ran ahead to examine the locomotive. One bodyguard followed her, the other two took care of the luggage, and Thomas escorted Anita to the awaiting train. Ten minutes later, the engine puffed, and the wheels turned. Looking out the rain-spattered window, they saw Thomas waving to them. Sonja waved back until he was out of sight.

An hour later, he boarded a train heading in the same direction.

CHAPTER THIRTY-NINE
South of the River Cher
April 25, 5:30 am

COLETTE RAN FROM the cottage yard, desperate to find shelter. Despite the hour, the road was too risky. Beyond her stashed bike, she made out a worn path leading south across a field. It looked promising. The whinnying she heard earlier might mean a barn was nearby. She headed up the trail on foot, hoping to find a place to get warm sooner than later.

There was still no sign of shelter as the first rays of dawn began to silhouette the treetops. Shivering, she thought of turning back. Instead, she quickened her pace—until a low snort stopped her. In a clearing ahead, she could make out a penned horse. A farmhouse with a dim light in the window was just beyond.

Desperate and out of options, she snuck up to the back door and listened. Muted voices unnerved her, but she made her choice and timidly knocked. The talking stopped, but nothing else happened. A minute later, she knocked harder. The latch clicked, and the door cracked ajar. She recognized the man instantly. In her condition, the thought of it being his place hadn't crossed her mind. But now, the proximity to the river and his being awake at this hour made sense. There was nothing to do but improvise.

"I'm sorry, sir. I've had an accident and wondered if I could please come in to warm up."

The man said nothing at first and just stared back at the miserable-looking young lady standing before him.

"Uh, of course." He motioned for her to follow.

He led her to a chair in the kitchen, then stepped away and returned with a severe-looking woman trailing him. He shrugged at her as if to ask, *What could I do?* and left the room, leaving her to tend to the stranger.

Seeing the woman, Colette lowered her chin and let some damp locks droop over her face. With different clothes, a mop for hair, and a doubtless dreadful appearance, she hoped the woman from Loches wouldn't recognize her.

"Jesus, what's happened to you? Your clothes are soaked. It's not even raining out." Afraid her voice might give her away, Colette remained silent. The woman left the room and returned with a robe draped over one arm. "Stand up." Colette complied. Flora threw the robe onto the table and stepped behind her. "Put your arms up."

Without warning, her shirt was pulled over her head. Appearing unappreciative wouldn't help. Despite her apprehension, she let the undressing continue. While standing in nothing but her panties, she felt the woman's hands begin pulling them down.

"Oh, it's okay. I can keep those on."

"Don't be ridiculous. You're not going around with wet panties clinging to you."

Colette conceded, felt them around her ankles, and stepped out.

The woman grabbed the robe off the table. Any thought that it would be handed over was premature. She placed an index finger under Colette's chin, lifted it, and began an examination. Her hand flicked away matted, black curls. She studied Colette's face, turning her head from side to side. Flora Gagnon stepped back as though captivated by a sculpture, took in the entirety of the female figure before her, and resumed her methodical assessment. After examining from all vantage points, she finally returned to face her. Auguste entered the room, stopped dead in his tracks, and gaped. His wife took no notice of him.

Colette pointed at the robe still held by the woman. "Do you mind if I—I'm quite cold."

"Oh, yes. I suppose you are." She handed it over after appearing to stamp the unveiled vision into her brain.

The robe warmed her immediately. Exhausted and unsure of the time, Colette sat down.

"Thank you. It was very nice of you to—"

"You are an exquisite representative," Flora said under her breath.

"I'm sorry?"

"Of our gender."

Colette felt flush. "I—"

"What happened that brought you to our door at this hour?"

"And the back door at that," Auguste threw in. "You're lucky we were up."

It would have been a fair expectation to ask the couple why they were awake at such an early hour, but she wasn't about to go down that path. Questioning them about it wasn't necessary and might make them suspicious.

"It's a long story, I'm afraid," she began—with no idea what tale she might drum up.

The woman cut her off before she could fumble out any more words. "Have we met? I feel like I've seen you before."

The question was unnerving. As unsure as she was about concocting a believable story, she wished to return to it. "I don't think so. I live near Saint Martin le Beau, but I've no idea where I am now. My dog ran away, and I thought he was drowning. I jumped into the river, but he swam to the other side and ran off. Maybe he was scared. I tried to follow but got completely lost. I'm sorry to intrude."

~ ~ ~

Flora looked to her husband to gauge his reaction, but got nothing useful. She motioned to him, and they left the kitchen.

"Her story's plausible, I suppose," Auguste whispered.

"I don't know. Maybe it is, but I don't like coincidences," she countered. "She shows up here in the middle of the night? A night that's been nothing but strange from the start?"

"I don't like coincidences either, but I can't see her making up a story about jumping into the river after her dog. I mean, she's miserable and looks like a drowned rat. Why else would someone be—"

Flora saw her husband's brain switch gears. "What is it?" He remained lost in thought, staring blankly at the floor. "What? What?" she whispered. He motioned for her to follow him further from the kitchen. "Well?" she begged.

"Something happened when I was with Schmid, but I thought nothing of it." Her eyes widened, urging him to continue. "We heard a splash at the river. He sent me to investigate, but I saw nothing. We figured it was a fish, animal, falling branch...whatever." He paused and thought more. "Maybe that's all it was, but what if it wasn't?"

They were each silent, their thoughts swirling independently.

"Alright," Flora whispered at last. "If she was there, why on earth come here? Wouldn't she have gone home? She's soaking wet, and we're not exactly an obvious destination." She thought about it. "Unless she—could she have followed you?"

Auguste shook his head. "Hell, I don't see that. I left just after Schmid, and I was riding. I think she came here by accident. Or maybe we're just being paranoid."

"Auguste, she could be telling the truth, but we can't take the chance. We need to keep her here until we know more."

"What do you propose? We roll out the welcome mat?"

Flora looked to the kitchen and bit her lower lip. "You saw her. That's exactly what I propose."

Auguste looked at his wife and grinned. "It's been a long time."

"Mmm. Far too long."

~ ~ ~

Madame Gagnon's ogling exam was beyond creepy, and fleeing shot through Colette's mind. But her hunger, fatigue, and robe made it an unrealistic option.

Returning to the kitchen, the woman had dramatically softened. She offered a warm bite to eat and an invitation to spend the night in the guest room. Colette knew her absence would make Philippe a wreck, but given everything she'd been through and the kindly turnabout, the offer was impossible to turn down.

At the upstairs landing, Auguste turned left and went to their bedroom. She followed her hostess in the opposite direction to a spare guest room.

"We have few visitors, but we always keep the bedding fresh."

"Oh, my," Colette said, entering. "I've never seen a bed so big."

"We like our guests to be comfortable. I'm sorry that I don't have anything for you to wear. You may sleep in the robe if you wish."

She was asleep within minutes.

~ ~ ~

Flora crawled into bed next to her husband. "Do you think it odd she never asked why we were awake and are just now going to bed?"

"I suppose so," he answered. "And does something about her make you feel...I don't know—"

"Aroused?" Flora offered.

Auguste smirked. "I was thinking, more like, uncomfortable."

Flora felt something similar in her gut. "The more I talk to her, the more I swear we've met. I can't place the face, but even her voice is familiar. Anyway, I'm sure looking forward to her. We'll do it like we used to. I go first."

"Hmph," her husband grunted. "I still get to watch."

"Yes, yes, but give me some time. Anyway, she'll be much better after some sleep. I can use it too. And if you plan on performing, I suggest you do the same."

"Damn, she is pretty, isn't she?"

"It's all I can do to keep my hands off her," Flora groaned. "She reminds me of that beauty I saw in—" She brought a hand to her mouth. "Jesus almighty."

"What?"

"Loches. It's her."

"Who? What are you saying? You think it's the same girl you saw in Loches? Are you seriously suggesting—."

"It makes sense," she interrupted, as though unraveling a riddle. "Follows us to Loches. Follows you to the landing. Ends up here." She turned her eyes to her husband. "She's spying on us."

"Spying? Who for?"

Flora's thoughts were spinning. "The French, the British...hell, the Germans for all I know. But it's her. It fits." She stopped again to think. "Not the Germans. They'd be more direct, and Schmid wouldn't have sent you to investigate the splashing." She was thinking on the fly. "Or, is the cell spying on us? On Schmid?"

He couldn't argue any of it. "It could be anything."

"Merde," she uttered. "It doesn't matter. If any of it's true, she could ruin us."

"We need to stop her," said Auguste.

"No. We can't," Flora countered. "Schmid has to deal with this. If we take it into our own hands, I guarantee that son of a bitch will pin anything he can on us."

"Okay," Auguste agreed. "We'll take her to him."

"Yes." A smile spread across her face. "But not until we show our guest some Gagnon hospitality."

CHAPTER FORTY
Bléré
April 25, Pre-dawn

PHILIPPE RENAUD GOT no sleep at the rented room in Bléré. The pull to sit at the small table and watch out the window outweighed the urge to pace. After two hours of sitting in the dark, a lone vehicle appeared on the barren street below. Passing under a street lamp's glow, the sole occupant was unmistakable. Everyone in the cell knew the man. But this was good. He expected Lieutenant Schmid to return about now if all had gone according to plan. More importantly, he was returning alone. It was time to wait some more.

They approved of his idea. Colette would return to Philippe after her night at the river. Anyone at the boat landing would need to clear out before she could risk leaving. Then, she'd have to return during curfew without being seen. That meant possibly ditching the bike and walking the entire distance. He needed to be patient.

Taking a break from the window, he arched his shoulders and stretched his neck one way, then the other. He felt tense and exhausted, but now wasn't the time to rest. The pot of weak coffee in the kitchen had cooled. He gave it no thought, poured a cup, and spent the time convincing himself she was okay. She probably needed to lie low. He was sure she'd be back by five. His optimism waned the longer he waited. Nighttime was turning to dawn, and at six o'clock, he was panicked. He threw his jacket on.

A light was on at the blacksmith shop. A wiry man opened the back door, took one look at him, and asked, "What's wrong?"

Within minutes, the two agreed that Philippe should return to the heart of town and keep his eyes open and ears tuned to any gossip. The likely scenario was that she needed to remain longer than anticipated and could show up any minute. Then again, she might have gotten caught violating the curfew. Lieutenant Schmid returning by himself gave them hope.

Smith hung the fifth horseshoe on the outside wall as Philippe left. He would relay everything known and unknown to Jean-Paul.

CHAPTER FORTY-ONE
The Gagnon House
April 25, 9:30 am

COLETTE FELT THE mattress heave. The windowless room afforded no notion of time.

"Shh, it's still early," said a calm voice. "My husband is snoring again, and this bed's my sanctuary. Go back to sleep."

It caught her off guard, but she had slept alongside her mother, aunt, and other women. "It's okay," she said, and soon drifted off.

Sometime later, she awoke to a warm hand sliding between her thighs. "Madame," she whispered, "you're dreaming. Please wake up." The woman didn't respond and started petting. "Please don't!"

"Oh, honey, you're going to enjoy this."

"Please!" Colette pleaded, now aware the woman wasn't dreaming.

"Shh, shh. I meant to say that you'll enjoy it...or else." Madame Gagnon's voice flipped from sweet to sinister. "You see, sweetheart, I know who you are. You can choose Lieutenant Schmid or me. As you might imagine, he won't be as gentle."

Colette squirmed sideways, trying to dislodge the hand. "Who I am? What do you mean? I've never met—"

Flora Gagnon's hand remained firmly in place. "Don't play with me," she snapped. "I think you remember our little chat in Loches. Then you were inside the church. Now you're in our home. I should have recognized you right away. You're quite unmistakable. The only thing missing is your bicycle."

"Bicycle? I don't have a bicycle." Colette's reply was half-hearted. She was found out, and pretending otherwise was useless. Her comment was ignored.

"So, what will it be? A pleasant time here with me now, or a visit with you know who?"

Colette had no intention of choosing either option. Thrusting her hand between her legs, she grabbed the woman's wrist and wrenched it. She lunged to her left and scrambled off the mattress. A hard tug on her robe nearly pulled her down as she dashed around the bedpost. She spun, swung a fist wildly in the dark, and caught her attacker on the side of the head. Flora cried out but held on. Colette's only choice was to slip out of it. Naked, she reached the door, yanked it open, and splatted into the plump, hairy belly of Auguste Gagnon. She flailed furiously until he clenched her wrists and dragged her screaming into his bedroom. He slammed the door shut, slapped her hard across the face, and threw her onto the bed.

"You can have her!" came a shrill scream from the hallway.

CHAPTER FORTY-TWO
Amboise
April 25, Mid-morning

IT WAS MID-MORNING, and nobody had seen Marcel, so Henri started the meeting. He informed those present of everything he'd learned from Jean-Paul's messages. The news that Colette had yet to return to Bléré was distressing.

"We should never have sent her," said Charles, his glum expression revealing the guilt he felt for taking part in that decision. "Should never have put her in harm's way. Who knows what she's going through."

"We can learn from it, but hindsight won't help right now," said Georges. "We all agreed to it. She's smart and crafty. Let's not think the worst. Philippe is on the lookout in Bléré, and we'll get people spread out as soon as we're done here."

They were all aware, but Charles reminded them they had lost the entire Dubois family. Giselle was taken from his place, and nobody had heard anything about François and Louis since they went searching for her. Now Colette was missing and possibly in Nazi custody or, equally bad, the hands of collaborators or local police.

"Gagnon's a traitor. He's responsible for this," Henri fumed. "His wife, too! Colette confirmed it."

"Has anyone seen his wife before?" Charles asked. "Do we even know what she looks like?"

"Good question," said Georges. "We need more than just a name to chase. I'll be right back."

A tapping came at the door as they were finalizing search assignments. Georges walked over and knocked back. Hearing the appropriate reply, he opened the door. Marcel Bouchet entered and began waving his hand for everyone to gather around.

"We've found François."

"What? Where?" came the nearly unanimous response.

He held up both hands to bring the excitement level down. "When I say 'found,' I mean we've got word about him and—"

"And Louis?" Charles called out.

"Yes, and Louis. We don't know exactly where, but a reliable source says they were heading to Orléans."

"Are they okay?" Henri asked. "Why Orléans?"

"Details are fuzzy, but he left us to find Giselle, so I suspect he caught wind of something. Word is they're moving Jews through there and on to Nancy. Who knows where after that."

"I heard it too," said Henri, "but Giselle isn't Jewish."

"They move anyone they don't want around," said Marcel. "It's likely she's in real danger."

"It's my fault," Charles mumbled. "Leaving her alone at my place like that."

"It's nobody's fault but the fucking Nazis!" Henri shouted. He whirled to Marcel. "How can we help?"

"I'm afraid it's up to François now. There's too much going on here—starting with Colette."

"So you've heard then," said Charles. "We've just been meeting about her."

"Thoughts so far?"

Henri filled him in. "We've got Philippe, Smith, and Jean-Paul scouring around Bléré. We're having others hit the towns west of there. Georges is hoping to dig up something on Flora Gagnon. We're trying to stay positive, but—"

"But we need to operate as though her life depends on us," Charles interrupted. "It very well may."

"Is Vouvray covered?" Marcel asked.

"Oui," said Henri.

"Tours?"

"Sending two."

"Good."

"What about Loches?" Charles suggested. "If they have her, could they take her south? Should we send word down there?"

"Let's start closer and fan out if we get nothing," said Marcel. "Stay positive. If someone has her, she could be holed up anywhere, and it'll be difficult."

Georges returned, laid out two photos of Flora Gagnon, and tossed down one of Auguste for good measure.

"I don't have copies, so commit them to memory."

"These are great," said Charles. "Where did you—"

"Just part of the job."

Everyone filtered past and took mental snapshots.

"Okay," said Marcel. "Let's get going. Be careful out there."

CHAPTER FORTY-THREE
The Gagnon House
April 25, Late Morning

DESPITE HER HORRIFYING night, pure exhaustion finally overwhelmed her. She was fast asleep when creaking floorboards stirred her. Flora Gagnon was standing at the bedside. Colette tried moving away, but ropes secured her legs and arms to the bedposts. She thrashed about as Flora threw the covers off.

"Get away from me!"

"I'd ask how your morning went, but my husband's mood tells me he's still having troubles. No spring chicken anymore," she chirped with an unambiguous lilt.

"What time is it?" Colette asked, ignoring the comment.

"Time to get going. He's back and waiting for us downstairs. Get dressed." Flora grabbed Colette's dried panties off the dresser and tossed them at her. "I'm untying these ropes now, and I better not have to call for help."

"Where are we going?"

The woman said nothing and handed over one item of clothing at a time. At last dressed, the pointing finger was clear. Colette headed for the stairs.

She sat in the kitchen, hands tied behind her back. Her stomach felt empty, but she was too proud and stubborn to ask for anything. The bigger worry was not knowing what the day had in store. The indiscreet conversation in the next room soon told her plenty.

"Why does he want to meet in Tours?" she heard Flora say.

"That's all they told me, and I chose not to question it."

"Why can't you take her yourself? We can tie her up secure and—"

"No!" Colette could hear Auguste's anger mounting. "We can't make a spectacle of this. What if the cell sent her? There's no way I can be seen bringing her to Schmid. Nobody knows what you look like."

"Well, somebody must be worried about her. And if she's with them, the entire damn cell could be out searching for her."

"That's precisely what I'm talking about," he griped. "I can't chance being seen!"

Colette heard nothing else significant but knew they were taking her to Tours to see Schmid. He might force her to reveal anything, as well as anyone who put her up to it. Betraying the others was what she feared most.

Auguste hitched up his horse, and they climbed onto the wagon. Colette spent most of the ride playing out the upcoming encounter with Schmid. Initial thoughts focused on the dread of the interrogation. Mentally holding up to him concerned her, but it could get worse. Being shipped away to Germany or taken away, never to be seen again, were real possibilities.

Nearing Tours, she expected her dread to grow. Instead, she felt more at ease. So far, her only encounter with Schmid was on the dirt road west of Bléré. He didn't see her in Loches. He hadn't seen her last night at the river. Maybe he wouldn't trust anything she'd say, but his one impression of her so far was positive. It was obvious. He was flirting with her, maybe smitten. Schmid and the Gagnon traitors were profiteering off the war at the expense of human lives and doing it behind the backs of everyone. They could never let that secret escape, but if she played it right, he might think twice about casting her aside. She gained confidence contemplating the upcoming encounter.

CHAPTER FORTY-FOUR
The Paris to Tours Train
April 25, Late Morning

ANITA HOLTZER CLOSED her book, closed her eyes, and relished the moment. Her daughter's energy hadn't waned the entire grueling day—until now. The train ride from Stuttgart to Paris was an especially relentless stream of questions, requests, and exclamations. Still, all of that paled compared to Sonja's enthrallment with the bustle and goings-on at the Gare de l'Est station in the capital city. It was everything Anita and her protectors could do to keep Sonja from running to and from each train, petting every animal in sight, and unnerving any vendor displaying bonbons, delicate baubles, or low-hanging trinkets. Half the mother in her wanted to holler, constrain, and admonish; the other half wanted to smile, relish, and reflect on the carefree joy of childhood. She did her best to compromise.

Anita had heard the rumblings of insurrections causing minor train delays, including occasional derailments, but such remote news had little lasting effect in the far-off comforts of her Stuttgart home. Those in her travel party also never discussed such occurrences, and, with the German army established in France, the thought never crossed her mind. Sonja was asleep, and all was bliss, twenty minutes removed from Paris on their way to Tours.

CHAPTER FORTY-FIVE
Gare de Tours
April 25, Afternoon

THE WAGONLOAD WAS unfairly heavy, and River Man attempted to hurry things along with his whip. The old mare ignored the pain and plodded on, disinclined to hasten her pace. Colette felt unnerved as they arrived at the city perimeter. Her two abductors didn't look to be faring much better.

"There's no way I'm meeting with him alone," Flora mumbled.

"You won't be alone," he growled. "You'll have that little bitch with you every step of the way."

"Damn it! I'm serious!"

"We've been through this!" Auguste exploded. "I can't chance being seen with her and Schmid, or we could be done!"

Flora sat back, crossed her arms, and scowled. "How the hell am I supposed to do it?"

He collected himself. "Again, I'll drop you at a safe distance. You'll walk her in with your wrists tied together so that nobody can see." He turned his eyes to Colette. "And not a sound or struggle out of you. Schmid will be watching. If you make one mistake, it'll be your last."

Already resigned to the meeting, Colette rolled her eyes and said nothing. Auguste continued with his wife.

"You'll go onto the platform between tracks one and two. There's a ramshackle office out there. Knock eight times and—"

"Why eight?" Flora cut him off.

"I don't know. Maybe nobody ever knocks eight times!" came the agitated reply. "That's it. That's all you need to do; no need to go in.

I'll follow at a distance and watch to ensure everything goes as planned. Then turn around and come find me where I drop you."

Flora turned and glared at Colette. "I'll be your worst nightmare if you try anything."

Colette turned away and gazed at some rundown industrial buildings in the distance.

There was an inconspicuous spot behind a warehouse three blocks from the station. River Man turned the horse toward it. Cutting a length of rope, he tied her and Flora's wrists together so that his wife's coat sleeve sufficiently disguised it. Colette considered telling him it wasn't necessary, but decided it was a waste of breath. He tugged on the rope until it hurt. An icy glare from his wife prompted him to loosen it.

Auguste gave last-second instructions to Flora, issued Colette some final threats, and looked around nervously before shooing them off the wagon.

~ ~ ~

A knock on the first-class cabin door woke Sonja. Anita gave the visitor an exasperated look that made him wince with understanding.

"I'm sorry, Frau Holtzer. I wanted to inform you that we're arriving any moment, on schedule."

"Thank you."

Sonja sat up, rubbed her eyes, and looked out the window. "Where are we, Mama?"

"We're here."

"Does Papa know?"

"I'm sure he does. He wanted to meet us at the station but couldn't make any promises."

"I hope he can. I can't wait to see him! Has it been a year, Mama?"

"No, it's only been three months. It just seems like a year."

True to her nature, her daughter's excitement and unrelenting questions resumed.

~ ~ ~

Flora Gagnon hadn't entered the station since before the war. It seemed far busier than she remembered, which was good. The crowd would make it easier for unimportant individuals like herself and Colette to blend in. She walked with purpose while avoiding the appearance of hauling a captive. They passed through the main hall and followed the signs as her husband instructed. The platform she sought was a long, broad, solid mass of concrete where trains could pull up on either side. One had just arrived on the left. Her husband said to look for a shabby office halfway out on the platform. She spotted it and tugged Colette by the hidden rope that bound them.

~ ~ ~

"I can't see Papa anywhere," said Sonja, her face pressed against the window. "Where is he?"

Anita Holtzer peered over her daughter's shoulder. "Well, he couldn't promise he'd be here, but maybe he's on his way."

The train made a final shudder and jerked to a stop. Sonja scrambled to get past her mother and stood behind two guardians, anxious for the door to open. The sights and sounds at the Tours station gripped her as she hopped off.

"Look, Mama!" she called back. "Another one's coming in!" With her father nowhere in sight, the anticipation of seeing him vanished.

She hurried across the platform to get a better look.

The two escorts looked at Anita wide-eyed.

"Oh, you know how she loves them. Just keep an eye on her."

Fifty meters out, the inbound train screeched as it slowed. Sonja stood near the platform edge, waving frantically. Her day was made when the conductor waved back from his side window.

~ ~ ~

Two pistol shots erupted in the station's terminal area, followed by an immediate, short burst of gunfire. A panic ensued, and a mass of people swarmed onto the platforms. Those already on them rushed further out. The shrieking crowd swallowed Anita's frantic cries for Sonja. One of the entourage grabbed her arm to steer her away from the crushing mass. She ripped herself away and dashed to where she'd last seen her daughter.

The gunshots had the same effect on Flora Gagnon. Halfway to the platform shack, she contributed to the mayhem, dragging Colette along—elbowing and plowing through anyone in her way. Near the platform edge, she had no regard for the little girl with a pink ribbon in her hair. She swiped her aside with her free arm, indifferent when the girl fell to the tracks below.

Little Sonja froze at the sight of the enormous train bearing down on her. The conductor watched in horror, knowing he couldn't stop in time. Seeing the tragedy unfolding, Colette threw all her weight into her captor, and the two plunged off the platform. Flora screamed in agony as her knee shattered on a steel rail, and Colette landed on top of her. The twisting fall loosened the rope binding. Colette was free. The train was nearly on them. She lunged for the girl, grabbed her arm, and dove for the platform base. The two lay cringing with eyes slammed shut as the train passed inches away.

A shrill scream was cut short; nobody heard the sound of bones crunching over the clamor. The locomotive engulfed the woman, obscuring the blood that spurted, spattered, and finally pooled around the body. The train squealed to a stop seconds later. Colette lay trembling with the sobbing girl—fully aware of what happened to the woman. Despite having never been so terrified, one thought filled her head: *Good riddance.*

Auguste Gagnon stood on another platform, doing his best to keep an eye on his wife through the commotion. What he saw couldn't be unseen. He looked on, terror-stricken as she vanished beneath the train.

Anita nearly fainted. She'd seen her daughter disappear from the platform edge just as the train arrived and frantically pushed her way through the crowd. With the panic subsiding, onlookers cheered as a young woman emerged near the engine and first-car coupling. Colette stood below and lifted the crying girl to two men. They sat the unharmed child down just as Anita arrived.

"It's my daughter!" she screamed, slumping to the concrete and engulfing Sonja in her arms.

Anita barely noticed a German officer reaching down and hauling a young woman up from the track bed below. She stood up with Sonja clinging to her. The crowd parted as the man strode by, Colette firmly in his grasp.

"Young lady!" Anita called out. "How can I ever—"

"Mind your own business!" the man thundered. "And put that thing on a leash if you want it alive."

Unaccustomed to verbal assaults, Anita's jaw dropped. "But my husband is coming and will insist on thanking her," she stammered.

Schmid stopped. "I couldn't give a shit about you or your damn husband." He yanked on Colette's arm and tramped to the office.

Auguste Gagnon was distraught and pressed through the crowd. Seeing a wall of approaching Nazis, he stopped. Uncertain of what to do, he stayed back and watched in horror as personnel crawled underneath the train, reported their findings, and began dealing with his wife's gruesome remains. He turned his head away.

~ ~ ~

Colette stumbled as Schmid pushed her through the office doors.

"Well, if it isn't you after all," was the first thing out of his mouth. "The thought crossed my mind, but I didn't dare believe I could be so lucky. And yet, here you are. Don't you love it when the stars align? Please, have a seat."

She remained standing. Scared and rattled by the events, she vowed to stay level-headed. "The stars aren't aligned for you. I know what you're up to and what you're about."

"That's why you and I are having this little chat. It seems we could be a thorn to each other, or..." he paused and rubbed his cheek scar, "we could help each other out."

"How could you possibly help me?"

Schmid snickered at the ridiculous question. "Well, for starters, I could let you live. It wouldn't be my obligation, but I might at least consider it."

She understood her delicate position and changed the conversation's direction. "Then how could I help you...if I'm alive, that is?"

"Hoping it was you, I've already given it considerable thought." He stared at her while tapping his fingers on the small desk. "But before that, you could keep your mouth shut."

She was right. Schmid was rogue, and his superiors were in the dark. "Wouldn't it be foolish to think I'd do that?"

"Would it? Ah, I forgot to mention another way I could help." He grinned. "If you're amenable to helping me, I might let your colleagues and family live."

"Colleagues?" she huffed. "I don't have colleagues."

Schmid shook his head slowly. "That may be the boldest lie anyone's ever tried on me...and I've heard countless."

"You don't know me, my friends, or my family."

"I don't think you're that naive," he sneered, "and I'm not concerned with my ability to coax missing pieces from you."

There were two sharp raps, and the door swung open. Major Viktor Holtzer dipped his head to avoid the overhead frame. Colette recognized him instantly from photos laid out by Georges in Amboise. He was more imposing in person, and she feared things were about to get worse than they already were.

~ ~ ~

Schmid stood at attention and gave a stiff-armed salute that was ignored. He was stunned by Holtzer's arrival and perplexed as to why he was there. Suddenly, he was acutely aware that his fate was in the young woman's hands.

"Why am I not surprised?" the major said, shaking his head. He returned to the door and motioned with his finger. The woman from the platform poked her nose inside, still hugging her child. Holtzer pointed to Colette.

"Yes, that's her!" the woman shouted. She then tugged on the major's arm, and he leaned down. Schmid watched helplessly as she whispered something and pointed his way.

He pieced it together and couldn't believe his bad luck. The woman he berated on the platform was Holtzer's wife. He looked on with dread as the major patted his daughter on the head and asked his wife to wait with the soldiers gathered for his protection.

Schmid attempted to say something. "Sir—"

Without looking at him, Holtzer held up a finger and approached Colette. He embraced her with his massive arms, lifting her off the ground. Schmid could only wait it out.

"So, you're the brave one who saved my daughter," he said, setting her back down. "If you hadn't risked your life—" He hesitated and shook his head. "Well, I can't think about that right now. What's your name, young lady?"

She spoke with pride. "My name is Colette, Sir. Colette Dubois."

Schmid was dumbfounded. *What? The beauty is the Dubois girl I've been looking for?*

Major Holtzer took a moment to reflect on her answer. "Dubois? Hmm...Is Dubois a common name in France?"

Colette gave a mousy shrug. "Maybe. I've never thought about it."

"I recently met with a Dubois. Big guy. Beard. Maybe you know him. His name's François Dubois."

Colette's eyes widened. "Yes! That's my father!" she shouted. "You say you've seen him?"

"I have."

"What? Where is he? Have you seen my mother?" she asked in rapid succession.

"Your mother? No, I can't say that I have." Holtzer's sideways glance at him further sapped Schmid's spirit.

"Yes, Sir. She's been missing for several days."

"I tell you what. Would you mind stepping out to wait with my family? I'll be there shortly." He opened the door, introduced Colette to his wife and daughter, and reentered the office.

"Sir, I had no idea—" Schmid began.

Holtzer spoke as though he hadn't heard a word. "I come to the station to greet my family. Some nut tries to shoot me before I'm barely through the door." Schmid could feel the man's eyes boring into him. "Then I hear from my wife that some lieutenant says he couldn't give a shit about me."

"Sir, I had no idea she was your—"

"As if those two things aren't enough, I hear this same lieutenant says he doesn't give a shit about my wife either."

He had to save himself. "Sir, it was chaotic. I had no idea she was— I pulled this girl in to question what happened out there. I meant no disrespect to you or your wife."

Holtzer strolled to the door and turned back. "So let me get it straight, Lieutenant. You regret disrespecting my wife and me, but were completely fine disrespecting a mother who nearly lost her child?"

"Sir, I didn't even know she was German."

"German?" Holtzer spat. "What the hell does that have to do with it? Jesus, Schmid, isn't the war brutal enough? I came here to enforce, but I also intend to keep the embers of dissent as dim as possible. And here you are, running around stoking the damn fires! They've got enough reason to hate us. Stop giving them more!"

He turned to rejoin his family. "By the way," he said without looking back, "it seems you found the daughter of François Dubois. Or at least she found you. A coincidence?"

Holtzer left him. Schmid threw his hat against the nearest wall. He dropped into a chair, fuming about his lousy luck but relieved there were no more questions to dodge. Now, he had to worry about what Colette Dubois might say.

~ ~ ~

Security staff surrounded the family on the platform. Little Sonja and Anita were still doting on Colette when Major Holtzer appeared and asked her to join them for a meal. The chance he could shed some light on her father outweighed her fears. She accepted, but first had something to get off her mind.

"Thank you so much. I would love to. I've forgotten something inside. I'll be right back."

She closed the door behind her and walked straight for Schmid. "Where's my mother, you son of a bitch?"

Schmid raised his eyebrows. A smug look crossed his face. "Right. Your mother. Oh, she's fine. For now, that is. And you'll keep your mouth shut if you want to see her or your sneaky friends again. Ask yourself if squealing to the major is worth the price."

She was livid and knew Schmid could do nothing with Major Holtzer on the platform. "Bring her back, and I'll consider it."

"I'm sure we can work something out." He grinned and stood. "But you need to play by my rules. Meet me tomorrow at eleven in the lobby of Château Belmont. I keep a room there."

She scoffed. "Fat chance. I'll meet you, but not in your hotel. I'll meet you at Saint-Gatien."

"You don't call the shots, honey. I do."

She looked toward the door, then back. "Take it or leave it." She could see him mulling it over, weighing the pros and cons.

"I understand you were visiting Loches. Seeing me in churches is growing on you, huh? Okay. Tomorrow at eleven, inside...and don't bring anyone. I'll have men casing the area looking for your little friends. You can make this easy on them or finish them off. Just a little warning as a favor."

"And why do me a favor?" she asked, knowing she would never risk bringing anyone.

Schmid shrugged. "Maybe I just want you to myself."

"Go fuck yourself," she sneered. The word surprised her, having never uttered it before.

"Oh, I've got other ideas about that."

She scoffed again. "See you at eleven."

Outside on the platform, Sonja greeted her cheerfully.

Auguste Gagnon waited in the shadows and watched Major Holtzer depart the station with his entourage—and Colette.

~ ~ ~

"She killed her!" Auguste yelled, barging into the office.

Flora Gagnon was the least of Lieutenant Schmid's concerns. "The Dubois girl got away because of her!" he fired back. "Your wife was a casualty of war. C'est la vie. Isn't that how you French say it?"

Gagnon's eyes went blank. "That's my wife...dead. That bitch killed her," he sputtered.

Schmid felt no pity. "How long were you married?"

"Almost thirty-five years."

"Then what the hell's your problem? You should have had your fill of each other by now. She wasn't exactly a...never mind. There are two things you need to know. First off, our business arrangement continues as is." He leaned back in his chair. "Second. You no longer have to share your cut with her." Schmid watched as the man's face turned blood red, aware that cowardice would throttle any incendiary remarks or thoughts of retaliation.

"That little bitch killed her," said Auguste, switching the subject of his rage. "I watched her do it. I'll have her hide if it's the last thing I do! And with what she knows—" Auguste shook his head. "We need to eliminate her."

Schmid was mildly impressed by Gagnon's fire. "It pains me to say it, but I agree with you. She's a threat to our operation, which means she threatens our livelihood...and our lives." He rubbed the back of his fingers against his cheek scar. "I have an idea how I can help you. In return, you can help us both."

Auguste's eyes fired up. "What?"

"There's a catch, though. If I put her in your hands, I'll have to kill you with my own if you ever say a word about this."

"Give her to me. That's all I care about."

Schmid pondered some more. "I have unfinished business with her. Pleasure, really. But I'll let you know where and when I need you."

"I'll be there!" Auguste fumed.

CHAPTER FORTY-SIX
A Restaurant in Tours
April 25, Late Afternoon

COLETTE WASN'T SURE if it was a late lunch or early supper. Either way, she hoped the time spent at the restaurant with Major Holtzer would help her learn something about her family. She was also aware of the fine line between wanting to ask questions and not having to answer them in return.

Holtzer said he and her father departed on cordial terms after their meeting. She believed him. To her disappointment, he knew nothing about her mother, but she thanked him when he offered to have staff ask around. Not wanting to press her luck, she let the conversation branch elsewhere. Sonja made serious discussion difficult anyway. Colette was bombarded with questions about life in France and had to navigate her memory when Sonja insisted on hearing about every animal she had. Her family's farm sure was no secret, and she willingly shared tidbits.

"Don't you have a horse?" the girl asked, stabbing at her peas.

"Well, we used to, but others needed it more," Colette explained.

"Do you have an auto?"

"No, no auto."

Sonja looked up from her plate. "Then how do you get places?" Her eyes lit up. "Train?"

"Well, I guess I mostly walk."

With no horse or train, Sonja lost interest in the subject and reached to play with the leather sheath around her father's waist. He gently set her hand back on the table.

"Mama, tell the story about the wild boar and the boy," she urged.

"No, dear. You know that story isn't a happy one."

She swung around to Colette. "The boy lives, but his sister—"

"Sonja!"

"I like when Uncle Thomas tells the story. The boy lost part of his thumb but lived." An idea struck her. "Papa, can you tell the story?"

"Perhaps another time, sweetheart."

She motioned for Colette to lean down and whispered, "Papa has a bad thumb, too."

Holtzer took care of the bill, and they stepped outside. Sonja held her arms wide and beckoned Colette to come down to her level for a hug. Anita gave her a similar show of affection.

Major Holtzer put his hand on her shoulder. "I'll never be able to fully express my gratitude. Our lives would've changed forever. And I'm sorry for what you had to see today with the woman who fell."

Doesn't he wonder why I was at the station? Maybe it's unimportant. Colette was happy to keep it to herself. Explaining Flora Gagnon or Lieutenant Schmid's role on the platform could open her up to questions she didn't trust herself to navigate. *The woman's dead. Let it be.* Schmid? She'd continue that saga tomorrow.

"Hopefully, I can get to the bottom of things," he added. "Lieutenant Schmid brought your father to me. I'll start with him." Before leaving with his family, he furrowed his brow. "You're missing both your parents. Are you staying with somebody here in Tours?"

She thought fast. "Um, no, Sir. I'm just looking for them."

"Well, I don't know if you're coming or going, but you're here now. Where are you staying?"

"I guess I haven't decided or figured that out yet. I'm just going from town to town."

"Oh, she must spend the night with us," Anita implored.

"Yes, Papa!" Sonja shrieked.

Viktor Holtzer smiled. "Well, then that's settled. I'm afraid I'll be scarce this evening, but my wife and daughter will be happy to help you with anything you need." Sonja beamed and clamped her two hands around one of Colette's.

They weren't kidding about needing to improvise.

CHAPTER FORTY-SEVEN
Amboise
April 25, Late Evening

ONE OF THE resistance men searching for Colette in Tours had investigated the news of a disturbance at the station. He learned of a death on the tracks—a tragedy seemingly caused by a panicked crowd. The assassination attempt on Holtzer concerned him more than the unfortunate woman, and he wondered if someone from the cell went rogue in retaliation for Roland Viard. Arriving, he had seen Colette and Major Holtzer led to a car by a team of guards and could only watch as it sped away. News about her and the events in Tours was whisked off to Amboise.

"It can't be," said Charles, shaking his head. "I've seen the fire in her, but there's no way."

Henri was staring blankly at the table. "She's the only one that wasn't here when we told everyone to stay calm...that we're working on a plan."

"Let's think this through," Marcel cut in. "We know she first went to the river, then later to Loches. Despite tense moments, she returned safely from both. Philippe was with her last night before she set out in the dark for the river. She never returned to Bléré as planned, but the next day she's in Tours? How? Bicycle? Why? To assassinate Holtzer? That's unlikely."

"Highly," Georges agreed. "Something's not adding up."

"Fire or not, she's level-headed," Charles added.

"If she got caught," Marcel continued, "it would've been by Schmid or River Man, right?"

"More than likely," said Georges, "but she was seen in Tours. She's alive. Wouldn't they have just dealt with—"

"I don't know," Marcel thought out loud. "Schmid's a brown nose if he thinks it'll serve him. He might take her straight to Holtzer, hoping to win some grand prize."

"But Philippe said Schmid returned to Bléré by himself as expected," said Charles. "Maybe Auguste got her."

"Well, if he did, he would have told Schmid. Could the lieutenant have ordered her to kill the major?" Marcel's question was worth consideration.

Henri answered first. "Holtzer's arrival could jeopardize Schmid's operation...even his life."

"Colette and Holtzer were put into the back of the same car?" Georges asked nobody in particular.

"That's how it was reported anyway," said Marcel. "A woman and child were also with them."

Georges looked puzzled. "No Nazi, or anyone for that matter, puts a high-ranking officer into a car with a killer and then adds a woman and child for good measure. It wouldn't happen."

"No, it wouldn't," Marcel agreed.

Nobody spoke for a while.

"Georges, who does Holtzer have for family?" Henri asked.

"A wife and daughter are pretty much it."

Marcel tried a quick scenario. "So, he's at the station to pick them up. Somebody catches wind of it and takes a shot at him. His security detail takes him to a car...along with Colette and his family."

"It wouldn't happen that way if she were any kind of threat," said Georges. "Holtzer was either protecting her, or she did something to help him or his family. Any assassin would have been blown away on the spot."

"They would need extra staff to clean up the mess," said Henri.

Charles grimaced. "Is it possible somebody from the team went off the deep end?"

"Don't know," said Marcel. "I doubt it, but plenty of angry people are roaming about."

"Well, you can't blame their patriotism," said Henri.

"No, but you can question their intelligence," Marcel grumbled. "They could get innocent people killed."

"Or us," said Charles.

Marcel thought for a second. "We need to get more eyes in Tours. Get word to Bléré to have Philippe head there. I'll go now and start digging around. Charles, you can get back to your work. Henri and Georges, keep your ears open here while figuring out what you can about François and Giselle. I'll be back by midday tomorrow."

CHAPTER FORTY-EIGHT
Tours
April 26, Early Morning

WALKING ALONG THE Rue Nationale in Tours, Philippe Renaud received a start when a man passed behind him and said, "Follow me shortly." Turning his head, he saw the backside of Marcel Bouchet walking away down Rue Colbert.

Two right turns later, he arrived at a garden space. Marcel was sitting on a bench reading the daily paper.

"You reminded me of something I need to work on," said Philippe, taking a seat at the other end of the bench.

"What's that?" Marcel asked without looking up.

"I startle too easily."

Marcel turned the page. "I saw you on the bridge...opposite side. When did you arrive?"

"I started walking from Bléré late last night, but it's damn far. I stole a bicycle and got in about sunrise. I've been out here since."

"Any trouble with curfew?"

"I stayed on back roads. Slipped into the shadows a handful of times, but that was it."

"Anything yet?"

Philippe shook his head. "Nothing. I'm heading to the station next to sniff around."

"Okay, I'm on my way to City Hall."

Philippe doubted Marcel would have luck finding his government contacts on a Sunday, but wasn't about to question it. "After the station, I thought I'd head to German headquarters."

Marcel considered it. "We're good there. I've got two men watching the entries now."

"Could two look suspicious?"

"They're separate. Both are reading journals. They'll be fine, but you should stay mobile. Look for official cars and German security details. I'll be heading back to Amboise after making some inquiries. Send word there at once if you learn anything."

"I will." Philippe stood and looked down at Marcel. "We have to find her."

"We will."

Philippe left the garden square, turned right, and headed for the train station.

Marcel waited until his young comrade was out of sight, then discarded his newspaper and headed for German headquarters.

CHAPTER FORTY-NINE
Tours
April 26, 11:00 am

THE MORNING SKY looked uneasy, and the parks had taken on a grayish hue. The sidewalks were busy with Sunday parishioners: some scurrying, most plodding along, keeping to themselves. Colette chose Saint-Gatien for their meeting, knowing they wouldn't be alone. She hoped Schmid would be oblivious to the day of the week when making her stipulation.

Morning service had finished, but several church-goers were prone to loiter. Outside, Colette watched Schmid from a distance. She dreaded the upcoming encounter but was oddly satisfied to see him looking out of his element when entering the church. Within seconds, stragglers filed out—silently making haste to get anywhere else. His threat about bringing a team to snare her 'little friends' was needless. He was profiteering off the war; the fewer people involved, the better. She suspected his pursuit of resistance cells was a perk, not a priority.

Choosing a place of worship was wise, but it still risked the appearance of collaboration. Patriotic types were eager to throw the word around—and it could permeate like skunk spray. She suspected nobody would recognize her, and meeting in the relative safety of a church was worth the trade-off.

Their time in the back pew was getting her nowhere. She had planned on doing the talking, hoping to limit any questions about Loches, Bléré, and the river. But Schmid seemed distracted, asked nothing about her escapades, and didn't even mention her family.

"Stop," he said, cutting her off mid-sentence. He rose to his feet.

"It's time to go."

"Go? What do you mean?" She felt somewhat safe in the church. Anywhere else wasn't part of the deal. "We agreed to meet here."

"Do you want to see your mother again?"

She looked around at the empty pews, glared at him, and stood.

"Where are we going?"

"Come on."

She followed him to the car. The driver opened the door, and Schmid motioned for her to get in.

"I'm not getting in until you tell me where we're going."

"Shopping." He motioned again. She returned a skeptical look and climbed in. He slid in beside her.

"Shopping? For what?" She looked out the window. Curious bystanders turned away.

"Clothes. For you."

"Clothes? Holtzer's wife gave me these. What's wrong with them?"

"We need something more...elegant. A shop owner has agreed to a private visit."

"Mmm. Agreed, huh?"

After she modeled a half dozen dresses, he approved of one. Surprisingly, she loved his choice. He then told her to select any pair of shoes she liked. When finished, the shop owner packaged it all neatly, and he walked out without paying. Colette apologized and thanked her for her time.

"One more stop," Schmid announced outside.

"Now what?" she said, exasperated.

"Patience. You'll see."

Four blocks away, the driver pulled to the curb. A woman biting her nails stood in the doorway of an upscale beauty shop.

Colette rolled her eyes. "Is this necessary?"

He shrugged. "I have an engagement tonight, and I need you to be...engaging. You look beautiful, but I want you to look divine."

An hour later, his wish had come true. Her hair was perfect, and the final makeup touches were complete. Looking in the mirror, she barely recognized herself. Schmid again walked out without paying.

Colette turned to the woman. "I'm terribly sorry."

On her way to the car, she looked up. The skies were menacing. *Improvise.*

~ ~ ~

Before taking her to his room, Schmid had Colette wait on a sofa in the hotel lobby. Placing a call from the phone booth, he looked out at her. *I've created a goddess.*

Though nothing would stop him from enjoying his influence—his power—to the fullest, he felt his afternoon would be more fruitful if he behaved with a decorum that wasn't his custom. He held himself together as they entered his room, keenly aware of one thing: She'd have to get undressed to get into her new dress.

"Ahh," Schmid said, pleased at the sound of a light knock on the door. "Entrez, s'il vous plaît."

The concierge entered with a tall brass wine holder, placed it beside an armchair, and was promptly excused. It held a bottle of champagne engulfed in ice. Schmid lifted it out, popped the cork, and poured two glasses. He clinked his on hers.

"Santé."

~ ~ ~

Colette seldom drank but accepted it, hoping to buy time. Beyond her obvious and immediate concern, she had other questions and doubts. The morning excursions were strange. *Is this part of his fantasy? What good does it do him to show me off tonight? Will my mother really be there?* It felt unlikely, but she held onto hope. Even if true, how could he let them live given what she knew? Disguised as small talk, she tried to learn more.

"Fancy dress, fancy hair." She took a small sip. "I have a feeling you're taking me somewhere nice."

"I think you'll like it. We both will." He pointed at her. "As long as you behave yourself."

"Etiquette is a strength of mine."

"I noticed you can have a foul mouth."

"Mmm." She gave him that one and feigned a sip.

Another knock came; a small piece of paper appeared at the foot of the door.

"What the hell?" Schmid set down his glass, walked over, and picked it up. He flung the door open and looked both ways down the hall. "Arghh!"

"What is it?" she asked, gathering that it was good news for her.

He crumpled the message in his fist and threw it at her feet.

Urgent. Needed at headquarters. Do not delay.

"Get dressed," he grumped. "We may not have time to stop back."

His crushing look of disappointment spoke volumes, but Colette felt relieved. She took her new dress and shoes behind a four-panel room divider and changed before he got other ideas.

CHAPTER FIFTY
Château de Chenonceau
April 26, Early Afternoon

VIOLETTE BURST INTO the study without knocking. Simone Menier gave a quizzical look but said nothing—convinced the purpose for the intrusion would soon be revealed.

"Madame Menier!" the out-of-breath girl panted.

Simone remained seated and motioned for Violette to close the door. She placed an index finger in front of her lips as a reminder the walls might have ears.

"Compose yourself, dear. Have a seat."

Violette heeded the advice and started over. "Madame Menier, I've just overheard!" Her hushed voice did little to conceal her excitement. "She's coming here! She's coming to the château!"

"I trust this visitor is worth being excited about. But when you say 'she', could you be more specific?"

"Colette! Colette is coming here. I just now heard!"

The news caught her off guard. "Coming here?" Simone whispered. "How do you mean? Come closer. What did you hear?"

Violette pulled her chair around the desk and drew it up as near as possible. "As you asked, I was eavesdropping on Captain Eicher and others. They have a meeting this evening."

Simone gave a quick nod. "And?"

"And he said she was being brought here."

"Why? Who said?"

"A man told Captain Eicher about some lieutenant boasting that he was bringing a French 'beauty' tonight."

"Go on," said Simone, rolling her hand.

"At first, they all laughed. Captain Eicher said it was unlikely. Another was especially skeptical and said the lieutenant couldn't get an old pauper lady to look at him, let alone a beautiful French woman. But the man had asked who she was, and the lieutenant told him— Colette Dubois! I guess he acted proud as a peacock about it." Violette took another breath and looked anxiously at Madame for her response.

"Did you catch the name of this lieutenant?"

"I was focused on translating, but it sounded like Smith or something like that."

Simone leaned back in her chair and sighed. "No...it's not Smith."

"Are you okay, Madame?"

She set her hand on Violette's knee. "I'm afraid our friend is in trouble. She'd only be coming here with him if she were caught."

"Oh no! Poor Colette!"

"The others may already know, but I need to make sure. Have the stable fashion me a carriage at once."

"Where to, Madame?"

"Amboise. And not a word about this to anyone."

CHAPTER FIFTY-ONE
Tours
April 26, Mid-Afternoon

AUGUSTE GAGNON WATCHED Schmid's car pull up to the hotel, waited ten minutes, then entered. He found a far-off chair in the busy hotel lobby and waited, thoughts of sexual violence racing through his head. He could avenge his wife's murder in limitless ways and could hardly bear the wait. However, disobeying Schmid's instructions wouldn't help. *Okay, stick to the plan—one hour.*

The elevator door opened. Auguste shrank and hid behind a paper. *What the?* He couldn't approach Schmid without causing a scene. While others in the lobby stopped everything and gaped, he kept his eye on Schmid. After making a lengthy inquiry at the reception desk, the lieutenant suddenly escorted the lady out the front door. *What the fuck is he doing? This isn't the plan!* Auguste shuffled to the window and watched the car pull away. He had to think fast.

"Monsieur!" he called to the man behind the desk. "The lieutenant who just left—I was supposed to deliver some papers, and I missed him. He's probably furious! Did he say when he'd return?"

"He was called to headquarters," the clerk said dismissively. "After that, your guess is as good as mine. For all I know, he could stay at Château de Chenonceau overnight. By the look of things, I'd say he's planning on having a good time. You'd best send them by messenger if they're that important."

"Oui, Monsieur. A very good idea. Merci."

Auguste shuffled outside. German headquarters was out of the question. Incensed, he fixated on getting to the château.

CHAPTER FIFTY-TWO
Amboise
April 26, Mid-Afternoon

SIMONE KEPT TO the back streets to avoid familiar faces and headed for a nearby café. The coffee and bakery offerings were no better than elsewhere, but the owner was. He was a reliable confidant.

At once, a messenger boy was sent out. She had no time for near-certain social encounters and went to a cramped booth in the rear to lay low and wait. Twenty minutes later, a man approached.

"Oh, thank goodness you're here," she whispered.

"You look upset," said Marcel Bouchet, squeezing into the bench opposite her. "What's going on?"

"It's Innocent. I fear it's bad news."

"We're trying to figure out her predicament. What do you know?"

"I've just learned she's to come to the château. Lieutenant Schmid is bringing her to a meeting with Captain Eicher."

"Schmid?" he said in a forced whisper. "The château? How did she end up with—" His voice trailed off.

She could see his mind racing. "What do you suppose it's about?"

He sat in thought. "No idea," he said at last, "but your timing's perfect. I've just returned from Tours. One of my men saw her being whisked off in a car yesterday evening with Major Holtzer. Then I got word she slipped away this morning and hasn't been seen since. When is this meeting?"

"That's just it. Tonight! The usual time's about eight. Right after they dine and smoke."

"How many?"

"Five or ten, I suspect. The captain usually tells me if a larger number is expected."

"Bringing Colette? Maybe an interrogation? But why there?" he muttered, mulling it over.

"Honestly, it sounded more like an invitation than an interrogation. My assistant said he was boasting about bringing her. Not like one would brag about a prisoner...more like being pompous about having a beautiful woman on his arm."

"Well, that does sound like Schmid. But by now, the man knows what she knows about him. She may be in extreme danger, or he could try blackmailing her into revealing everything about the rest of us."

"Blackmail? How?"

"His favorite way. Family. Mother, maybe."

"How can I help?" she asked.

"You already have. We lost her. You found her." He took hold of her hand and kissed the back of it. "I'll take it from here. We haven't much time." He slid off the bench and was gone.

Seconds later, three ebullient women converged on her booth to say hello and fill her ear with the daily blather. Simone smiled warmly and briefly obliged them.

CHAPTER FIFTY-THREE
Tours
April 26, Late Afternoon

LIEUTENANT SCHMID HAD Colette wait in the foyer. He crossed the marble floor. "What's so urgent?" he asked the woman behind the desk. "Why was I summoned?"

Miss Fassbender stopped typing and looked up. "I don't believe you're needed here, Lieutenant."

"What? Then who sent the telegram?"

"I haven't the faintest notion."

"Where's Major Holtzer?" he demanded.

"He's been out all afternoon. But if he wanted to see you, I can assure you I'd know about it."

Schmid turned and stomped off. Though confused, he felt relief that it wasn't Holtzer who needed him, but he was no closer to finding out why he was contacted.

His driver spent the next hour taking him from one place to another. Colette sat in the back seat while he failed to discover the telegram's purpose. No place needed him, and nobody knew of urgent developments to explain the message.

At last, his anger boiled up, realizing it was a wild goose chase. He looked at his watch. There was no time to get Colette into bed. An idea struck him: *The château!* It was the perfect place to enjoy the perfect woman—and he had nothing pressing that required a return to Tours tonight.

"To Château de Chenonceau!" he commanded his driver.

Half a block behind, a tall man in a trench coat held out his left hand and felt raindrops splat onto it. He adjusted his leather fedora, settled into the driver's seat, tested the windshield wipers, and set off down the same road as Schmid.

CHAPTER FIFTY-FOUR
Château de Chenonceau
April 26, Evening

SIMONE MENIER HAD no choice but to politely cut her admirers short at the café in Amboise and return to the château. It began drizzling as she pulled up. A freshened, neatly dressed, and anxious-looking Violette Lebon awaited her at the door.

"Madame, a hot bath is being drawn for you, and I set out some items for your consideration. Any will look lovely."

She appreciated her devoted assistant's enthusiasm but couldn't help ribbing her. "Dear, you do know the captain's having a few visitors, not hosting a gala."

"Oh, yes! I was only hoping to save you some time."

"You're very thoughtful. I'm sure it will."

"I'm glad you beat the rain."

"You can count on rain in April," Simone said, looking up at the threatening sky.

Entering her chamber, she closed her eyes and shook her head. She anticipated finding a couple of items to consider—not a dozen. She completed her choice of shoes, dress, and jewelry within seconds and returned the rest to her wardrobe. Having time to wind down before dinner, the bath felt exquisite after the long, dust-laden trip to Amboise and back. While soaking, her mind juggled the evening's possibilities and responsibilities—especially regarding Colette.

~ ~ ~

Violette received word to join Madame Menier in her study for dinner. Madame often dined there or in her private quarters, but seldom invited others. Sitting across from her, Violette felt uneasy. Having given little thought to her eating habits, she now self-assessed every move. Should she eat one item first in its entirety or some of each? Was it proper or excessive to take a sip after each bite? If there was soup, would she slurp it? Would a knife be required? The prospect of clanking utensils worried her. Mimicking Madame's behaviors would be embarrassingly obvious. To play it safe, she decided on a somewhat delayed shadowing of her mentor's actions.

"Bon appétit," said Madame before remaining reflective and quiet while they ate.

The silence made it especially difficult. Despite her mindfulness, Violette inwardly winced as each interaction of her knife with the china seemed amplified. At last, seeing Madame place her napkin on the table, she paused before doing the same, then set her fork and knife to the right of her plate. The silence finally broke.

"Violette, I must say that dress looks lovely on you. I don't recall seeing it before."

"Oh, thank you! I've saved it for a special occasion."

"I see. It's a bit disappointing knowing I'm the only one without an invitation tonight," Madame chided.

Violette blushed. "Oh, I wasn't invited, but—"

"You do know that we never greet the captain's visitors. He has able staff for that."

"I do, and I've never wanted to before," she replied anxiously, "but this feels different."

"It does. I can't argue that. I, too, would like to see Colette and get a sense of her well-being." Violette opened her mouth to speak, but Simone held up a finger and continued. "We must remain composed.

There's no reason we should know who Colette is, and even less reason to know she's coming here. We cannot make that mistake. Keeping their trust is imperative."

Violette nodded, but her wheels kept spinning. "I can check on her. Maybe bring some refreshments to their meeting."

Madame seemed to consider her suggestion. "We'll see. Your passion, loyalty, and eagerness are qualities I admire and wish to foster, but there's a risk to you both if you're near each other. Something could slip, even if it's just an expression or acknowledgment of each other. But thank you. It has given me an idea, and I hope it's okay that I'll need your help."

Violette's eyes lit up. "Oh, my. Yes, of course!"

"Good. By the way, I know it's only been two days, but have you seen any patterns with the guards?"

"Oui, Madame, but it may still be too soon. Give me two or three more days, and I'll know better."

"Smart thinking. Now, give me some time. I'll call on you shortly."

~ ~ ~

They were only minutes from the château when Schmid finally stopped sulking about the fiasco in Tours, and a satisfying feeling began to surface. He could hardly wait to present the showpiece he'd brought along. Those black locks flowing over her form-fitting white dress would leave them speechless and quash any debate about her unmatched beauty.

The wind was picking up, and a steady rain fell as they drove up the long, tree-lined approach and passed between two stone lions flanking the inner drive. Colette had kept quiet but leaned forward to look out the front windshield at the majestic sight.

"To think people live there," she whispered in awe.

The driver slowed and stopped near the guard tower to the right of the château.

"How long will we be?" she asked.

"I haven't decided," said Schmid. "We might spend the night if the hospitality is everything Captain Eicher says it is. Then again, my hotel bed is extremely comfortable." He stepped out and peeked back to gauge her reaction. She did nothing but sigh as though hearing a bad joke. Feeling exhilarated and confident, Schmid addressed his driver. "Hand the woman an umbrella. You've got the night off. Be here at six-thirty in the morning."

"Are you sure, Sir?" his driver asked, unable to hide his disbelief.

"Don't test me, Private."

A fidgety young sentry greeted them at the main entrance. Schmid brushed past him without regard, pulling Colette by the elbow. Her open umbrella caught the door frame and fell to the floor.

"No funny business," he whispered in her ear. "I'm not taking my eye off you."

~ ~ ~

Inside, a corporal escorted them to a great hall that spanned the River Cher. Colette saw two officers conversing. One nudged the other and pointed her way. The man dropped what he was doing. Lieutenant Schmid steered her that way.

"Good evening, Captain," Schmid began with a formal salute.

"Good evening, Lieutenant," Captain Eicher replied without taking his eyes off her. "I'd forgotten the bluster that preceded your arrival, but I see now that it was warranted. May I have the pleasure of being introduced to your guest?"

"Mademoiselle Dubois, Sir. Colette Dubois of Indre-et-Loire."

"Catchy." The captain took her hand and kissed the back of it. "Welcome to Château de Chenonceau, Mademoiselle."

"Thank you, Sir. It's beautiful."

"Ah, you've never been before? To what do we owe the pleasure?"

"The lieutenant is reuniting me with my mother here tonight." Schmid's stunned reaction was brief but didn't escape her. She slipped him a steely glance.

"Ah, excellent," said the captain. "I'm pleased you're here, no matter the reason, but the evening should be especially gratifying for you. Our meeting may take some time, but I hope we can visit more."

Schmid jumped in. "I'm sure that won't be a problem, Sir. I'll arrange a comfortable place for her to wait."

The captain kissed her hand again and excused himself. Schmid walked Colette to the far end of the long hall and out of earshot.

"Wait here until I come for you," he ordered.

"Where's my mother? You said she'd be here."

"Was that what I said? Or is that what you heard? Or maybe you came along because you want me. Not to worry; we'll have time for that later. Now sit down and don't even think about moving."

Colette seethed inside but kept her composure. Minutes later, she brightened. A woman appeared in a doorway near where the men sat. Captain Eicher stood, and the others followed suit. It never dawned on her that she might see Madame Menier. She rose in hopes of being seen. The woman never looked her way and walked directly to the man in charge.

~ ~ ~

"Captain, it has come to my attention that you have a guest this evening who may have some free time. It is contrary to my sense of etiquette and courtesy to leave her sitting idly by when I could offer a modicum of hospitality. May I have the pleasure of offering her a tour?" Simone correctly assumed the captain wouldn't consider how it came to her attention.

"Of course, Madame. You're speaking of the young lady just down the hall." He pointed her out. "It seems her mother is expected here this evening. Lieutenant Schmid has arranged for them to reunite."

"Oh, my. How wonderful," she played along.

Schmid overheard and stepped over to express his discomfort with the arrangement. "Captain, I'd rather not. Her mother may arrive, and I've been looking forward to—"

Eicher stopped him. "Where are your manners, Lieutenant? She's a charming young woman, but don't be greedy. Madame Menier won't steal her from you; nobody will steal your thunder. Would you rather refuse this gracious offer and leave her sitting alone while we take care of business?"

"I appreciate the offer, Sir. But yes, I'd prefer she wait here with us."

"Well, she's not with us. She's over there. Honestly, Schmid," Eicher said, shaking his head, "sometimes, you seem smart. Are you aware that we also value common sense?"

"Of course, Sir."

Eicher turned to Simone. "Yes, Madame Menier. By all means. And thank you for your generosity." Simone gave a curt nod and walked down the great hall to greet Colette.

Schmid slouched as Madame Menier escorted his guest out.

~ ~ ~

Auguste Gagnon had returned home as fast as his horse would take him. It was the first time he'd been in the house since his wife died, and the solitude struck him—but not for long. His despair and emptiness reverted to bitterness, anger, and hatred as he dressed in his nicest clothes and reached for his rain cloak.

Approaching the château, he made no effort to go unnoticed. Stealth and agility weren't in his skill set, and his horse and cart would be heard well before he arrived. There was a clearing to the side of the long entry drive. Tying the mare to a tree, he walked the remaining distance and was surprised to see only one guard manning the entry.

"Good evening, Sir," Auguste said, doffing his rain-soaked hat.

"Hello, Sir. Please state your business."

"Of course. I am here at the request of Lieutenant Schmid." The sentry appeared apprehensive. "He's expecting me."

Auguste stepped in from the rain and waited. Left alone, he stepped back outside, preferring that Schmid not spot him from a distance. Three minutes later, he heard footsteps approaching.

"He was right here when I...ah, Sir, this man claims he's come at your request," the sentry said, seeing Auguste step into view.

Schmid looked like he would explode, but said nothing and walked away, waving his arm for Auguste to follow.

"What in the hell are you doing?" he snapped.

Auguste put aside his usual cowardice for the first time. "We had a deal at the hotel," he complained. "Did you forget about me?"

"Honestly, yes," Schmid growled through clenched teeth. "Things changed. I got called away at the last—" He stopped. "Why the hell am I explaining it to you?"

"She killed my wife! Something needs to be done, and I plan on doing it. As we agreed!"

"So, you're going to march into a building full of Germans and be stupid? If you want to get caught and shot, that's a good way to do it."

"Where is she?" Auguste demanded.

"I don't know...wandering this place somewhere. And I wouldn't tell you if I knew. You'll get yourself killed; then everybody will start asking questions. I can't have that."

"You promised."

Schmid ran a hand through his oily hair. "Okay. This is how option one goes. I get my time with her, and then you do the dirty work for me late tonight...outside."

"That suits me fine. What's option two?"

"I eliminate you right now and restart everything from scratch. Finding the right people will take some doing, but I'm willing to go that route. Which do you prefer?"

"I'll do the dirty work. It's why I'm here. When?"

"It could be a while. I'm in a meeting, and you won't see her until I've had my fun."

"I'll wait all night if I have to," Auguste grumbled.

Schmid opened some nearby doors and found a darkened room with two chairs. "Wait here for me, and stay out of sight. I've got to get back. When I return, I'll let you know when and where."

~ ~ ~

The study door opened. Violette sprang to her feet and nearly squeezed the breath out of the visitor. Considering they'd only met once before, Colette was warmed by the affectionate display.

"You look wonderful," said Violette, stepping back and looking her over from top to bottom.

"All right, that's enough," Madame Menier broke in. "Violette is quite right, of course, but we have much to discuss. Fortunately, it's a big place, and it won't surprise them if we're away long." She patted

Colette's shoulder. "A real tour must come another time. Please have a seat. We knew you were coming, and we're so excited to see you, but —" Simone started over. "Tell us why you're here. What's happened? Everyone's been worried sick. Violette and I still are!"

"What? How did you know I was coming?" Colette wasn't sure what she could divulge to the two women. "So much has happened, but I'm not sure I should—"

"Ah, I see your dilemma," said Madame Menier. "I can help with that. You see," she said, looking to Violette, "Mademoiselle Lebon may not know it yet, but she is in training, just as you were."

The announcement surprised them both, and it took Colette a second to unravel the meaning.

"Oh, Madame!" Violette cried out. "You mean I can help—"

"You already are, dear. But first things first." She turned again to Colette. "Yes, we're all in this together, and each has a part. To answer your question about how we knew, Violette overheard and brought it to my attention. But we didn't know the purpose. And looking at how you're dressed, I still don't."

It was fuzzy to Colette, too. She described how Schmid brought her there like any trophy he'd want to show off. Both women were infuriated to hear that he planned on sleeping with her, including tonight at the château. Asked how it came about that she was with the lieutenant, Colette recounted everything from her trip to Loches and the Gagnon-Schmid connection to her capture by Auguste and his wife and how she ended up with Schmid here tonight. She chose to omit specific nightmarish events from the Gagnon house.

"Schmid tried luring me to meet with him, but I went voluntarily. He said he'd bring my mother here tonight. I had to hope and maybe buy time, but I've been naive. I'm not sure what's next. Given what I know, he'll want to get rid of me permanently...after he gets me into his bed, anyway."

"That's not going to happen," said Simone. "You're a brave woman, and you are right to hope...especially now among friends. Thanks to Violette, I was able to get word to Monsieur Bouchet that you were coming here tonight."

"I'm unsure what can be done, but thank you."

"It's another reason to hope. As far as your mother goes, you're correct in assuming Schmid won't keep his word. But Violette has some news." Simone motioned for her assistant to elaborate.

"Colette, I overheard some officers talking, and her name came up. I wish I had more details, but your mother is either in Orléans or on the way there."

"Orléans? Why?"

"I'm not sure, but we've learned your father knows about it, and he's going there with your brother to find her."

Simone spoke up. "You can be sure the lieutenant's bluffing about bringing her here tonight. I suspect he deported her." She chose not to mention how Orléans was notorious as a staging area for shipping prisoners farther east.

"If she's there, my father will find her. Do you think that's what happened to Madame Viard?"

"It's likely, but there's still no word about her or her son, Paul."

"And I haven't heard her name mentioned," Violette added.

Colette tried to stay positive. "When I was with Major Holtzer, he said he'd try to help. Maybe I'm being foolish, but he seemed sincere."

Simone shrugged. "It's quite possible. People say horrible things about him, but knowing what to believe is hard. Your encounter with his daughter may have been fortunate. Perhaps he's a man of honor and feels indebted."

"Maybe," said Colette, "but I don't think I'll be around long enough to ever find out."

"Don't say that!" Violette scolded.

"Anyway, I've been away from Schmid for a while. He may start getting suspicious."

"I agree," said Simone, "and trying to sneak you out would be futile. I'll walk you back."

"There's one more thing, Madame." Colette looked down and shook her head. "I don't know, though."

"What is it?"

"It's from the other day at the café in Bléré. I've been thinking about the château. Violette said that one end sits in occupied France, and the other in Free France."

"It does!" Violette perked up.

"An oddity of geography," said Simone.

"Well, for better or worse, we've been trying to help people escape occupied France. It turns out one of our own is a traitor. I suppose for the money. Schmid is the leader, and I don't think other Germans know. I'm sure he's doing it behind their backs."

"Yes, I'm aware. Bad news travels fast."

"Well, I haven't had the chance to speak to anyone about it, but what if we could move people across the border right here at the château? I don't know. It's just a thought. It would be dangerous."

"Go on," said Simone.

"The Germans are stationed here, and, well, they probably have guards keeping watch. Now that I think more, it would require you and Violette to take unfair risks."

"Nothing is fair in wartime, Colette. It's something we should all get accustomed to."

"I know, but—"

"I like that you've thought about it." She looked to her assistant.

"And the two of us agree." Colette and Violette both looked puzzled. "During the Great War," Simone continued, "brave soldiers were brought here and nursed back to health. Now, through some quirk of fate, divine intervention, or geographical whim, the château is again being called on to contribute. We'll discuss it more, but I've recently asked Violette to track the guard posts overseeing the river. It won't be long before we have some useful information to share."

Before escorting her back, Simone handed her a black satin handbag. "It's something I'd like you to have."

"Oh, my. It's beautiful! But I could never accept—"

"You're rejecting my gift?" Simone asked wryly.

"Oh, my. No. I'm sorry. Of course. It's lovely." She turned it to examine all sides. "Thank you so much. I love it. What will I tell Lieutenant Schmid?"

"If he insists on being nosy, tell him it's a gift from me."

Violette looked solemn. She stepped over and hugged Colette. "Don't forget to look inside," she whispered.

Madame Menier led the way downstairs and to the meeting.

"If you don't mind, is there a place I could freshen up a little?" Colette asked. Simone made a short detour and showed her to the salle de bain. "I can find them from here. Thank you for everything, Madame Menier. Wish me luck."

"I'll let the captain know you're on your way. Perhaps I'll send Violette down to peek in on you."

CHAPTER FIFTY-FIVE
Château de Chenonceau
April 26, Dusk

AUGUSTE PUT HIS ear to the door. Female voices were approaching in the corridor. He waited, turned the knob, and peeked out. From behind, he didn't recognize the woman she was with, but his wife's murderer was unmistakable. His life was torn apart only yesterday, and here she was: gussied up, shiny, and waltzing around a castle like a fucking princess. His blood boiled.

He never blinked until the two parted. Nothing would stand in his way, no matter what Schmid wanted. He gave it a little time, looked again, and was about to step out when the unknown woman appeared at the end of the hall. He slipped back into the room, quietly latched the door, and waited for the footsteps to fade.

~ ~ ~

Colette set her new handbag down, looked in the mirror, and made a few adjustments. It was not for Schmid's benefit; something about Madame Menier's comportment inspired her. While fluffing her hair, she remembered what Violette whispered in her ear. Undoing the bag's clasp, she peeked in and frowned. She ran her fingers inside. Nothing. Pulling her hand out, her knuckles brushed against something hard. Tilting the bag toward the vanity lamp revealed a large interior flap of black material stitched near the top and hanging in a way that concealed the inner lining on one side. She slipped her fingers under it and discovered a hidden pocket. The ornate brass letter opener she pulled out was a surprise, and Violette's somber attitude suggested it might be for more than opening envelopes. Colette shuddered at the thought, dropped it back inside, and hung the bag on a hook next to the wash basin.

She suspected she had dawdled long enough, but washing her hands was a final way of delaying her dreaded return to Schmid. She didn't hear the groaning door over the running water. Shutting off the faucet and grabbing a neatly folded handtowel, she looked in the mirror one last time.

"Wha!" she cried, petrified at the reflection of a man behind her.

"Remember me?" Auguste Gagnon's voice chilled her spine. "I'm the man who watched you murder his wife."

She caught her breath, struggled to regain herself, and turned. "The stars know what to do with traitors."

The last word had hardly left her mouth when a fierce blow struck the left side of her head. She staggered and crumpled against the wall.

"Never mind about that," he said, pushing his shirt sleeves up. "It's *your* fate that should worry you now."

The only way out was through him. She tried to buy time. "Schmid won't like that you're messing up his prize."

"I'll deal with him and his consequences later."

He grabbed her with both hands and threw her like she was weightless. She slammed against the unyielding wall. Instinctively wiping at a warm trickle near her right eye, her fingers turned red.

"He'll kill you," she muttered, "and nobody in France will complain about one less thief, rapist, and murderer." She thought of the letter opener. "Why did you do it?" she said through gritted teeth.

"In case you haven't heard, France is a lost cause. While you're getting yourself killed, I'm getting rich."

Scared but defiant, she got her feet under her and stood. River Man still blocked the way.

"A lot of good it'll do you. They all know." She tried to keep his mind occupied while inching toward the handbag. "I've told everyone. And if they don't get you, Schmid will. He can't trust you any more than we can. You're a murderer and a fool. Your wife is gone, and you're next."

"No, YOU'RE NEXT!" he roared.

She lunged for the bag. Auguste rushed at her. She clutched the heavy opener in her right hand and swung for his chest. He saw it coming and grabbed her forearm. He pried it from her grip with his free hand, tossed it behind him, and threw her backward over the sink. Her head slammed into the mirror, and glass pieces rained down. He kept coming. She flailed her feet and swiped at him with a large shard, gashing his forehead.

"Argh! You bitch!" Throwing her to the floor, he pinned her down with his knees and seized her neck. "Nothing will compare to doing it with my bare hands!"

It felt like a vice squeezing from all directions. Unable to breathe, things began to blur. She sensed a loud noise. The suffocating grip stopped, and she gasped, her lungs desperate for air. The vice tightened again. Everything went dark.

Something wet spattered her face, and the crushing stopped. Gulping for air triggered a fit of coughing. She regained her senses but struggled to focus. On the floor at her side was Auguste Gagnon, motionless—a brass handle protruding from the base of his skull. She pushed him away with her legs. His head flopped to the side, revealing a blade sticking out of his right eye.

"Careful there." A strained voice startled her. She turned her head. "Try not to move. That glass can cut you good."

A bloodied man sat propped against the far wall. "Who—," she croaked, unable to finish.

"Don't speak just yet."

~ ~ ~

Violette was sent downstairs by Madame Menier under the auspices of tending to Captain Eicher's needs. She had a strict directive to avoid eye contact with Colette. Before arriving, a crashing noise down the hallway made her change course. Passing the washroom, she heard a man's voice and stopped to knock.

"Hello?" she called softly. "Is everything okay?"

"No. Please help us."

The man's voice seemed strangely calm, given his reply. Cautiously opening the door, she peeked in.

"Colette!" She rushed over and knelt at her side. "You're hurt! What can I—." Colette patted her shoulder with a blood-free hand and pointed to the man sitting on the opposite wall. Violette struggled to look away from the dead stranger slumped on the floor with Madame Menier's letter opener sticking out of his eye.

The man motioned with his right arm for Violette to come to his side. Colette nodded her approval. There was fresh blood soaking the injured man's shirt below his ribcage. His left arm looked severely out of place or broken.

"Sir, you're badly hurt!"

"My arm is dislocated...possibly broken. But I suspect this bleeding is the bigger problem."

"I'll fetch someone to help you!"

"Thank you, but in a moment. This young woman may still be in danger. Please take her to Madame Menier as fast as you can. Afterward, I'd welcome your assistance."

She sprang back to Colette, helping her stand. "Are you okay?"

"My whole body hurts," she wheezed, "but I don't think anything's broken or missing."

Violette poked her nose into the hall. She turned and mouthed the words 'thank you' to the stranger. He motioned with his good arm for her to hurry.

~ ~ ~

Lieutenant Schmid wasn't actively participating in the meeting. Colette's continued absence was the only thing on his mind. At last, he'd had enough.

"Sir, will you please excuse me? I need to check on my guest and ensure she's okay."

"If you must," said Captain Eicher, "but make it quick."

Schmid went door to door, hoping to find the powder room with Colette inside. He soon received an unexpected shock. Lying on the floor, plainly dead, was Auguste Gagnon. A second man sat against the far wall, applying pressure to a bleeding wound with a coat and one good arm.

"Where's the girl?" Schmid demanded.

The man looked up. "Are you from the infirmary?"

"WHERE?" he bellowed.

"Who?" came the casual reply.

Schmid stormed out of the room and ran for the château entrance.

"Private!" he yelled at the sentry. "Did a woman come this way?"

"No, Sir. Nobody has come in or out since the Frenchman who asked for you."

For the first time, Schmid focused on the young man. "Wagner? Just my fucking luck. Wagner?"

"Uh...Wegner, Sir. Yes, Sir. I'm stationed here now."

"Whatever. Take me to Madame Menier's room."

"And leave the post unattended, Sir?"

"That's an order!"

"Yes, Sir! Do you mean her bedroom or study?"

"I don't know. Both! Move it!"

Simone's study was their first stop.

"Open it!" he ordered.

The private tried the handle. "It's locked, Sir."

Schmid stepped up and pounded on the door. "Open up immediately!" He heard hushed voices. "NOW!"

The lock clicked, and he slammed the door open, nearly toppling Madame Menier.

"Lieutenant, your lady guest was attacked. I'm tending to her."

"What has she told you?" he fumed.

"About what?"

"Don't play dumb with me!"

He grabbed Colette's arm and yanked her from the room.

"I'll deal with you two later," he snapped at Simone and Violette. "Private, watch them. They don't leave this room until I return!"

Schmid pulled her down the stairs to the main floor and headed for the entry. He couldn't afford to be seen by Eicher or the others. They'd ask questions, and she might blurt out undesired answers.

A woman was dusting furniture at the far end of the hall.

"A gentleman in the salle de bain needs help!" Colette called out.

When the maid was out of sight, he slapped her, knocking her to the floor. Before she could stand, he dragged her out the front door and across the drive, through one puddle after another.

"Get up! What the fuck happened in there!"

"He attacked me!" she cried, struggling to her feet.

"The other one. Who is he?"

"I've never seen him before, but he saved my life from that monster." Her legs were scraped and bleeding. She pulled at the soaking-wet dress clinging to her.

"This has gone too far. *You've* gone too far!" He took a second to compose himself. "You know too much. That man in there, whoever he is...I'll take care of him, too. And your friends. I'll hunt them all down. There's no more help coming for you."

"You're a murderer and a thief," she snarled. "Anyone who doesn't know that is a fool. Two weeks ago, I was that fool. I didn't even know people like you existed."

"Oh, I'll exist long after your pretty ass is ten feet under. Your time has come, and it's a shame. We could've had fun." He saw her gazing at the moat and the Cher flowing just beyond it. "I can't have you do that," he said. "It's unlikely, but what if you somehow survived?"

He'd calmed down but was disappointed and frustrated that the time to eliminate his goddess had come before he could do everything he wanted to her.

~ ~ ~

The last light of dusk was gone. The heavy clouds and steady rain made everything colorless. The two were getting wetter by the second, but Colette took no notice and began accepting her fate.

"Your own people will soon be onto you," she mumbled. "It's just a matter of time."

"Hah! Try again. A promotion's inevitable when I capture the Brit spy and American officer Tuesday morning." A smug, rain-soaked grin spread across his face, highlighting his suddenly grotesque scar. "You didn't think I knew about that, did you?"

The team's deception plan had slipped her mind with everything else going on.

"You're an idiot," she scoffed. Schmid's expression turned severe. He backhanded her across the face, staggering her. "Do you honestly believe that?" she went on. "Even if it wasn't a ruse to fool a fool, who would row the boat now? It sure won't be the dead asshole with the leaking eyeball." Colette could see his brain racing with the realization he'd been outwitted.

"What a waste," he finally said, examining his handgun.

"You're just going to shoot me in cold blood?"

"No." He pointed to the château. "I'm the one who chased down and shot an escaping murderer."

Colette came to terms with Fate, and her thoughts shifted. "What's become of my family?"

"Fair enough. There's no reason you can't know. I honestly have no idea of your father's whereabouts. He's a crafty son of a bitch. Quite good at acting innocent, too. You take after him that way...but I'll find him."

"Not if he finds you first. And my mother?"

"Ah, yes. Your mother. She was on her way to Orléans. But I've washed my hands of her. I suspect she's already been shipped off to another camp. Anywhere we send undesirables."

"You have a fucked up sense of what's undesirable."

Schmid backhanded her again, knocking her to the ground.

"My father will bring her back," she said, looking up. "Then he'll hunt you down."

"You don't get it, do you?" Schmid said, reexamining his pistol. "Most of France does, but some of you are too damn stubborn or blind to see it. It's over, got it? France is now Germany. And for those that don't accept it—" He paused and glared at her. "I'll be the one doing the hunting."

"We'll see," she said in a near whisper.

"You sure as hell won't," he sneered. "Now get up. I don't usually shoot women in the back, but I have no choice if you're escaping."

She realized she'd been sitting in a growing pool of cold rainwater and slowly stood. Her impending doom didn't heighten her senses. They were dull.

"Turn and run," Schmid commanded.

She had no intention of appeasing him.

CHAPTER FIFTY-SIX
Château de Chenonceau
April 26, Nightfall

COLETTE FELT NOTHING. Her thoughts drifted to her family.

"If you won't run, I need you to turn away." Schmid's voice sounded distant and unimportant. She wasn't opposed to following the instruction, but something vague distracted her.

A glint in her eye caused Schmid to turn. Two approaching lights cut through the murk. "Verdammt! Who the fuck is this?" He looked back at her. "It makes no difference. You sealed your fate when you killed that Frenchman."

The vehicle stopped thirty meters out and sat idling. The headlights soon silhouetted someone walking toward them.

He squinted. "Who the—" The answer became apparent as the figure neared. "Perfect," he hissed. "This man came to Tours to deal with people like you. I'll gladly take credit for your capture."

The imposing man approached but said nothing. She, too, remained silent. Schmid spoke first.

"Sir, I've apprehended this woman for the murder of a civilian inside the château. If you don't recognize her, she's also responsible for killing the woman on the tracks in Tours."

Major Holtzer considered him, then looked down at Colette. "Are these accusations true?"

"This man is the murderer," she murmured, "and he's robbing people blind. French *and* German. It doesn't matter to him."

Schmid jumped in. "Sir, she's delusional and will say anything to save her hide. I've caught her red-handed. She may look innocent and sure as hell can act it, but she's a spy, a murderer, and a threat to the entire Reich."

"Hmm, the entire Reich, huh? We may need to up our game." Holtzer looked her over as though considering Schmid's assessment. "A spy?" He tilted his head. "It's possible. They come in all shapes, sizes, ages...and genders." He considered her longer. "A murderer? You're right. She doesn't look the part. Few do, I suppose. She looks innocent enough, but I've only just arrived and may have to take your word for it. And, if what you say is true," he continued, "I can see how she'd be a threat."

The lieutenant brightened. Colette accepted her fate.

~ ~ ~

Schmid felt emboldened and offered his advice. "Sir, she's a murdering spy and needs to be executed."

"Perhaps, Lieutenant. But prior to that, have we learned everything we can from her?"

Schmid cringed inside. *This can't drag out. If she talks, somebody might believe her—or at least look into it.*

"Yes, Sir. I have."

"Alright."

Yes! He had finally turned the corner. The major would soon be added to his list of those he could influence and manipulate. "Sir, I'm prepared to handle this right now."

Major Holtzer nodded, looked sadly at Colette, and asked her to turn around. She looked at him with resigned dignity, tears glazing her eyes. Schmid slipped her a steely grin and raised his gun. Holtzer stopped him.

"Put your gun away, Lieutenant. I came here to bring order and lead by example." His eyes scanned the château and surrounding property. "If anyone's to be executed, it will be by my hand."

"I understand, Sir."

~ ~ ~

It felt dreamlike: opaque, unreal, but not nightmarish. Colette again took in the grand château, then the Cher and the trees on the far bank. It was beautiful. So near Free France, it was a fitting place to die. She closed her eyes and breathed in La Mère de la Terre's sweet night air. She thought of her family and smiled.

Time was lost on her. It may have been a fraction of a second or minutes before she realized she was still standing—still alive. Something felt strangely heavy against the back of her legs. Someone grasped her elbow and pulled her forward. She opened her eyes.

"Stay right there." The major let go of her arm and stooped down. The blade of a knife rested deep between Lieutenant Schmid's ribs. Viktor Holtzer wrenched the handle violently and yanked it out. The body made a final spasm. He wiped the blade clean on the dead man's rain-soaked jacket and settled it back into its sheath.

Colette stared at the scene, confused. Blood had mixed with water, creating different shades of swirling gray in a pool around the body. She looked at the major, speechless.

Holtzer looked down the entry drive. A vehicle flashed its lights. He held up three fingers, then five, then seven. The headlights flashed again.

"Let's get you inside." She didn't respond. He took her arm and walked her to the château.

At the entrance, she turned to look back at the lifeless body. "I don't understand."

~ ~ ~

Viktor Holtzer expected to find someone to assist him inside the château, but found nobody.

"Can you show me to Madame Menier?" he gently asked her.

"Yes." She pointed the way.

He helped her ascend the staircase. They were approaching the study when she stopped. "A man saved me in the salle de bain on the main floor. Now you did. What's going on?"

"A German soldier?" Holtzer asked.

"No. I don't think so. He had plain clothes, and he's been hurt."

"Do you know if he's still there?"

"I'm not sure. I hope he's being taken care of. There's also a dead man in there. His name's Auguste Gagnon."

"Let's get you some help first."

A private abruptly saluted when he opened the study door.

"Wegner?" Then it dawned on him. "Right. Miss Fassbender said you were assigned here. Thank you for keeping these women safe."

"Huh? Um, yes. Of course, Sir."

"Madame Menier, this young lady has some injuries. She's cold and soaked through. Could you tend to her, please?"

Simone and Violette rushed to Colette's side.

"You poor thing. We'll take care of you," Violette said, trying to comfort her.

"Madame Menier, when you're ready, will the three of you return here and wait for me?"

"Of course."

The two hurried Colette from the study.

Major Holtzer turned to the private. "Show me the washroom on the main floor. Something's happened."

~ ~ ~

Private Wegner led Major Holtzer to the main floor, down a hallway, and around the corner. Inside the washroom, they found blood, broken glass, and a man slumped on the floor. The private looked on, shocked, as the major grasped the handle of a letter opener, slid it from the skull, wiped matter from each blade face onto the dead man's jacket, and held it up to examine its artistry.

"Any idea who this fellow is?"

"Uh, no, Sir," Wegner answered, unable to avert his eyes from the gruesome scene. "He arrived earlier to see Lieutenant Schmid. Otherwise, I've never seen him before."

"Did you see another man? Civilian clothes?"

"No, Sir."

"No, I suspect not. Tell Captain Eicher I'm here and will visit him shortly, then keep watch at the main entry."

"Yes, Sir. That's my post this evening. Lieutenant Schmid asked me to leave it unattended."

"Are you the only one posted?"

"It's usually pretty quiet around here, Sir."

"Mmm, then I'd say this evening's an exception. You'll see a car idling outside. After you inform the captain, bring everyone inside, escort them to Madame Menier's study, and immediately return to your post. Nobody comes in or out."

"What if someone outranks me, Sir?"

"Tell them it's by my orders."

"Yes, Sir!" he saluted, buoyed by the responsibility.

"But first, how do I get to the infirmary?"

After telling Major Holtzer the way, the private told Captain Eicher of the impending visitor. The announcement seemed to catch the captain off guard, but having no more details to provide, Wegner was excused.

"Private?" Captain Eicher called after him. "If you see Lieutenant Schmid, tell him I'm—. Never mind, I'll tell him myself."

"Yes, Sir."

~ ~ ~

Holtzer was impressed. He had no reason to doubt the infirmary's cleanliness, but it was larger and better equipped than expected. It was also empty—except for a bed at the far end with two women tending to a patient. He walked over and introduced himself to the caregivers. The patient's left arm was splinted and immobilized. His torso was wrapped in heavy gauze held in place by large swaths of tape.

"Fine, skilled nurses here, Viktor," said the man. "Shoulder's back in place; arm's immobilized. It took some effort, but they also stopped me from bleeding to death."

"It wasn't a surety," said one of the nurses, "but he'll be fine with follow-up care and a few months rest."

"Months, huh? Thank you, mesdames. I need to speak with him if that's okay."

"Please make it quick," the same nurse said with trepidation.

"I promise."

The nurses gave them privacy. Holtzer pulled a chair beside the bed, grinned, and shook his head. "Well, my friend, you can outdo yourself when I ask you to watch somebody."

"In truth," said Thomas, "it wasn't how I foresaw the day unfolding when I woke this morning."

The major changed his tone. "All kidding aside, my family would be devastated if anything happened to you. Sonja was upset enough thinking you're back in Germany and can't be seen for weeks."

The injured man smiled. "Well, tell her I'll see her soon."

"I will."

Thomas' face turned serious. "It was luck, Viktor. Any later, I might not have saved her."

"But you did. A day doesn't go by that I don't think of lives I wish I'd saved." He produced the brass weapon he'd been carrying and examined it. "I'm not sure where you got this multi-purpose letter opener, but you sure put it to good use."

"I don't know either. It was just there on the floor," Thomas said, shaking his head. "Any idea who he is?"

"The young Dubois woman said his name is Auguste Gagnon. Ever heard of him?"

"Gagnon? No, but he and Schmid know each other somehow. I followed her from your place to the church. From there, Schmid was stuck to her like glue. He took her to a boutique, a beautician, and then his hotel. I couldn't chance what he might do there, so I concocted a telegram that he was needed. This Gagnon watched them from the lobby. You're right about Schmid, Viktor. He's up to no good. I'm guessing she stumbled onto something she shouldn't have, and he brought Gagnon here to do his dirty work."

"I'm sorry I almost got you killed, but you did good, Thomas. I owe you."

"Unhh." The patient winced from a surge of pain. "Just a day's work. I haven't spotted Schmid since he went into the meeting. She may still be in danger."

"The lieutenant is no longer of consequence, and I'll make arrangements for the young lady until she's reunited with her family."

Holtzer glanced across the room, saw two concerned nurses staring back, and stood. "Now, get some rest. We'll talk soon. I don't think this uniform has much clout in here." He left his friend in good hands and departed for the ongoing meeting.

As he entered the great hall, everyone stood in unison and saluted. He paused briefly, taking in the château's grandeur for the first time.

"Impressive office you have here, Captain."

"Thank you, Sir. I quite agree. To what do we owe the pleasure of your first visit?"

"No pleasure. I won't take long. Lieutenant Schmid will not be rejoining your meeting. His corruption is limitless, and his disloyalty to the homeland is unpardonable. He's been dealt with accordingly." Everyone sat in stunned silence. "Any questions?"

"Uh, no, Sir. Thank you for informing us," Captain Eicher answered. The others remained silent.

"Regarding his female guest this evening," Holtzer continued. "His intentions were dishonorable, immoral, malicious, and incompatible with my expectations...hopefully with anyone's expectations. If that isn't clear for any of you, speak up now." Nobody said a word. "I'll make arrangements for her care. Thank you, Captain."

The group again saluted. Holtzer turned and walked out.

~ ~ ~

Having treated the bumps, bruises, and cuts, Madame Menier left the room—leaving her assistant to take care of any remaining matters. Colette was patient as Violette made deliberate and discriminating wardrobe selections. The shoes were a bit large, but she wasn't particular and graciously accepted every item presented. She let Violette dote on her as she wished, including brushing her hair. At last finished, they returned to the study.

A shriek filled the usually tranquil room. Colette ran to embrace Philippe and Marcel.

"How...how did you get here? Why are you here?" she stammered, stepping back to see Philippe beaming.

Marcel grinned. "We're here because of your friends. Madame Menier rushed word that you were coming. This young lady," he said, pointing at Violette, "is the only reason anyone knew."

A woman standing to one side was unknown to her.

"I'm sorry, do I know—"

"Where are my manners?" said Marcel. "Colette and Violette, this is Miss Fassbender, Major Holtzer's aide. She drove us here."

"Drove you?" Colette gave the stranger a confused look. The woman returned a kind smile.

"It's a bit complicated," said Marcel. "Madame Menier has been filled in, and—"

There was a sudden knock. Major Holtzer stepped into the room and closed the door. "Please, everyone, have a seat."

Simone's study was spacious but not equipped for a gathering of seven. Colette didn't argue when Philippe slid a chair behind her. The others remained standing.

She turned and looked up at him, stunned. "Philippe, did you come here with...with Major Holtzer?"

"I did."

"I don't understand. What's going on?"

Most in the room were equally unsure of the answer and turned their eyes to the major. He obliged them.

"Monsieur Bouchet got word to Miss Fassbender earlier this evening that Lieutenant Schmid was bringing you here. I was busy, but they rightly understood the urgency and tracked me down. The three of us set out right away."

She looked again at Philippe. "But how did you end up—"

"Pure chance," Holtzer interrupted. "Monsieur Bouchet saw him on the streets of Tours searching for you, and we picked him up."

Philippe tapped his chest. "I about had a heart attack when a black car with German flags pulled up, and someone called my name. But," he shrugged, "my feet were getting sore, so I hopped in."

"What? I still don't understand. How did anyone know to—" She turned to Marcel. "What had you go to Major Holtzer?"

"Like I was saying: It's complicated."

"Suffice it to say," said Holtzer, "Lieutenant Schmid wasn't desirable to France *or* Germany."

"But the other man I told you about—" Colette began. "The one who saved my life. Did you find him?"

"Yes. The nurses here are extraordinary, and he's on the mend. Thank you for that, Madame Menier."

"Does anybody know who he is or why he's here?" Simone asked.

"He's a friend of mine," said Holtzer. "A discreet one when necessary. He's my eyes and ears whenever and wherever I need him. I asked him to keep an eye on Colette, so when I learned she was being brought here, I expected I might also find him."

"These were brought to me. I believe they're his," said Simone. She held up a long charcoal-gray trench coat and a matching leather fedora. "I think the hat survived, but it's unlikely the coat will recover from these bloodstains."

"He was using it as a compress when I returned," said Violette. "I offered him a towel, but he didn't care. Said it was just a coat."

"Thank God he's okay. He saved my life." Colette turned to Major Holtzer. "But I don't understand why you had him following me. Was I to be arrested?"

Holtzer smiled. "Oh, I hope I have more important things to do than arrest young French women. No, think of it more like watching over rather than following."

"Watching over me is what he did...like an angel." A somber expression came over her, and she switched subjects. "Violette overheard that my mother was on her way to Orléans. And maybe my father and Louis are heading there to find her. Is there any news?"

The room went silent. Philippe put his hand on her shoulder. "Nothing yet."

Her eyes were glazed. "Do I go home and wait? Should I go to Orléans and try to find them? I'm not sure what to do."

"You'll do neither," said Violette. "You're staying here at the château with Madame Menier and me until your family's found."

Colette looked to Simone, who nodded.

CHAPTER FIFTY-SEVEN
Outskirts of Amboise
April 29, Morning

PHILIPPE AGREED WHEN Marcel requested that he accompany him to the Tours station. Some patriotic colleagues were arriving there, but not until midday. He was thrilled by the suggestion that they first stop at the château to check on Colette. Madame Menier arranged for them to be picked up at a junction just south of Amboise, so that's where they sat, awaiting their ride.

"I don't know anyone with a car," said Philippe. "She seems well-connected, non?"

"Indeed, and I trust her. Let's see what happens."

"Good enough for me."

After several minutes, Marcel asked him what he thought about inviting Colette to the station with them. Nothing could've made him happier, but he thought she might be hesitant, given what happened the last time she was there.

Marcel gave an understanding nod. "What is it they say...the American cowboys...about getting back on a horse?"

"Yeah, yeah. I know it! It's like not giving up...or maybe doing something again soon. You know...before it gets in your head and you can't ever do it again."

"Well, this may be a good chance. Nothing negative about it. A nice change from her last time there."

Philippe looked up. "Not to mention, it's a beautiful day. Maybe she'll want to get out."

"It's a thought, anyway," said Marcel. "It can't hurt to ask."

Philippe pointed out a black car creeping their way. "It looks lost."

It slowed even more when passing them, stopped, and backed up. The driver stepped out.

"Château de Chenonceau?" the sentry from the château asked.

Marcel raised a finger; the driver opened the back door.

A few minutes down the road, Philippe rolled down the window to create noise and leaned toward Marcel. "I sure wasn't expecting a Nazi to give us a ride," he whispered.

"She has a way about her," Marcel whispered back.

CHAPTER FIFTY-EIGHT
Château de Chenonceau
April 29, Midday

MADAME MENIER AND Violette were reviewing sentry logs when Private Wegner brought Marcel and Philippe to the study and excused himself. After exchanging pleasantries, Philippe asked how Colette was doing.

"She's well," said Simone, "other than being worried sick about her family and upset at the lack of information. She doesn't know you're here. She'll be delighted."

"It's all we can do to keep her from running off to Orléans," said Violette. "I think we convinced her to give the others a chance."

"Her body and mind heal quickly," said Simone. "It's amazing. Despite her ordeal, she's eager to get back in the mix of things."

"She'd rather risk the dangers and be helping people than doing nothing and helping nobody," Violette added.

Philippe liked what he was hearing and glanced over to get Marcel's reaction.

"That does sound like her," he said. "Do you think she's ready for an outing to the station in Tours with Philippe and me?"

"Oh, I suspect so. Let's ask. Violette, would you please bring her?"

The two entered a minute later. Colette ran to kiss them both.

"You look great," Philippe gushed. "Weren't you the one who nearly drowned in an icy river, almost got run over by a train, and narrowly escaped being strangled and shot?"

She cringed. "Thanks for the reminder. Anyway, I have no choice with this one around." She gave Violette a sweet look. "Honestly, she pampers me far too much."

"Why shouldn't I?" said Violette. "You deserve it, and it makes me feel good."

"I can't believe you're living in a castle," said Philippe.

"Oh, it's not a castle," Colette corrected, "it's a château."

"Really? What's the diff—"

"Madame Menier says you're doing well," Marcel interrupted.

"Everyone is so kind and supportive. But I can't stop worrying about my parents and Louis. If I don't hear anything in the next day or two, I'll try to catch a train for Orléans."

Marcel bobbed his head. "I understand and expected as much. If it gets to that point, I'll have others escort you. We have people looking hard. In the meantime, speaking of trains, I wondered if you might consider joining Philippe and me. We're heading to Tours to greet some important passengers. Given your recent experience there, I'd understand if you'd rather not."

"No, it's a nice day. I'd like to come. And my father always said to climb back on the horse if you fall off." Philippe and Marcel looked at each other. "What is it?" she asked.

"Oh, nothing," said a perplexed Philippe.

Marcel patted her arm. "We're just glad you'll join us."

"Good, it's settled," said Simone. "Private Wegner will have a car waiting for you outside."

"Excellent," said Marcel. "If you would all step out a moment, Madame Menier and I have something to discuss. I'll be there shortly."

CHAPTER FIFTY-NINE
Gare de Tours
April 29, Late Afternoon

COLETTE FOLLOWED MARCEL and Philippe into the station. They walked to the near end of the scheduled arrival platform to wait on a bench. Philippe couldn't stop fidgeting and looked like he had something on his mind.

"Spit it out," said Marcel. "What is it?"

Philippe turned to Colette. "I hate to ask, but would you be okay showing me where it happened?"

Marcel shrugged and also admitted his curiosity. She motioned for them to follow her.

"It was much busier four days ago, and it was chaos after the gunshots...but about there," she said, pointing with a circular motion.

The two men walked to the platform edge, hesitated, and peeked over. Philippe looked incredulous. "Damn, there isn't much room down there."

They returned to the bench and waited. All stood when the train rolled into sight.

"I'm not sure which car they'll be on," said Marcel. "From here, we may only see people disembark from the first two or three. But they know what I look like, and I have their description. Anyway, everyone has to pass by us here."

The train belched smoke and came to a stop. She and Philippe watched the passengers step off without knowing who to look for. The first two cars unloaded nothing but German soldiers. Their eyes drifted to the third.

"Anything?" Philippe asked.

"Hmm, not yet," said Marcel.

"Hah!" Colette spouted. "That boy getting off the third car reminds me of—" She froze. A woman stepped off behind the lad, followed by a big, bearded man. Colette gasped and cupped her hands over her mouth. She turned to Marcel with a glazed look. He returned a smile and dipped his head.

She whirled and raced down the platform. "MAMA!"

Marcel put his arm around Philippe and gave him a wink. "It's good to have them back, non?"

Philippe stared back at him, speechless.

CHAPTER SIXTY
The Dubois Farm
April 30

COLETTE AND HER family returned to their quiet farmhouse northwest of Amboise and were left alone to enjoy each other in peace. Charles Touchard, who cared for the animals when not immersed in his forging efforts, departed to allow the family their private time.

There was much to tend to, but the animals were fine, and her father insisted that several things could wait. The four sat together and shared their harrowing, exciting, and sometimes uplifting stories. Her parents could hardly believe everything she'd been through. She expected both of them to be angry, but it was clear that their pride outweighed other feelings.

She and her brother cried when their parents decided to tell them about Paul and his folks before they heard it from others. Later, she stood at the window with her mother and teared up watching Louis wander off toward the old footbridge. After allowing him some time to himself, they went to join him.

Early in the evening, while Giselle prepared supper, François invited his children to join him in making rounds of the property. As always, her brother scampered ahead. Approaching a shed, Louis stopped in his tracks.

"Papa?"

François held up a hand, signaling for Colette to stop. "What is it, son?" he called out. Louis just turned his back to them and pointed. They caught up. Not ten meters from them was a horse harnessed to a wagon. "What in the—" François muttered.

"Is it lost, Papa?" Louis wondered.

Colette walked up to the old mare and stroked her cheek. "No, she's not lost. She's right where she belongs."

CHAPTER SIXTY-ONE
The Dubois Farm
May 1

TWENTY-FOUR HOURS OF family time seemed plenty to the others. Two days after the reunion at the station, well-wishers and curiosity seekers converged on the Dubois farm to welcome them back and hear their stories.

There was a solemn air as many needed to speak of their departed friends. François relieved his wife from the burden of recounting the events. While captive, Giselle learned about a woman and boy who met their demise the day before her arrival. The woman had arranged to smuggle her son out of the camp but was double-crossed. The boy was apprehended, and the mother shackled. They were marched into the center of the yard and made examples of. An execution-style shot to the head killed Regina Viard, but not before being forced to watch her son, Paul, slowly hang to death from a guard tower.

Marcel, Henri, and Georges stood apart from the others. "Was Schmid's death mollifying for anyone?" Marcel asked.

"For now, maybe," said Georges. "It gives them a chance to grieve rather than focus on hatred and revenge."

"Nothing will ever make up for Roland and his family," said Henri, "but I plan on trying. Schmid was an evil bastard. They all are."

"I don't know about *all*, but I suspect Fate keeps a closer eye on some," said Marcel, his fingers fiddling with something.

"What have you got there?" asked Georges.

"Oh, Colette handed me these earlier." Marcel held out two diamond stones. "More from River Man's dropped bag, I'm guessing.

Anyway, they'll come in handy."

Henri's hatred for Auguste Gagnon resurfaced. "God only knows how much he stole in jewels, money, artwork, or whatever."

"Or was paid off by Schmid," Georges added.

"I'm hoping to find that out before people notice he's missing," said Marcel. "Jean-Paul and a team went down yesterday to turn his place inside out. Risky to spend, so I suspect they stashed most of it."

"If so, they'll find it," said Georges, "but it won't help the poor souls it belonged to."

"No, it won't," Marcel agreed, "but we'll put it to good use."

Philippe spotted the three men and joined them. He looked back at Colette. She stood between Simone and Charles in a group gathered around her parents. Everyone was captivated by the retelling of events that led to their return.

"I'm so glad Madame Menier and Violette could make it," he said, his eyes still fixed on Colette. "She was thrilled to see them, though I've hardly seen Violette since they arrived."

"Simone filled me in on some intriguing ideas she's discussed with Violette and Colette," Marcel said. "We'll talk later."

"Any hints?" Henri asked.

"When you were complaining about Auguste that night at the river, I asked if there was any other option."

"I remember."

"Well, we may have found one."

"I heard some resistance cells are naming themselves," Philippe said out of the blue. "You know...the whole group, not just the people. Maybe we should, too. What do you think?"

Marcel, Henri, and Georges looked at each other.

"We've been talking about that very thing," said Marcel. "How about everyone considers it, and we'll discuss it at the next meeting?"

They tuned in to François across the room.

"Louis and I stayed positive," they heard him say. "We kept the faith, but I'd be lying if I said I was confident. It would be difficult just finding where they brought her."

"How did you?" someone asked.

"Well, the first place we went, they treated us like dirt. The guards ignored me until I became insistent. That's when they knocked the wind out of me with the butt of a rifle. I told Louis we'd come back later. The holding sites are always near the tracks, so we moved on to the next one and asked again: Can you tell me if a Giselle Dubois is being held here?"

François paused for effect.

"And?" a spellbound listener asked.

"Strangest damned thing. The two guards stopped what they were doing, looked me over from top to bottom, and did the same to Louis. Then, instead of ignoring or threatening me, one said, 'We were told you might come. Wait here.' He walked away. Ten minutes later, my heart stopped. He was returning with—" He couldn't finish.

Giselle stepped in. "The guard found me and told me to grab my stuff. He said I had a visitor. I had no idea what he was talking about. I never saw anyone get visitors, and I didn't have any stuff. I followed him, fearing the worst. Then, I saw—" Her eyes watered. "I'm sorry. I didn't think I'd ever feel joy like that again...until I saw Colette running toward us at the station."

"I had no idea what was happening," François sniffed. "A car pulled up. We were driven to a hotel in the heart of Orléans and given a room for the night." Waving a hand before his nose, he added, "We all appreciated a nice bath."

"Even Louis approved," Giselle said, shaking her head. "Whenever I asked François what was happening, he just shrugged."

"I'm still shrugging. I have no idea what happened, but I don't care. I have her back. I have everyone back," he said, smiling at his daughter.

Violette appeared with Louis at her side. She looked winded.

"Where did you disappear to?" Simone asked, looking her over. "And where are your shoes?"

"They're full of mud. I left them at the back door. Louis insisted on giving me a tour of the farm. I think I've seen everything...some things more than once. But I couldn't refuse. He's adorable."

Louis smiled at her. "You like it, right?"

"I love it," she corrected.

Marcel, Henri, Georges, and Philippe stood aside, taking it all in.

"So, with what Colette's been through, do you think she's still on board?" Henri asked no one in particular.

"Oh, she's on board all right," Philippe chirped.

"Great!" said Georges.

Marcel showed no surprise at Philippe's response. "I spoke with François. After everything his wife's seen, heard, and been through, Nazi Germany now has the entire Dubois clan to contend with."

Henri looked dubious. "What about her family?" he asked.

"They'll always be Giselle's priority, but she just lost her best friend and says that doing nothing guarantees nothing."

"And she's right," said Georges. "I guess we know where Colette gets it from. I wish everyone could see it that way."

"Well, we'll take them one at a time," said Henri. "It's good to have her support."

"Support?" Marcel turned his eyes to him. "I don't think you understand. The fire's been lit. Giselle's already giving François ideas on ways she can help. Said she's been thinking ever since she was taken from Charles' place."

"Excellent!" said Georges. "No sense quelling the flames."

"No, there isn't," Marcel agreed.

They looked back at the gathered group.

"Okay, I've just got to say it," said Philippe, changing subjects. "I'm confused. Everything from the release of Madame Dubois to this Major Holtzer. I watched from the car the other night at the château, and I still don't understand what I saw."

Georges gave his take. "The Great War took his father. A wild boar killed his sister. The state took his mother away, never to be seen again. Maybe things aren't always what they seem."

Marcel was silent, then reconsidered. "I've had a chance to meet the man and learn some things. I'll share them when the time's right."

Colette looked their way, locked eyes with Philippe, and grinned from ear to ear.

His heart melted. "Do you remember when Charles and Georges first brought her to Chançay?"

"I do," said Marcel. "Would you believe that was only two weeks ago? Hard to imagine it's the same person. And I think I missed the mark on her nom de guerre. Innocent seemed appropriate at the time."

"I think Georges is right," Philippe said, smiling. "Maybe things aren't always what they seem."

Author's Note

This novel is a product of my imagination and is meant to be entirely fictitious. Any similarities to specific historical events or organizations are entirely coincidental and unintentional. The characters and names are also intended to be fictional—save one. Although her dialog and actions in the novel are imagined, Simone Menier is a true French heroine and former Lady of Chenonceau.

Acknowledgments

I'm indebted to many for their contributions to my first novel. Firstly, I would like to thank Kathryn Fletcher of Quill & Books for leading me to my editor, Beverly Mardis. Beverly was enthusiastic, discerning, insightful, and otherwise enormously helpful. Her assistance with matters big and small was delivered in a guiding way while encouraging me to write as I liked without feeling beholden to one style or another. Others who played an early and important part in the journey include Karen Skogman, Kim Obermiller, Paul Kurzweg, Teresa Dettle, Catherine Clark, Coco Venturin, Stephanie Haugan, Judith Zasada, Linda Archambault, and Erica Ellis. Finally, I'd like to thank Bonnie Newgard (especially for her patience) and my children, Drake and Alexa, who unwittingly inspired me to write a novel.

Author Bio

J.D. Maxwell has lived most of his life in the Twin Cities and currently lives in Saint Paul, Minnesota. He is a self-proclaimed history buff, particularly regarding World War II and the American Civil War, and always wished to have a go at writing a work of fiction. The idea for this, his first novel, came to him while visiting France and the Indre-et-Loire region with his friend April Johnson in 2016. While walking the halls and grounds of Château de Chenonceau (near the town of Chenonceaux, France), he overheard an equally awe-struck visitor tell her travel companion: "Someone should write a book about this place!" The author couldn't have agreed more and eventually used his imagination to do so.

www.ingramcontent.com/pod-product-compliance
Lightning Source LLC
Chambersburg PA
CBHW021531250626
47154CB00006BA/2061